TALES OF HEROES, GODS & MONSTERS
NATIVE AMERICAN
STORIES & LEGENDS

FLAME TREE PUBLISHING
6 Melbray Mews, Fulham,
London SW6 3NS, United Kingdom
www.flametreepublishing.com

First published and copyright © 2025
Flame Tree Publishing Ltd

25 27 29 28 26
1 3 5 7 9 10 8 6 4 2

ISBN: 978-1-83562-261-2

All rights reserved. No part of this publication may be reproduced,
stored in a retrieval system, or transmitted in any form or by any means, electronic,
mechanical, photocopying, recording or otherwise, without the prior
written permission of the publisher.

Cover and pattern art was created by Flame Tree Studio, with elements
courtesy of Shutterstock.com
Inside ornaments courtesy Shutterstock.com/Tancha.

Judith John (Glossary) is a writer and editor specializing in literature and history. A
former secondary school English Language and Literature teacher, she has subsequently
worked as an editor on major educational projects, including *English A: Literature* for
the Pearson International Baccalaureate series. Judith's major research interests include
Romantic and Gothic literature, and Renaissance drama.

The stories in this book are selected and edited from the following original sources:
Folklore and Legends: North American Indian by W.W. Gibbings 1890; *The Myth of
Hiawatha, and Other Oral Legends, Mythologic and Allegoric, of the North American Indians*
by Henry R. Schoolcraft, 1856; *Myths and Legends of the Sioux* by Marie L. McLaughlin,
1916; *Creation Myths of Primitive America* by Jeremiah Curtin, 1898; *The Algonquin Legends
of New England* by Charles G. Leland, 1884; *American Indian Fairy Tales* by Margaret
Compton, 1903; *Myths and Legends of British North America* series 1910–1917; *Historical and
Statistical Information Respecting the History, Condition, and Prospects of the Indian Tribes
of the United States* series, 1851–1857.

A copy of the CIP data for this book is available
from the British Library.

Designed and created in the UK | Printed and bound in China

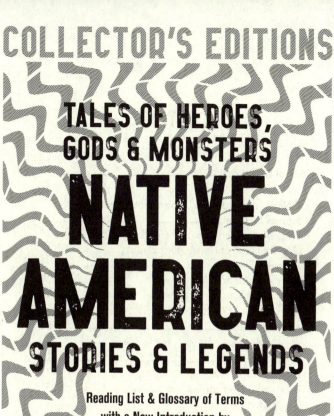

COLLECTOR'S EDITIONS

TALES OF HEROES, GODS & MONSTERS

NATIVE AMERICAN STORIES & LEGENDS

Reading List & Glossary of Terms
with a New Introduction by
DR. ANGELO BACA

FLAME TREE PUBLISHING

CONTENTS

Series Foreword 10

**A New Introduction to Native American
Stories & Legends** 16
Personal History of Family Storytelling 18
Oral Traditions of Native Americans 19
A World of Stories 22
Representation and Perspective 25
Native American Myths Book 27

Further Reading 31

Origin stories 33
How the World Was Made 33
Creation Myth of the Iroquois 36
Osage Creation Story 41
The Great Deeds of Michabo 43
The Origin of the Three Races 45
The First Appearance of Man 47
The Old Chippeway 49
The Discovery of the Upper World 51
The Evil Maker 54
Machinitou, the Evil Spirit 55
Piqua 63
The First Fire 78
The Finding of Fire 80
The Funeral Fire 85

CONTENTS

The Origin of Medicine 90
Origin of Strawberries 94
Legend of the Corn 96
Omaha Sacred legend 98
The Flood and the Rainbow 101
The Wonderful Rod 102
The Sacred Pole 103
The Legend of the Peace Pipes 105

Animal Tales 108
The Beaver Medicine Legend 108
Opeche, the Robin-redbreast 113
The Broken Promise 117
The Sacred Bundle 122
The Serpent-men 128
The Girl who Became a Bird 131
The Maiden who Loved a Fish 133
The Man-fish 136
Pauppukkeewis 141
Manabozho the Wolf 156
The Buffalo and the Grizzly Bear 161
The Bird Chief 163
The Race Between Humming Bird and Crane 164
Why the Turkey Gobbles 165
Unktomi and the Bad Songs 165
Ikto and the Rabbit 168
How Rabbit Escaped from the Wolves 168
Why the Possum Plays Dead 169
How the Deer Got His Horns 170

Heroes, Monsters & the Supernatural 174
The Legend of Scar-face 174
The Legend of Hiawatha 183
Ganusquah, Last of the Stone Giants 188

The Legend of O-na-wut-a-qut-o 192
Great Head and the Ten Brothers 197
White Feather and the Six Giants 202
The Gift of Corn 211
Michabo Defeats the King of Fishes 215
The Sun Ensnared 219
The Spirits and the Lovers 224
Sayadio and the Magic Cup 232
The Land of Souls 235
The Strange Guests 240
The Undying Head 247
The Man who Shot a Ghost 264
The Woman of Stone 266
The Indian who Wrestled with a Ghost 267
The Ghost's Resentment 270

Love & Marriage 275
Moowis, the Snow-husband 275
Osseo, Son of Evening Star 280
The Fire Plume 286
The Southern Bride 290
Aggo-dah-gauda 291
The Girl who Married the Pine-tree 294
The Sun and the Moon 295
The Faithful Lovers 297
Sukonia's Wives and the Ichpul Sisters 302
The Two Sisters, Haka Lasi and Tsore Jowa 309
The Sioux who Married the Crow Chief's Daughter 322
Peeta Kway, or The Foam Woman 326
A Lazy Man 329
The Invisible One 333
Snowbird and the Water-Tiger 337

A Glossary of Myth & Folklore 344

CONTENTS

NATIVE AMERICAN STORIES & LEGENDS

TALES OF HEROES, GODS & MONSTERS
NATIVE AMERICAN
STORIES & LEGENDS

SERIES FOREWORD

Stretching back to the oral traditions of thousands of years ago, tales of heroes and disaster, creation and conquest have been told by many different civilizations in many different ways. Their impact sits deep within our culture even though the detail in the tales themselves are a loose mix of historical record, transformed narrative and the distortions of hundreds of storytellers.

Today the language of mythology lives with us: our mood is jovial, our countenance is saturnine, we are narcissistic and our modern life is hermetically sealed from others. The nuances of myths and legends form part of our daily routines and help us navigate the world around us, with its half truths and biased reported facts.

The nature of a myth is that its story is already known by most of those who hear it, or read it. Every generation brings a new emphasis, but the fundamentals remain the same: a desire to understand and describe the events and relationships of the world. Many of the great stories are archetypes that help us find our own place, equipping us with tools for self-understanding, both individually and as part of a broader culture.

For Western societies it is Greek mythology that speaks to us most clearly. It greatly influenced the mythological heritage of the ancient Roman civilization and is the lens through which we

SERIES FOREWORD

still see the Celts, the Norse and many of the other great peoples and religions. The Greeks themselves learned much from their neighbours, the Egyptians, an older culture that became weak with age and incestuous leadership.

It is important to understand that what we perceive now as mythology had its own origins in perceptions of the divine and the rituals of the sacred. The earliest civilizations, in the crucible of the Middle East, in the Sumer of the third millennium BCE, are the source to which many of the mythic archetypes can be traced. As humankind collected together in cities for the first time, developed writing and industrial scale agriculture, started to irrigate the rivers and attempted to control rather than be at the mercy of its environment, humanity began to write down its tentative explanations of natural events, of floods and plagues, of disease.

Early stories tell of Gods (or god-like animals in the case of tribal societies such as African, Native American or Aboriginal cultures) who are crafty and use their wits to survive, and it is reasonable to suggest that these were the first rulers of the gathering peoples of the earth, later elevated to god-like status with the distance of time. Such tales became more political as cities vied with each other for supremacy, creating new Gods, new hierarchies for their pantheons. The older Gods took on primordial roles and became the preserve of creation and destruction, leaving the new gods to deal with more current, everyday affairs. Empires rose and fell, with Babylon assuming the mantle from Sumeria in the 1800s BCE, then in turn to be swept away by the Assyrians of the 1200s BCE; then the Assyrians and the Egyptians were subjugated by the Greeks, the Greeks by the Romans and so on, leading to the spread and assimilation of common themes, ideas and stories throughout the world.

The survival of history is dependent on the telling of good tales, but each one must have the 'feeling' of truth, otherwise it will be ignored. Around the firesides, or embedded in a book or a computer, the myths and legends of the past are still the living materials of retold myth, not restricted to an exploration of origins. Now we have devices and global communications that give us unparalleled access to a diversity of traditions. We can find out about Native American, Indian, Chinese and tribal African mythology in a way that was denied to our ancestors, we can find connections, match the archaeology, religion and the mythologies of the world to build a comprehensive image of the human experience that is endlessly fascinating.

The stories in this book provide an introduction to the themes and concerns of the myths and legends of their respective cultures, with a short introduction to provide a linguistic, geographic and political context. This is where the myths have arrived today, but undoubtedly over the next millennia, they will transform again whilst retaining their essential truths and signs.

Jake Jackson
General Editor

TALES OF HEROES, GODS & MONSTERS

NATIVE AMERICAN

STORIES & LEGENDS

NATIVE AMERICAN STORIES & LEGENDS

INTRODUCTION
& FURTHER READING

A NEW INTRODUCTION TO NATIVE AMERICAN STORIES & LEGENDS

"Ya'at'eeh! Angelo Baca yinishe."
Translation: "Hello! My name is Angelo Baca."

I am introducing myself in the traditional Navajo way, using my Navajo clans to identify myself and say who my relatives are in my kin networks of our communities. My clans are: the Red Bottom People, Hopi People, Bitter Water and Mexican People clans. As a Diné (Navajo) resident of San Juan County, I learned about our histories in the broader Montezuma Creek/Aneth, Utah region. I have lived in Blanding, Aneth and Monument Valley, Utah my entire life. Most importantly, I bring an intimate familiarity with the region's culture, history and language, mostly Navajo and Hopi, including Zuni, Ute, Ute Mountain Ute and other nations of the broader Colorado Plateau. As someone raised by Navajo grandparents, I am blessed to know our culture, traditions, language and ceremonies, which are the foundation of who I am in the world today, and can trace my lineage all the way back to the beginning of my ancestors.

I am a Navajo and Hopi filmmaker and scholar. I like to make documentary films because they reflect the world's reality and the problems we must fix as people who co-exist in the world together. However, it has dawned on me that I am in fact a traditional storyteller; I just use the mediums of film and video. I'm carrying

INTRODUCTION

on an indigenous tradition, just as my ancestors would have done back in their day. As Native American filmmaker and scholar Beverly Singer notes in *Wiping the Warpaint Off the Lens* (2001), 'Traditional Native American storytelling practices and oral histories are a key source of our recovery of our authentic identity.' Singer identifies how these practices, particularly storytelling, contribute to Native American priorities in our culture and identity. In my research I use these as a way to aid protection of the sacred Bears Ears landscape, practicing our traditions and ceremonies and revitalizing our culture and language.

My graduate research consisted of analyzing visual media narratives and representations by the Ute Indian Tribe, Hopi, Diné (Navajo), Ute Mountain Ute and Zuni nations of the Bears Ears National Monument, a protected area in southeastern Utah, from the moment of the proclamation of the monument through the subsequent administration. The Bears Ears National Monument was established on 28 December, 2016. In 2017, one of the first acts of the next sitting president was to reduce this national monument significantly – from 1.35 million acres to 220,200 acres, an 85 percent illegal land reduction. It was the first time a national monument was cut by a sitting president using an executive order carried out without the approval of Congress. This event mobilized the Bears Ears Inter-Tribal Coalition, and dynamic, progressive activism at a grassroots, community, intra-community, national and international level emerged. Part of the strategy for protecting sacred indigenous lands includes the media narratives that we help to shape. My film work and research focused on using narratives about Bears Ears with the surrounding communities to educate the wider general public. Centrally, it is about storytelling and education, reflecting who we are as the indigenous people of Bears Ears, and why it matters to us, and should matter to everyone.

At first, when asked to write an introduction to this Native American Myths book, I was unsure if I was qualified or if it made sense for me to comment on the oral traditions as a mostly dedicated filmmaker. However, I soon changed my mind when I remembered that storytelling is a family tradition. It has been an honor to discuss the importance and utmost value of storytelling and oral traditions in indigenous cultures, such as ours in the Navajo Nation and beyond.

PERSONAL HISTORY OF FAMILY STORYTELLING

My grandfather, Hugh Yellowman, was a traditional storyteller who shared Navajo stories during the winter seasons. He was known for his ceremonial and traditional knowledge and sought to participate in local and regional cultural activities requiring his expertise. Hugh's handmade moccasins were highly sought-after in the Southwest's Four Corners region, consisting of the four states of Utah, Colorado, New Mexico and Arizona, a traditional territory that intersects to form four perpendicular border corners. Navajo families and folklore academics alike respected his wisdom and would seek his counsel.

Barre Toelken (1935–2018), an academic from Utah State University, became a lifelong friend of the Yellowman family, while working prospecting for uranium in the remote region of southeastern Utah in the 1950s. In the desert he found himself disoriented, tired, dehydrated and sick. He almost died alone, were it not for my grandfather who found him and brought him back to the family hogan. There, he woke up from his sickness, and saw that the entire community was there to sing him back to health in a ceremony. He credited Yellowman for saving his life. Toelken collaborated with the Navajo community, learned the language, attended ceremonies and cultural gatherings, and would eventually, alongside Hugh Yellowman, become a collaborative partner in gathering stories from the Navajo culture, acknowledging Hugh as an equal in his folklore pursuits.

His colleagues heavily criticized Toelken's work as a folklorist because he refused to accept that indigenous 'informants' were not to be considered equals or accorded the same respect as other knowledge holders, such as professors in academia. When Navajo families requested to have Toelken's research material returned, he did not hesitate to explain in *Native American Oral Traditions* (2001): 'It remains for us, and for our many colleagues engaged in the study of Native American oral traditions, to continue opening up the mutually responsive, mutually responsible dialogues, that will bring forth the hundreds of other tribal literatures and languages of America.' Both of these brilliant men have 'walked on' now and leave us with a rich collection of stories and adventures in Toelken's published books, which cover the course of nearly half a century. Toelken, along with the Yellowman family, believed in collaboration on equal and respectful terms with his indigenous and non-indigenous colleagues.

ORAL TRADITIONS OF NATIVE AMERICANS

Oral traditions are perhaps the last bastion of authentic Native American and indigenous identity, representation and presence in our increasingly narrative-saturated world, filled with social media, internet content and competing real-world and fake news sources. Technology radically shifted the ability to make and share stories, giving us the tools to share as many stories as possible. With new sophisticated versions of Artificial Intelligence, humans are increasingly left out of the equation with each successive day. As this tech evolves, non-human storytelling gets better and better. But storytelling will always be a human endeavor. As traditional storyteller and Lower Elwha Sk'llalam tribal elder Roger Fernandes explains at a speaking event: *Native American Storytellers Share Vital Knowledge with RISD Students* (March 18, 2023), 'Before there was the internet, there was television. Before television, there was radio. Before radio, there were books. Before books, there was storytelling.'

At a time when we are all told to use a microphone and a camera to share our thoughts individually, we can look to the past, when the world was about our collective survival, knowledge and wisdom. Technology is more accessible than it has ever been, but only requires a short attention span for quick bursts of storytelling. Increasingly, it is harder to stay focused with longer stories and listen deeply just as our ancestors did during storytelling. At the first annual indigenous storytelling event at Rhode Island School of Design (RISD), Roger Fernandes began his storytelling set by addressing the audience directly while holding his traditional drum and projecting his voice loudly, saying, 'I won't be using the microphone to tell these stories. I don't want to put my spirit through a machine.'

Re-imagining this storytelling event at RISD, we wanted to keep it as close to original indigenous cultural protocols as possible, such as performing storytelling in the winter season,

INTRODUCTION

commonly agreed as the best time to do so. In indigenous communities, winter is the time to share stories and food, reflect on the year, while contemplating the coming new spring season, and pondering the histories and lessons passed down from generation to generation. As such, we also wanted to limit the use of technology and requested that attendees not record, video, write or document the stories. Still, they were allowed to listen and draw, sketch or otherwise create during the storytelling to let the creative energy express itself in whatever form it would take. We wanted the students and community members to feel and imagine the stories connected with them. Many of these creations were given to our guest storytellers as gifts, a form of reciprocity in acknowledging their time and energy to share stories that spanned generations, reaching ears not from their culture for the first time. We wanted to honor these storytellers as traditional knowledge-holders on equal and respectful grounds as with other artists who are experts, professors and recognized specialists inside and outside of the academy.

Now, as I teach Native American Oral Traditions, Native American Film and Media, and an Introduction to Indigenous Philosophy at RISD, I realize every indigenous teacher I have ever had contributed to me accumulating the stories and experiences of those teachers, elders and mentors, making me who I am today. I am merely an extension of their teachings and wisdom, lucky enough to be able to share and teach them to young people now. What they poured into me is a fraction compared to the other oral traditions and teachings I learned from childhood into adulthood, giving me strength and direction to survive an uncertain world impacted by the external forces of a violent settler-colonial history, theft of traditional territories and greedy land rushes to take the world's last remaining natural resources from the places that indigenous people call 'Home'. Indigenous storytelling contemporaries like me and other Native colleagues are the living manifestations of the prayers of our ancestors for what they wanted for their future children.

A WORLD OF STORIES

The world is a collection of stories. Our realities become colored by our beliefs, which are then reinforced by our stories. When these stories are passed down from generation to generation, they also pass along the realities of ancestors long gone. Yet, in many indigenous cultures, those ancestors are never far away, so we are not alone in this life. Stories of our loved ones and heroes and villains live in these narratives. We might be able to ask the same question as our ancestors in their time: 'If I were in the same position as the character in this story, what would I do?' The more we learn and know our own stories, the more we know our place – they are the constellation of stars that guide us in the night of our contemporary misinformation darkness.

In today's published academic literature, stories of indigenous people are rarely told from their own perspective. Often, in the fields of folklore and oral histories, interviews document the stories that are known only in the hearts and minds of the storytellers of these native cultures. In early ethnology collection efforts, along with many other salvage ethnography projects, much was made of field workers who went out to 'Indian' tribes, before they 'disappeared' or 'vanished' as modernity encroached upon them. Scottish anthropologist and folklorist Lewis Spence

INTRODUCTION

states in *The Myths of the North American Indians* (1989): 'Many treatises of the utmost value on the ethnology, mythology and tribal customs of the North American Indians have been issued by this conscientious and enterprising State department. These are written by men who possess first-hand knowledge of Indian life and languages, many of whom have faced great privations and hardships in order to collect the material they have published.' Yet it is important to note that the material they collected was often done in return for monetary compensation or some form of payment. Academia and government work could be a secondary source of income for storytellers, whether authentic or not. As time went on, story-sharing included different modalities. In some cases, documentation in audio recordings or other forms like video is applied as a tool in oral traditions that are supplementary to stories. These tools help do this work, but they can never replace the face-to-face interaction of oral traditions, or we risk losing the nuances and details accompanying stories, and the knowledge gained from this necessary contact with other human beings.

Indigenous intellectual properties are indigenous oral traditions. Such content belongs to indigenous peoples, particularly tribal nations. In many traditional artforms, like pottery and basketry, there are certain aspects that may be headed or led by certain family groups, clanships, communities or societies. This may require specific cultural knowledge belonging to those groups. How do we know what songs and prayers must be said when we harvest certain materials like plants, paints and medicines? What is the responsibility of the harvester to reciprocate a mutually beneficial relationship with these living landscapes in exchange for their gifts?

Consider what else might be lost in translation when communicating the story to a live audience of listeners. The articulation of vast sums of knowledge is told through different lenses, and holders of the stories differ from those who held them before. Each storyteller has a distinct style and delivery, varied strengths and abilities to tell a story in a way that isn't like anyone else. Sometimes, storytellers have a different take and interpretation of the stories altogether. Author Ella E. Clark in *Indian Legends of the Pacific Northwest Vol.18* (1953) writes: 'A skilful Indian storyteller is actor as well as narrator. His facial expressions are lively, his eyes twinkle, he gestures not only with his hands but with his feet, he changes his voice to fit the characters. When one of his characters sings, the storyteller sings. Sometimes a tale that was delightful when I heard it lacked life when put on paper, for the dramatic quality of the person who related it had been lost.' How many versions of the Raven or Coyote stories exist in the world and have traveled extensively across geographies, trade networks and generations?

Navajos say we will keep our identity and culture alive 'as long as the stories are wet with our breath'. A people without their stories and origins are without a history and doomed to repeat it. We realized a long time ago that our lineages and ancestors, and the stories that accompany them, are essential to carry with us wherever we go. Our embodied selves are given animation and dynamism through our breath and the literal wind of life that inhabits our bodies. Toelken said in *Dynamics of Folklore* (1996), 'Basically, we can say that a clear delineation of genre or structure of a folk item is only one small part of understanding a folk performance. Without the whole live context and the comments of the performers, it is unlikely that we will ever get very close to understanding – or even seeing – the dynamics that underlie the traditional process.' If we don't say these stories with our own breath and mother tongues, the power of these stories will lack efficacy. We can write them down but must not forget to perform and share them. We must honor the spirit that moves us and talks from within, which is the ageless connection of what every human experiences when they are a 'five-fingered being' or 'Dine' Bila'ashla'ii'.

These oral traditions are no less adventurous and timeless in their relevance. We have all battled the same foes before in human history, seemingly insurmountable antagonists such as hunger, greed, violence, selfishness or death. Native American storytelling takes us on these journeys through their eyes. Yet it is a human experience that translates the enormity of life across cultures in all its abstract forms, which we can make more tangible and less frightening by knowing it through stories. If we have heard a story hundreds of times before, it is a different experience to revisit it anew, with time and distance away from it. One has accumulated experiences, histories and outlook on life; where they once heard or read a story before, it does not land the same as it once did. Like a good book by a well-known author or a popular beloved classic movie, it means different things to us at various stages of our lives.

REPRESENTATION AND PERSPECTIVE

Indigenous narratives have had a history of erasure and little to no representation. Whenever there was representation, it was usually stereotypical and incorrect. The old, outdated tropes native peoples have endured were directly impacting the ways that their communities and nations have been treated since colonial outsiders invaded their original territories. These narrative omissions are related to their negative perception in, first, settler colonial ventures to the Americas, then, secondly, in the minds and imaginations of Americans in the political, cultural and economic realms of life.

Indigenous stories have always been distant from much more established literary traditions from the Western academic world. Authored stories were given more primacy and weight than those from indigenous oral traditions simply because they were written down. In the view of Euro-American dominant culture, some written works, like those from William Shakespeare (1564–1616) or Charles Dickens (1812–70), are now interpreted as classics. The crushing weight of the written word expressed itself early and often in the form of one of the earliest oral traditions to have been born before contact with the Americas turned into a fixed textual form: the Christian Bible.

How ironic it is that the world's largest and most popular religions also began as oral traditions! But since they were written down, systematized and bureaucratically contained into a managed hierarchy of power and influence, many lessons and teachings in these stories were lost or made to fulfill the purposes of man rather than re-establish and renew the lost relationships of humans to other humans or, humans to non-human beings. Everyone had their peacemaker – whether Jesus, Mohammed, Buddha, Hiawatha or Deganawida. Saying there is one singular true religion is like saying there is only a singular true, authentic version of an oral tradition above others. These are all just valuable stories connecting our roots from a shared sacred tree, growing from Mother Earth.

INTRODUCTION

Oral traditions can be very fluid in the ways they engage the world and other realities beyond the one we inhabit as human beings. Shifting seamlessly between these worlds and among other dimensions is displayed in the stories effortlessly. It is problematic for two-legged beings considered human to make such dramatic changes experienced as a regular part of life. It demonstrates how limited we are in our thinking of human abilities and intellect. Living as a human being in the world does not mean we are at the pinnacle of nature or at the top of the food chain. Clearly, we still have much to learn as human beings, learning to co-exist in the world with other beings, spirits, deities and people. When will we respect and recognize that our collective survival depends on shifting our perspectives to others, for non-human and human relatives, so we can thrive together?

NATIVE AMERICAN MYTHS BOOK

This book reflects the ideals and values that many Native American cultures and societies held close to their hearts. Authors Richard Erdoes and Alfonso Ortiz express in *American Indian Myths and Legends* (1984): 'Creation myths deal with both how the physical world as we know it came to be and how the many features of specific cultures originated.' Such descriptions do little justice explaining stories because they are derived from Western thought-oriented concepts and do not reflect the holistic approach of existence within indigenous realities. Despite this, it should be no surprise these values show up in indigenous stories.

In the section 'Origin Stories', the theme of 'beginning' shows up again and again. Creation stories are alive with vital, powerful characters who interchangeably hold titles of deities, spirits and gods. Nonetheless, 'Creation Stories' set the tone and stage for later stories. Native foods appear in the Arikara *Legend of the Corn* and the Cherokee story of the *Origin of Strawberries* who also appear as characters in their own stories. Explanations of different worlds above or below, or how specific groupings of man came to be, and the appearance of elemental forces of nature, such as fire, came into relationship with humans also emerge.

In the 'Animal Tales' section, our other-than-human associates are arguably the older and wiser of the world in which we co-exist. From birds, beavers, wolves, buffalo, serpents, fish, bears, rabbits, deer and possums, many animals appear to parallel the human experience; they speak, experience hunger, scheme, sing and create just as people do. Our animal friends share teachings and exciting adventures to learn from. They are, in fact, from an indigenous perspective, people of a different kind.

In the 'Heroes, Monsters, and the Supernatural' section, we learn that beings beyond us challenge our finite states of human existence in this world and the next. Stories of spirits amongst us let us know we are not alone. Tales of overwhelming odds are part of the typical journey of heroes, no matter the setting or period in history, conquering foes from giants, hunger and grief. Some inspire us, like *The Legend of Hiawatha* who helped lead his people into forming the Haudenosaunee Confederacy.

In the 'Love and Marriage' section, we see relationships have always been part of our lives, and these stories remain relevant to us. Commemorating love through story celebrates the experience, not just for human beings but it weaves worlds together like in *The Sun and the Moon* describing the balance of night and day. Marriage, searching, longing and loss are all part of living in the world. Yet classic love stories of being from two different worlds, sometimes literally, allow us to see how similar we all are.

Metaphorically speaking, oral traditions are like the tip of an iceberg. We only see the surface but the more we look under the iceberg, we see the stories have deeper levels. Usually, entertaining and exciting aspects of these unique stories stand out. But if one looks deeper, we see beyond the obvious. As Toelken states in *Anguish of Snails: Native American Folklore in the West* (2003): 'The survival of an orally transmitted story is in itself a testimony to its ongoing validity as an expression of cultural meaning in dramatic terms. A narrative is a sequence of related events, acted out by characters who experience an important complication and then witness its resolution. Of course, most narratives must be interesting and entertaining, or else why keep telling them?' Indigenous oral traditions are packed with lessons, histories and teachings, so vitally important that their content and characters are components of the holistic and overall value of the story – a reason why such stories keep getting handed down from generation to generation.

Taking the iceberg metaphor further, today's anxieties are about melting icecaps, droughts and climate change. It is contemporary concerns of our daily modern lives that are slowly eroding our own abilities in storytelling in the ways our ancestors used to do, just like the icebergs in the Arctic north are slowly eroding in record high temperatures. The shrinking of these cohesive and solid stories, no matter where they come from, have always done what their purpose has been for generations before us – make sense of a changing world. But what does it mean when the world is changing so fast that the stories do not have a chance to keep up, and stories of seasonal changes, weather phenomena and certain regional natural phenomena of plants, animals and landscapes are at risk?

We get to revisit Native American myths, oral traditions and stories with new experiences that change our perception over time. With each victory and tragedy, our views on the dialectics of the world and how each of us have conversations with other beings begin to shift because nothing in the world stays the same, nor is black and white. Tricksters and transformers show us many shades of gray. If there is anything the universe offers to teach us, it is that we are all truly diverse and still exist because we do, in fact, need each other. You need an example, you say? Well, there's a story for that…

Dr. Angelo Baca

FURTHER READING

Clark, Ella Elizabeth, *Indian legends of the Pacific Northwest*, Vol. 18. (Berkeley and Los Angeles: University of California Press, 1953)

Erdoes, Richard, and Alfonso Ortiz, *American Indian Myths and Legends*, (Pantheon, 1984)

Evers, Larry, and Barre Toelken, *Native American Oral Traditions*, (Logan, Utah: Utah State University Press, 2001)

Spence, Lewis, *The Myths of the North American Indians*, (New York: Dover Publications, 1989)

Toelken, Barre, *Dynamics of Folklore*, (Logan, Utah: Utah State University Press, 1996)

Toelken, Barre, *Anguish of Snails: Native American Folklore in the West*, (Logan, Utah: University Press of Colorado, 2003)

Dr. Angelo Baca (Diné/Hopi) is a cultural activist, scholar, filmmaker and public lands advocate at Rhode Island School of Design's History, Philosophy and Social Sciences Department. His primary research focuses on the tribally led initiative of the Bears Ears National Monument. His research interests include Indigenous international repatriation, food sovereignty, public lands and protection of sacred lands. He is committed to collaborative research with Indigenous communities, empowering traditional knowledge-keepers in stewarding stories and landscapes. He is deeply dedicated to Western and Indigenous knowledge on equal and respectful terms.

ORIGIN STORIES

Chosen from among the ancient folklore of a number of widely scattered tribes, the stories which follow are a very broad selection of some of the most popular and characteristic of Native American legends. Creation stories are an important theme in any mythology due to our innate nature to wonder where we, and everything around us, came from. The various tribes had different stories about how the earth came to be, how man was first created and the origins of basic elements and foods; but common ideas proliferate throughout. What were also evidently very important were stories on the origins of the different tribes, and tracing their heritage back to the very beginning of how they came to be formed.

HOW THE WORLD WAS MADE

The Cherokees believed the following about how the world was made. The earth is a great floating island in a sea of water. At each of the four corners there is a cord hanging down from the sky. The sky is of solid rock. When the world grows old and worn out, the cords will break, and then the earth will sink down into the ocean. Everything will be water again. All the people will be dead. The Indians are much afraid of this.

In the long time ago, when everything was all water, all the animals lived up above in Galun'lati, beyond the stone arch that made the sky. But it was very much crowded. All the animals wanted more room. The animals began to wonder what was below the water and at last Beaver's grandchild, little Water Beetle, offered to go and find out. Water Beetle darted in every direction over the surface of the water, but it could find no place to rest. There was no land at all. Then Water Beetle dived to the bottom of the water and brought up some soft mud. This began to grow and to spread out on every side until it became the island which we call the earth. Afterwards this earth was fastened to the sky with four cords, but no one remembers who did this.

At first the earth was flat and soft and wet. The animals were anxious to get down, and they sent out different birds to see if it was yet dry, but there was no place to alight; so the birds came back to Galun'lati. Then at last it seemed to be time again, so they sent out Buzzard; they told him to go and make ready for them. This was the Great Buzzard, the father of all the buzzards we see now. He flew all over the earth, low down near the ground, and it was still soft. When he reached the Cherokee country, he was very tired; his wings began to flap and strike the ground. Wherever they struck the earth there was a valley; whenever the wings turned upwards again, there was a mountain. When the animals above saw this, they were afraid that the whole world would be mountains, so they called him back, but the Cherokee country remains full of mountains to this day.

When the earth was dry and the animals came down, it was still dark. Therefore they got the sun and set it in a track to go every day across the island from east to west, just overhead. It was too hot this way. Red Crawfish had his shell scorched a bright red, so that his meat was spoiled. Therefore the Cherokees do not eat it.

Then the medicine men raised the sun a handsbreadth in the air, but it was still too hot. They raised it another time; and then another time; at last they had raised it seven handsbreadths so that it was just under the sky arch. Then it was right and they left it so. That is why the medicine men called the high place "the seventh height." Every day the sun goes along under this arch on the under side; it returns at night on the upper side of the arch to its starting place.

There is another world under this earth. It is like this one in every way. The animals, the plants, and the people are the same, but the seasons are different. The streams that come down from the mountains are the trails by which we reach this underworld. The springs at their head are the doorways by which we enter it. But in order to enter the other world, one must fast and then go to the water, and have one of the underground people for a guide. We know that the seasons in the underground world are different, because the water in the spring is always warmer in winter than the air in this world; and in summer the water is cooler.

We do not know who made the first plants and animals. But when they were first made, they were told to watch and keep awake for seven nights. This is the way young men do now when they fast and pray to their medicine. They tried to do this. The first night, nearly all the animals stayed awake. The next night several of them dropped asleep. The third night still more went to sleep. At last, on the seventh night, only the owl, the panther, and one or two more were still awake. Therefore, to these were given the power to see in the dark, to go about as if it were day, and to kill and eat the birds and animals which must sleep during the night.

Even some of the trees went to sleep. Only the cedar, the pine, the spruce, the holly, and the laurel were awake all seven nights. Therefore they are always green. They are also sacred trees. But to the other trees it was said, "Because you did not stay awake, therefore you shall lose your hair every winter."

After the plants and the animals, men began to come to the earth. At first there was only one man and one woman. He hit her with a fish. In seven days a little child came down to the earth. So people came to the earth. They came so rapidly that for a time it seemed as though the earth could not hold them all.

CREATION MYTH OF THE IROQUOIS

At the dawn of creation, before mankind ever existed, the universe comprised two separate worlds. The lower world was a place of eternal darkness, peopled only by creatures of the water, while the upper world, a kingdom of bright light, was inhabited by the Great Ruler and his family. The goddess Atahensic was daughter of the Great Ruler, and at this time she was heavy with child and very close to her time of confinement. As the hour drew near, her relatives persuaded her to lie down on a soft mattress, wrapping her in a ray of light, so that her weary body would gather strength and refreshment for the task ahead. But as soon as she had closed her eyes, the bed on which she lay began to sink without warning through the thick clouds, plunging rapidly towards the lower world beneath her.

Dazzled and alarmed by the descending light, the monsters and creatures of the great water held an emergency council to decide what should be done.

'If the being from above falls on us,' said the Water-hen, 'it will surely destroy us. We must quickly find a place where it can rest.'

'Only the oeh-da, the earth which lies at the very bottom of the water, will be strong enough to hold it,' said the Beaver. 'I will swim down and bring some back with me.' But the Beaver never returned from his search.

Then the Duck volunteered himself for the same duty, but soon his dead body floated up to the surface. Finally, however, the Muskrat came forward:

'I know the way better than anyone,' he told the others, 'but the oeh-da is extremely heavy and will grow very fast. Who is prepared to bear its weight when I appear with it?'

The Turtle, who was by far the most capable among them, readily agreed to suffer the load. Shortly afterwards, the Muskrat returned with a small quantity of the oeh-da in his paw which he smoothed on to the turtle's back. It began to spread rapidly, and as soon as it had reached a satisfactory size for the light to rest on, two birds soared into the air and bore the goddess on their outstretched wings down towards the water and safely on to the turtle's back. From that day onwards, the Turtle became known as the Earth Bearer, and whenever the seas rise up in great waves, the people know that it is the Turtle stirring in his bed.

A considerable island of earth now floated on the waves, providing a timely shelter, for soon Atahensic began to hear two voices within her womb, one soft and soothing, the other loud and aggressive, and she knew that her mission to people the island was close at hand. The conflict continued within, as one of her twin infants sought to pass out under the side of his mother's arm, while the other held him back, attempting to spare his mother this unnecessary pain. Both entered into the world in their own individual way, the first bringing trouble and strife, the second bringing freedom and peace. The goddess wisely accepted that it must be so, and named her children Hahgwehdiyu, meaning Good Mind, and Hahgwehdaetgah, meaning Bad Mind. Each went his way, Hahgwehdiyu anxious to bring beauty to the island, Hahgwehdaetgah determined that darkness and evil should prevail.

Not long after she had given birth, Atahensic passed away and the island grew dim in the dawn of its new life. Knowing the goddess would not have wished it this way, Hahgwehdiyu lifted his palm high into the air and began moulding the sky with his fingers. After he had done this, he took his mother's head from her body and placed it firmly in the centre of the firmament:

'You shall be known as the Sun', he announced, 'and your face shall light up this new world where you shall rule forever.'

But his brother saw all of this good work and set darkness in the west sky, forcing the Sun down behind it. Hahgwehdiyu would not be beaten, however, and removing a portion of his mother's breast, he cast it upwards, creating an orb, inferior to the sun, yet capable of illuminating the darkness. Then he surrounded the orb with numerous spots of light, giving them the name of stars and ordering them to regulate the days, nights, seasons and years. When he had completed this work above, he turned his attention to the soil beneath his feet. To the barren earth he gave the rest of his mother's body from which the seeds of all future life were destined to spring forth.

The Good Mind continued the works of creation, refusing all rest until he had accomplished everything he had set out to do. All over the land he formed creeks and rivers, valleys and hills, luscious pastures and evergreen forests. He created numerous species of animals to inhabit the forests, from the smallest to the greatest, and filled the seas and lakes with fishes and mammals of every variety and colour. He appointed thunder to water the earth and winds to scatter pollen so that, in time, the island became fruitful and productive. But all was not yet complete, for Hahgwehdiyu wisely observed that a greater being was needed to take possession of the Great Island. And so, he began forming two images from the dust of the ground in his own likeness. To these he gave the name of Eagwehowe, meaning the Real People, and by breathing into their nostrils he gave them living souls.

When the earth was created and Hahgwehdiyu had bestowed a protective spirit upon every object of his creation, he went out in search of his brother, hoping to persuade him to abandon his evil and vicious existence. But the Bad Mind was already hard at work, intent on destroying all evidence of Hahgwehdiyu's remarkable labour. Without much effort, he overcame the guardian spirits he encountered and marched throughout the island, bending the rivers, sundering the mountains, gnarling the forests and destroying food crops. He created lethal reptiles to injure mankind, led ferocious monsters into the sea and gathered great hurricanes in the sky. Still dissatisfied with the devastation, however, he began making two images of clay in the form of humans, aiming to create a more superior and destructive race. But he was quickly made to realize that he had not been blessed with the same creative powers as the Good Mind, for as he breathed life into them, his clay figures turned into hideous apes. Infuriated by this discovery, the Bad Mind thundered through the island like a terrible whirlwind, uprooting fruit-trees and wringing the necks of animals and birds. Only one thing would now satisfy his anger, a bloody and ruthless combat to the death, and with this purpose in mind, he hastened towards his twin-brother's dwelling.

Weary of the destruction he had witnessed, the Good Mind willingly submitted himself to the contest that would decide the ruler of the earth. The Bad Mind was keen to discover anything that might help to destroy his brother's temporal life and began to question him rather slyly on the type of weapons they should use.

'Tell me,' he said, 'what particular instrument would cause you the most injury, so that I may avoid its use, as a gesture of goodwill.'

Hahgwehdiyu could see through this evil strategy, however, and falsely informed him that he would certainly be struck down by a lotus arrow.

'There is nothing I fear,' the Bad Mind boasted, but Hahgwehdiyu knew this to be untrue, and wisely remembered that ever since childhood the horns of a stag had always induced feelings of terror in his brother.

The battle began and lasted for two days and two nights, causing panic and disruption throughout the earth as mountains shook violently under the strain of the combat and rivers overflowed with the blood of both brothers. At last, however, the Bad Mind could no longer ignore the temptation to shoot the lotus arrow in his brother's direction. The Good Mind responded by charging at him with the stag-horns, impaling him on their sharp points until he screamed in pain and fell to the ground begging for mercy.

Hahgwehdiyu, the supreme ruler of the earth, immediately banished his evil brother to a dark pit beneath the surface of the world, ordering him never to return. Gathering together as many hideous beasts and monsters as he could find, he flung them below so that they might share with their creator a life of eternal doom. Some escaped his grasp, however, and remained on the earth as Servers, half-human and half-beasts, eager to continue the destructive work of the Bad Mind who had now become known as the Evil Spirit.

Hahgwehdiyu, faithful to the wishes of his grandfather, the Great Ruler, carried on with his good work on the floating island, filling the woodlands with game, slaying the monsters, teaching the Indians to make fires and to raise crops, and instructing them in many of the other arts of life until the time had come for him to retire from the earth to his celestial home.

OSAGE CREATION STORY

Way beyond, once upon a time, some of the Osages lived in the sky. They did not know where they came from, so they went to Sun. They said, "From where did we come?"

He said, "You are my children."

Then they wandered still further and came to Moon.

Moon said, "I am your mother; Sun is your father. You must go away from here. You must go down to the earth and live there."

So they came to the earth but found it covered with water. They could not return up above. They wept, but no answer came to them. They floated about in the air, seeking help from some god; but they found none.

Now all the animals were with them. Elk was the finest and most stately. They all trusted Elk. So they called to Elk, "Help us."

Then Elk dropped into the water and began to sink. Then he called to the winds. The winds came from all sides and they blew until the waters went upwards, as in a mist. Now before that the winds had traveled in only two directions; they went from north to south and from south to north. But when Elk called to them, they came from the east, from the north, from the west, and from the south. They met at a central place; then they carried the waters upwards.

Now at first the people could see only the rocks. So they traveled on the rocky places. But nothing grew there and there was nothing to eat. Then the waters continued to vanish. At last the people could see the soft earth. When Elk saw the earth, he was so joyous, he rolled over and over on the earth. Then all the loose hairs clung to the soil. So the hairs grew, and from them sprang beans, corn, potatoes, and wild turnips, and at last all the grasses and trees.

Now the people wandered over the land. They found human footsteps. They followed them. They joined with them, and traveled with them in search of food.

The Hoga came down from above, and found the earth covered with water. They flew in every direction. They sought for gods who would help them and drive the water away. They found not one. Then Elk came. He had a loud voice and he shouted to the four corners of the sky. The four winds came in answer. They blew upon the water and it vanished upwards, in a mist. Then the people could see the rocks. Now there was only a little space on the rocks. They knew they must have more room.

The people were crowded. So they sent Muskrat down into the water. He did not come back. He was drowned. Then they sent Loon down. He did not come back. He was drowned. Then they sent Beaver down into the water. The water was too deep. Beaver was drowned. Then Crawfish dived into the water. He was gone a long time. When he came up there was a little mud in his claws. Crawfish was so tired he died. But the people took the mud out of his claws and made the land.

THE GREAT DEEDS OF MICHABO

A very powerful manitto once visited the earth and, falling in love with its only inhabitant, a beautiful young maiden, he made her his wife. From this union were born four healthy sons, but in giving birth the mother sadly passed away. The first son was named Michabo and he was destined to become the friend of the human race. Michabo, supreme deity of the Algonquin Indians, is very often represented as an invincible god, endowed with marvellous powers. Sometimes, however, he is given a far more human treatment, and is depicted as a trickster, or troublemaker, as in the story to follow. The second, Chibiabos, took charge of the dead and ruled the Land of Souls. The third, Wabassa, immediately fled to the north, transforming himself into a rabbit-spirit, while the fourth, Chokanipok, who was of a fiery temperament, spent his time arguing, especially with his eldest brother.

Michabo, the strongest and most courageous of the four, had always attributed the death of his mother to Chokanipok, and the repeated combats between the two were often fiercely savage. During one particularly brutal confrontation, Michabo carved huge fragments of flesh from the body of his brother which, as soon as they fell to the ground, were transformed into flintstones. In time, the children of men found a use for these stones and used them to create fire, giving Chokanipok the name of Firestone, or Man of Flint.

After a long and tortuous battle, Chokanipok was finally slain by Michabo who tore out his bowels and changed them into long twining vines from which the earth's vegetation sprung forth. After this, Michabo journeyed far and wide, carrying with him all manner of tools and equipment which he distributed among men. He gave them lances and arrow-points; he taught them how to make axes or agukwats; he devised the art of knitting nets to catch fish; he furnished the hunter with charms and signs to use in his chase, and he taught mankind to lay traps and snares. In the course of his journeys he also killed the ferocious beasts and monsters threatening the human race and cleared the rivers and streams of many of the obstructions which the Evil Spirit had placed there.

When he saw that all this was done, Michabo placed four good spirits at the four cardinal points of the earth, instructing mankind that he should always blow the smoke from his calumet in each of these four directions as a mark of respect during the sacred feasts. The Spirit of the North, he told them, would always provide snow and ice, enabling man to hunt game. The Spirit of the South would give them melons, maize and tobacco. The Spirit he had placed in the West would ensure that rain fell upon the crops, and the Spirit of the East would never fail to bring light in place of darkness.

Then, retreating to an immense slab of ice in the Northern Ocean, Michabo kept a watchful eye on mankind, informing them that if ever the day should arrive when their wickedness forced him to depart the earth, his footprints would catch fire and the end of the world would come; for it was he who directed the sun in his daily walks around the earth.

THE ORIGIN OF THE THREE RACES

Having resolved to create a new species, the Great Spirit took himself off to a place of solitude and began the labour that was to last him several days. He toiled long and hard and at length he produced a being, different from anything else he had ever before created. The figure, whose skin was black as the night, enthralled the Great Spirit, and at first he was deeply satisfied with his work. But soon, he felt that a single example of the new species was not enough and he decided to embark upon a second attempt, hopeful that the result would bring him equal pleasure.

On the next occasion, his creation proved to be a being with a red skin colour. Placing him alongside his brother, the Great Spirit smiled. He was even more pleased with the fruits of his labour, but once again, after only a short time, he became anxious to try his hand a third time.

'This will be my last effort,' he told himself, and he wandered off to complete his final creation. The being he produced this time had a white skin colour, far lighter than the other two. It proved to be the Great Spirit's favourite, and so utterly satisfied him that he spent several minutes turning it over in the palm of his hand before releasing it to the company of its two elder brothers.

Calling the three men before him one day soon afterwards, the Great Spirit pointed to three boxes lying in the earth. The first box contained books, papers and quills; the second was filled with bows and arrows, tomahawks and spears; the third held a collection of spades, axes, hoes and hammers. The Great Spirit then addressed his children with these words:

'My sons, what you see before you are the means by which you shall live. Each of you must choose one of the boxes for your future use.' And saying this, he beckoned to his favourite, the white man, instructing him to make the first choice.

The youngest brother passed by the working-tools, the axes, hoes and hammers, without paying them any attention whatsoever and moved towards the weapons of war and hunting. Here, he hesitated, lifting a number of them from the box so that he might examine them more closely. The red-skinned brother trembled, for with his whole heart he longed to take possession of these instruments and feared that he was close to losing them. But the white man deliberated only a moment longer and then passed swiftly on to the box of books and writing tools, signalling to the Great Spirit that he had finally reached his decision.

The red-skinned brother came next, and he sprang forward and immediately seized upon the bows and arrows, the tomahawks and spears, delighted with himself that he was now the owner of so valuable a collection.

Last of all, the black man stepped forward, the Great Spirit's first offspring. Having no choice left, he lifted the remaining box filled with tools of the land and humbly carried it all the way back to his dwelling.

It was in this manner, according to ancient Seminole legend, that the three races came into being.

THE FIRST APPEARANCE OF MAN

A great many years ago the Navajos, Pueblos and the white man all lived beneath the earth's surface as one people at the place known as Cerra Naztarny, on the Rio San Juan. The underground world they lived in had no light, and in those days they survived entirely on the flesh of whatever animal they managed to capture in the darkness. But in spite of every difficulty, their world was a peaceful one. The people shared the same outlook and the same language and even the same dwelling, a large and comfortable cave, where each man lived on equal terms with his neighbour.

Among the Navajos there were two dumb men who were skilled in a great many things, but especially in the art of playing the Indian flute. One evening, the elder of the two, having reached a particularly rousing point in his performance, stood up with his flute, tilting it high in the air. Quite by accident, he cracked the instrument against the roof of the cave, producing a peculiarly hollow sound which excited his curiosity. Determined to discover what lay above their heads, the dumb man called to a raccoon nearby, requesting his assistance. The raccoon ascended to the roof of the cave using the flute as a ladder and began digging furiously. But after a reasonable length of time, when he became convinced he was not making any progress, the raccoon came back down the ladder allowing the moth-worm to ascend in his place.

It was several hours before the moth-worm succeeded in boring through the roof, but his perseverance was rewarded when at last a tiny stream of light filtered into the cave. Wriggling through the opening he had made, he soon found himself upon a mountain, surrounded by water. He was more than pleased at the sight, and began throwing up a little mound on which to rest. As he sat there, looking around him more attentively, he noticed four large white swans, placed at the four cardinal points, each carrying an arrow under either wing.

The swan from the north was the first to spot the little visitor, and as soon as he did so he rushed upon him, thrusting both of his arrows through the body of the moth-worm. When he saw that the arrows had drawn blood, the swan withdrew each of them and examined them closely.

'He is of my race,' he then called aloud to his three brothers, and they, in turn, came forward and subjected the moth-worm to the same peculiar ceremony. After the ordeal was gone through, each of the swans resumed its former station and began tunnelling in the earth until it had created a great ditch into which the water swiftly flowed, leaving behind a mass of soft, sticky mud.

The worm carefully descended to the dumb man and related to him all that had happened. The raccoon was then sent through the hole in the roof to verify the tiny creature's story, but as soon as he leaped to the ground, he became stuck in the mud almost to his thighs, staining his paws and legs so that the black marks have remained to this day. After a struggle, the disgruntled raccoon managed to free himself and made his way back down to the cave where the dumb man called upon the wind to come forth and blow upon the mud until it had dried out.

Once this task had been completed, a throng of men and animals gathered at the opening in the roof, anxious to explore the new world for themselves. The larger beasts poured from the cave in a steady stream and scattered directly to the plains. The birds and smaller animals headed straightaway for the woodlands, while the people, the last to emerge, immediately separated into different groups, each with its own new language. The Navajos, who were the first to appear, commenced a large painting in the sand. The Pueblos cut their hair and began building houses. The white man set off towards the point where the sun rises, and was not heard from again for a great many years.

THE OLD CHIPPEWAY

The old man Chippeway, the first of men, when he first landed on the earth, near where the present Dogribs have their hunting-grounds, found the world a beautiful world, well stocked with food, and abounding with pleasant things. He found no man, woman, or child upon it; but in time, being lonely, he created children, to whom he gave two kinds of fruit, the black and the white, but he forbade them to eat the black. Having given his commands for the government and guidance of his family, he took leave of them for a time, to go into a far country where the sun dwelt, for the purpose of bringing it to the earth.

After a very long journey, and a long absence, he returned, bringing with him the sun, and he was delighted to find that his children had remained obedient, and had eaten only of the white food.

Again he left them to go on another expedition. The sun he had brought lighted up the earth for only a short time, and in the land from which he had brought it he had noticed another body, which served as a lamp in the dark hours. He resolved therefore to journey and bring back with him the moon; so, bidding adieu to his children and his dwelling, he set forth once more.

While he had been absent on his first expedition, his children had eaten up all the white food, and now, when he set out, he forgot to provide them with a fresh supply. For a long time they resisted the craving for food, but at last they could hold out no longer, and satisfied their hunger with the black fruit.

The old Chippeway soon returned, bringing with him the moon. He soon discovered that his children had transgressed his command, and had eaten the food of disease and death. He told them what was the consequence of their act—that in future the earth would produce bad fruits, that sickness would come amongst men, that pain would rack them, and their lives be lives of fatigue and danger.

Having brought the sun and moon to the earth, the old man Chippeway rested, and made no more expeditions. He lived an immense number of years, and saw all the troubles he declared would follow the eating of the black food. At last he became tired of life, and his sole desire was to be freed from it.

"Go," said he, to one of his sons, "to the river of the Bear Lake, and fetch me a man of the little wise people (the beavers). Let it be one with a brown ring round the end of the tail, and a white spot on the tip of the nose. Let him be just two seasons old upon the first day of the coming frog-moon, and see that his teeth be sharp."

The man did as he was directed. He went to the river of the Bear Lake, and brought a man of the little wise people. He had a brown ring round the end of his tail, and a white spot on the tip of his nose. He was just two seasons old upon the first day of the frog-moon, and his teeth were very sharp.

"Take the wise four-legged man," said the old Chippeway, "and pull from his jaws seven of his teeth."

The man did as he was directed, and brought the teeth to the old man. Then he bade him call all his people together, and when they were come the old man thus addressed them—

"I am old, and am tired of life, and wish to sleep the sleep of death. I will go hence. Take the seven teeth of the wise little four-legged man and drive them into my body."

They did so, and as the last tooth entered him the old man died.

THE DISCOVERY OF THE UPPER WORLD

The **Minnatarees, and all of the other Indians** who are not of the stock of the grandfather of nations, were once not of this upper air, but dwelt in the bowels of the earth. The Good Spirit, when he made them, meant, no doubt, at a proper time to put them in enjoyment of all the good things which he had prepared for them upon earth, but he ordered that their first stage of existence should be within it. They all dwelt underground, like moles, in one great cavern. When they emerged it was in different places, but generally near where they now inhabit. At that time few of the Indian tribes wore the human form. Some had the figures or semblances of beasts. The Paukunnawkuts were rabbits, some of the Delawares were ground-hogs, others tortoises, and the Tuscaroras, and a great many others, were rattlesnakes. The Sioux were the hissing-snakes, but the

Minnatarees were always men. Their part of the great cavern was situated far towards the mountains of snow.

The great cavern in which the Indians dwelt was indeed a dark and dismal region. In the country of the Minnatarees it was lighted up only by the rays of the sun which strayed through the fissures of the rock and the crevices in the roof of the cavern, while in that of the Mengwe all was dark and sunless. The life of the Indians was a life of misery compared with that they now enjoy, and it was endured only because they were ignorant of a fairer or richer world, or a better or happier state of being.

There were among the Minnatarees two boys, who, from the hour of their birth, showed superior wisdom, sagacity, and cunning. Even while they were children they were wiser than their fathers. They asked their parents whence the light came which streamed through the fissures of the rock and played along the sides of the cavern, and whence and from what descended the roots of the great vine. Their father could not tell them, and their mother only laughed at the question, which appeared to her very foolish. They asked the priest, but he could not tell them; but he said he supposed the light came from the eyes of some great wolf. The boys asked the king tortoise, who sulkily drew his head into his shell, and made no answer. When they asked the chief rattlesnake, he answered that he knew, and would tell them all about it if they would promise to make peace with his tribe, and on no account kill one of his descendants. The boys promised, and the chief rattlesnake then told them that there was a world above them, a beautiful world, peopled by creatures in the shape of beasts, having a pure atmosphere and a soft sky, sweet fruits and mellow water, well-stocked hunting-grounds and well-filled lakes. He told them to ascend by the roots, which were those of a great grape-vine. A while after the boys were missing; nor did they come back till the Minnatarees had celebrated their death, and the lying priest had, as he falsely said, in a vision seen them inhabitants of the land of spirits.

The Indians were surprised by the return of the boys. They came back singing and dancing, and were grown so much, and looked so different from what they did when they left the cavern, that their father and mother scarcely knew them. They were sleek and fat, and when they walked it was with so strong a step that the hollow space rang with the sound of their feet. They were covered with the skins of animals, and had blankets of the skins of racoons and beavers. They described to the Indians the pleasures of the upper world, and the people were delighted with their story. At length they resolved to leave their dull residence underground for the upper regions. All agreed to this except the ground-hog, the badger, and the mole, who said, as they had been put where they were, they would live and die there. The rabbit said he would live sometimes above and sometimes below.

When the Indians had determined to leave their habitations underground, the Minnatarees began, men, women, and children, to clamber up the vine, and one-half of them had already reached the surface of the earth, when a dire mishap involved the remainder in a still more desolate captivity within its bowels.

There was among them a very fat old woman, who was heavier than any six of her nation. Nothing would do but she must go up before some of her neighbours. Away she clambered, but her weight was so great that the vine broke with it, and the opening, to which it afforded the sole means of ascending, closed upon her and the rest of her nation.

THE EVIL MAKER

The Great Spirit made man, and all the good things in the world, while the Evil Spirit was asleep. When the Evil Spirit awoke he saw an Indian, and, wondering at his appearance, he went to him and asked—

"Who made you?"

"The Great Spirit," replied the man.

"Oh, oh," thought the Evil Spirit, "if he can make such a being so

can I."

So he went to work, and tried his best to make an Indian like the man he saw, but he made some mistake, and only made a black man. When he saw that he had failed he was very angry, and in that state was walking about when he met a black bear.

"Who made you?" he asked.

"The Great Spirit," answered the bear.

"Then," thought the Evil Spirit, "I will make a bear too."

To work he went, but do what he would he could not make a black bear, but only a grizzly one, unfit for food. More disgusted than before, he was walking through the forest when he found a beautiful serpent.

"Who made you?" he asked.

"The Great Spirit," replied the serpent.

"Then I will make some like you," said the Evil Maker.

He tried his best, but the serpents he made were all noisome and poisonous, and he saw that he had failed again.

Then it occurred to him that he might make some trees and flowers, but all his efforts only resulted in his producing some poor deformed trees and weeds.

Then he said—

"It is true, I have failed in making things like the Great Spirit, but I can at least spoil what he has made."

And he went off to put murder and lies in the hearts of men.

MACHINITOU, THE EVIL SPIRIT

Chemanitou, being the Master of Life, at one time became the origin of a spirit that has ever since caused him and all others of his creation a great deal of disquiet. His birth was owing to an accident. It was in this wise:—

Metowac, or as the white people now call it, Long Island, was originally a vast plain, so level and free from any kind of growth that it looked like a portion of the great sea that had suddenly been made to move back and let the sand below appear, which was, in fact, the case.

Here it was that Chemanitou used to come and sit when he wished to bring any new creation to life. The place being spacious and solitary, the water upon every side, he had not only room enough, but was free from interruption.

It is well known that some of these early creations were of very great size, so that very few could live in the same place, and their strength made it difficult for even Chemanitou to control them, for when he has given them certain powers they have the use of the laws that govern those powers, till it is his will to take them back to himself. Accordingly it was the custom of Chemanitou, when he wished to try the effect of these creatures, to set them in motion upon the island of Metowac, and if they did not please him, he took the life away from them again. He would set up a mammoth, or other large animal, in the centre of the island, and build it up with great care, somewhat in the manner that a cabin or a canoe is made.

Even to this day may be found traces of what had been done here in former years, and the manner in which the earth sometimes sinks down shows that this island is nothing more than a great cake of earth, a sort of platter laid upon the sea for the convenience of Chemanitou, who used it as a table upon which he might work, never having designed it for anything else, the margin of the Chatiemac (the stately swan), or Hudson river, being better adapted to the purposes of habitation.

When the Master of Life wished to build up an elephant or mammoth, he placed four cakes of clay upon the ground, at proper distances, which were moulded into shape, and became the feet of the animal.

Now sometimes these were left unfinished, and to this day the green tussocks to be seen like little islands about the marshes show where these cakes of clay were placed.

As Chemanitou went on with his work, the Neebanawbaigs (or water-spirits), the Puck-wud-jinnies (little men who vanish), and, indeed, all the lesser manitoes, used to come and look on, and wonder what it would be, and how it would act.

When the animal was completed, and had dried a long time in the sun, Chemanitou opened a place in the side, and, entering in, remained there many days.

When he came forth the creature began to shiver and sway from side to side, in such a manner as shook the whole island for leagues. If its appearance pleased the Master of Life it was suffered to depart, and it was generally found that these animals plunged into the open sea upon the north side of the island, and disappeared in the great forests beyond.

Now at one time Chemanitou was a very long time building an animal of such great bulk that it looked like a mountain upon the centre of the island, and all the manitoes from all parts came to see what it was. The Puck-wud-jinnies especially made themselves very merry, capering behind its great ears, sitting within its mouth, each perched upon a tooth, and running in and out of the sockets of the eyes, thinking Chemanitou, who was finishing off other parts of the animal, would not see them.

But he can see right through everything he has made. He was glad to see the Puck-wud-jinnies so lively, and he bethought him of many new creations while he watched their motions.

When the Master of Life had completed this large animal, he was fearful to give it life, and so it was left upon the island, or work-table of Chemanitou, till its great weight caused it to break through, and, sinking partly down, it stuck fast, the head and tail holding it in such a manner as to prevent it slipping further down.

Chemanitou then lifted up a piece of the back, and found it made a very good cavity, into which the old creations which failed to please him might be thrown.

He sometimes amused himself by making creatures very small and active, with which he disported awhile, and finding them of very little use in the world, and not so attractive as the little vanishers, he would take out the life, taking it to himself, and then cast them into the cave made in the body of the unfinished animal.

In this way great quantities of very odd shapes were heaped together in this Roncomcomon, or Place of Fragments.

He was always careful before casting a thing he had created aside to take out the life.

One day the Master of Life took two pieces of clay and moulded them into two large feet, like those of a panther. He did not make four—there were two only.

He put his own feet into them, and found the tread very light and springy, so that he might go with great speed and yet make no noise.

Next he built up a pair of very tall legs, in the shape of his own, and made them walk about a while. He was pleased with the motion. Then followed a round body covered with large scales, like those of the alligator.

He now found the figure doubling forward, and he fastened a long black snake, that was gliding by, to the back part of the body, and wound the other end round a sapling which grew near, and this held the body upright, and made a very good tail.

The shoulders were broad and strong, like those of the buffalo, and covered with hair. The neck thick and short, and full at the back.

Thus far Chemanitou had worked with little thought, but when he came to the head he thought a long while.

He took a round ball of clay into his lap, and worked it over with great care. While he thought, he patted the ball of clay upon the top, which made it very broad and low, for Chemanitou was thinking of the panther feet and the buffalo neck. He remembered the Puck-wud-jinnies playing in the eye sockets of the great unfinished animal, and he bethought him to set the eyes out, like those of a lobster, so that the animal might see on every side.

He made the forehead broad and full, but low, for here was to be the wisdom of the forked tongue, like that of the serpent, which should be in its mouth. It should see all things and know all things. Here Chemanitou stopped, for he saw that he had never thought of such a creation before, one with two feet—a creature that should stand upright, and see upon every side.

The jaws were very strong, with ivory teeth and gills upon either side, which rose and fell whenever breath passed through them. The nose was like the beak of the vulture. A tuft of porcupine-quills made the scalp lock.

Chemanitou held the head out the length of his arm, and turned it first upon one side and then upon the other. He passed it rapidly through the air, and saw the gills rise and fall, the lobster eyes whirl round, and the vulture nose look keen.

Chemanitou became very sad, yet he put the head upon the shoulders. It was the first time he had made an upright figure. It seemed to be the first idea of a man.

It was now nearly right. The bats were flying through the air, and the roar of wild beasts began to be heard. A gusty wind swept in from the ocean and passed over the island of Metowac, casting the light sand to and fro. A wavy scud was skimming along the horizon, while higher up in the sky was a dark thick cloud, upon the verge of which the moon hung for a moment and was then shut in.

A panther came by and stayed a moment, with one foot raised and bent inward, while it looked up at the image and smelt the feet that were like its own.

A vulture swooped down with a great noise of its wings, and made a dash at the beak, but Chemanitou held it back.

Then came the porcupine, the lizard, and the snake, each drawn by its kind in the image.

Chemanitou veiled his face for many hours, and the gusty wind swept by, but he did not stir.

He saw that every beast of the earth seeks its kind, and that which is like draws its likeness to itself.

The Master of Life thought and thought. The idea grew into his mind that at some time he would create a creature who should be made, not after the things of the earth, but after himself.

The being should link this world to the spirit world, being made in the likeness of the Great Spirit, he should be drawn unto his likeness.

Many days and nights—whole seasons—passed while Chemanitou thought upon these things. He saw all things.

Then the Master of Life lifted up his head. The stars were looking down upon the image, and a bat had alighted upon the forehead, spreading its great wings upon each side. Chemanitou took the bat and held out its whole leathery wings (and ever since the bat, when he rests, lets his body hang down), so that he could try them over the head of the image. He then took the life of the bat away, and twisted off the body, by which means the whole thin part fell down over the head of the image and upon each side, making the ears, and a covering for the forehead like that of the hooded serpent.

Chemanitou did not cut off the face of the image below, but went on and made a chin and lips that were firm and round, that they might shut in the forked tongue and ivory teeth, and he knew that with the lips the image would smile when life should be given to it.

The image was now complete save for the arms, and Chemanitou saw that it was necessary it should have hands. He grew more grave.

He had never given hands to any creature. He made the arms and the hands very beautiful, after the manner of his own.

Chemanitou now took no pleasure in the work he had done. It was not good in his sight.

He wished he had not given it hands. Might it not, when trusted with life, create? Might it not thwart the plans of the Master of Life himself?

He looked long at the image. He saw what it would do when life should be given it. He knew all things.

He now put fire in the image, but fire is not life.

He put fire within and a red glow passed through and through it. The fire dried the clay of which the image was made, and gave the image an exceedingly fierce aspect. It shone through the scales upon the breast, through the gills, and the bat-winged ears. The lobster eyes were like a living coal.

Chemanitou opened the side of the image, but he did not enter. He had given it hands and a chin.

It could smile like the manitoes themselves.

He made it walk all about the island of Metowac, that he might see how it would act. This he did by means of his will.

He now put a little life into it, but he did not take out the fire. Chemanitou saw the aspect of the creature would be very terrible, and yet that it could smile in such a manner that it ceased to be ugly. He thought much upon these things. He felt that it would not be best to let such a creature live—a creature made up mostly from the beasts of the field, but with hands of power, a chin lifting the head upward, and lips holding all things within themselves.

While he thought upon these things he took the image in his hands and cast it into the cave. But Chemanitou forgot to take out the life.

The creature lay a long time in the cave and did not stir, for its fall was very great. It lay amongst the old creations that had been thrown in there without life.

Now when a long time had passed Chemanitou heard a great noise in the cave. He looked in and saw the image sitting there, and it was trying to put together the old broken things that had been cast in as of no value.

Chemanitou gathered together a vast heap of stones and sand, for large rocks are not to be had upon the island, and stopped the mouth of the cave. Many days passed and the noise within the cave grew louder. The earth shook, and hot smoke came from the ground. The manitoes crowded to Metowac to see what was the matter.

Chemanitou came also, for he remembered the image he had cast in there of which he had forgotten to take away the life.

Suddenly there was a great rising of the stones and sand, the sky grew black with wind and dust.

Fire played about on the ground, and water gushed high into the air.

All the manitoes fled with fear, and the image came forth with a great noise and most terrible to behold. Its life had grown strong within it, for the fire had made it very fierce.

Everything fled before it and cried—

"Machinitou! machinitou," which means a god, but an evil god.

DIQUA

A great while ago the Shawanos nation took up the war-talk against the Walkullas, who lived on their own lands on the borders of the Great Salt Lake, and near the Burning Water. Part of the nation were not well pleased with the war. The head chief and the counsellors said the Walkullas were very brave and cunning, and the priests said their god was mightier than ours. The old and experienced warriors said the counsellors were wise, and had spoken well; but the Head Buffalo, the young warriors, and all who wished for war, would not listen to their words. They said that our fathers had beaten their fathers in many battles, that the Shawanos were as brave and strong as they ever were, and the Walkullas much weaker and more cowardly. They said the old and timid, the faint heart and the failing knee, might stay at home to take care of the women and children, and sleep and dream of those who had never dared bend a bow or look upon a painted cheek or listen to a war-whoop, while the young warriors went to war and drank much blood. When two moons were gone they said they would come back with many prisoners and scalps, and have a great feast. The arguments of the fiery young men prevailed with all the youthful warriors, but the elder and wiser listened to the priests and counsellors, and remained in their villages to see the leaf fall and the grass grow, and to gather in the nut and follow the trail of the deer.

Two moons passed, then a third, then came the night enlivened by many stars, but the warriors returned not. As the land of the Walkullas lay but a woman's journey of six suns from the villages of our nation, our people began to fear that our young men had been overcome in battle and were all slain.

The head chief, the counsellors, and all the warriors who had remained behind, came together in the great wigwam, and called the priests to tell them where their sons were. Chenos, who was the wisest of them all (as well he might be, for he was older than the oak-tree whose top dies by the hand of Time), answered that they were killed by their enemies, the Walkullas, assisted by men of a strange speech and colour, who lived beyond the Great Salt Lake, fought with thunder and lightning, and came to our enemies on the back of a great bird with many white wings. When he had thus made known to our people the fate of the warriors there was a dreadful shout of horror throughout the village. The women wept aloud, and the men sprang up and seized their bows and arrows to go to war with the Walkullas and the strange warriors who had helped to slay their sons, but Chenos bade them sit down again.

"There is one yet living," said he. "He will soon be here. The sound of his footsteps is in my ear as he crosses the hollow hills. He has killed many of his enemies; he has glutted his vengeance fully; he has drunk blood in plenteous draughts. Long he fought with the men of his own race, and many fell before him, but he fled from the men who came to the battle armed with the real lightning, and hurling unseen death. Even now I see him coming; the shallow streams he has forded; the deep rivers he has swum. He is tired and hungry, and his quiver has no arrows, but he brings a prisoner in his arms. Lay the deer's flesh on the fire, and bring hither the pounded corn. Taunt him not, for he is valiant, and has fought like a hungry bear."

As the wise Chenos spoke these words to the grey-bearded counsellors and warriors the Head Buffalo walked calm and cool into the midst of them. There he stood, tall and straight as a young pine, but he spoke no word, looking on the head chief and the counsellors. There was blood upon his body, dried on by the sun, and the arm next his heart was bound up with the skin of the deer. His eye was hollow and his body gaunt, as though he had fasted long. His quiver held no arrows.

"Where are our sons?" inquired the head chief of the warrior.

"Ask the wolf and the panther," he answered.

"Brother! tell us where are our sons!" exclaimed the chief. "Our women ask us for their sons. They want them. Where are they?"

"Where are the snows of last year?" replied the warrior. "Have they not gone down the swelling river into the Great Lake? They have, and even so have your sons descended the stream of Time into the great Lake of Death. The great star sees them as they lie by the water of the Walkulla, but they see him not. The panther and the wolf howl unheeded at their feet, and the eagle screams, but they hear them not. The vulture whets his beak on their bones, the wild-cat rends their flesh, both are unfelt, for your sons are dead."

When the warrior told these things to our people, they set up their loud death-howl. The women wept; but the men sprang up and seized their weapons, to go to meet the Walkullas, the slayers of their sons. The chief warrior rose again—

"Fathers and warriors," said he, "hear me and believe my words, for I will tell you the truth. Who ever heard the Head Buffalo lie, and who ever saw him afraid of his enemies? Never, since the time that he chewed the bitter root and put on the new moccasins, has he lied or fled from his foes. He has neither a forked tongue nor a faint heart. Fathers, the Walkullas are weaker than us. Their arms are not so strong, their hearts are not so big, as ours. As well might the timid deer make war upon the hungry wolf, as the Walkullas upon the Shawanos. We could slay them as easily as a hawk pounces into a dove's nest and steals away her unfeathered little ones. The Head Buffalo alone could have taken the scalps of half the nation. But a strange tribe has come among them—men whose skin is white as the folds of the cloud, and whose hair shines like the great star of day. They do not fight as we fight, with bows and arrows and with war-axes, but with spears which thunder and lighten, and send unseen death. The Shawanos fall before it as the berries and acorns fall when the forest is shaken by the wind in the beaver-moon. Look at the arm nearest my heart. It was stricken by a bolt from the strangers' thunder; but he fell by the hands of the Head Buffalo, who fears nothing but shame, and his scalp lies at the feet of the head chief.

"Fathers, this was our battle. We came upon the Walkullas, I and my brothers, when they were unprepared. They were just going to hold the dance of the green corn. The whole nation had come to the dance; there were none left behind save the sick and the very old. None were painted; they were all for peace, and were as women. We crept close to them, and hid in the thick bushes which grew upon the edge of their camp, for the Shawanos are the cunning adder and not the foolish rattlesnake. We saw them preparing to offer a sacrifice to the Great Spirit. We saw them clean the deer, and hang his head, horns, and entrails upon the great white pole with a forked top, which stood over the roof of the council wigwam. They did not know that the Master of Life had sent the Shawanos to mix blood with the sacrifices. We saw them take the new corn and rub it upon their hands, breasts, and faces. Then the head chief, having first thanked the Master of Life for his goodness to the Walkullas, got up and gave his brethren a talk. He told them that the Great Spirit loved them, and had made them victorious over all their enemies; that he had sent a great many fat bears, deer, and moose to their hunting-ground, and had given them fish, whose heads were very small and bodies very big; that he had made their corn grow tall and sweet, and had ordered his suns to ripen it in the beginning of the harvest moon, that they might make a great feast for the strangers who had come from a far country on the wings of a great bird to warm themselves at the Walkullas' fire. He told them they must love the Great Spirit, take care of the old men, tell no lies, and never break the faith of the pipe of peace; that they must not harm the strangers, for they were their brothers, but must live in peace with them, and give them lands and wives from among their women. If they did these things the Great Spirit, he said, would make their corn grow taller than ever, and direct them to hunting-grounds where the moose should be as thick as the stars.

"Fathers and warriors, we heard these words; but we knew not what to do. We feared not the Walkullas; the God of War, we saw, had given them into our hands. But who were the strange tribe? Were they armed as we were, and was their Great Medicine (Great Spirit) like ours? Warriors, you all knew the Young Eagle, the son of the Old Eagle, who is here with us; but his wings are feeble, he flies no more to the field of blood. The Young Eagle feared nothing but shame, and he said—

"'I see many men sit round a fire, I will go and see who they are!'

"He went. The Old Eagle looks at me as if he would say, 'Why went not the chief warrior himself?' I will tell you. The Head

Buffalo is a head taller than the tallest man of his tribe. Can the moose crawl into the fox's hole? Can the swan hide himself under a little leaf? The Young Eagle was little, save in his soul. He was not full-grown, save in his heart. He could go and not be seen or heard. He was the cunning black-snake which creeps silently in the grass, and none thinks him near till he strikes.

"He came back and told us there were many strange men a little way before us whose faces were white, and who wore no skins, whose cabins were white as the snow upon the Backbone of the Great Spirit (the Alleghany Mountains), flat at the top, and moving with the wind like the reeds on the bank of a river; that they did not talk like the Walkullas, but spoke a strange tongue, the like of which he had never heard before. Many of our warriors would have turned back to our own lands. The Flying Squirrel said it was not cowardice to do so; but the Head Buffalo never turns till he has tasted the blood of his foes. The Young Eagle said he had eaten the bitter root and put on the new moccasins, and had been made a man, and his father and the warriors would cry shame on him if he took no scalp. Both he and the Head Buffalo said they would go and attack the Walkullas and their friends alone. The young warriors then said they would also go to the battle, and with a great heart, as their fathers had done. Then the Shawanos rushed upon their foes.

"The Walkullas fell before us like rain in the summer months. We were as a fire among rushes. We went upon them when they were unprepared, when they were as children; and for a while the Great Spirit gave them into our hands. But a power rose up against us that we could not withstand. The strange men came upon us armed with thunder and lightning. Why delays my tongue to tell its story? Fathers, your sons have fallen like the leaves of a forest-tree in a high wind, like the flowers of spring after a frost, like drops of rain in the sturgeon moon! Warriors, the sprouts which sprang up from the withered oaks have perished, the young braves of our nation lie food for the eagle and the wild-cat by the arm of the Great Lake!

"Fathers, the bolt from the strangers' thunder entered my flesh, yet I did not fly. These six scalps I tore from the Walkullas, but this has yellow hair. Have I done well?"

The head chief and the counsellors answered he had done very well, but Chenos answered—

"No. You went into the Walkullas' camp when the tribe were feasting to the Great Spirit, and you disturbed the sacrifice, and mixed human blood with it. Therefore has this evil come upon us, for the Great Spirit is very angry."

Then the head chief and the counsellors asked Chenos what must be done to appease the Master of Breath.

Chenos answered—

"The Head Buffalo, with the morning, will offer to him that which he holds dearest."

The Head Buffalo looked upon the priests, and said—

"The Head Buffalo fears the Great Spirit. He will kill a deer, and, in the morning, it shall be burned to the Great Spirit."

Chenos said to him—

"You have told the council how the battle was fought and who fell; you have shown the spent quiver and the scalps, but you have not spoken of your prisoner. The Great Spirit keeps nothing hid from his priests, of whom Chenos is one. He has told me you have a prisoner, one with tender feet and a trembling heart."

"Let any one say the Head Buffalo ever lied," replied the

warrior. "He never spoke but truth. He has a prisoner, a woman taken from the strange camp, a daughter of the sun, a maiden from the happy islands which no Shawano has ever seen, and she shall live with me, and become the mother of my children."

"Where is she?" asked the head chief.

"She sits on the bank of the river at the bend where we dug up the bones of the great beast, beneath the tree which the Master of Breath shivered with his lightnings. I placed her there because the spot is sacred, and none dare disturb her. I will go and fetch her to the council fire, but let no one touch her or show anger, for she is fearful as a young deer, and weeps like a child for its mother."

Soon he returned, and brought with him a woman. She shook like a reed in the winter's wind, and many tears ran down her cheeks. The men sat as though their tongues were frozen. Was she beautiful? Go forth to the forest when it is clothed with the flowers of spring, look at the tall maize when it waves in the wind, and ask if they are beautiful. Her skin was white as the snow which falls upon the mountains beyond our lands, save upon her cheeks, where it was red,—not such red as the Indian paints when he goes to war, but such as the Master of Life gives to the flower which grows among thorns. Her eyes shone like the star which never moves. Her step was like that of the deer when it is a little scared.

The Head Buffalo said to the council—

"This is my prisoner. I fought hard for her. Three warriors, tall, strong, and painted, three pale men, armed with red lightning, stood at her side. Where are they now? I bore her away in my arms, for fear had overcome her. When night came on I wrapped skins around her, and laid her under the leafy branches of the tree to keep off the cold, and kindled a fire, and watched by her till the sun rose. Who will say she shall not live with the Head Buffalo, and be the mother of his children?"

Then the Old Eagle got up, but he could not walk strong, for he was the oldest warrior of his tribe, and had seen the flowers bloom many times, the infant trees of the forest die of old age, and the friends of his boyhood laid in the dust. He went to the woman, laid his hands on her head, and wept. The other warriors, who had lost their kindred and sons in the war with the Walkullas, shouted and lamented. The woman also wept.

"Where is the Young Eagle?" asked the Old Eagle of the Head Buffalo. The other warriors, in like manner, asked for their kindred who had been killed.

"Fathers, they are dead," answered the warrior. "The Head Buffalo has said they are dead, and he never lies. But let my fathers take comfort. Who can live for ever? The foot of the swift step and the hand of the stout bow become feeble. The eye grows dim, and the heart of many days quails at the fierce glance of warriors. 'Twas better they should die like brave men in their youth than become old men and faint."

"We must have revenge," they all cried. "We will not listen to the young warrior who pines for the daughter of the sun."

Then they began to sing a mournful song. The strange woman wept. Tears rolled down her cheeks, and she often looked up to the house of the Great Spirit and spoke, but none could understand her. All the time the Old Eagle and the other warriors begged that she should be burned to revenge them.

"Brothers and warriors," said Chenos, "our sons did wrong when they broke in upon the sacred dance the Walkullas made to their god, and he lent his thunder to the strange warriors. Let us not draw down his vengeance further by doing we know not what. Let the beautiful woman remain this night in the wigwam of the council, covered with skins, and let none disturb her. Tomorrow we will offer a sacrifice of deer's flesh to the Great Spirit, and if he will not give her to the raging fire and the torments of the avengers, he will tell us so by the words of his mouth. If he does not speak, it shall be done to her as the Old Eagle and his brothers have said."

The head chief said—

"Chenos has spoken well; wisdom is in his words. Make for the strange woman a soft bed of skins, and treat her kindly, for it may be she is a daughter of the Great Spirit."

Then they all returned to their cabins and slept, save the Head Buffalo, who, fearing for the woman's life, laid himself down at the door of the lodge, and watched.

When the morning came the warrior went to the forest and killed a deer which he brought to Chenos, who prepared it for a sacrifice, and sang a song while the flesh lay on the fire.

"Let us listen," said Chenos, stopping the warriors in their dance. "Let us see if the Great Spirit hears us."

They listened, but could hear nothing. Chenos asked him why he did not speak, but he did not answer. Then they sang again.

"Hush!" said Chenos listening. "I hear the crowing of the Great Turkey-cock. I hear him speaking."

They stopped, and Chenos went close to the fire and talked with his master, but nobody saw with whom he talked.

"What does the Great Spirit tell his prophet?" asked the head chief.

"He says," answered Chenos, "the young woman must not be offered to him. He wills her to live and become the mother of many children."

Many were pleased that she was to live, but those who had lost brothers or sons were not appeased, and they said—

"We will have blood. We will go to the priest of the Evil Spirit, and ask him if his master will not give us revenge."

Not far from where our nation had their council fire was a great hill, covered with stunted trees and moss, and rugged rocks. There was a great cave in it, in which dwelt Sketupah, the priest of the Evil One, who there did worship to his master. Sketupah would have been tall had he been straight, but he was more crooked than a bent bow. His hair was like a bunch of grapes, and his eyes like two coals of fire. Many were the gifts our nation made to him to gain his favour, and the favour of his master.

Who but he feasted on the fattest buffalo hump? Who but he fed on the earliest ear of milky corn, on the best things that grew on the land or in the water?

The Old Eagle went to the mouth of the cave and cried with a loud voice—

"Sketupah!"

"Sketupah!" answered the hoarse voice of the Evil One from the hollow cave. He soon came and asked the Old Eagle what he wanted.

"Revenge for our sons who have been killed by the Walkullas and their friends. Will your master hear us?"

"My master must have a sacrifice; he must smell blood," answered Sketupah. "Then we shall know if he will give revenge. Bring hither a sacrifice in the morning."

So in the morning they brought a sacrifice, and the priest laid it on the fire while he danced around. He ceased singing and listened, but the Evil Spirit answered not. Just as he was going to commence another song the warriors saw a large ball rolling very fast up the hill to the spot where they stood. It was the height of a man. When it came up to them it began to unwind itself slowly, until at last a little strange-looking man crept out of the ball, which was made of his own hair. He was no higher than one's shoulders. One of his feet made a strange track, such as no warrior had ever seen before. His face was as black as the shell of the butter-nut or the feathers of the raven, and his eyes as green as grass. His hair was of the colour of moss, and so long that, as the wind blew it out, it seemed the tail of a fiery star.

"What do you want of me?" he asked.

The priest answered—

"The Shawanos want revenge. They want to sacrifice the beautiful daughter of the sun, whom the Head Buffalo has brought from the camp of the Walkullas."

"They shall have their wish," said the Evil Spirit. "Go and fetch her."

Then Old Eagle and the warriors fetched her. Head Buffalo would have fought for her, but Chenos commanded him to be still.

"My master," he said, "will see she does not suffer." Then they fastened her to the stake. The head warrior had stood still, for he hoped that the priest of the Great Spirit should snatch her away from the Evil One. Now he shouted his war-cry and rushed upon Sketupah. It was in vain. Sketupah's master did but breathe upon the face of the warrior when he fell as though he had struck him a blow, and never breathed more. Then the Evil One commanded them to seize Chenos.

"Come, my master," cried Chenos, "for the hands of the Evil One are upon me."

As soon as he had said this, very far over the tall hills, which Indians call the Backbone of the Great Spirit, the people saw two great lights, brighter and larger than stars, moving very fast towards the land of the Shawanos. One was just as high as another, and they were both as high as the goat-sucker flies before a thunderstorm. At first they were close together, but as they came nearer they grew wider apart. Soon our people saw that they were two eyes, and in a little while the body of a great man, whose head nearly reached the sky, came after them. Brothers, the eyes of the Great Spirit always go before him, and nothing is hid from his sight. Brothers, I cannot describe the Master of Life as he stood before the warriors of our nation. Can you look steadily on the star of the morning?

When the Evil Spirit saw the Spirit of Good coming, he began to grow in stature, and continued swelling until he was as tall and big as he. When the Spirit of Good came near and saw how the Evil Spirit had grown, he stopped, and, looking angry, said, with a voice that shook the hills—

"You lied; you promised to stay among the white people and the nations towards the rising sun, and not trouble my people more."

"This woman," replied the Evil Spirit, "comes from my country; she is mine."

"She is mine," said the Great Spirit. "I had given her for a wife to the warrior whom you have killed. Tell me no more lies, bad manito, lest I punish you. Away, and see you trouble my people no more."

The cowardly spirit made no answer, but shrank down to the size he was when he first came. Then he began as before to roll himself up in his hair, which he soon did, and then disappeared as he came. When he was gone, the Great Spirit shrank till he was no larger than a Shawano, and began talking to our people in a soft sweet voice—

"Men of the Shawanos nation, I love you and have always loved you. I bade you conquer your enemies; I gave your foes into your hands. I sent herds of deer and many bears and moose to your hunting-ground, and made my suns shine upon your corn. Who lived so well, who fought so bravely as the Shawanos? Whose women bore so many sons as yours?

"Why did you disturb the sacrifice which the Walkullas were offering to me at the feast of green corn? I was angry, and gave your warriors into the hands of their enemies.

"Shawanos, hear my words, and forget them not; do as I bid you, and you shall see my power and my goodness. Offer no further violence to the white maiden, but treat her kindly. Go now and rake up the ashes of the sacrifice fire into a heap, gathering up the brands. When the great star of evening rises, open the ashes, put in the body of the Head Buffalo, lay on much wood, and kindle a fire on it. Let all the nation be called together, for all must assist in laying wood on the fire, but they must put on no pine, nor the tree which bears white flowers, nor the grape-vine which yields no fruit, nor the shrub whose dew blisters the flesh. The fire must be kept burning two whole moons. It must not go out; it must burn night and day. On the first day of the third moon put no wood on the fire, but let it die. On the morning of the second day the Shawanos must all come to the heap of ashes—every man, woman, and child must come, and the aged who cannot walk must be helped to it. Then Chenos and the head chief must bring out the beautiful woman, and place her near the ashes. This is the will of the Great Spirit."

When he had finished these words he began to swell until he had reached his former bulk and stature. Then at each of his shoulders came out a wing of the colour of the gold-headed pigeon. Gently shaking these, he took flight from the land of the Shawanos, and was never seen in those beautiful regions again.

The Shawanos did as he bade them. They raked the ashes together, laid the body of Head Buffalo in them, lighted the fire, and kept it burning the appointed time. On the first day of the third moon they let the fire out, assembled the nation around, and placed the beautiful woman near the ashes. They waited, and looked to see what would happen. At last the priests and warriors who were nearest began to shout, crying out—

"Piqua!" which in the Shawanos tongue means a man coming out of the ashes, or a man made of ashes.

They told no lie. There he stood, a man tall and straight as a young pine, looking like a Shawanos, but handsomer than any man of our nation. The first thing he did was to cry the war-whoop, and demand paint, a club, a bow and arrows, and a hatchet,—all of which were given him. Looking around he saw the white woman, and he walked up to her, and gazed in her eyes. Then he came to the head chief and said—

"I must have that woman for my wife."

"What are you?" asked the chief.

"A man of ashes," he replied.

"Who made you?"

"The Great Spirit; and now let me go, that I may take my bow and arrows, kill my deer, and come back and take the beautiful maiden for my wife."

The chief asked Chenos—

"Shall he have her? Does the Great Spirit give her to him?"

"Yes," replied the priest. "The Great Spirit has willed that he shall have her, and from them shall arise a tribe to be called Piqua."

Brothers, I am a Piqua, descended from the man made of ashes. If I have told you a lie, blame not me, for I have but told the story as I heard it. Brothers, I have done.

THE FIRST FIRE

In the beginning there was no fire and the world was cold. Then the Thunders, who lived up in Galun'lati, sent their lightning and put fire into the bottom of a hollow sycamore tree which grew on an island. The animals knew it was there because they could see the smoke coming out at the top, but they could not get to it on account of the water, so they held a council to decide what to do. This was a long, long time ago.

Every animal was anxious to go after the fire. Raven offered. He was large and strong, so he was sent first. He flew high and far across the water, and lighted on the sycamore tree. There he perched, wondering what to do next. Then he looked at himself. The heat had scorched his feathers black. Raven was so frightened he flew back across the water without any fire.

Then little Wa-hu-hu, the Screech Owl, offered to go. He flew high and far across the water and perched upon a hollow tree. As he sat there looking into the hollow tree, wondering what to do, a blast of hot air came up and hurt his eyes. Screech Owl was frightened. He flew back as best he could, because he could hardly see. That is why his eyes are red even to this day.

Then Hooting Owl and the Horned Owl went, but by the

time they reached the hollow tree, the fire was blazing so fiercely that the smoke nearly blinded them. The ashes carried up by the breeze made white rings around their eyes. So they had to come home without fire. Therefore they have white rings around their eyes.

None of the rest of the birds would go to the fire. Then Uk-su-hi, the racer snake, said he would go through the water and bring back fire. He swam to the island and crawled through the grass to the tree. Then he went into the tree by a small hole at the bottom. But the heat and smoke were dreadful. The ground at the bottom of the tree was covered with hot ashes. The racer darted back and forth trying to get off the ashes, and at last managed to escape through the same hole by which he had entered. But his body had been burned black. Therefore he is now the black racer. And that is why the black racer darts around and doubles on his track as if trying to escape.

Then great Blacksnake, "The Climber," offered to go for fire. He was much larger than the black racer. Blacksnake swam over to the island and climbed up the tree on the outside, as the blacksnake always does, but when he put his head down into the hole the smoke choked him so that he fell into the burning stump. Before he could climb out, he, too, was burned black.

So the birds, and the animals, and the snakes held another council. The world was still very cold. There was no fire. But all the birds, and the snakes, and all the four-footed animals refused to go for fire. They were all afraid of the burning sycamore.

Then Water Spider said she would go. This is not the water spider that looks like a mosquito, but the other one—the one with black downy hair and red stripes on her body. She could run on top of the water, or dive to the bottom.

The animals said, "How can you bring back fire?"

But Water Spider spun a thread from her body and wove it into a tusti bowl which she fastened on her back. Then she swam over to the island and through the grass to the fire. Water Spider put one little coal of fire into her bowl, and then swam back with it.

That is how fire came to the world. And that is why Water Spider has a tusti bowl on her back.

THE FINDING OF FIRE

The Yanas have their own story about first finding fire. Names in brackets in the story below signify the creature or thing into which the personage was changed subsequently.

In the beginning Au Mujaupa (master of fire) had fire very far down south on the other side of a big river. The people in this country had no real fire; they had a kind of fire, but it wasn't good. It just warmed a little; it wouldn't cook like the fire which we have now. People killed deer and fished, but they had to eat fish and venison raw.

In the west people had fire, but it wouldn't cook. In the north there were many people, and in the east; but they had no fire that would cook.

"There must be fire in some place," said the people at Pawi; "how can we find it?"

"I will go out to-night to look," said Ahalamila (grey wolf).

That night he went to look for fire. He went to the top of Wahkanopa, looked east and west, saw no fire in either place. Next he looked north; no fire in the north. He looked south; saw no fire anywhere.

Ahalamila came home and talked to the chief and people. "I saw no fire," said he; "I could not see any, but I will go to a better place the next time and take some one with me. I will go to-morrow night to the top of Wahkalu. Who here has a good head, who a sharp eye to see fire? I want to look for fire to-morrow night from the top of Wahkalu; from that place I will look all around the whole world to find fire."

"We have a man here," said the chief, "who can see through a tree, who can see down through the earth to bed rock, who can see through a mountain. You can take him to-morrow night with you. He is Siwegi (a small bird)."

Ahalamila went to Siwegi. "Will you go to-morrow night to look for fire?" asked he.

"I will go if the way is not too long."

"Oh," said Ahalamila, "it will not be long. I will shorten it."

Siwegi agreed to go; and when the time came, they started. Ahalamila doubled up the trail and made it short; in an hour they were on the top of Wahkalu, both ready now to look for fire. The night is very dark; they can see the smallest fire easily.

They look to the east, look with great care, look a good while, see no fire; they look to the north in the same way, see no fire; they look to the west, no fire there. Now Ahalamila looks south, looks a long time, and sees nothing: he looks half an hour to the south, sees a little glimmer like a light very far away.

"Siwegi," said he, "I see a small light down south; it seems like fire far away. I think it is fire."

"Look again," said Siwegi, "look sharply. Maybe it is fire."

"I have looked enough, I think it is fire," said Ahalamila; "but I want you to see it, I want you to look now."

Siwegi looked a little while. "Yes, that is fire," said he.

"Well," said Ahalamila, "we see fire, we know that it is far off in the south."

Ahalamila made the road short, and they were back at Pawi in an hour. "We have found fire," said Ahalamila to the chief and the people. "We know where fire is, we can have fire now."

"We must have that fire," said the people.

"There is no way to get the fire but to go for it," said Ahalamila.

"Well," said the chief, "since Ahalamila saw the fire he will go for it; but the road is long. Who will go and help him? Who will go for fire with Ahalamila?"

About fifty men offered to go, and they started next morning. The journey was long and very hard. Soon two or three men were tired and went home; not long after more were tired, and when they had gone far down to a great river, just north of where the fire was, of the fifty who started only three were left,—Ahalamila, Metsi (coyote), and old Shushu Marimi (dog woman).

Just south of the great river Au Mujaupa had a very big village, and in the village a large sweat-house.

In that house he kept the fire, and had a great crowd of people living in the country outside who served him, and kept every one in the world from stealing his fire. These people were Patcha (snow), Chil Wareko (big rain), Chil Daiauna (big hail), Sabil Keyu (small hail), Juhauju (west wind), Juwaju (south wind), Jukami (north wind), Jukilauju (east wind).

The three, Ahalamila, Metsi, and old Shushu Marimi, were at the northern end of the bridge, and sat there watching till all at the sweat-house was quiet. The bridge was very narrow and slippery; so Ahalamila put pitch on his feet and hands, and on Metsi's and Shushu's feet and hands. All three crossed without slipping, and found every one asleep in the sweat-house.

The old chief, Au Mujaupa, had covered the fire well with ashes. All was silent within and without. Ahalamila, Metsi, and Shushu crept onto the sweat-house quietly, and looked in. All were asleep.

"I will go down first," said Metsi.

"No, I will go first," said Ahalamila. "I will get the fire and reach it to you; you take it and run very fast."

Ahalamila slipped down. Metsi and Shushu remained on the roof. Ahalamila opened the fire carefully, took out a good piece and handed it to the old woman. She put it in her ear. He handed her another; she put it in her other ear, slipped down from the top of the sweat-house, ran across the bridge, and hurried away.

Ahalamila gave Metsi two pieces. He put them in his two ears and started. Ahalamila filled his own ears and followed.

The three had run over two mountains when Au Mujaupa woke up and saw that the ashes had been opened, and that fire had been taken, that a coal had fallen near the central pillar. He sprang up, went to the top of the sweat-house, shouted, called to all his people,—

"Fire has been stolen! Fire has been stolen! Go, you, and follow!"

Now Patcha, Chil Wareko, Chil Daiauna, Sabil Keyu, and all the wind people rose up and followed, raced and stormed in every direction. So much rain came that the whole country was covered with water.

Now Juwaju was ahead of all Au Mujaupa's people chasing the three robbers. Chil Wareko came too, and fell upon the three furiously; he drenched and chilled them. Next came Jukami and Patcha, who nearly froze them.

Metsi was almost dead; the fire went out in both his ears. Ahalamila lost his fire, too. Chil Wareko, Juwaju, and Patcha quenched it, and then he let it fall.

Old Shushu was behind a good way, but she ran all the time. She kept her hand on one ear as she ran. She lost the fire out of her other ear, and when the piece fell out it broke in two and fell apart. Chil Wareko picked up the fire and took it back; he found six pieces, thought that he had all. He and the others stopped following.

Ahalamila and Metsi ran ahead, left old Shushu to get on the best she could, and reached home first. They were wet, very cold, and tired.

"Where is your fire?" asked the chief.

"I have none; Chil Wareko took my fire," said Ahalamila.

"Where is your fire?" asked the chief.

"Chil Wareko took it," said Metsi.

The chief was very sorry, and all the people were sorry. The old woman did not come, and the people said, "She must be frozen dead."

At sundown old Shushu came back; she came very slowly, was terribly tired, but courageous. She reached the sweat-house, came in, said nothing, lay down wet and cold.

"Where is the fire?" asked she; "did not Ahalamila and Metsi bring fire? They are young and strong, and had plenty of fire."

After a while she stood up, drew some wood-dust together, then sat down, opened her ear and held it over the dust; a big piece of fire came out. Wood was brought quickly, and soon the whole sweat-house was warm. The people who were cold before were warm now and glad.

"Bring meat and we will try how it tastes when 'tis roasted," said the chief.

He cut some venison and roasted it. One and another tasted the meat. "It is very good," said they; a third one said, "I'll try it," and Gagi (crow) took a taste. "Oh, it is sweet, very good," said Gagi.

Each one roasted meat and ate heartily. Next day all went to hunt, and had a great feast in the evening. A chief from another place came to the feast and got fire, took it home with him. Soon all people had fire; every one had fire in all parts of the country.

THE FUNERAL FIRE

For several nights after the interment of a Chippewa a fire is kept burning upon the grave. This fire is lit in the evening, and carefully supplied with small sticks of dry wood, to keep up a bright but small fire. It is kept burning for several hours, generally until the usual hour of retiring to rest, and then suffered to go out. The fire is renewed for four nights, and sometimes for longer. The person who performs this pious office is generally a near relative of the deceased, or one who has been long intimate with him. The following tale is related as showing the origin of the custom.

A small war party of Chippewas encountered their enemies upon an open plain, where a severe battle was fought. Their leader was a brave and distinguished warrior, but he never acted with greater bravery, or more distinguished himself by personal prowess, than on this occasion. After turning the tide of battle against his enemies, while shouting for victory, he received an arrow in his breast, and fell upon the plain. No warrior thus killed is ever buried, and according to ancient custom, the chief was placed in a sitting posture upon the field, his back supported by a tree, and his face turned towards the direction in which his enemies had fled. His headdress and equipment were accurately adjusted as if he were living, and his bow leaned against his shoulder. In this posture his companions left him. That he was dead appeared evident to all, but a strange thing had happened. Although deprived of speech and motion, the chief heard distinctly all that was said by his friends. He heard them lament his death without having the power to contradict it, and he felt their touch as they adjusted his posture, without having the power to reciprocate it. His anguish, when he felt himself thus abandoned, was extreme, and his wish to follow his friends on their return home so completely filled his mind, as he saw them one after another take leave of him and depart, that with a terrible effort he arose and followed them. His form, however, was invisible to them, and this aroused in him surprise, disappointment, and rage, which by turns took possession of him. He followed their track, however, with great diligence. Wherever they went he went, when they walked he walked, when they ran he ran, when they encamped he stopped with them, when they slept he slept, when they awoke he awoke. In short, he mingled in all their labours and toils, but he was excluded from all their sources of refreshment, except that of sleeping, and from the pleasures of participating in their conversation, for all that he said received no notice.

"Is it possible," he cried, "that you do not see me, that you do not hear me, that you do not understand me? Will you suffer me to bleed to death without offering to stanch my wounds? Will you permit me to starve while you eat around me? Have those whom I have so often led to war so soon forgotten me? Is there no one who recollects me, or who will offer me a morsel of food in my distress?"

Thus he continued to upbraid his friends at every stage of the journey, but no one seemed to hear his words. If his voice was heard at all, it was mistaken for the rustling of the leaves in the wind.

At length the returning party reached their village, and their women and children came out, according to custom, to welcome their return and proclaim their praises.

"Kumaudjeewug! Kumaudjeewug! Kumaudjeewug! they have met, fought, and conquered!" was shouted by every mouth, and the words resounded through the most distant parts of the village. Those who had lost friends came eagerly to inquire their fate, and to know whether they had died like men. The aged father consoled himself for the loss of his son with the reflection that he had fallen manfully, and the widow half forgot her sorrow amid the praises that were uttered of the bravery of her husband. The hearts of the youths glowed with martial ardour as they heard these flattering praises, and the children joined in the shouts, of which they scarcely knew the meaning. Amidst all this uproar and bustle no one seemed conscious of the presence of the warrior-chief. He heard many inquiries made respecting his fate. He heard his companions tell how he had fought, conquered, and fallen, pierced by an arrow through his breast, and how he had been left behind among the slain on the field of battle.

"It is not true," declared the angry chief, "that I was killed and left upon the field! I am here. I live; I move; see me; touch me. I shall again raise my spear in battle, and take my place in the feast."

Nobody, however, seemed conscious of his presence, and his voice was mistaken for the whispering of the wind.

He now walked to his own lodge, and there he found his wife tearing her hair and lamenting over his fate. He endeavoured to undeceive her, but she, like the others, appeared to be insensible of his presence, and not to hear his voice. She sat in a despairing manner, with her head reclining on her hands. The chief asked her to bind up his wounds, but she made no reply. He placed his mouth close to her ear and shouted—

"I am hungry, give me some food!"

The wife thought she heard a buzzing in her ear, and remarked it to one who sat by. The enraged husband now summoning all his strength, struck her a blow on the forehead. His wife raised her hand to her head, and said to her friend—

"I feel a slight shooting pain in my head."

Foiled thus in every attempt to make himself known, the warrior-chief began to reflect upon what he had heard in his youth, to the effect that the spirit was sometimes permitted to leave the body and wander about. He concluded that possibly his body might have remained upon the field of battle, while his spirit only accompanied his returning friends. He determined to return to the field, although it was four days' journey away. He accordingly set out upon his way. For three days he pursued his way without meeting anything uncommon; but on the fourth, towards evening, as he came to the skirts of the battlefield, he saw a fire in the path before him. He walked to one side to avoid stepping into it, but the fire also changed its position, and was still before him. He then went in another direction, but the mysterious fire still crossed his path, and seemed to bar his entrance to the scene of the conflict. In short, whichever way he took, the fire was still before him,—no expedient seemed to avail him.

"Thou demon!" he exclaimed at length, "why dost thou bar my approach to the field of battle? Knowest thou not that I am a spirit also, and that I seek again to enter my body? Dost thou presume that I shall return without effecting my object? Know that I have never been defeated by the enemies of my nation, and will not be defeated by thee!"

So saying, he made a sudden effort and jumped through the flame. No sooner had he done so than he found himself sitting on the ground, with his back supported by a tree, his bow leaning against his shoulder, all his warlike dress and arms upon his body, just as they had been left by his friends on the day of battle. Looking up he beheld a large canicu, or war eagle, sitting in the tree above his head. He immediately recognised this bird to be the same as he had once dreamt of in his youth—the one he had chosen as his guardian spirit, or personal manito. This eagle had carefully watched his body and prevented other ravenous birds from touching it.

The chief got up and stood upon his feet, but he felt himself weak and much exhausted. The blood upon his wound had stanched itself, and he now bound it up. He possessed a knowledge of such roots as have healing properties, and these he carefully sought in the woods. Having found some, he pounded some of them between stones and applied them externally. Others he chewed and swallowed. In a short time he found himself so much recovered as to be able to commence his journey, but he suffered greatly from hunger, not seeing any large animals that he might kill. However, he succeeded in killing some small birds with his bow and arrow, and these he roasted before a fire at night.

In this way he sustained himself until he came to a river that separated his wife and friends from him. He stood upon the bank and gave that peculiar whoop which is a signal of the return of a friend. The sound was immediately heard, and a canoe was despatched to bring him over, and in a short time, amidst the shouts of his friends and relations, who thronged from every side to see the arrival, the warrior-chief was landed.

When the first wild bursts of wonder and joy had subsided, and some degree of quiet had been restored to the village, he related to his people the account of his adventures. He concluded his narrative by telling them that it is pleasing to the spirit of a deceased person to have a fire built upon the grave for four nights after his burial; that it is four days' journey to the land appointed for the residence of the spirits; that in its journey thither the spirit stands in need of a fire every night at the place of its encampment; and that if the friends kindle this fire upon the spot where the body is laid, the spirit has the benefit of its light and warmth on its path, while if the friends neglect to do this, the spirit is subjected to the irksome task of making its own fire each night.

THE ORIGIN OF MEDICINE

In the old days, there was peace throughout the earth and mankind lived in friendship and harmony with the great beasts of creation. But as time progressed, the human race multiplied rapidly and became so large that the animals were forced to surrender their settlements and seek out new homes in the forests and deserts. Although cramped and unhappy, they did not complain too vociferously, but embraced these changes with an open mind, hoping that mankind would now remain satisfied. Sadly, however, this was not the case, and within a short time, man began to equip himself with a variety of weapons – bows, arrows, axes, spears and hooks – which he used to attack the beasts of the forests, slaughtering them for their flesh and valuable skins.

The animals, at first incredulous, soon became enraged by this show of bloodthirsty contempt and began to consider measures that would guarantee them their survival and safety. The bear tribe was the first to meet in council under Kuwahi mountain, presided over by White Bear, their chief. One after another, members of the tribe stood up and reported the appalling atrocities their families had suffered. Mankind had mutilated their bodies, devoured their flesh, skinned them to make superfluous clothing and displayed their severed heads on wooden stakes as trophies. There was only one way to deal with such hostility, it was unanimously agreed, and it involved wholesale war.

The bears sat down to deliberate their strategy more seriously, but as soon as someone asked about weapons, they all fell silent, knowing that humans had one distinct advantage over them in this respect.

'We should turn man's own instruments upon him,' announced one of the elder bears. 'Let us go and find one of these bows, together with some arrows, and copy their design.'

A messenger returned shortly afterwards with these objects and the group gathered round to examine them carefully. A strong piece of locust wood was called for by the chief and with this he constructed a bow. Then, one of the younger bears provided a piece of his gut for the string and soon the weapon was completed, ready for its first testing.

The strongest, most agile bear volunteered his services. He had little trouble drawing back the bow, but as soon as he attempted to let the arrow fly, his long claws became entangled in the string and the shot was ruined. He quickly realized that he would have to trim his claws, and when he had done this, he let a second arrow fly which hit its target successfully. Delighted with himself, he turned to face the chief, but White Bear did not appear at all pleased by the result.

'We need our claws to climb trees,' he wisely proclaimed. 'If we cut off our claws we will not be able to climb or hunt down prey and soon we would all starve together.' And saying this, he ordered the group to scatter amongst the woods, instructing them to reappear before him when they had found a better solution.

The deer also held a similar council under their chief, Little Deer. After they had aired their grievances and lamented the death of their comrades, they came to a decision that if any human hunter should attempt to slay one of them without first asking suitable pardon, he would be struck down by rheumatism. Notice of this decision was sent out to all the Indian villages nearby and the people were instructed what to do if ever necessity demanded that they kill one of the deer tribe.

So now, whenever a deer is hit by an arrow, Little Deer, who moves faster than the wind and can never be wounded, runs to the spot where the victim has fallen and, bending over the pool of blood, asks the spirit of the deer whether or not he has heard the hunter's plea for pardon. If the reply is 'yes', the hunter remains fit and well, but if the answer is 'no', then Little Deer tracks him to his cabin and strikes him down with rheumatism, transforming him into a helpless cripple.

The fishes and reptiles were the next to gather together to determine an appropriate punishment for their aggressors. They held a council which lasted only a few minutes, where it was quickly decided that those who tortured or killed any of their species would be tormented by nightmarish visions of slimy serpents with foul breath twining around their limbs and throats, very slowly choking them to death. Or else, these brutal attackers would dream, day and night, of eating raw, decaying fish, causing them to refuse all food and to sicken and die as a result.

Finally, the birds, insects and smaller animals held their own meeting, presided over by a grub-worm. Each creature, he announced, should come forward and state his point of view and if the consensus was against mankind, the entire race should be put to death by the most cruel and painful means.

Frog was the first to leap forward and he delivered his tirade in a loud and angry voice:

'Something will have to be done to stop the spread of this human menace,' he thundered. 'See how they have kicked me and beaten me with sticks because they think I'm ugly. Now my back is covered with sores that will never disappear.' And he pointed to the spots on his skin for everyone around him to examine.

Next a group of birds hopped forward and began to condemn mankind for the way in which he ruthlessly set out to burn their feet, impaling them on a stick over a fire as soon as he had trapped them, and turning them slowly until their claws and feathers were singed black.

Others then followed with a string of complaints and criticisms, so that apart from the ground-squirrel, who had seldom been a victim because of his tiny size, there was not one among the gathering who showed any restraint or compassion towards the human species. Hurriedly, they began to devise and name various lethal diseases to be released among the human population. As the list grew longer, the grub-worm shook with laughter and glee, until he suddenly fell over backwards and could not rise to his feet again, but had to wriggle off on his back, as he has done ever since that day.

Only the plants remained friendly towards man, and before long every tree, shrub and herb, down even to the wild grasses and mosses, agreed to provide some remedy for the diseases now hanging thick in the air.

'We will help mankind in his hour of need,' each plant affirmed. 'Every one of us shall assist in the struggle against sickness and disease and hope that in return, the earth will be restored to order.'

Even the weeds in the fields were endowed with healing properties and, in time, every tribe boasted a shaman, a great healer, capable of hearing the spirit-voices of the plants speaking to him whenever he was in doubt about a cure.

It was in this way that the very first medicine came into being, ensuring the survival of a human race which had come so perilously close to destruction.

ORIGIN OF STRAWBERRIES

The following is a Cherokee story about the first strawberries. When the world was new, there was one man and one woman. They were happy; then they quarreled. At last the woman left the man and began to walk away toward the Sunland, the Eastland.

The man followed. He felt sorry, but the woman walked straight on. She did not look back.

Then Sun, the great Apportioner, was sorry for the man. He said,

"Are you still angry with your wife?"

The man said, "No."

Sun said, "Would you like to have her come back to you?"

"Yes," said the man.

So Sun made a great patch of huckleberries which he placed in front of the woman's trail. She passed them without paying any attention to them. Then Sun made a clump of blackberry bushes and put those in front of her trail. The woman walked on. Then Sun created beautiful service-berry bushes which stood beside the trail. Still the woman walked on.

So Sun made other fruits and berries. But the woman did not look at them.

Then Sun created a patch of beautiful ripe strawberries. They were the first strawberries. When the woman saw those, she stopped to gather a few. As she gathered them, she turned her face toward the west. Then she remembered the man. She turned to the Sunland but could not go on. She could not go any further.

Then the woman picked some of the strawberries and started back on her trail, away from the Sunland. So her husband met her, and they went back together.

LEGEND OF THE CORN

The Arikara were the first to find the maize. A young man went out hunting. He came to a high hill. Looking down a valley, he saw a buffalo bull near where two rivers joined. When the young man looked to see how he could kill the buffalo, he saw how beautiful the country was. The banks of the two rivers were low, with many trees. The buffalo faced the north; therefore he could not get within bowshot of him. He thought he should wait until the buffalo moved close to the banks of one of the rivers, or to a ravine where there were bushes and shrubs. So the young man waited. The sun went down before the buffalo moved.

Nearly all night the hunter lay awake. He had little food. He felt sorry he could not reach the buffalo. Before the sun rose, he hurried to the top of the hill. The buffalo stood just where it had, but it faced the east. Again he waited for it to move. He waited all day. When the sun went down, the buffalo still stood in the same place.

Nearly all night the young man lay awake. He had very little food indeed. The next morning he rose early, and came to the top of the hill, just as the sun came up. The buffalo was still standing in the same place; but now it faced the south. He waited all day. Then the sun went down.

Now the next morning, when he arose early, the buffalo stood in the same place; this time it faced the west. All day the young man waited, but the buffalo did not move.

Now the young man thought, "Why does not the buffalo move?" He saw it did not drink, did not eat, did not sleep. He thought some power must be influencing it.

Now the next morning, the young man hurried to the top of the hill. The sun had risen and everything was light. The buffalo was gone. Then he saw where the buffalo had stood there was a strange bush.

He went to the place; then he saw it was a plant. He looked for the tracks of the buffalo. He saw where it had turned to the east and to the south and to the west. In the centre there was one track; out of it the small plant had grown. There was no track to show where the buffalo had left the place.

Then the hunter hurried to his village. He told the chiefs and the people of the strange buffalo and the plant. So all the chiefs and the people came to the place. They saw the tracks of the buffalo as he had stood, but there were no tracks of his coming or going.

So all the people knew that Wahkoda had given this strange plant to the people. They knew of other plants they might eat. They knew there was a time when each plant was ripe. So they watched the strange plant; they guarded it and protected it.

Then a flower appeared on the plant. Afterwards, at one of the joints, a new part of the plant pushed out. It had hair. At first the hair was green; then it was brown. Then the people thought, "Perhaps this fruit is ripe." But they did not dare touch it. They met together. They looked at the plant.

Then a young man said, "My life has not been good. If any evil comes to me, it will not matter."

So the people were willing, and the young man put his hand on the plant and then on its fruit. He grasped the fruit boldly. He said to the people, "It is solid. It is ripe." Then he pulled apart the husks, and said, "It is red."

He took a few of the grains and showed them to the people. He ate some. He did not die. So the people knew Wahkoda had sent this plant to them for food.

Now in the fall, when the prairie grass turned brown, the leaves of this plant turned brown also. Then the fruit was plucked, and put away. After the winter was over, the kernels were divided. There were four to each family.

Then the people moved the lodges to the place where the plant had grown. When the hills became green, they planted the seed of the strange plant. But first they built little mounds like the one out of which it grew. So the fruit grew and ripened. It had many colours; red, and yellow, and white, and blue.

Then the next year there were many plants and many ears of corn. So they sent to other tribes. They invited them to visit them and gave them of the new food. Thus the Omahas came to have corn.

OMAHA SACRED LEGEND

In the beginning the people were in water. They opened their eyes, but they could see nothing. As the people came out of the water, they first saw the daylight. They had no clothing. Then they took weeds and grasses and from them wove clothing.

The people lived near a large body of water; it was in a wooded country where there was game. The men hunted the deer with clubs; they did not know the use of the bow. The people wandered about the shores of the great water. They were poor and cold. The people thought, "What shall we do to help ourselves?" So they began chipping stones. They found a bluish stone that was easily flaked and chipped; so they made knives and arrowheads out of it. But they were still poor and cold. They thought, "What shall we do?"

Then a man found an elm root that was very dry. He dug a hole in it and put a stick in and rubbed it. Then smoke came. He smelled it. Then the people smelled it and came near. Others helped him to rub. At last a spark came. They blew this into a flame. Thus fire came to warm the people and to cook their food.

After this the people built grass houses; they cut the grass with the shoulder blade of a deer. Now the people had fire and ate their meat roasted. Then they grew tired of roast meat. They thought, "How shall we cook our meat differently?"

A man found a piece of clay that stuck well together. Then he brought sand to mix with it. Then he moulded it as a pot. Then he gathered grass until he had a large heap of it; he put the clay pot into the midst of the grass and set it on fire. This made the clay hard. After a time he put water into the pot; the water did not leak out. This was good. So he put water into it and then meat into it, and put the pot over the fire. Thus the people had boiled meat to eat.

Now their grass coverings would grow fuzzy and drop off. It was hard to gather and keep these coverings. The people were not satisfied. Again they thought, "What can we do to have something different to wear?"

Before this, they had been throwing away the hides from the game which they killed. But now they took their stone knives to scrape down the hides and make them thin. They rubbed the hides with grass and with their hands to make them soft. Then they used the hides for clothing. Now they had clothing and were warm.

Now the women had to break the dry wood to keep up the fires. They had no tools. So the men made a stone ax with a groove. Then they put a handle on the grooved stone and fastened it with rawhide. This was used. Then they wanted something better to break the wood. So they made wedges of stone.

Now the grass shelter came to pieces easily. Then the people thought, "What shall we do? How can we get something that will not come to pieces?" Then they tried putting skins on poles.

First they tried deerskins. But they were too small. They tried elk skins. But they became hard and stiff in the rain and sun. Then they did not try skins longer. They used bark to cover the poles of their tepees.

But the bark houses were not warm. Then the people took the leg bone of the deer and splintered it So they made sharp pieces for awls. Then they took buffalo skins and sinews, and with the awl they fastened the skins together. So they made comfortable covers for their tepees.

Then a man wandered around a long time. One day he found some small pieces of something which were white, and red, and blue. He thought they must be something of great value, so he hid them in a mound of earth. Now one day he went to see if they were safe. Behold! When he came to the mound, green stalks were growing out of it. And on the stalks were small kernels of white, and red, and blue. Behold! It was corn. Then the man took the corn, and gave it to the people. They tried it for food. They found it good, and have ever since called it their life.

Now when the people found the corn good, they thought to hide it in mounds as the first man had done. So they took the shoulder blade of an elk and made mounds. Then they hid the corn in it. So the corn grew and the people had food.

Now as the people wandered around, they came to a forest where the birch trees grew. There was a great lake there. Then they made canoes of birch bark. They traveled in them on the water. Then a man found two young animals. He carried them home. He fed them so they grew bigger. Then he made a harness which he placed upon them and fastened it to poles. So these animals became burden bearers. Before that, every burden had to be carried on the back. Now the dogs helped the people.

THE FLOOD AND THE RAINBOW

The Lenni-Lenapi are the First People, so that they know this story is true. After the Creation of the earth, the Mysterious One covered it with a blue roof. Sometimes the roof was very black. Then the Manitou of Waters became uneasy. He feared the rain would no longer be able to pour down upon the earth through this dark roof. Therefore the Manitou of Waters prayed to the Mysterious One that thewaters from above be not cut off.

At once the Mysterious One commanded to blow the Spirit of the Wind, who dwells in the Darkening Land. At once thick clouds arose. They covered all the earth, so that the dark roof could no longer be seen.

Then the voice of the Mysterious One was heard amongst the clouds. The voice was deep and heavy, like the sound of falling rivers.

Then the Spirit of Rain, the brother of the Spirit of Waters and the Spirit of the Winds, poured down water from above. The waters fell for a long time. They fell until all the earth was covered. Then the birds took refuge in the branches of the highest trees. The animals followed the trails to the mountain peaks.

Then the Manitou of Waters feared no longer. Therefore the Mysterious One ordered the rain to cease and the clouds to disappear. Then Sin-go-wi-chi-na-xa, the rainbow, was seen in the sky.

Therefore the Lenni-Lenapi watch for the rainbow, because it means that the Mysterious One is no longer angry.

THE WONDERFUL ROD

The Choctaws had for many years years found a home in regions beyond the Mountains of Snow, far away to the west of the Mississippi. They, however, decided, for some reason or other, to leave the place in which they dwelt, and the question then arose in what direction they should journey. Now, there was a jossakeed (priest) who had a wonderful rod, and he said that he would lead them.

For many years, therefore, they travelled, being guided by him. He walked before them bearing the rod, and when night was come he put it upright in the earth, and the people encamped round it. In the morning they looked to see in what direction the rod pointed, for each night the rod left its upright position, and inclined one way or another. Day after day the rod was found pointing to the east, and thither the Choctaws accordingly bent their steps.

"You must travel," said the jossakeed, "as long as the rod directs you pointing to the direction in which you must go, but when the rod ceases to point, and stands upright, then you must live there."

So the people went on until they came to a hill, where they camped, having first put up the rod so that it did not lean at all. In the morning, when they went to see which direction the rod pointed out for them to take, they found it upright, and from it there grew branches bearing green leaves. Then they said—

"We will stop here."

So that became the centre of the land of the Choctaws.

THE SACRED POLE

A young man who had been wandering came back to his village. When he reached his home he said, "Father, I have seen a wonderful tree." Then he told his father about it. The old man was silent because all was not yet settled between the tribes. The Cheyenne, the Arikara, the Omaha, Ponca, and Iowa were having a great council, so as to adopt rules concerning the hunting of game, and of peace, and war.

After a while, the young man went to visit the tree. When he reached home, he told his father again of it. The old man was silent, for the chiefs were still holding their council. At last, when the council was over and the rules decided upon, the old man sent for the chiefs. He said, "My son has seen a wonderful tree. The Thunder Birds come and go upon this tree. They make a trail of fire which leaves four paths on the burnt grass that stretch towards the Four Winds. When the Thunder Birds alight upon the tree, it bursts into flame. The fire mounts to the top. The tree stands burning, but no one can see the fire except at night."

When the chiefs heard this tale, they sent runners to see what this tree might be. The runners came back and told the same story. In the night they had seen the tree burning as it stood. Then all the people held a council as to what this might mean. The chiefs said,

"We shall run for it. Put on your ornaments and prepare as if for battle."

The warriors painted themselves as if for war. They put on their ornaments. They set out for the tree, which stood near a lake. They ran as if it were a race to attack the enemy. All the men ran. A Ponca was the first to reach the tree and he struck it as if it were an enemy.

Then they cut the tree down. Four men, walking in a straight line, carried it on their shoulders to the village. The chiefs for four nights sang the songs made in honour of the tree. They held a council about the tree. A tent was made for it, and it was set up in the circle of lodges. The chiefs worked upon it; they trimmed it and called it a human being. They made a basket of twigs and feathers and tied it half way up the tree. Then they said, "It has no hair!" So they sent out to get a large scalp lock and they put it on top of Pole for hair. Afterwards the chiefs told the criers to tell the people that when Pole was completed they should see it.

Then they painted Pole and set it up before the tent. They leaned it on a crotched stick. Then they called all the people and all the people came. Men, women, and children came.

When they were all together, the chiefs said, "This is a mystery. Whenever we meet with trouble, we shall bring all our prayers to Pole. We shall make offerings to him. We shall ask him for what we need. When we ask anything, we must make gifts. If anyone desires to become a chief, he shall make presents to the Keepers of the Pole, and they shall give him authority to be a chief."

When all was finished the people said, "Let us appoint a time when we shall again paint Pole; when we shall act before him the battles we have fought." So they fixed the time in the moon when the buffaloes bellow.

THE LEGEND OF THE PEACE PIPES

The people came across a great water on logs tied together. They pitched their tents on the shore. Then they thought to make for themselves certain bounds within which they were to live and rules which should govern them. They cleared a space of grass and weeds so they could see each other's faces. They sat down and there was no obstruction between them.

While they were holding a council, an owl hooted in the trees near by. The leader said, "That bird is to take part in our council. He calls to us. He offers us his aid."

Immediately afterward they heard a woodpecker. He knocked against the trees. The leader said, "That bird calls to us. He offers us his aid. He will take part in our council."

Then the chief appointed a man as servant. He said, "Go into the woods and get an ash sapling." The servant came back with a sapling having a rough bark.

"We do not want that," said the leader. "Go again and get a sapling with a smooth bark, bluish in colour at the joint where a branch comes." So the servant went out, and came back with a sapling of the kind described.

When the leader took up the sapling, an eagle came and soared about the council which was sitting in the grass. He dropped a downy feather; it fell. It fell in the centre of the cleared space. Now this was the white eagle. The chief said, "This is not what we want," so the white eagle passed on.

Then the bald eagle came swooping down, as though attacking its prey. It balanced itself on its wings directly over the cleared space. It uttered fierce cries, and dropped one of its downy feathers, which stood on the ground as the other eagle's feather had done. The chief said, "This is not what we want." So the bald eagle passed on.

Then came the spotted eagle, and soared over the council, and dropped its feather as the others had done. The chief said, "This is not what we want," and the spotted eagle passed on.

Then the imperial eagle, the eagle with the fantail, came, and soared over the people. It dropped a downy feather which stood upright in the centre of the cleared space. The chief said, "This is what we want."

So the feathers of this eagle were used in making the peace pipes, together with the feathers of the owl and woodpecker, and with other things. These peace pipes were to be used in forming friendly relations with other tribes.

When the peace pipes were made, seven other pipes were made for keeping peace within the tribe. One pipe was to prevent revenge. If one man should kill another, the chief took this pipe to the relatives and offered it to them. If the relatives of the dead man refused to accept it, it was offered again. It was offered four times. If it was refused four times, the chief said, "Well, you must take the consequences. We will do nothing, and you cannot now ask to see the pipes." He meant if they took revenge and any trouble came to them, they could not ask for help or for mercy.

Each band had its own pipe.

ANIMAL TALES

Animals feature heavily in and form an integral part of many of the stories in North American mythology. With the similar desire to explain the world around them that we saw in the chapter above, the Native Americans had many tales which explain why the animals have the characteristics and physical attributes that they do. There are also many stories where the animals take on an almost human role in the action – able to speak, help or trick people – though perhaps possessing superhuman powers, and even narratives of animal husbands and wives were not uncommon. The relationship and coexistence between humans and animals is explored in great detail in these stories – another way of explaining the world in which they live.

THE BEAVER MEDICINE LEGEND

Nopatsis, son of a noble Indian chief, dwelt with his younger brother, Akaiyan, in a lodge at the foot of the mountains. Nopatsis was a well-meaning and gentle soul, but he did not share his brother's intelligence, and was renowned for the most impulsive behaviour.

One day he returned home accompanied by a young woman he proceeded to introduce to his younger brother as his wife. He

ANIMAL TALES

knew little about her, he told Akaiyan, and was certain only of one thing, that he had fallen in love with her as soon as he had set eyes on her. Akaiyan welcomed the woman into their lodge, respecting his brother's choice, and did all that he could to make his new sister-in-law as comfortable as possible.

The weeks passed by quite smoothly, and the two brothers remained as close as they had always been since the day, many years before, when they had been tragically orphaned and left alone to care for each other. Nopatsis, although now a married man, always set aside time in the evenings to sit with his brother while the two discussed the day's events and watched the sun sinking into the clouds. The new wife was not so pleased to see this, however, and it was not long before she began pestering her husband to be rid of Akaiyan.

'He is my only brother,' Nopatsis explained to her, 'and I would not be parted from him for all the wealth in the world.'

But the young woman would not be put off by these words and decided that she must find a more devious way of persuading her husband to do as she wanted.

Her evil mind soon hit upon the perfect solution, and one day shortly afterwards, when she knew she had been left alone in the lodge with Akaiyan, she removed herself to her bedroom and began tearing at her clothes and clawing at her skin and hair. Nopatsis returned at sundown to find his wife sobbing and trembling by the door. In a quivering voice, she divulged to him that Akaiyan had treated her brutally, after having first sworn her to a silence she simply could not keep.

Nopatsis, whose misguided perception led him to accept all things at face value, was deeply disturbed by what he heard. Silently he listened, storing up hatred in his heart for his younger brother. Not once did he pause to consider that Akaiyan might be innocent; not once did he allow him an opportunity to defend himself. As his wife had planned it, Nopatsis became consumed by thoughts of revenge, debating in his mind night and day precisely how he would get rid of his brother.

The warmth of summer soon filled the air and with its arrival a large number of wild water-fowl gathered on the island of the great lake where it was customary for them to shed their brightly coloured feathers. Every year, the tribal warriors collected these feathers, using them to decorate their arrows. Nopatsis and Akaiyan now began making the raft that would take them to the island, binding logs together securely with strips of buffalo-hide. When their craft was ready, they set sail, reaching their destination before midday.

The two brothers agreed to separate in their search for feathers and Akaiyan wandered far off along the strand, stooping regularly to salvage the plumes washed up among the pebbles. Raising himself up from his crouched position after an interval of about ten minutes, he was astonished to see Nopatsis aboard their raft sailing back towards the mainland. He called out loudly to him:

'Nopatsis, have you gone mad? What are you doing? Please return at once, I have no way of getting back home.'

But Nopatsis rowed onwards, hurling abuse at his brother for what he had done. Akaiyan protested and swore solemnly that he had not injured his sister-in-law in any way, but his cries were ignored all the more and Nopatsis increased his speed, satisfied that he had served up a proper punishment.

Akaiyan sat down and wept bitterly, knowing that he would

certainly perish on the island without food and clean drinking water. As night closed in, he began praying earnestly to the spirits of nature and to the sun and the moon for guidance, after which he felt a little more at ease. He took some branches and built himself a shelter, lining the earth with feathers on which he lay until sleep finally conquered his troubled spirit.

The next morning when he awoke he became aware of a little beaver standing in the doorway of his hut.

'My father would like you to visit him at his dwelling,' said the animal. 'I will lead you there if you care to follow.'

Akaiyan agreed to accept the invitation and promptly arose from his bed. Soon he approached a well-constructed lodge where Great Beaver, attended by his wife and family, waited to receive him. His host was indeed the most ancient and revered of all beavers, a wise old animal with a coat as white as snow and large, curling whiskers trailing the ground. Akaiyan immediately felt that he would be understood in such a place and he began to relate to Great Beaver the story of his ill-treatment.

The wise old animal listened and offered his sympathy and it was soon decided among the community that Akaiyan should spend the winter with them where he would be well cared for and introduced to a great many wonderful things he had never before experienced. Akaiyan was deeply touched by the family's kindness and when the beavers closed up their lodge for the winter he happily took up shelter with them. They kept him warm by placing their thick, fur-coated bodies alongside his and they taught him many secrets, including the art of healing, the planting and smoking of tobacco, and various sacred dances, songs and ceremonial prayers associated with the great mystery of medicine.

Summer returned and Akaiyan appeared above ground once more, hoping to find some way to reach the mainland. As luck would have it, his brother, Nopatsis, had set sail for the island that same morning intent on discovering whether or not his younger brother had survived the winter months. Akaiyan soon recognized the vessel, which now lay unattended, and quickly decided that fate might never again offer him a more favourable opportunity. Racing towards Great Beaver's lodge, he entered one last time and sadly took leave of his friends.

'Choose something to take with you as a parting gift,' Great Beaver urged him, 'some small item you may remember us by.' Gazing around him, Akaiyan's eyes fell upon Great Beaver's youngest child with whom he had formed a very special bond during his stay. At first, the wise old animal would not agree to Akaiyan's request, for he prized his little one above all other things, but finally he surrendered to the wishes of both Akaiyan and his pleading child, counselling Little Beaver to construct a sacred Beaver Bundle as soon as he arrived on the mainland.

Akaiyan was soon walking towards his native village in the company of Little Beaver. Many of the warriors he had hunted with in the past ran forward to greet him, surprised and relieved to see him alive. They longed to hear of his adventures and soon the chief had ordered a great fire to be lit, around which they all sat as Akaiyan told them his story. Little Beaver then stood up and proceeded to explain to the people, as his father had bid him, the mystery of medicine with its accompanying songs and sacred dances. He called for a Beaver Bundle to be made and to this each man contributed a relic conveying good or ill luck, including feathers, animal-skins, bones, rocks and stone-pipes. Long into the evening, they watched Little Beaver as he danced, and many chiefs of the animal tribes joined in the ceremony, honoured to receive the Beaver Medicine that had been brought to them from the island.

When he was satisfied that he had accomplished his task of instruction, Little Beaver agreed to be returned to his parents. On the island, Akaiyan found the bones of his vengeful brother and was grateful that he had escaped a fate intended for him. Great Beaver presented the young warrior with a sacred pipe in exchange for his child and taught him the songs and dances that would speed the growth of the tobacco plants on the plains.

Every spring Akaiyan set off on his little raft to visit the beavers, and on each occasion he received some important object to add to his Beaver Medicine Bundle, until it reached a great size, bringing him prosperity and good fortune. Soon afterwards, he married a wholesome woman and together they founded a race of medicine-men who never failed to pass on the traditions and ceremonials of the Beaver Medicine to their own offspring, ensuring that the good works of Akaiyan and Little Beaver have remained with us even to this day.

OPECHE, THE ROBIN-REDBREAST

Iadilla **was the only son** of an old man and his wife living in the northern woodlands. The couple had watched the boy grow up to be a fine and strong young warrior and they were fiercely proud of his every achievement. The father, in particular, was extremely ambitious for his son and made no secret of the fact that he fully expected him to rise to the position of chief one day. To this end, he carefully supervised Iadilla's every activity, determined that he should surpass all others in whatever he set out to do.

It was of the utmost importance to the old man that Iadilla obtain a very powerful guardian spirit when the time arrived for him to undergo the customary ceremony. He insisted that his son prepare himself with great solemnity and gave him the most meticulous instructions for his conduct, urging him, above all, to acquit himself with a manly spirit no matter how relentless the suffering ahead.

On the chosen morning, the old man led his son deep into the forest towards the sweating-lodge. Having remained within the lodge for as long as his father deemed necessary, the boy reappeared and plunged into the cold water of the river. This process was repeated twice more until his father was satisfied that his purification had been completed. Then he led Iadilla to another, more isolated lodge expressly prepared for him, and ordered him to lie down upon a straw mat woven by his mother. Soon afterwards, Iadilla heard the sound of his father's retreating footsteps and he lay in silence with his face covered, patiently awaiting the approach of the spirit with the power to decide his good or evil fortune in life.

Every morning his father came to the door of the little lodge and offered his son gentle words of encouragement, never failing to remind him of the honour and renown that would attend him should he reach the end of the twelve days without food or water. For over a week Iadilla managed to fulfil his father's expectations without uttering a single word of complaint, but as nightfall approached on the eighth day, his strength began to fail rapidly, so that when he awoke on the following morning he was unable to move his limbs.

As soon as he could hear his father coming towards the lodge, Iadilla broke his silence and cried out weakly:

'Father, I do not have enough strength to endure my fast any longer. My dreams are not good and the spirits who visit me seem to oppose your wishes. Give me permission to break my fast now and I promise I will continue it another time.'

But the old man would not entertain such a thought and replied rather impatiently: 'My son, have you any idea what you are asking? You have only three days left and you must strive a little longer if only for the sake of your ageing parents.'

Overcome by guilt, Iadilla covered his face again and lay perfectly still, neither moving nor speaking until the eleventh day. But as soon as his father appeared in the morning at the door of the lodge, he could not prevent himself repeating the same request.

'Only a very short time now remains,' the old man answered. 'At dawn tomorrow I will visit you carrying a meal prepared with my own hands. Please do not bring shame upon the family just when you are so close to your goal.'

'I will not shame you, father,' replied Iadilla and he lay his head back wearily, his breathing scarcely audible in the still, dark silence of the lodge.

Before the sun had even risen on the twelfth morning, the old man leaped out of bed excitedly and set off to greet his son, carrying with him the meal he had prepared the evening before. Drawing near to the little lodge, he was surprised to hear voices coming from within and stooped to peer through a small crack in one of the walls. He was astonished to discover his son sitting up, not only talking to himself, but in the act of painting his breast and shoulders a rich vermilion colour.

'My father was set to destroy me,' Iadilla muttered to himself. 'Although I was obedient to him, he pushed me beyond my strength and would not listen to my requests. Now he will have to respect my wishes, for my guardian spirit has been kind and just and has given me the shape I desire. At last, I am free. It is time for me to go.'

Hearing these words, the old man broke into the lodge and began pleading through his tears: 'Ningwis! Ningwis! My son, my son, please do not leave me.'

But even as he spoke, Iadilla was transformed into a bird with a beautiful red breast that flew to the top of the lodge and addressed the old man with these words:

'Do not mourn the change you see in me, father. I could not fulfil your expectations of me as a warrior, but in this form I will always seek to cheer you with my song and strive to lift your spirits whenever you are low. I have been released from the cares and sufferings of human life. The fields and mountains will furnish me with food. The clean, bright air will serve as my path. I shall be happier in my present shape than I ever was before as a man.'

Then, stretching himself on his toes, Iadilla spread his wings and took his first, glorious flight, disappearing high above the feathered clouds. But he did not forget his promise and soon returned to build his nest in the highest branch of the tree overlooking his father's lodge. Every morning, as soon as the old man awoke, he was heard to call aloud, 'Opeche, Opeche', and his call was answered by the sweetest song, as the red-breasted bird sang to him, soothing his troubled spirit and filling his heart with a lasting joy.

THE BROKEN PROMISE

At the heart of a solitary forest, a hunter had built for himself and his family a small wooden lodge, having decided once and for all to withdraw from the company of his tribe. Their deceit and cruelty had caused him to turn from them and he had chosen the loneliest spot he could find, adamant that his three young children should never fall under their poisonous influence.

The years passed by and the family remained happy and peaceful in their new home until, one day, the father fell gravely ill, and took to his couch with little or no hope of a recovery. Day and night the family lovingly attended the sick man, exhausting all of their simple medicines on him, yet never failing to whisper words of encouragement in his ear. But at last, they resigned themselves to the fact that he would not regain his health and gathered around him in the dimly lit room, awaiting the departure of his spirit.

As death drew near, the sick man called for the skin door of the lodge to be thrown open so that he might witness the sun sinking in the evening sky one last time. Then he motioned to his eldest son to raise him up in the bed and with these words he addressed his grieving family:

'I must leave you very shortly,' he said, 'but I am satisfied that I have been a good father and that I have provided you with ample food and protected you from the storms and cold of our harsh climate.

'You, my partner in life,' he continued, casting his eyes upon his wife, 'you, I can leave behind with an easy conscience, for you do not have much longer here and will soon join me in the Isle of the Blessed. But oh, my children who have only just set off on life's great journey, you have every wickedness before you from which I can no longer offer you protection. The unkindness and ingratitude of men caused me to abandon my tribe, and while we have lived here in peace and harmony, those very men have caused the forests to echo with the cries of war.

'My wish for you is that you remain pure at heart and never follow the evil example of such men. I will go tranquilly to my rest only if I am certain that you will always cherish one other.

'My eldest son, my eldest daughter, promise to obey my dying command and never forsake your younger brother, for he is most in need of your care.'

The sick man then closed his eyes and spoke no more, and after a few minutes' silence, when his family came to his bedside and called him by name, they found that his spirit did not answer, for it was already well on its way to the Land of Souls. After eight months, the mother sadly passed away also, but in her last moments she was careful to to remind the two eldest children of the promise they had made to their father. During the winter that followed her death, they could not have been more attentive to the delicate younger child, but as soon as the winter had passed, the older brother became restless and struggled increasingly to conceal his uneasy mood. Before long, he had reached a decision to break his promise to his father and to search out the village of his father's tribe.

'I am lonely and wretched here,' he told his sister one morning. 'Must I forever pretend that we are the only people in the world and sacrifice my youth to this miserable existence? No! I am determined to seek out the society of our fellow-men and nothing you can say will prevent me leaving.'

ANIMAL TALES

'My brother,' replied his sister, 'I do not blame you for harbouring these desires, but we have made a solemn promise to cherish each other always and to protect the youngest of our family from all harm. Neither pleasure nor pain should separate us, for if we follow our own inclinations, he will surely become a victim of our neglect.'

The young man made no reply to this and for some weeks afterwards continued on with his work as normal, every day exerting himself in the hunt to supply the wants of the family. But then, one evening, he failed to return home and when she searched his corner of the lodge, his sister found that all of his possessions had vanished. Turning aside from her little brother, she began to weep silently, knowing in her heart that he might never return and that, from now on, she would carry the burden of responsibility her father had placed upon them.

Five moons had waned, during which the young girl tenderly watched over her younger brother, feeding him, clothing him, and building a great fire every day to protect them both from the bitter winds. But soon the solitude of her life began to weary her unspeakably. She had nobody to converse with save the birds and beasts about her, nothing ever to look forward to and she felt at the bottom of her heart that she was entirely alone. Her younger brother was the only obstacle preventing her enjoying the companionship of others and there were times when she wished him dead so that she might escape and have a new life of her own.

At last, when she felt her patience had been entirely exhausted, she gathered into the lodge a large store of food and firewood and announced to her little brother: 'My child, I must go in search of our older brother, but I have provided for you until my return. Do not leave the lodge until I reappear and you will remain safe.'

Then she embraced the young boy warmly and set off with her bundle in search of the village of her father's tribe. Soon she had arrived at her destination and found her brother nicely settled with a wife of his own and two healthy sons. She had been prepared to chastize him severely, but she discovered quite quickly that there was much about the village that appealed to her own starved curiosity. Within a few weeks she had accepted a proposal of marriage from one of the most handsome warriors of the tribe and abandoned all thought of ever returning to the solitary lodge in the forest.

The poor younger brother had fully expected his sister to return, but the months passed by and soon he discovered he had eaten all of the food she had provided him with. Forced to trudge through the woods in search of food, he began picking whatever berries he could find and digging up roots with his pale, slender hands. These satisfied his hunger as long as the weather remained mild, but winter arrived briskly and now the berries were blighted by frost or hidden from view by a thick carpet of snow.

With each new day he was obliged to wander farther and farther from the lodge, sometimes spending the night in the clefts and hollows of old trees, glad of the opportunity to scavenge any scraps of food the wolves might leave for him.

At first fearful of these animals, in time he grew so desperate for food that he would sit waiting a few feet from their circle watching while they devoured their meat, patiently awaiting his share. The wolves themselves became accustomed to the sight of him, and seeming to understand his plight, developed a habit of leaving something behind for him to eat. In this way the little boy lived on through the savage winter, saved from starvation by the generosity of the wild beasts of the woods.

When spring had come and the ice sheets on the Great Lake began melting slowly, the boy followed the wolf pack to the pebbled shore. It so happened that on the same day he arrived, the older brother, whom he had almost entirely forgotten about, was fishing on the lake in his canoe and, hearing the cry of a child, stood up and listened with all his attention, wondering how any human creature could survive in such a bleak and hostile environment. Again, he heard the cry, but this time it sounded very familiar and so he hastened to the shore to confront its source. Here he came face to face with his little brother who had begun singing a mournful little song:

Nesia, Nesia, shug wuh, gushuh!
Ne mien gun-iew! Ne mien gun-iew!
My brother, my brother,
I am almost a wolf!
I am almost a wolf!

The wailing voice touched him deeply and as the song drew to a close, the young boy howled long and loudly, exactly like a wolf. Approaching closer to the spot, the elder brother was startled to see that the little fellow had indeed half changed into a wolf.

'My brother, my brother, come to me,' he pleaded, but the boy fled, leaving behind paw-prints in the sand while he continued to sing:

Ne mien gun-iew! Ne mien gun-iew!
I am almost a wolf.

The more eagerly the older brother called, the faster his brother fled from him and the more rapidly the change continued, until with a prolonged, mournful howl, his whole body was transformed.

The elder brother, sick with remorse, and hearing again the voice of his dying father, continued to cry out in anguish: 'My brother! my brother!'

But the young boy leaped upon a bank and looking back, his eyes filled with a deep reproach, exclaimed: 'I am a wolf!'

Then he bounded swiftly away into the depths of the forest and was never heard of again.

THE SACRED BUNDLE

In a certain village of the Pawnee tribe, there lived a vain young man who always insisted upon wearing the finest clothes and the richest ornaments, no matter how ordinary and uneventful the day that lay ahead. Although unmarried and extremely handsome, he showed no interest in the maidens of the village, but concentrated exclusively on improving his hunting skills, inviting himself to join whatever party happened to be planning an excursion. Among his most prized possessions, he had the down feather of an eagle which he always wore on his head, believing it possessed strange magical properties.

One morning, while he was out hunting, the young man became separated from his companions and, to pass the time, he began following a herd of buffalo for some considerable distance. The animals eventually scattered, with the exception of a young cow, who had become stuck in a mud-hole. Pleased that fate had presented him with such a favourable target, the young man raised his bow and arrow and was about to take aim when he noticed the cow had disappeared, and in its place stood a beautiful young woman. The hunter remained deeply perplexed, for he could not understand where the animal had disappeared to, nor could he comprehend where the maiden had suddenly sprung from.

Warily, he approached the girl, but was surprised to find that she was most friendly towards him and that her presence filled him with a strange delight he had never before experienced. The two sat down and chatted together for many hours, and so enamoured was the hunter by the end of this time that he asked the young maiden to marry him and return with him to his tribe. Graciously she consented, but only on the condition that they set up home in the precise spot where he had discovered her.

To this, the hunter readily agreed and removed from around his neck a string of blue and white beads which he gave to his new wife as a wedding gift.

The two lived very happily together for many months until the evening the young man returned home after a day's hunting to find his lodge surrounded by the marks of many hooves and not a trace of his wife in sight. For weeks he scoured the woodlands and neighbouring countryside, but still he could not discover any sign of her whereabouts. Defeated and dejected, he resolved that he had no option but to return to his own tribe in an attempt to rebuild something of the life he had left behind.

The years passed by, and even though he had a great many

offers of marriage, the handsome young man refused to choose for himself a new bride. Try as he might, he could not remove from his mind an image of the beautiful maiden and he mourned her loss with an ever-increasing passion.

One summer's morning, however, as he stood chatting to a number of his friends, he noticed a young boy walking towards him. The child wore around his neck a string of blue and white beads and his clothing revealed that he had come from a distant village.

'Father,' said the boy, 'mother would like to speak to you.'

Annoyed by the interruption, the young hunter replied curtly: 'I am not your father, go away and do not pester me.'

The boy went away, and the hunter's companions began laughing loudly, amused by the fact that the man whose reputation for spurning women was famous throughout the village should ever have been addressed as 'father'. But at length the boy returned only to repeat exactly the same words. He was again dismissed in an angry fashion, but still he did not give up. On the third occasion when he reappeared, some of the men suggested that it might be a good idea for the hunter to follow the child to see what he wanted. This seemed a sensible suggestion and so he set off on the trail of the boy, keen to get to the bottom of the mystery once and for all.

The blue and white beads he had spotted around the boy's neck had begun to agitate the hunter. He could not place them exactly, but then, up ahead, he saw a buffalo cow with her calf running across the prairie and suddenly he began to remember the clearest details of his former life. Taking his bow and arrows, he followed the buffalo whom he now recognized as his wife and child. But the woman, angry that her husband had not come when he had been repeatedly summoned, made sure that the chase was long and wearisome. She dried up every creek they came to, so that the hunter feared he would die of thirst, and frightened off any deer he attempted to pursue, so that he grew pale and weak with hunger. But for the kindness of his child, the young man might well have perished, but the boy took pity on him and managed to obtain food and drink at intervals, enough to sustain the hunter until they arrived at the home of the buffalo.

The leader of the herd, who was father of the buffalo cow, had never approved of his daughter's marriage and it was he who had kidnapped her from the nuptial home many years before. His resentment was still as strong as it had ever been, and as soon as he laid eyes on the young man, he desired only to kill him. But at last, after lengthy deliberations, the great chief agreed that the hunter would be free to live if he survived a number of rigorous trials designed by the elders of the herd.

To begin with, six cows were placed in a row before the hunter, and he was told that his life would be spared if he could identify his wife among them. It was an impossible feat, since each of the cows was almost identical in appearance to the next, but once again the young child intervened to help his father, and secretly indicated to him where his mother stood in the parade. The old bulls were more than surprised at his success, but very irritated at the same time, and insisted that the hunter surrender himself to a second test. This time, they lined up six buffalo calves and asked him to pick out his son from among them. But the hunter felt certain that his son would give him some small clue to his identity, and so, when one of the calves swished its tail high in the air, the hunter pointed to it and successfully located his own son.

The leader of the herd still remained dissatisfied and was determined to rid himself of the intruder even though he had passed all of their tests. Having promised the young man that he would now bring his wife to him, he asked him to sit on the ground until he had returned with his daughter. The hunter had no sooner complied with this request however, when he heard a noise like thunder approaching, and looking up, he saw the entire buffalo herd rushing towards him. One by one the buffalo charged past the spot, coming to a halt only after they felt satisfied that they had trampled him to pieces. But when they turned around to examine their mighty work, they were astonished to find the young hunter sitting calmly in the centre of the circle, a white feather proudly positioned in his hair.

The chief bull, who had never imagined his son-in-law to possess such magical powers, now moved forward respectfully and lifted him off the ground. He had won back his buffalo-wife and child, the chief told him, but there remained one final thing for him to do before he could be welcomed into the buffalo camp. He must go off and gather together a selection of gifts from his tribe and bring them back to the buffalo herd as a mark of his respect.

The young man set off with his wife and son towards his village making a list in his mind of the fine things he intended to gather together to impress the buffalo chief – corn, maize, the finest fruit and the most succulent deer-flesh. But when he arrived at his home, he was shocked to discover that there was no food to be had, for a great famine had descended upon the people causing many to die of starvation. The buffalo-wife, who was quick to notice the distress her husband suffered, quietly withdrew from his company, and it was not long before she reappeared, pulling from under her robe a great slab of buffalo meat which she presented to the starving people. Every day for a whole month she repeated this act of kindness so that the people soon recovered their strength and began to smile anew. As a way of thanking the young man and his wife, they gathered together the very best of their possessions to present to the buffalo chief and sent the family on its way once more, back to the great camp.

But having returned home, the young son could not rest, knowing his father's people were constantly in want of food. At length, he went and spoke with his grandfather, the chief of the herd, and soon they had worked out a solution to the problem.

Transforming himself into a buffalo, the young boy led the whole herd back towards the village, accompanied by his mother and father in human shape. When they had reached their destination, the father, as his son had commanded him, addressed the people with the following words:

'From this day forward you may hunt the buffalo for food, but you must not kill my son, who is among them, for it is he who generously provides you with the yellow calf.

'The time will come when you will be directed to kill the yellow calf and sacrifice it to the god Tirawa. Then you must tan its hide and form a bundle of its skin, placing within it an ear of corn and other things sacred to your tribe.

'Every year, you must look among the herd for another yellow calf. This too, you should sacrifice and keep a piece of its flesh to add to the bundle. Then, whenever food is scarce and famine threatens, you must gather in council around your sacred bundle and pray to Tirawa who will answer your need, and send another yellow calf to you.'

All this was done as the young boy had instructed, and before long food became plentiful and the father rose to become a chief, greatly respected by the people. He lived for many long and happy years among the villagers with his buffalo-wife and when he died the sacred bundle was long preserved and guarded religiously by the tribe who always used it in times of need as a magic charm to bring the buffalo.

THE SERPENT-MEN

After over a month on the warpath, an eminent band of Sioux warriors accompanied by their chief, were returning home to their encampment in the hills. When they were still quite a long way off, they were suddenly gripped by a savage hunger and decided amongst themselves to scatter in search of wild game to sustain them on the rest of their journey. Some dispersed to the woodlands while others headed for the plains, agreeing that the first to locate an animal should signal to the others to join in the pursuit, for no great warrior could ever enjoy the flesh of a creature he had not helped to track down.

They had been on the hunt for some time without having anything to show for their efforts when suddenly one of the braves, placing his ear to the ground, declared that he could hear a herd of buffalo approaching in the distance. The prospect of such an enjoyable chase greatly cheered the young warriors and they gathered around their chief, anxious to assist in the plan to intercept the animals.

Closer and closer came the sound of the herd. The chief and his men lay very still in the undergrowth, their arrows poised and ready to shoot as soon as the buffalo came into view. Suddenly, their target appeared, but to their absolute horror the group came face to face, not with the four-legged animals they had been expecting, but with a gigantic snake, its rattle held menacingly in the air, as large as a man's head. Although almost paralysed with terror, the chief somehow managed to raise his weapon and shot an arrow through the air which lodged itself in the snake's throat. The huge creature immediately keeled over and lay squirming and hissing in the earth for some minutes until all life had passed out of it.

Even though it lay dead, the Sioux warriors did not dare to approach the snake for quite some time but remained instead at a safe distance, debating what they should do with the carcass. Hunger beckoned once more and for the first time the chief was struck by the thought that they had, in fact, provided themselves with a perfectly good, if unusual, meal. He called up his men and ordered them to build a fire and soon they were helping themselves to a delicious stew, as flavoursome as the tenderest buffalo meat. Only one brave refused to partake of the meal. Even his extreme hunger could not conquer his scruples and he remained adamant that he would not join the others in tasting the body of a great rattling snake.

When the meal was over, the warriors felt both satisfied and drowsy and lay down beside the camp-fire for a brief rest in preparation for their ongoing journey. It was several hours before the chief awoke, but as he slowly opened his eyes, he imagined he must still be dreaming, for he observed that all around him, his men had turned to snakes. Then he gazed at his own body and cried out in alarm, for he himself was already half snake, half man. Hastily, he slithered towards his transformed warriors and observed that only one among them had not suffered the same fate as the others – the young brave who had earlier refused to try any of the food.

The serpent-men and their chief placed themselves under the protection of the young brave, requesting that he gather them together in a large robe and carry them to the summit of the high hill overlooking their village. Terrified by the sight of them and fearing he might soon be attacked, the boy raced all the way to the hill-top and flung the robe beneath some trees. But the snakes broke free quickly and, moving towards him, coiled themselves around his ankles. They had no wish to harm him, they assured him, and soon he discovered that they treated him very kindly, sharing with him their strange wisdom and their many mysterious charms.

'You must return to the village and visit our families for us,' they said to him. 'Tell the people not to be afraid, and say to our wives and children that we shall visit them in the summer when they should come out to greet us.'

The young brave readily agreed to deliver this message and set off homewards without further delay. Tears filled the eyes of every villager as he informed them of the fate of their chief and the other great warriors of the tribe, but the people were determined not to let grief destroy them, and took some comfort in the news that they would at least see their loved ones again.

It was a hot summer's morning when the snakes arrived at the little village, striking up a loud, hissing chorus that immediately attracted the attention of every man, woman and child. Abruptly, the villagers gathered together and walked cautiously in the direction of the snakes, taking with them moccasins, leggings, saddles and weapons that once belonged to the missing warriors. Their hearts were filled with fear as they drew closer to the creatures and they stood, still at a safe distance, fully prepared to turn on their heels. But the chief, who sat at the centre of the serpent-men, rose up from the earth and spoke to his people reassuringly: 'Do not be afraid of us,' he called to them. 'Do not flee from us, we mean you no harm.'

From that moment, the people grew in confidence and moving boldly forwards, they formed a circle around the serpent-men and chatted to them long into the evening.

In the winter the snakes vanished altogether, but every summer, for as long as the villagers could remember, they returned, wearing a new and brilliant coat. The villagers always treated them with the greatest respect and taught their children to revere the serpent, so that even today if a snake appears in the pathway of a tribal warrior, he will always stop and talk to it, offering it some token of his friendship and regard.

THE GIRL WHO BECAME A BIRD

The father of Ran-che-wai-me, the flying pigeon of the Wisconsin, would not hear of her wedding Wai-o-naisa, the young chief who had long sought her in marriage. The maiden, however, true to her plighted faith, still continued to meet him every evening upon one of the tufted islets which stud the river in great profusion. Nightly, through the long months of summer, did the lovers keep their tryst, parting only after each meeting more and more endeared to each other.

At length Wai-o-naisa was ordered off upon a secret expedition against the Sioux, and so sudden was his departure that he had no opportunity of bidding farewell to his betrothed. The band of warriors to which he was attached was a long while absent, and one day there came the news that Wai-o-naisa had fallen in a fight with the Menomones.

Ran-che-wai-me was inconsolable, but she dared not show her grief before her parents, and the only relief she could find from her sorrow was to swim over by starlight to the island where she had been accustomed to meet her lover, and there, calling upon his name, bewail the loss of him who was dearer to her than all else.

One night, while she was engaged in this lamentation, the sound of her voice attracted some of her father's people to the spot. Startled by their appearance the girl tried to climb a tree, in order to hide herself in its branches, but her frame was bowed with sorrow and her weak limbs refused to aid her.

"Wai-o-naisa!" she cried, "Wai-o-naisa!"

At each repetition of his name her voice became shriller, while, as she endeavoured to screen herself in the underwood, a soft plumage began to cover her delicate limbs, which were wounded by the briers. She tossed her arms to the sky in her distress and they became clothed with feathers. At length, when her pursuers were close upon her, a bird arose from the bush they had surrounded, and flitting from tree to tree, it fled before them, ever crying—

"Wai-o-naisa! Wai-o-naisa!"

THE MAIDEN WHO LOVED A FISH

There was once among the Marshpees, a small tribe who have their hunting-grounds on the shores of the Great Lake, near the Cape of Storms, a woman whose name was Awashanks. She was rather silly, and very idle. For days together she would sit doing nothing. Then she was so ugly and ill-shaped that not one of the youths of the village would have aught to say to her by way of courtship or marriage. She squinted very much; her face was long and thin, her nose excessively large and humped, her teeth crooked and projecting, her chin almost as sharp as the bill of a loon, and her ears as large as those of a deer. Altogether she was a very odd and strangely formed woman, and wherever she went she never failed to excite much laughter and derision among those who thought that ugliness and deformity were fit subjects for ridicule.

Though so very ugly, there was one faculty she possessed in a more remarkable degree than any woman of the tribe. It was that of singing. Nothing, unless such could be found in the land of spirits, could equal the sweetness of her voice or the beauty of her songs. Her favourite place of resort was a small hill, a little removed from the river of her people, and there, seated beneath the shady trees, she would while away the hours of summer with her charming songs. So beautiful and melodious were the things she uttered, that, by the time she had sung a single sentence, the branches above her head would be filled with the birds that came thither to listen, the thickets around her would be crowded with beasts, and the waters rolling beside her would be alive with fishes, all attracted by the sweet sounds. From the minnow to the porpoise, from the wren to the eagle, from the snail to the lobster, from the mouse to the mole,—all hastened to the spot to listen to the charming songs of the hideous Marshpee maiden.

Among the fishes which repaired every night to the vicinity of the Little Hillock, which was the chosen resting-place of the ugly songstress, was the great chief of the trouts, a tribe of fish inhabiting the river near by. The chief was of a far greater size than the people of his nation usually are, being as long as a man, and quite as thick.

Of all the creatures which came to listen to the singing of Awashanks none appeared to enjoy it so highly as the chief of the trouts. As his bulk prevented him from approaching so near as he wished, he, from time to time, in his eagerness to enjoy the music to the best advantage, ran his nose into the ground, and thus worked his way a considerable distance into the land. Nightly he continued his exertions to approach the source of the delightful sounds he heard, till at length he had ploughed out a wide and handsome channel, and so effected his passage from the river to the hill, a distance extending an arrow's-flight. Thither he repaired every night at the commencement of darkness, sure to meet the maiden who had become so necessary to his happiness. Soon he began to speak of the pleasure he enjoyed, and to fill the ears of Awashanks with fond protestations of his love and affection. Instead of singing to him, she soon began to listen to his voice. It was something so new and strange to her to hear the tones of love and courtship, a thing so unusual to be told she was beautiful, that it is not wonderful her head was turned by the new incident, and that she began to think the voice of her lover the sweetest she had ever heard. One thing marred their happiness. This was that the trout could not live upon land, nor the maiden in the water. This state of things gave them much sorrow.

They had met one evening at the usual place, and were discoursing together, lamenting that two who loved one another so should be doomed to always live apart, when a man appeared close to Awashanks. He asked the lovers why they seemed to be so sad.

The chief of the trouts told the stranger the cause of their sorrow.

"Be not grieved nor hopeless," said the stranger, when the chief had finished. "The impediments can be removed. I am the spirit who presides over fishes, and though I cannot make a man or woman of a fish, I can make them into fish. Under my power Awashanks shall become a beautiful trout."

With that he bade the girl follow him into the river. When they had waded in some little depth he took up some water in his hand and poured it on her head, muttering some words, of which none but himself knew the meaning. Immediately a change took place in her. Her body took the form of a fish, and in a few moments she was a complete trout. Having accomplished this transformation the spirit gave her to the chief of the trouts, and the pair glided off into the deep and quiet waters. She did not, however, forget the land of her birth. Every season, on the same night as that upon which her disappearance from her tribe had been wrought, there were to be seen two trouts of enormous size playing in the water off the shore. They continued these visits till the pale-faces came to the country, when, deeming themselves to be in danger from a people who paid no reverence to the spirits of the land, they bade it adieu for ever.

THE MAN-FISH

A very great while ago the ancestors of the Shawanos nation lived on the other side of the Great Lake, half-way between the rising sun and the evening star. It was a land of deep snows and much frost, of winds which whistled in the clear, cold nights, and storms which travelled from seas no eyes could reach. Sometimes the sun ceased to shine for moons together, and then he was continually before their eyes for as many more. In the season of cold the waters were all locked up, and the snows overtopped the ridge of the cabins. Then he shone out so fiercely that men fell stricken by his fierce rays, and were numbered with the snow that had melted and run to the embrace of the rivers. It was not like the beautiful lands—the lands blessed with soft suns and ever-green vales—in which the Shawanos now dwell, yet it was well stocked with deer, and the waters with fat seals and great fish, which were caught just when the people pleased to go after them. Still, the nation were discontented, and wished to leave their barren and inhospitable shores. The priests had told them of a beautiful world beyond the Great Salt Lake, from which the glorious sun never disappeared for a longer time than the duration of a child's sleep, where snow-shoes were never wanted—a land clothed with perpetual verdure, and bright with never-failing gladness. The Shawanos listened to these tales till they came to loathe their own simple comforts; all they talked of, all they appeared to think of, was the land of the happy hunting-grounds.

Once upon a time the people were much terrified at seeing a strange creature, much resembling a man, riding along the waves of the lake on the borders of which they dwelt. He had on his head long green hair; his face was shaped like that of a porpoise, and he had a beard of the colour of ooze.

If the people were frightened at seeing a man who could live in the water like a fish or a duck, how much more were they frightened when they saw that from his breast down he was actually fish, or rather two fishes, for each of his legs was a whole and distinct fish. When they heard him speak distinctly in their own language, and when he sang songs sweeter than the music of birds in spring, or the whispers of love from the lips of a beautiful maiden, they thought it a being from the Land of Shades—a spirit from the happy fishing-grounds beyond the lake of storms.

He would sit for a long time, his fish-legs coiled up under him, singing to the wondering ears of the Indians upon the shore the pleasures he experienced, and the beautiful and strange things he saw in the depths of the ocean, always closing his strange stories with these words, shouted at the top of his voice—

"Follow me, and see what I will show you."

Every day, when the waves were still and the winds had gone to their resting-place in the depths of the earth, the monster was sure to be seen near the shore where the Shawanos dwelt. For a great many suns they dared not venture upon the water in quest of food, doing nothing but wander along the beach, watching the strange creature as he played his antics upon the surface of the waves, listening to his songs and to his invitation—

"Follow me, and see what I will show you."

The longer he stayed the less they feared him. They became used to him, and in time looked upon him as a spirit who was not made for harm, nor wished to injure the poor Indian. Then they grew hungry, and their wives and little ones cried for food, and, as hunger banishes all fear, in a few days three canoes with many men and warriors ventured off to the rocks in quest of fish.

When they reached the fishing-place, they heard as before the voice shouting—

"Follow me, and see what I will show you."

Presently the man-fish appeared, sitting on the water, with his legs folded under him, and his arms crossed on his breast, as they had usually seen him. There he sat, eying them attentively. When they failed to draw in the fish they had hooked, he would make the water shake and the deep echo with shouts of laughter, and would clap his hands with great noise, and cry—

"Ha, ha! there he fooled you."

When a fish was caught he was very angry. When the fishers had tried long and patiently, and taken little, and the sun was just hiding itself behind the dark clouds which skirted the region of warm winds, the strange creature cried out still stronger than before:

"Follow me, and see what I will show you."

Kiskapocoke, who was the head man of the tribe, asked him what he wanted, but he would make no other answer than—

"Follow me."

"Do you think," said Kiskapocoke, "I would be such a fool as to go I don't know with whom, and I don't know where?"

"See what I will show you," cried the man-fish.

"Can you show us anything better than we have yonder?" asked the warrior.

"I will show you," replied the monster, "a land where there is a herd of deer for every one that skips over your hills, where there are vast droves of creatures larger than your sea-elephants, where there is no cold to freeze you, where the sun is always soft and smiling, where the trees are always in bloom."

ANIMAL TALES

The people began to be terrified, and wished themselves on land, but the moment they tried to paddle towards the shore, some invisible hand would seize their canoes and draw them back, so that an hour's labour did not enable them to gain the length of their boat in the direction of their homes. At last Kiskapocoke said to his companions—

"What shall we do?"

"Follow me," said the fish.

Then Kiskapocoke said to his companions—

"Let us follow him, and see what will come of it."

So they followed him,—he swimming and they paddling, until night came. Then a great wind and deep darkness prevailed, and the Great Serpent commenced hissing in the depths of the ocean. The people were terribly frightened, and did not think to live till another sun, but the man-fish kept close to the boats, and bade them not be afraid, for nothing should hurt them.

When morning came, nothing could be seen of the shore they had left. The winds still raged, the seas were very high, and the waters ran into their canoes like melted snows over the brows of the mountains, but the man-fish handed them large shells, with which they baled the water out. As they had brought neither food nor water with them, they had become both hungry and thirsty. Kiskapocoke told the strange creature they wanted to eat and drink, and that he must supply them with what they required.

"Very well," said the man-fish, and, disappearing in the depths of the water, he soon reappeared, bringing with him a bag of parched corn and a shell full of sweet water.

For two moons and a half the fishermen followed the man-fish, till at last one morning their guide exclaimed—

"Look there!"

Upon that they looked in the direction he pointed out to them and saw land, high land, covered with great trees, and glittering as the sand of the Spirit's Island. Behind the shore rose tall mountains, from the tops of which issued great flames, which shot up into the sky, as the forks of the lightning cleave the clouds in the hot moon. The waters of the Great Salt Lake broke in small waves upon its shores, which were covered with sporting seals and wild ducks pluming themselves in the beams of the warm and gentle sun. Upon the shore stood a great many strange people, but when they saw the strangers step upon the land and the man-fish, they fled to the woods like startled deer, and were no more seen.

When the warriors were safely landed, the man-fish told them to let the canoe go; "for," said he, "you will never need it more." They had travelled but a little way into the woods when he bade them stay where they were, while he told the spirit of the land that the strangers he had promised were come, and with that he descended into a deep cave near at hand. He soon returned, accompanied by a creature as strange in appearance as himself. His legs and feet were those of a man. He had leggings and moccasins like an Indian's, tightly laced and beautifully decorated with wampum, but his head was like a goat's. He talked like a man, and his language was one well understood by the strangers.

"I will lead you," he said, "to a beautiful land, to a most beautiful land, men from the clime of snows. There you will find all the joys an Indian covets."

For many moons the Shawanos travelled under the guidance of the man-goat, into whose hands the man-fish had put them, when he retraced his steps to the Great Lake. They came at length to the land which the Shawanos now occupy. They found it as the strange spirits had described it. They married the daughters of the land, and their numbers increased till they were so many that no one could count them. They grew strong, swift, and valiant in war, keen and patient in the chase. They overcame all the tribes eastward of the River of Rivers, and south to the shore of the Great Lake.

PAUPPUKKEEWIS

A man of large stature and great activity of mind and body found himself standing alone on a prairie. He thought to himself—

"How came I here? Are there no beings on this earth but myself? I must travel and see. I must walk till I find the abodes of men."

So as soon as his mind was made up he set out, he knew not whither, in search of habitations. No obstacles diverted him from his purpose. Prairies, rivers, woods, and storms did not daunt his courage or turn him back. After travelling a long time he came to a wood in which he saw decayed stumps of trees, as if they had been cut in ancient times, but he found no other traces of men. Pursuing his journey he found more recent marks of the same kind, and later on he came to fresh traces of human beings, first their footsteps, and then the wood they had cut lying in heaps.

Continuing on he emerged towards dusk from the forest, and beheld at a distance a large village of high lodges, standing on rising ground. He said to himself—

"I will arrive there at a run."

Off he started with all his speed, and on coming to the first lodge he jumped over it. Those within saw something pass over the top, and then they heard a thump on the ground.

"What is that?" they all said.

One came out to see, and, finding a stranger, invited him in. He found himself in the presence of an old chief and several men who were seated in the lodge. Meat was set before him, after which the chief asked him where he was going and what his name was. He answered he was in search of adventures, and that his name was Pauppukkeewis (grasshopper). The eyes of all were fixed upon him.

"Pauppukkeewis!" said one to another, and the laugh went round.

Pauppukkeewis made but a short stay in the village. He was not easy there. The place gave him no opportunity to display his powers.

"I will be off," he said, and taking with him a young man who had formed a strong attachment for him and who might serve him as a mesh-in-au-wa (official who bears the pipe), he set out once more on his travels. The two travelled together, and when the young man was fatigued with walking Pauppukkeewis would show him a few tricks, such as leaping over trees, and turning round on one leg till he made the dust fly in a cloud around him. In this manner he very much amused his companion, though at times his performance somewhat alarmed him.

One day they came to a large village, where they were well received. The people told them that there were a number of manitoes who lived some distance away and who killed all who came to their lodge.

The people had made many attempts to extirpate these

manitoes, but the war parties that went out for this purpose were always unsuccessful.

"I will go and see them," said Pauppukkeewis.

The chief of the village warned him of the danger he would run, but finding him resolved, said—

"Well, if you will go, since you are my guest, I will send twenty warriors with you."

Pauppukkeewis thanked him for this. Twenty young men offered themselves for the expedition. They went forward, and in a short time descried the lodge of the manitoes. Pauppukkeewis placed his friend and the warriors near him so that they might see all that passed, and then he went alone into the lodge. When he entered he found five horrible-looking manitoes eating. These were the father and four sons. Their appearance was hideous. Their eyes were set low in their heads as if the manitoes were half starved. They offered Pauppukkeewis part of their meat, but he refused it.

"What have you come for?" asked the old one.

"Nothing," answered Pauppukkeewis.

At this they all stared at him.

"Do you not wish to wrestle?" they all asked.

"Yes," replied he.

A hideous smile passed over their faces.

"You go," said the others to their eldest brother.

Pauppukkeewis and his antagonist were soon clinched in each other's arms. He knew the manitoes' object,—they wanted his flesh,—but he was prepared for them.

"Haw, haw!" they cried, and the dust and dry leaves flew about the wrestlers as if driven by a strong wind.

The manito was strong, but Pauppukkeewis soon found he

could master him. He tripped him up, and threw him with a giant's force head foremost on a stone, and he fell insensible.

The brothers stepped up in quick succession, but Pauppukkeewis put his tricks in full play, and soon all the four lay bleeding on the ground. The old manito got frightened, and ran for his life. Pauppukkeewis pursued him for sport. Sometimes he was before him, sometimes over his head. Now he would give him a kick, now a push, now a trip, till the manito was quite exhausted. Meanwhile Pauppukkeewis's friend and the warriors came up, crying—

"Ha, ha, a! Ha, ha, a! Pauppukkeewis is driving him before him."

At length Pauppukkeewis threw the manito to the ground with such force that he lay senseless, and the warriors, carrying him off, laid him with the bodies of his sons, and set fire to the whole, consuming them to ashes.

Around the lodge Pauppukkeewis and his friends saw a large number of bones, the remains of the warriors whom the manitoes had slain. Taking three arrows, Pauppukkeewis called upon the Great Spirit, and then, shooting an arrow in the air, he cried—

"You, who are lying down, rise up, or you will be hit."

The bones at these words all collected in one place. Again Pauppukkeewis shot another arrow into the air, crying—

"You, who are lying down, rise up, or you will be hit," and each bone drew towards its fellow.

Then he shot a third arrow, crying—

"You, who are lying down, rise up, or you will be hit," and the bones immediately came together, flesh came over them, and the warriors, whose remains they were, stood before Pauppukkeewis alive and well.

He led them to the chief of the village, who had been his friend, and gave them up to him. Soon after, the chief with his counsellors came to him, saying—

"Who is more worthy to rule than you? You alone can defend us."

Pauppukkeewis thanked the chief, but told him he must set out again in search of further adventures. The chief and the counsellors pressed him to remain, but he was resolved to leave them, and so he told the chief to make his friend ruler while he himself went on his travels.

"I will come again," said he, "sometime and see you."

"Ho, ho, ho!" they all cried, "come back again and see us."

He promised that he would, and set out alone.

After travelling for some time, he came to a large lake, and on looking about he saw an enormous otter on an island. He thought to himself—

"His skin will make me a fine pouch," and, drawing near, he drove an arrow into the otter's side. He waded into the lake, and with some difficulty dragged the carcass ashore. He took out the entrails, but even then the carcass was so heavy that it was as much as he could do to drag it up a hill overlooking the lake. As soon as he got it into the sunshine, where it was warm, he skinned the otter, and threw the carcass away, for he said to himself—

"The war-eagle will come, and then I shall have a chance to get his skin and feathers to put on my head."

Very soon he heard a noise in the air, but he could see nothing. At length a large eagle dropped, as if from the sky, on to the otter's carcass. Pauppukkeewis drew his bow and sent an arrow through the bird's body. The eagle made a dying effort and lifted the carcass up several feet, but it could not disengage its claws, and the weight soon brought the bird down again.

Then Pauppukkeewis skinned the bird, crowned his head with its feathers, and set out again on his journey.

After walking a while he came to a lake, the water of which came right up to the trees on its banks. He soon saw that the lake had been made by beavers. He took his station at a certain spot to see whether any of the beavers would show themselves. Soon he saw the head of one peeping out of the water to see who the stranger was.

"My friend," said Pauppukkeewis, "could you not turn me into a beaver like yourself?"

"I do not know," replied the beaver; "I will go and ask the others."

Soon all the beavers showed their heads above the water, and looked to see if Pauppukkeewis was armed, but he had left his bow and arrows in a hollow tree a short distance off. When they were satisfied they all came near.

"Can you not, with all your united power," said he, "turn me into a beaver? I wish to live among you."

"Yes," answered the chief, "lie down;" and Pauppukkeewis soon found himself changed into one of them.

"You must make me large," said he, "larger than any of you."

"Yes, yes," said they; "by and by, when we get into the lodge, it shall be done."

They all dived into the lake, and Pauppukkeewis, passing large heaps of limbs of trees and logs at the bottom, asked the use of them. The beavers answered—

"They are our winter provisions."

When they all got into the lodge their number was about

one hundred. The lodge was large and warm.

"Now we will make you large," said they, exerting all their power. "Will that do?"

"Yes," he answered, for he found he was ten times the size of the largest.

"You need not go out," said they. "We will bring your food into the lodge, and you shall be our chief."

"Very well," answered Pauppukkeewis. He thought—

"I will stay here and grow fat at their expense," but very soon a beaver came into the lodge out of breath, crying—

"We are attacked by Indians."

All huddled together in great fear. The water began to lower, for the hunters had broken down the dam, and soon the beavers heard them on the roof of the lodge, breaking it in. Out jumped all the beavers and so escaped. Pauppukkeewis tried to follow them, but, alas! they had made him so large that he could not creep out at the hole. He called to them to come back, but none answered. He worried himself so much in trying to escape that he looked like a bladder. He could not change himself into a man again though he heard and understood all the hunters said. One of them put his head in at the top of the lodge.

"Ty-au!" cried he. "Tut-ty-au! Me-shau-mik! King of the beavers is in."

Then they all got at Pauppukkeewis and battered in his skull with their clubs. After that seven or eight of them placed his body on poles and carried him home. As he went he reflected—

"What will become of me? My ghost or shadow will not die after they get me to their lodges."

When the party arrived home, they sent out invitations to a grand feast. The women took Pauppukkeewis and laid him in the snow to skin him, but as soon as his flesh got cold, his jee-bi, or spirit, fled.

Pauppukkeewis found himself standing on a prairie, having assumed his mortal shape. After walking a short distance, he saw a herd of elks feeding. He admired the apparent ease and enjoyment of their life, and thought there could be nothing more pleasant than to have the liberty of running about, and feeding on the prairies. He asked them if they could not change him into an elk.

"Yes," they answered, after a pause. "Get down on your hands and feet." He did so, and soon found himself an elk.

"I want big horns and big feet," said he. "I wish to be very large."

"Yes, yes," they said. "There," exerting all their power, "are you big enough?"

"Yes," he answered, for he saw he was very large.

They spent a good time in playing and running.

Being rather cold one day he went into a thick wood for shelter, and was followed by most of the herd. They had not been there long before some elks from behind passed them like a strong wind. All took the alarm, and off they ran, Pauppukkeewis with the rest.

"Keep out on the plains," said they, but he found it was too late to do so, for they had already got entangled in the thick woods. He soon smelt the hunters, who were closely following his trail, for they had left all the others to follow him. He jumped furiously, and broke down young trees in his flight, but it only served to retard his progress. He soon felt an arrow in his side. He jumped over trees in his agony, but the arrows clattered thicker and thicker about him, and at last one entered his heart. He fell to the ground and heard the whoop of triumph given by the warriors. On coming up they looked at the carcass with astonishment, and, with their hands up to their mouths, exclaimed—

"Ty-au! ty-au!"

There were about sixty in the party, who had come out on a special hunt, for one of their number had, the day before, observed Pauppukkeewis's large tracks in the sand. They skinned him, and as his flesh got cold his jee-bi took its flight, and once more he found himself in human shape.

His passion for adventure was not yet cooled. On coming to a large lake, the shore of which was sandy, he saw a large flock of brant, and, speaking to them, he asked them to turn him into a brant.

"Very well," said they.

"But I want to be very large," said he.

"Very well," replied the brant, and he soon found himself one of them, of prodigious size, all the others looking on at him in amazement.

"You must fly as leader," they said.

"No," replied Pauppukkeewis, "I will fly behind."

"Very well," said they. "One thing we have to say to you. You must be careful in flying not to look down, for if you do something may happen to you."

"Be it so," said he, and soon the flock rose up in the air, for they were bound for the north. They flew very fast with Pauppukkeewis behind. One day, while going with a strong wind, and as swift as their wings would flap, while they passed over a large village, the Indians below raised a great shout, for they were amazed at the enormous size of Pauppukkeewis. They made such a noise that Pauppukkeewis forgot what had been told him about not looking down. He was flying as swift as an arrow, and as soon as he brought his neck in, and stretched it down to look at the shouters, his tail was caught by the wind, and he was blown over and over. He tried to right himself, but without success. Down he went from an immense height, turning over and over. He lost his senses, and when he recovered them he found himself jammed in a cleft in a hollow tree. To get backward or forward was impossible, and there he remained until his brant life was ended by starvation. Then his jee-bi again left the carcass, and once more he found himself in human shape.

Travelling was still his passion, and one day he came to a lodge, in which were two old men whose heads were white from age. They treated him well, and he told them he was going back to his village to see his friends and people. The old men said they would aid him, and pointed out the way they said he should go, but they were deceivers. After walking all day he came to a lodge very like the first, and looking in he found two old men with white heads. It was in fact the very same lodge, and he had been walking in a circle. The old men did not undeceive him, but pretended to be strangers, and said in a kind voice—

"We will show you the way."

After walking the third day, and coming back to the same place, he discovered their trickery, for he had cut a notch in the door-post.

"Who are you," said he to them, "to treat me so?" and he gave one a kick and the other a slap that killed them. Their blood flew against the rocks near their lodge, and that is the reason there are red streaks in them to this day. Then Pauppukkeewis burned their lodge.

He continued his journey, not knowing exactly which way to go. At last he came to a big lake. He ascended the highest hill to try and see the opposite shore, but he could not, so he made a canoe and took a sail on the water. On looking down he saw that the bottom of the lake was covered with dark fish, of which he caught some. This made him wish to return to his village, and bring his people to live near this lake. He sailed on, and towards evening came to an island, where he stopped and ate the fish.

Next day he returned to the mainland, and, while wandering along the shore, he encountered a more powerful manito than himself, named Manabozho. Pauppukkeewis thought it best, after playing him a trick, to keep out of his way. He again thought of returning to his village, and, transforming himself into a partridge, took his flight towards it. In a short time he reached it, and his return was welcomed with feasting and songs. He told them of the lake and of the fish, and, telling them that it would be easier for them to live there, persuaded them all to remove. He immediately began to lead them by short journeys, and all things turned out as he had said.

While the people lived there a messenger came to Pauppukkeewis in the shape of a bear, and said that the bear-chief wished to see him at once at his village. Pauppukkeewis was ready in an instant, and getting on the messenger's back was carried away. Towards evening they ascended a high mountain, and came to a cave, in which the bear-chief lived. He was a very large creature, and he made Pauppukkeewis welcome, inviting him into his lodge.

As soon as propriety allowed he spoke, and said that he had sent for him because he had heard he was the chief who was leading a large party towards his hunting-grounds.

"You must know," said he, "that you have no right there, and I wish you to leave the country with your party, or else we must fight."

"Very well," replied Pauppukkeewis, "so be it."

He did not wish to do anything without consulting his people, and he saw that the bear-chief was raising a war-party, so he said he would go back that night. The bear-king told him he might do as he wished, and that one of the bears was at his command; so Pauppukkeewis, jumping on its back, rode home. Then he assembled the village, and told the young men to kill the bear, make ready a feast, and hang the head outside the village, for he knew the bear spies would soon see it and carry the news to their chief.

Next morning Pauppukkeewis got all his young warriors ready for the fight. After waiting one day, the bear war-party came in sight, making a tremendous noise. The bear-chief advanced, and said that he did not wish to shed the blood of the young warriors, but if Pauppukkeewis would consent they two would run a race, and the winner should kill the losing chief, and all the loser's followers should be the slaves of the other. Pauppukkeewis agreed, and they ran before all the warriors. He was victor; but not to terminate the race too quickly he gave the bear-chief some specimens of his skill, forming eddies and whirlwinds with the sand as he twisted and turned about. As the bear-chief came to the post Pauppukkeewis drove an arrow through him. Having done this he told his young men to take the bears and tie one at the door of each lodge, that they might remain in future as slaves.

After seeing that all was quiet and prosperous in the village, Pauppukkeewis felt his desire for adventure returning, so he took an affectionate leave of his friends and people, and started off again. After wandering a long time, he came to the lodge of Manabozho, who was absent. Pauppukkeewis thought he would play him a trick, so he turned everything in the lodge upside down and killed his chickens. Now Manabozho calls all the fowl of the air his chickens, and among the number was a raven, the meanest of birds, and him Pauppukkeewis killed and hung up by the neck to insult Manabozho. He then went on till he came to a very high point of rocks running out into the lake, from the top of which he could see the country as far as eye could reach. While he sat there, Manabozho's mountain chickens flew round and past him in great numbers. So, out of spite, he shot many of them, for his arrows were sure and the birds many, and he amused himself by throwing the birds down the precipice. At length a wary bird called out—

"Pauppukkeewis is killing us: go and tell our father."

Away flew some of them, and Manabozho soon made his appearance on the plain below.

Pauppukkeewis slipped down the other side of the mountain. Manabozho cried from the top—

"The earth is not so large but I can get up to you."

Off Pauppukkeewis ran and Manabozho after him. He ran over hills and prairies with all his speed, but his pursuer was still hard after him. Then he thought of a shift. He stopped, and climbed a large pine-tree, stripped it of all its green foliage, and threw it to the winds. Then he ran on. When Manabozho reached the tree, it called out to him—

"Great Manabozho, give me my life again. Pauppukkeewis has killed me."

"I will do so," said Manabozho, and it took him some time to gather the scattered foliage. Then he resumed the chase.

Pauppukkeewis repeated the same trick with the hemlock, and with other trees, for Manabozho would always stop to restore anything that called upon him to give it life again. By this means Pauppukkeewis kept ahead, but still Manabozho was overtaking him when Pauppukkeewis saw an elk. He asked it to take him on its back, and this the animal did, and for a time he made great progress. Still Manabozho was in sight. Pauppukkeewis dismounted, and, coming to a large sandstone rock, he broke it in pieces, and scattered the grains. Manabozho was so close upon him at this place that he had almost caught him, but the foundation of the rock cried out—

"Haye! Ne-me-sho! Pauppukkeewis has spoiled me. Will you not restore me to life?"

"Yes," replied Manabozho, and he restored the rock to its previous shape. He then pushed on in pursuit of Pauppukkeewis, and had got so near as to put out his arm to seize him, when Pauppukkeewis dodged him, and raised such a dust and commotion by whirlwinds, as to make the trees break, and the sand and leaves dance in the air. Again and again Manabozho's hand was put out to catch him, but he dodged him at every turn, and at last, making a great dust, he dashed into a hollow tree, which had been blown down, and, changing himself into a snake, crept out at its roots. Well that he did; for at the moment Manabozho, who is Ogee-bau-ge-mon (a species of lightning) struck the tree with all his power, and shivered it to fragments. Pauppukkeewis again took human shape, and again Manabozho, pursuing him, pressed him hard.

At a distance Pauppukkeewis saw a very high rock jutting out into a lake, and he ran for the foot of the precipice, which was abrupt and elevated. As he came near, the manito of the rock opened his door and told him to come in. No sooner was the door closed than Manabozho knocked at it.

"Open," he cried in a loud voice.

The manito was afraid of him, but said to his guest—

"Since I have sheltered you, I would sooner die with you than open the door."

"Open," Manabozho cried again.

The manito was silent. Manabozho made no attempt to force the door open. He waited a few moments.

"Very well," said he, "I give you till night to live."

The manito trembled, for he knew that when the hour came he would be shut up under the earth.

Night came, the clouds hung low and black, and every moment the forked lightning flashed from them. The black clouds advanced slowly and threw their dark shadows afar, and behind was heard the rumbling noise of the coming thunder. When the clouds were gathered over the rock the thunders roared, the lightning flashed, the ground shook, and the solid rock split, tottered, and fell. Under the ruins lay crushed the mortal bodies of Pauppukkeewis and the manito.

It was only then that Pauppukkeewis found that he was really dead. He had been killed before in the shapes of different animals, but now his body, in human shape, was crushed.

Manabozho came and took his jee-bi, or spirit. "You," said he to Pauppukkeewis, "shall not be again permitted to live on the earth. I will give you the shape of the war-eagle, and you shall be the chief of all birds, and your duty shall be to watch over their destinies."

MANABOZHO THE WOLF

Manabozho set out to travel. He wished to outdo all others, and see new countries, but after walking over America, and encountering many adventures, he became satisfied as well as fatigued. He had heard of great feats in hunting, and felt a desire to try his power in that way.

One evening, as he was walking along the shores of a great lake, weary and hungry, he encountered a great magician in the form of an old wolf, with six young ones, coming towards him. The wolf, as soon as he saw him, told his whelps to keep out of the way of Manabozho.

"For I know," said he, "that it is he we see yonder."

The young wolves were in the act of running off, when Manabozho cried out—

"My grandchildren, where are you going? Stop, and I will go with you."

He appeared rejoiced to see the old wolf, and asked him whither he was journeying. Being told that they were looking out for a place where they could find the most game, and best pass the winter, he said he should like to go with them, and addressed the old wolf in these words—

"Brother, I have a passion for the chase. Are you willing to change me into a wolf?"

The old wolf was agreeable, and Manabozho's transformation was effected.

He was fond of novelty. He found himself a wolf corresponding in size with the others, but he was not quite satisfied with the change, crying out—

"Oh! make me a little larger."

They did so.

"A little larger still," he cried.

They said—

"Let us humour him," and granted his request.

"Well," said he, "that will do." Then looking at his tail—

"Oh!" cried he, "make my tail a little longer and more bushy."

They made it so, and shortly after they all started off in company, dashing up a ravine. After getting into the woods some distance, they fell in with the tracks of moose. The young wolves went after them, Manabozho and the old wolf following at their leisure.

"Well," said the wolf, "who do you think is the fastest of my sons? Can you tell by the jumps they take?"

"Why," replied he, "that one that takes such long jumps; he is the fastest, to be sure."

"Ha, ha! You are mistaken," said the old wolf. "He makes a good start, but he will be the first to tire out. This one who appears to be behind will be the first to kill the game."

Soon after they came to the place where the young ones had killed the game. One of them had dropped his bundle there.

"Take that, Manabozho," said the old wolf.

"Esa," he replied, "what will I do with a dirty dog-skin?"

The wolf took it up; it was a beautiful robe.

"Oh! I will carry it now," said Manabozho.

"Oh no," replied the wolf, who at the moment exerted his magic power. "It is a robe of pearls."

From that moment he lost no opportunity of displaying his superiority, both in the hunter's and magician's art, over his conceited companion.

Coming to a place where the moose had lain down, they saw

that the young wolves had made a fresh start after their prey.

"Why," said the wolf, "this moose is poor. I know by the tracks, for I can always tell whether they are fat or not."

They next came to a place where one of the wolves had tried to bite the moose, and, failing, had broken one of his teeth on a tree.

"Manabozho," said the wolf, "one of your grandchildren has shot at the game. Take his arrow. There it is."

"No," replied he, "what will I do with a dirty tooth?"

The old wolf took it up, and, behold! it was a beautiful silver arrow.

When they overtook the young ones, they found they had killed a very fat moose. Manabozho was very hungry, but, such is the power of enchantment, he saw nothing but bones, picked quite clean. He thought to himself—

"Just as I expected. Dirty, greedy fellows!"

However, he sat down without saying a word, and the old wolf said to one of the young ones—

"Give some meat to your grandfather."

The wolf, coming near to Manabozho, opened his mouth wide as if he had eaten too much, whereupon Manabozho jumped up, saying—

"You filthy dog, you have eaten so much that you are ill. Get away to some other place."

The old wolf, hearing these words, came to Manabozho, and, behold! before him was a heap of fresh ruddy meat with the fat lying all ready prepared. Then Manabozho put on a smiling-face.

"Amazement!" cried he, "how fine the meat is!"

"Yes," replied the wolf; "it is always so with us. We know our work, and always get the best. It is not a long tail that makes a hunter."

Manabozho bit his lip.

They then commenced fixing their winter quarters, while the young ones went out in search of game, of which they soon brought in a large supply. One day, during the absence of the young wolves, the old one amused himself by cracking the large bones of a moose.

"Manabozho," said he, "cover your head with the robe, and do not look at me while I am at these bones, for a piece may fly in your eye."

Manabozho covered his head, but, looking through a rent in the robe, he saw all the other was about. At that moment a piece of bone flew off and hit him in the eye. He cried out—

"Tyau! Why do you strike me, you old dog!"

The wolf said—

"You must have been looking at me."

"No, no," replied Manabozho; "why should I want to look at you?"

"Manabozho," said the wolf, "you must have been looking, or you would not have got hurt."

"No, no," said Manabozho; and he thought to himself, "I will repay the saucy wolf for this."

Next day, taking up a bone to obtain the marrow, he said to the old wolf—

"Cover your head, and don't look at me, for I fear a piece may fly in your eye."

The wolf did so. Then Manabozho took the leg-bone of the moose, and, looking first to see if the old wolf was well covered, he hit him a blow with all his might. The wolf jumped up, and cried out—

"Why do you strike me so?"

"Strike you?" exclaimed Manabozho. "I did not strike you!"

"You did," said the wolf.

"How can you say I did, when you did not see me. Were you looking?" said Manabozho.

He was an expert hunter when he undertook the work in earnest, and one day he went out and killed a fat moose. He was very hungry, and sat down to eat, but fell into great doubts as to the proper point in the carcass to begin at.

"Well," said he, "I don't know where to commence. At the head? No. People would laugh, and say, 'He ate him backward!'"

Then he went to the side.

"No," said he, "they will say I ate him sideways."

He then went to the hind-quarter.

"No," said he, "they will say I ate him forward."

At last, however, seeing that he must begin the attack somewhere, he commenced upon the hind-quarter. He had just got a delicate piece in his mouth when the tree just by began to make a creaking noise, rubbing one large branch against another. This annoyed him.

"Why!" he exclaimed, "I cannot eat when I hear such a noise. Stop, stop!" cried he to the tree.

He was again going on with his meal when the noise was repeated.

"I cannot eat with such a noise," said he; and, leaving the meal, although he was very hungry, he went to put a stop to the noise. He climbed the tree, and having found the branches which caused the disturbance, tried to push them apart, when they suddenly caught him between them, so that he was held fast. While he was in this position a pack of wolves came near.

"Go that way," cried Manabozho, anxious to send them away

from the neighbourhood of his meat. "Go that way; what would you come to get here?"

The wolves talked among themselves, and said, "Manabozho wants to get us out of the way. He must have something good here."

"I begin to know him and all his tricks," said an old wolf. "Let us see if there is anything."

They accordingly began to search, and very soon finding the moose made away with the whole carcass. Manabozho looked on wistfully, and saw them eat till they were satisfied, when they left him nothing but bare bones. Soon after a blast of wind opened the branches and set him free. He went home, thinking to himself—

"See the effect of meddling with frivolous things when certain good is in one's possession!"

THE BUFFALO AND THE GRIZZLY BEAR

Grizzly Bear was going somewhere, following the course of a stream, and at last he went straight towards the headland. When he got in sight, Buffalo Bull was standing beneath it. Grizzly Bear retraced his steps, going again to the stream, following its course until he got beyond the headland. Then he drew near and peeped. He saw that Buffalo Bull was very lean, and standing with his head bowed, as if sluggish. So Grizzly Bear crawled up close to him, made a rush, seized him by the hair of his head, and pulled down his head. He turned Buffalo Bull round and round, shaking him now and then, saying, "Speak! Speak! I have been coming to this place a long time, and they say you have threatened to fight me. Speak!" Then he hit Buffalo Bull on the nose with his open paw.

"Why!" said Buffalo Bull, "I have never threatened to fight you, who have been coming to this country so long."

"Not so! You have threatened to fight me." Letting go the buffalo's head, Grizzly Bear went around and seized him by the tail, turning him round and round. Then he left, but as he did so, he gave him a hard blow with his open paw.

"Oh! Oh! Oh! Oh! Oh! you have caused me great pain," said Buffalo Bull. Bobtailed Grizzly Bear departed.

Buffalo Bull thought thus: "Attack him! You too have been just that sort of a person."

Grizzly Bear knew what he was thinking, so he said, "Why! what are you saying?"

"I said nothing," said Buffalo Bull.

Then Grizzly Bear came back. He seized Buffalo Bull by the tail, pulling him round and round. Then he seized him by the horns, pulling his head round and round. Then he seized him again by the tail and hit him again with the open paw. Again Grizzly Bear departed. And again Buffalo Bull thought as he had done before. Then Grizzly Bear came back and treated Buffalo Bull as he had before.

Buffalo Bull stepped backward, throwing his tail into the air.

"Why! Do not flee," said Grizzly Bear.

Buffalo threw himself down, and rolled over and over. Then he continued backing, pawing the ground.

"Why! I say, do not flee," said Grizzly Bear. When Buffalo Bull backed, making ready to attack him, Grizzly Bear thought he was scared.

Then Buffalo Bull ran towards Grizzly, puffing a great deal.

When he neared him, he rushed on him. He sent Grizzly Bear flying through the air.

As Grizzly Bear came down towards the earth, Buffalo Bull caught him on his horns and threw him into the air again. When Grizzly Bear fell and lay on the ground, Buffalo Bull made at him with his horns to gore him, but just missed him. Grizzly Bear crawled away slowly, with Buffalo Bull following him step by step, thrusting at him now and then, though without striking him. When Grizzly Bear came to a cliff, he plunged over headlong, and landed in a thicket at the foot. Buffalo Bull had run so fast he could not stop at the edge where Grizzly Bear went over, but followed the cliff for some distance. Then he came back and stood with his tail partly raised. Grizzly Bear returned to the bank and peeped.

"Oh, Buffalo Bull," said Grizzly Bear. "Let us be friends. We are very much alike in disposition."

THE BIRD CHIEF

All the birds were called together. To them was said, "Whichever one of you can fly farthest into the sky shall be chief."

All the birds flew to a great height. But Wren got under the thick feathers of Eagle and sat there as Eagle flew. When all the birds became wing-tired, they flew down again; but Eagle flew still higher. When Eagle had gone as far as he could, Wren flew still higher.

When all the birds reached the ground, Eagle alone returned, after a great while. Behold! Wren only was absent. So they awaited him. At last he returned. Eagle had too highly been thinking of himself, being sure of being made chief; and behold! Wren was made chief.

THE RACE BETWEEN HUMMING BIRD AND CRANE

Humming Bird and Crane were both in love with a pretty woman. She liked Humming Bird, who was handsome. Crane was ugly, but he would not give up the pretty woman. So at last to get rid of him, she told them they must have a race, and that she would marry the winner. Now Humming Bird flew like a flash of light; but Crane was heavy and slow.

The birds started from the woman's house to fly around the world to the beginning. Humming Bird flew off like an arrow. He flew all day and when he stopped to roost he was far ahead.

Crane flew heavily, but he flew all night long. He stopped at daylight at a creek to rest. Humming Bird waked up, and flew on again, and soon he reached a creek, and behold! there was Crane, spearing tadpoles with his long bill. Humming Bird flew on.

Soon Crane started on and flew all night as before. Humming Bird slept on his roost.

Next morning Humming Bird flew on and Crane was far, far ahead. The fourth day, Crane was spearing tadpoles for dinner when Humming Bird caught up with him. By the seventh day Crane was a whole night's travel ahead. At last he reached the beginning again. He stopped at the creek and preened his feathers, and then in the early morning went to the woman's house. Humming Bird was far, far behind.

But the woman declared she would not marry so ugly a man as Crane. Therefore she remained single.

ANIMAL TALES

WHY THE TURKEY GOBBLES

In the old days, Grouse had a good voice and Turkey had none. Therefore Turkey asked Grouse to teach him. But Grouse wanted pay, so Turkey promised to give him some feathers for a collar. That is how the Grouse got his collar of turkey feathers.

So the Grouse began to teach Turkey. At last Grouse said, "Now you must try your voice. You must halloo."

Turkey said, "Yes."

Grouse said, "I'll stand on this hollow log, and when I tap on it, you must halloo as loudly as you can."

So Grouse climbed upon a log, ready to tap on it, but when he did so, Turkey became so excited that when he opened his mouth, he only said, "Gobble, gobble, gobble!"

That is why the Turkey gobbles whenever he hears a noise.

UNKTOMI AND THE BAD SONGS

Unktomi was going along; his way lay along by the side of a lake. Out on the lake there were a great many ducks, geese, and swans swimming. When Unktomi saw them he went backward out of sight, and picking some grass, bound it up in a bundle. He placed this on his back and so went again along by the side of the lake.

"Unktomi, what are you carrying?" asked the ducks and the geese and the swans.

"These are bad songs I am carrying," said Unktomi.

The ducks said, "Unktomi, sing for us."

Unktomi replied, "But the songs are very bad."

But the ducks insisted upon it. Then Unktomi said, "Make a grass lodge." So they went to work and made a large grass lodge.

"Now, let all the ducks, geese, and swans gather inside the lodge and I will sing for you," said Unktomi. So all the ducks and the geese and the swans gathered inside and filled the grass lodge. Then Unktomi took his place at the door of the lodge and said, "If I sing for you, no one must look, for that is the meaning of the song."

Then he began to sing:

> *Dance with your eyes shut;*
> *If you open your eyes*
> *Your eyes shall be red!*
> *Your eyes shall be red!*

When he said and sang this, the geese, ducks, and swans danced with their eyes shut. Then Unktomi rose up and said:

> *I even, even I*
> *Follow in my own;*
> *I even, even I,*
> *Follow in my own.*

So they all gabbled as they danced, and Unktomi, dancing among them, commenced twisting off the necks of the fattest of the geese and ducks and swans. But when he tried to twist off the neck of a large swan and could not, he only made him squawk. Then a small duck, called Skiska, partly opened his eyes. He saw Unktomi try to break the swan's neck, and he made an outcry:

Look ye, look ye! Unktomi will destroy us all. Look ye, look ye!

At once they all opened their eyes and attempted to go out. But Unktomi threw himself in the doorway and tried to stop them. They rushed upon him with their feet and wings, and smote him and knocked him over, walking on his stomach, and leaving him as though dead. Then Unktomi came to life, and got up, and looked around.

But they say that the Wood Duck, which looked first, had his eyes made red.

Then Unktomi gathered up the ducks and geese and swans he had killed and carried them on his back. He came to a river and traveled along by the side of it till he came to a long, straight place where he stopped to boil his kettle. He put all the ducks and geese and swans whose necks he had twisted into the kettle, and set it on the fire to boil, and then he lay down to sleep.

As he lay there, curled up on the bank of the river, he said, "Mionze [familiar spirit], if anyone comes you wake me up." So he slept.

Now a mink came paddling along on the river, and coming close to Unktomi's boiling place, saw him lying fast asleep. Then he went there. While Unktomi slept, he took out all the boiling meat and ate it up, putting the bones back into the kettle. Then Unktomi woke up. He sat up and saw no one.

"Perhaps my boiling is cooked for me," he said.

He took the kettle off the fire. He poked a stick into it and found only bones. Then he said, "Indeed, the meat has all fallen off." So he took a spoon and dipped it out; nothing was there but bones.

This is the story of Unktomi and the Bad Songs.

IKTO AND THE RABBIT

The Tetons believed that Ikto was the first person in this world. He is more cunning than human beings. He it was who named all the animals and people. But sometimes Ikto was tricked by the beings he had created.

One day Ikto was hungry; just then he caught a rabbit. He was about to roast him.

Suddenly Rabbit said, "Oh, Ikto, I will teach you a magic art."

Ikto said, "I have created all things."

"But I will show you something new," said Rabbit. Therefore Ikto consented. He let go of Rabbit.

Rabbit stood in front of Ikto and said, "Elder brother, if you wish snow to fall at any time, take some hair such as this,"—and he pulled out some of his rabbit fur—"and blow it in all directions; there will be a blizzard."

Rabbit made a deep snow in this way, though the leaves were green.

At once, Ikto began to pull his own fur and say magic words. Rabbit made a long leap and ran away. Ikto pulled his fur and blew it about. But there was no snow. Then he pulled more fur, and blew it about. Still there was no snow. It was only rabbit fur that made the snow.

HOW RABBIT ESCAPED FROM THE WOLVES

Once upon a time, Wolves caught Rabbit. They were going to eat him, but Rabbit said he would show them a new dance.

Now the Wolves knew that Rabbit was a good dancer, so they made a ring around him.

Rabbit pattered with his feet and began to dance around in a circle, singing,

On the edge of the field I dance about, Ha' nia lil! lil! Ha' nia lil! lil!

Then the Rabbit stopped a minute. He said, "Now when I sing 'on the edge of the field,' I dance that way"—and he danced over in that direction; "and when I sing 'lil! lil!' you must all stamp your feet hard."

The Wolves liked that. They liked new dances.

Rabbit began singing the same song, dancing nearer to the field, while all the Wolves stamped their feet. He sang the song again, dancing still nearer the edge of the field. The fourth time he sang it, while the Wolves were stamping their feet as hard as they could, Rabbit made one jump off and leaped through the long grass. The Wolves raced after him, but Rabbit ran for a hollow stump and climbed inside. When the Wolves got there, one of them put his head inside, but Rabbit hit him on the eye and he pulled his head out. The others were afraid to try, so they went away and left Rabbit in the stump.

WHY THE POSSUM PLAYS DEAD

Rabbit and Possum each wanted a wife, but no one would marry either of them. They talked over the matter and Rabbit said, "We can't get wives here. Let's go to the next village. I'll say

I'm messenger for the council and that everybody must marry at once, and then we'll be sure to get wives."

Off they started for the next town. As Rabbit traveled the faster, he got there first. He waited outside the village until people noticed him and took him into the council lodge. When the chief asked his business, Rabbit said he brought an important message: everyone must be married at once. So the chief called a great council of the people and told them the message.

Every animal took a mate at once, and thus Rabbit got a wife.

But Possum traveled slowly. Therefore he reached the village so late that all the men were married and there was no wife for him. Rabbit pretended to be sorry. He said, "Never mind. I'll carry the same message to the next village."

So Rabbit traveled ahead to the next village. He waited outside until they invited him to the council lodge. There he told the chief he brought an important message: there had been peace so long, there must be war at once. The war must begin in the council lodge.

The animals all began to fight at once, but Rabbit got away in just four leaps. Then Possum reached the lodge. Now Possum had brought no weapons. So all the animals began to fight Possum. They hit him so hard that after a while he rolled over in a corner and shut his eyes and pretended to be dead. That is why Possum pretends to be dead when he finds the hunters after him.

HOW THE DEER GOT HIS HORNS

Long ago, in the beginning, Deer had no horns. His head was smooth like a doe's. Now Deer was a very fast runner, but Rabbit was a famous jumper. So the animals used to talk about it and wonder which could go the farther in the same time. They talked about it a great deal. They decided to have a race between the two, and they made a pair of large antlers to be given to whoever could run the faster. Deer and Rabbit were to start together from one side of a thicket, go through it, and then turn and come back. The one who came out of the thicket first was to receive the horns.

On a certain day all the animals were there. They put the antlers down on the ground to mark the starting point. Everyone admired the horns. But Rabbit said, "I don't know this part of the country; I want to look through the bushes where I am to run."

So the Rabbit went into the thicket, and stayed a long time. He was gone so long the animals suspected he was playing a trick. They sent a messenger after him. Right in the middle of the thicket he found Rabbit, gnawing down the bushes and pulling them away to make a clear road for himself.

The messenger came back quietly and told the animals. When Rabbit came back, they accused him of cheating. Rabbit said, "No," but at last they all went into the thicket and found the road he had made. Therefore the animals gave the antlers to Deer, saying that he was the better runner. That is why deer have antlers. And because Rabbit cut the bushes down, he is obliged to keep cutting them down, as he does to this day.

Rabbit began singing the same song, dancing nearer to the field, while all the Wolves stamped their feet. He sang the song again, dancing still nearer the edge of the field. The fourth time he sang it, while the Wolves were stamping their feet as hard as they could. Rabbit made one jump off and leaped through the long grass. The Wolves raced after him, but Rabbit ran for a hollow stump and climbed inside. When the Wolves got there, one of them put his head inside, but Rabbit hit him on the eye and he pulled his head out. The others were afraid to try, so they went away and left Rabbit in the stump.

HEROES, MONSTERS & THE SUPERNATURAL

Heroic legends featured sometimes reluctant but often brave and moral mortals who would undertake great tasks or journeys, some of which might be supernatural in nature. Native Americans believed emphatically in the existence of supernatural forces, both good and evil, and sought communion with nature as the most fruitful path to self-fulfilment. They held a strong belief in witchcraft and were convinced of the existence of a number of malevolent beings roaming the earth, among them the Stone Giants and the curious creature known as Great Head. The unknown aftermath of death is an ever-present question for humanity, and stories about the Land of Souls and ghostly figures are an obvious extension of wondering what happens, especially for such spiritual people.

THE LEGEND OF SCAR-FACE

In a far-off time, there lived an Indian who had a very beautiful daughter. Many young warriors desired to marry her, but at each request, she only shook her head and said she had no need of a husband.

'Why is this?' asked her father. A great many of these young men are rich and handsome, yet still you refuse them.'

'Why should I marry?' replied the girl, 'when I have all that I could possibly want here with you at our lodge.'

'It is a shame for us,' said her mother, 'that we should still have an unmarried daughter. People will begin to believe you keep a secret lover.'

At this, the girl bowed her head and addressed her parents solemnly: 'I have no secret lover, I promise you, but now hear the truth. The Sun-god above has decreed that I cannot marry and he has told me that I will live happily, to a great age, if I preserve myself for him alone.'

'Ah!' replied her father, 'if the Sun-god has spoken thus, then his wishes must be obeyed. It is not for us to question the ways of the gods.'

In a nearby village there dwelt a poor young warrior who had neither parents nor relatives. Left to fend for himself, he had become a mighty hunter with a brave and noble spirit. He would have been a very good-looking young man, but for a long scar on his cheek, left by the claw of a great grizzly bear he had slain in close combat. The other warriors of the village had ostracized the youth because of this disfigurement. They had given him the name of Scar-face and nothing pleased them more than to make a mockery of his appearance. Each of these young men had been unsuccessful in their attempt to win the hand of the beautiful young maiden and now, slightly embittered by failure, they made it an occasion to poke some fun at the poor, deformed youth.

'Why don't you ask that girl to marry you,' they taunted him. 'She could hardly refuse a man like you, so rich and handsome.'

They laughed a great deal to see that they had touched upon

a sensitive nerve, for Scar-face blushed from ear to ear at their suggestion and stared longingly in the direction of the young woman's lodge.

'I will go and do as you say,' he suddenly replied and marched off defiantly towards the river to deliver his proposal.

He found the young woman stooping by the banks gathering rushes. Respectfully, he approached her, and as she gazed upon him with bright, enticing eyes, he shyly announced his purpose: 'I know that I am poor and shabbily dressed,' he told her, 'but I have seen you refuse rich men clothed in luxurious fur. I am not handsome either, but you have shunned men of the noblest features. Would you consider having me for your husband? I cannot promise you wealth, but I can promise you love, as much of it as you care to receive from me.'

The young girl lowered her eyes and stared silently into the shallow water. After a time she turned towards Scar-face and spoke softly: 'It little matters to me that you are poor. My father is wealthy and would happily provide for us both. I am glad that a man of courage has finally asked me to marry him. But wait! I cannot accept your offer, for the Sun-god has reserved me for himself and has declared that I may never take a mortal husband. Seek him out, if you truly care for me, and beg him to release me from this covenant. If he agrees to do this, ask him to remove that scar from your face and I will treat it as a sign of his blessing.'

Scar-face was sad at heart to hear these words. He had no idea where to begin his search for the Sun-god and felt that a deity so powerful would almost certainly refuse to surrender to him his intended bride. But the young warrior had never before recoiled from a challenge, no matter how difficult it appeared, and the prospect of such a glorious reward seemed well worth risking his life for.

For many days and many nights he journeyed over the sweeping prairies and on through the dense forests, carrying a small sack of food, a spare pair of moccasins, and a simple bow and arrow. Every day his sack of food grew lighter, but he saved as much as he could, eating wild berries and roots and sometimes killing a small bird. At length, he came across a bear's cave and paused to ask directions to the lodge of the Sun-god.

'I have travelled far and wide,' the bear told him, 'but I have never come across the Sun-god's lodge. Stripe-face, who lives beyond in that hole, may be able to assist you. Go and ask him for his help.'

Scar-face moved towards the hole and stooping over it, called aloud to the animal within: 'O generous Stripe-face, O wise old badger, can you tell me the way to the lodge of the Sun-god?'

'I am old and frail and never journey very far,' replied the badger. 'I do not know where he lives. Over there, through the trees, you will find a wolverine. Go and speak with him.'

Scar-face obeyed the badger's instructions, but having called aloud for several minutes, he could find no trace of the wolverine. Wearily, he sat on the ground and began to examine what remained of his food: 'Pity me, wolverine,' he cried out despondently, 'my moccasins are worn through, my food is almost gone. Take pity on me, or I shall meet my death here.'

'How can I help you,' said a voice, and turning around, Scar-face came face to face with the wolverine.

'I have travelled a great distance in search of the Sun-god,' he told the animal, 'but no one can tell me where he lives.'

'I can show you where he lives,' replied the wolverine, 'but first you must rest, for the journey is long. Tomorrow, as soon as you awake, I will set you on the right path.'

Early the next morning, the wolverine took Scar-face to the edge of the forest and pointed out the trail he should follow. Scar-face set off and walked many miles until he came upon the shores of a vast lake whose waters stretched as far as the eye could see. His spirits fell at this sight, for the great lake presented him with a problem he could not hope to overcome.

'I cannot cross this black and fearful water,' he said to himself, 'and I do not have the strength to return home to my own people. The end has come and I must give up the fight.'

But help was not so very far away and soon two beautiful white swans advanced towards him on the water.

'You are not far from the object of your search,' they called to him. 'Lie on our backs and we will carry you to the other side.'

Scar-face rose up and waded into the water. Before long, he had safely reached dry land where he thanked the swans and began following once more the broad trail leading to the home of the Sun-god.

It was now past midday and still the young warrior had not reached his destination. But he refused to lose hope and before long his optimism was rewarded, for he soon stumbled upon an array of beautiful objects lying in the earth which he knew must be from another world. He had never seen such splendid, golden-tipped arrows, or a war shield so elaborately decorated with beads and precious stones. He felt tempted to remove these items from the earth, but decided that would be dishonourable of him, and tried to picture instead what the owner of such fine weapons might look like. He had moved a little further onwards when he observed quite the handsomest youth he had ever seen approaching in the distance. The young man wore clothing of the smoothest animal skin and moccasins sewn with brightly coloured feathers.

'I am searching for my bow and arrows, have you seen them?' the beautiful stranger inquired.

'Yes, I have seen them, back there, lying on the ground,' replied Scar-face.

'And you did not wish to seize these items for yourself?' the young man asked.

'No,' answered Scar-face, 'I felt that would be wrong of me. I knew that the owner would eventually return for them.'

'I admire your honesty, and you have saved me a tiring search,' said the stranger. 'Where is it you come from? You appear to be a very long way from home.'

'I am looking for the Sun-god,' Scar-face told him, 'and I believe I am not very far from his house.'

'You are right,' replied the handsome youth. 'The Sun-god is my father and I am Apisirahts, the Morning Star. Come, I will take you to my father's lodge. He will be pleased to meet a man of such honest character.'

They set off together and shortly afterwards Morning Star pointed to a great lodge, basked in glorious golden light, whose walls were covered with magnificent paintings of medicine animals and other rare and curious creatures. At the entrance to the lodge stood a beautiful woman, Morning Star's mother, Kikomikis, the Moon-goddess. She embraced her son and welcomed the footsore traveller into their home. Then, the great Sun-god made his appearance and he too greeted Scar-face kindly, inviting him to stay for as long as he needed and urging him to accept the guidance and friendship of his son, Apisirahts.

'He will show you the wonderful sights of our kingdom,' the Sun-god told Scar-face. 'Go with him wherever you please, but never hunt near the Great Water, for that is the home of the savage birds who bear talons as long as spears and bills as sharp as arrows. They have carried off many of our finest warriors and would not hesitate to kill you both.'

Scar-face listened carefully to all that was said and during the months which followed, he lived happily among his celestial friends, learning to love the Sun-god as a father and becoming more and more intimate with Apisirahts whom he came to regard as the brother he had always longed for in his earthly home.

One day, he set off with Apisirahts on a hunting excursion, but the two did not follow their usual route and soon they found themselves by the shores of the Great Water.

'We are the finest hunters in the kingdom,' said Morning Star, 'so let us wait no longer, but go and kill these savage birds that put terror into the hearts of our people.'

'Your father has already told us not to pursue them,' replied Scar-face, 'and I have promised to heed his warning.'

'Then I will go and hunt them alone,' said Morning Star and he jumped into the water, waving his spear and shouting his war-cry. Scar-face was forced to follow, for he did not wish to see his brother come to any harm. Soon he had overtaken Apisirahts and began lashing out boldly with his weapon, slaying the monstrous creatures that swooped down upon him, attempting to sink their barbed claws into his flesh. When he had slaughtered every last one of them, he severed their heads and the two young men carried these back towards the Sun-god's lodge, anxious to relate the details of their heroic conquest.

The Moon-goddess was shocked to see the carcasses of the

savage birds and scolded her son for his foolishness. But at the same time, she was relieved that Morning Star had escaped unharmed and ran to inform the Sun-god of his safe return, instinctively aware that she had Scar-face to thank for her son's safe delivery.

'I will not forget what you have done for us this day,' the Sun-god told Scar-face. 'If I can ever repay you, you must let me know at once and whatever you request of me shall be brought to you.'

Scar-face hesitated only a moment and then began to explain to the god the reason for his long journey away from home.

'You have never greedily demanded anything of us,' said the god, 'and you have suffered patiently all these months a great burden of anxiety, knowing that I alone have the power to decide your future with a woman you love and admire so earnestly. Your kindness and your patience have earned the young maiden her freedom. Return home now and make her your wife.

'One thing I will ask of you, however, when you return to your home. Build a lodge in honour of me, shape it like the world, round with thick walls, and paint it red so that every day you will be reminded of your visit here. It shall be a great Medicine Lodge and if your wife remains pure and true I will always be there to help you in times of illness or hardship.'

Then the god explained to Scar-face many of the intricacies of Sun-medicine and rubbed a powerful remedy into the skin on his cheek which caused his unsightly scar to disappear instantly. The young warrior was now ready to return home and the Moon-goddess gave him many beautiful gifts to take to his people. The Sun-god pointed to a short route through the Milky Way and soon he had reached the earth, ready to enter his village in triumph.

It was a very hot day and the sun shone brilliantly in the sky, forcing the people to shed their clothing and sit in the shade.

Towards midday, when the heat was at its fiercest, the chief of the village peered through the window of his lodge and caught sight of a figure, wrapped from head to foot in thick animal skins, sitting on a butte nearby.

'Who is that strange person sitting in winter clothing? The heat will certainly kill him, for I see that he has no food or water. Go and invite him to sit indoors with us.'

Some of the villages approached the stranger and called to him: 'Our chief is concerned for you. He wishes you to withdraw to the shade of his lodge.'

But they had no sooner spoken these words when the figure arose and flung his outer garments to the ground. The robe he wore underneath was of the most delicate, embroidered cloth and the weapons he carried were of an extraordinary, gleaming metal. Gazing upon the stranger's face, the villagers recognized in it something familiar, and at last, one of them cried out in surprise: 'It is Scar-face, the poor young warrior we thought had been lost forever. But look, the blemish on his face has disappeared.'

All the people rushed forward to examine the young man for themselves.

'Where have you been?' they asked excitedly. 'Who gave you all these beautiful things?'

But the handsome warrior did not answer. His eyes searched instead through the crowd until they fell upon the beautiful face of the maiden he had returned home to marry.

'The trail was long and tortuous,' he told her as he walked boldly forward, 'but I found the lodge of the Sun-god and I won his favour. He has taken away my scar and given me all these things as proof of his consent. Come with me now and be my wife for that is the Sun-god's greatest wish.'

The maiden ran towards him and fell upon his breast, tears of great joy flowing freely down her cheeks. That same day the young couple were married and before long they had raised a great Medicine Lodge to the Sun-god. During the long years ahead, they were never sick or troubled in any way and were blessed with two fine, strong children, a girl and a boy, whom they named Apisirahts and Kikomikis. This legend is attributed to the famous Blackfeet tribe of the western territories.

THE LEGEND OF HIAWATHA

A great many fanciful myths and legends have sprung up around Hiawatha, the famous Iroquois warrior and chief. Such a tradition is demonstrated, for example, by H. W. Longfellow, whose poem, Hiawatha, combines historical fact and mythical invention to produce a highly colourful demi-god figure akin to the Algonquin deity, Michabo. The real Hiawatha, an actual historical figure, lived in the sixteenth century and was renowned for promoting a very down-to-earth policy of tribal union. His greatest achievement was the formation of the original Five Nations Confederacy of the Iroquois people. The legend chosen here, although it too reveres Hiawatha as a man of mystical qualities, is based on that historical accomplishment and has been adapted from a story told by a nineteenth-century Onondaga chief.

Along the banks of Tioto, or Cross Lake as it was often called, there lived an eminent young warrior named Hiawatha. Also known as the Wise Man throughout the district, he exerted a powerful influence over the people.

No one knew exactly where Hiawatha had come from. They knew only that he was of a high and mysterious origin and investigated no further than this. He had a canoe, controlled by his will, which could move without the aid of paddles, but he did not use it for any common purpose and pushed it out into the water only when he attended the general council of the tribes.

It was from Hiawatha that the villagers sought advice when they attempted to raise corn and beans. As a direct result of his instruction, their crops flourished; even after they had harvested the corn, food was never in short supply for he taught them how to remove obstructions from watercourses and to clear their fishing grounds. The people listened to Hiawatha with ever-increasing respect, and as he continued to provide them with wise laws and proverbs for their development, they came to believe that he had been sent by the Great Spirit himself, for a short but precious stay amongst them.

After a time, Hiawatha elected to join the Onondagas tribe and it was not long before he had been elevated to a prime position of authority, next in line to its chief. The Onondagas enjoyed a long period of peace and prosperity under Hiawatha's guidance, and there was not one among the other tribes of the region that did not yield to their superiority.

But then, one day, a great alarm was suddenly raised among the entire people of the region. From north of the Great Lakes, a ferocious band of warriors advanced towards them [The Huron, ancient enemies of the Iroquois, although at one time part of the same race.], destroying whatever property they could lay their hands on and indiscriminately slaughtering men, women and children. Everyone looked to

HEROES, MONSTERS & THE SUPERNATURAL

Hiawatha for comfort and advice and, as a first measure, he called together a council of all the tribes from the east to the west and appointed a time for a meeting to take place on the banks of the Onondaga Lake.

By midday, a great body of men, women and children had gathered together in anticipation that they would shortly experience some form of deliverance. But after they had waited several hours they became anxious to know what had become of Hiawatha, for he appeared to be nowhere in sight. Three days elapsed and still Hiawatha did not appear. The crowd, beginning to fear that he was not coming at all, despatched a group of messengers to his home and here they found him sitting on the ground, seized by a terrible misgiving that some form of tragedy would follow his attendance at the meeting. Such fear was hastily overruled by the messengers, whose main concern was to pacify their beleaguered tribesmen. Soon, they had persuaded Hiawatha to follow them and, taking his daughter with him, he pushed his wonderful canoe into the water and set out for the council.

As soon as the people saw him, they sent up shouts of welcome and relief. The venerated warrior climbed ashore and began ascending the steep banks of the lake leading to the place occupied by the council. As he walked, however, he became conscious of a loud, whirring noise overhead. He lifted his eyes upwards and perceived something which looked like a small cloud descending rapidly towards the earth. Filled with terror and alarm, the crowd scattered in confusion, but Hiawatha stood still, instructing his daughter to do the same, for he considered it cowardly to flee, and futile, in any event, to attempt to escape the designs of the Great Spirit. The object approached with greater speed and as it came nearer, it revealed the shape of a gigantic white heron, whose wings, pointed and outstretched, masked all light in the sky. The creature descended with ever-increasing velocity, until, with a mighty crash, it fell upon the girl, instantly crushing her to death.

Hiawatha stared at the spot where the prostrate bird lay and then, in silent anguish, he signalled to a group of warriors nearby to lift the carcass from the earth. They came forward and did as he requested, but when they had moved the bird, not a trace of Hiawatha's daughter was discovered. No word was spoken. The people waited in silence, until at length, Hiawatha stooped to the ground and selected a feather from the snow-white plumage. With this, he decorated his costume, and after he had ensured that other warriors followed his example, he walked in calm dignity to the head of the council. [Since this event, the plumage of the white heron was used by the Onondagas as a decoration while on the warpath.] During that first day, he listened gravely and attentively to the different plans of the various tribal chiefs and speakers. But on the second day he arose and with a voice of great authority and strength he began to address his people:

'My friends and brothers, listen to what I say to you. It would be a very foolish thing to challenge these northern invaders in individual tribes. Only by uniting in a common band of brotherhood may we hope to succeed. Let us do this, and we shall swiftly drive the enemy from our land.

'You, the Mohawks, sitting under the shadow of the great tree whose roots sink deep into the earth, you shall be the first nation, because you are warlike and mighty.

'You, the Oneidas, who recline your bodies against the impenetrable stone, you shall be the second nation, because you have never failed to give wise counsel.

'You, the Onondagas, who occupy the land at the foot of the great hills, because you are so gifted in speech, you shall be the third nation.

'You, the Senecas, who reside in the depths of the forest, you shall be the fourth nation, because of your cunning and speed in the hunt.

'And you, the Cayugas, who roam the prairies and possess great wisdom, you shall be the fifth nation, because you understand more than any of us how to raise corn and build lodges.

'Unite ye five nations, for if we form this powerful alliance, the Great Spirit will smile down on us and we shall remain free, prosperous and happy. But if we remain as we are, always at variance with each other, he will frown upon us and we shall be enslaved or left to perish in the war-storm.

'Brothers, these are the words of Hiawatha. I have said all that I have to say.'

On the following day, Hiawatha's great plan was considered and adopted by the council. Once more, he stood up and addressed the people with wise words of counsel, but even as his speech drew to a close he was being summoned back to the skies by the Great Spirit.

Hiawatha went down to the shore and assumed the seat in his canoe, satisfied within that his mission to the Iroquois had been accomplished. Strange music was heard on the air at that moment and while the wondering multitude stood gazing at their beloved chief, he was silently wafted from sight, and they never saw him again.

GANUSQUAH, LAST OF THE STONE GIANTS

As a final desperate measure in the bloody battle to rid themselves of the Stone Giants, the Iroquois called upon the Upholder of the Heavens, Tahahiawagon, to come to their aid. For generations, they had bravely suffered the carnage and destruction alone, but were now so depleted in numbers they agreed they had nowhere else to turn. Tahahiawagon, who had generously provided them with their hunting grounds and fisheries, was already aware of their distress and had waited patiently for the day when he could again demonstrate his loyalty and devotion.

Determined to relieve the Iroquois of these merciless invaders, the great god transformed himself into a stone giant and descended to earth where he placed himself among the most influential of their tribes. Before long, the giants began to marvel at his miraculous strength and fearlessness in battle and soon they reached the unanimous decision that Tahahiawagon should act as their new chief. The great god brandished his club high in the air:

'Now we will destroy the Iroquois,' he roared. 'Come, let us make a feast of these puny warriors and invite all the Stone Giants throughout the earth to celebrate it with us.'

Carrying on with his façade, the new chief marched all the Stone Giants towards a strong fort of the Onondagas where he commanded them to lie low in a deep hollow in the valley until sunrise. At dawn, he told them, they would slaughter and destroy all the unsuspecting Indians while they still lay in their beds.

But during the night, Tahahiawagon scaled a great mountain nearby and began hewing the rock-face with an enormous chisel.

When he had produced a great mass of boulders he raised his foot and kicked them over the land below. Only one Stone Giant managed to escape the horrifying avalanche. His name was Ganusquah, and he fled as fast as his legs would carry him through the darkness, all the way to the Allegheny Mountains.

As soon as he had reached this spot, he secreted himself in a cave where he remained until he had grown to a huge size and strength. No human being had ever set eyes on him, for to look upon his face meant instant death. He was vulnerable to attack only at the base of his foot, but it was not within the power of any mortal to wound him. And so, Ganusquah used the whole earth as his path, carving out a massive trail through the forests and mountains where his footprints formed huge caverns that filled with water to make the lakes.

If a river obstructed his path, he would swoop it up in his huge hands and turn it from its course. If a mountain stood in his way, he would push his fists through it to create a great tunnel. If ever he were hungry, he would devour a whole herd of buffalo. If ever he were thirsty, he would drink the ocean dry. Even in the tumult of the storms, he made his presence felt, as his voice rose high above the booming of the clouds, warning the Thunderess to keep away from his cave.

It was during one of these terrific storms that Ganusquah came closer than ever before to one of the human species. A young hunter, blinded and bruised by the hail which hurled itself like sharp pebbles upon him, soon lost his trail and took refuge within the hollow of an enormous rock. Nightfall approached, casting deep shadows on the walls of his temporary shelter and soon the young warrior began to drift off to sleep, pleased to have found a place of warmth and safety. He had no sooner indulged this comforting thought, however, when the rock which housed him began to move, but in the queerest manner, almost as if it was being tilted from side to side with the weight of some vast and heavy burden. The swaying motion intensified and was soon accompanied by the most perplexing jumble of sounds, at one moment as sweet and relaxed as a babbling brook, and the next, as eerie and tormented as a death-cry.

The young warrior stood up in alarm, straining his eyes to find the opening of the cave. But too late, for suddenly he felt a gigantic hand on his shoulder and heard a loud voice rumbling in his ear:

'Young warrior, beware! You are in the cave of the stone giant, Ganusquah. Close your eyes and do not look at me, for no human has yet survived who has gazed upon my face. Many have wandered into this cave, but they have come to hunt me. You alone have come here for shelter and I will not, therefore, turn you away.

'I shall spare your life if you agree to obey my commands for as long as I consider necessary. Although I will remain unseen, you will hear my voice whenever I wish to speak to you, and I will always be there to help you as you roam the earth. From here you must go forth and live freely among the animals, the birds and the fish. All these are your ancestors and it will be your task hereafter to dedicate your life to them.

'You will encounter many of them along your way. Do not pass until you have felled a strong tree and carved their image in the wood grain. When you first strike a tree, if it speaks, know that it is my voice urging you on with your task. Each tree has a voice and you must learn the language of the entire forest.

'Now, go on your way. I will be watching you and guiding you.

Teach mankind kindness, the unspoken kindness of nature, and so win your way in life forever.'

The young hunter walked out into the darkness and when he awoke next morning he found himself seated at the base of a basswood tree which gradually transformed itself into a mask and began relating to him the great breadth of its power.

The mask was the supreme being of the forest. It could see behind the stars. It could conjure up storms and summon the sunshine. It knew the remedy for each disease and could overpower death. The venomous reptiles knew its threat and avoided its path. It knew every poisonous root and could repel their evil influence.

'I am Gogonsa,' said the mask. 'My tree is basswood and there is nothing like it in the forest. My wood is soft and will make your task easier. My timber is porous and the sunlight can enter its darkness. Even the wind can whisper to it and it will hear. Ganusquah has called upon me to help you and when he is satisfied with your work, I will lead you back to your people.'

The young hunter listened carefully to every word of advice Gogonsa offered him and then, forearmed with this knowledge, he set about the task of carving the gogonsasooh, the 'false faces' of the forest. On his travels he met many curious animals, birds, reptiles and insects, which he detained until he had carved them in the basswood, inviting them to stay with him until he had learned their language and customs. Guided by the voice of Ganusquah, he moved deeper into the forest and soon he had learned to interpret its many different voices, including the voices of the trees and grasses, mosses and flowers. He learned to love his surroundings and every last creature he encountered, and he knew he would be loathe to leave this world of his ancestors when the time eventually came for him to return to his own home.

A great many years were passed in this way until the hunter, who had entered the cave as a youth, had become an old man, bent in two with the burden of the gogonsasooh he carried with him from place to place. At last, he heard the voice of Ganusquah pronouncing an end to his labour and soon the mask appeared to guide him back to his own people. He wondered if he had the strength to make the journey, but he refused to abandon what he now considered his most precious possessions, the hundreds of gogonsasooh he had carved in basswood.

Wearily, he set off on the track, almost crushed by his heavy load, but after only a short time, he felt a sudden surge of energy. Slowly, his spine began to uncurl, his back began to broaden and strengthen and he felt himself growing taller until he had become a giant in stature, rising high above the trees. He stood up tall and proud and smiled, unaware that in the distance, a great cave had begun to crumble.

THE LEGEND OF O-NA-WUT-A-QUT-O

A long time ago there lived an aged Odjibwa and his wife on the shores of Lake Huron. They had an only son, a very beautiful boy, named O-na-wut-a-qut-o, or He that catches the clouds. The family were of the totem of the beaver. The parents were very proud of their son, and wished to make him a celebrated man; but when he reached the proper age he would not submit to the We-koon-de-win, or fast. When this time arrived they gave him charcoal instead of his breakfast, but he would not blacken his face. If they denied him food he sought bird's eggs along the shore, or picked up the heads of fish that had been cast away, and broiled them. One day they took away violently the food he had prepared, and cast him some coals in place of it. This act decided him. He took the coals and blackened his face and went out of the lodge. He did not return, but lay down without to sleep. As he lay, a very beautiful girl came down from the clouds and stood by his side.

"O-na-wut-a-qut-o," she said, "I am come for you. Follow in my footsteps."

The young man rose and did as he was bid. Presently he found himself ascending above the tops of the trees, and gradually he mounted up step by step into the air, and through the clouds. At length his guide led him through an opening, and he found himself standing with her on a beautiful plain.

A path led to a splendid lodge, into which O-na-wut-a-qut-o followed his guide. It was large, and divided into two parts. At one end he saw bows and arrows, clubs and spears, and various warlike instruments tipped with silver. At the other end were things exclusively belonging to women. This was the house of his fair guide, and he saw that she had on a frame a broad rich belt of many colours that she was weaving.

"My brother is coming," she said, "and I must hide you."

Putting him in one corner she spread the belt over him, and presently the brother came in very richly dressed, and shining as if he had points of silver all over him. He took down from the wall a splendid pipe, and a bag in which was a-pa-ko-ze-gun, or smoking mixture. When he had finished smoking, he laid his pipe aside, and said to his sister—

"Nemissa," (elder sister) "when will you quit these practices?

Do you forget that the greatest of the spirits has commanded that you shall not take away the children from below? Perhaps you think you have concealed O-na-wut-a-qut-o, but do I not know of his coming? If you would not offend me, send him back at once."

These words did not, however, alter his sister's purpose. She would not send him back, and her brother, finding that she was determined, called O-na-wut-a-qut-o from his hiding-place.

"Come out of your concealment," said he, "and walk about and amuse yourself. You will grow hungry if you remain there."

At these words O-na-wut-a-qut-o came forth from under the belt, and the brother presented a bow and arrows, with a pipe of red stone, richly ornamented, to him. In this way he gave his consent to O-na-wut-a-qut-o's marriage with his sister, and from that time the youth and the girl became husband and wife.

O-na-wut-a-qut-o found everything exceedingly fair and beautiful around him, but he found no other people besides his wife and her brother. There were flowers on the plains, there were bright and sparkling streams, there were green valleys and pleasant trees, there were gay birds and beautiful animals, very different from those he had been accustomed to. There was also day and night as on the earth, but he observed that every morning the brother regularly left the lodge and remained absent all day, and every evening his sister departed, but generally for only a part of the night.

O-na-wut-a-qut-o was curious to solve this mystery, and obtained the brother's consent to accompany him in one of his daily journeys. They travelled over a smooth plain which seemed to stretch to illimitable distances all around. At length

O-na-wut-a-qut-o felt the gnawings of hunger and asked his companion if there was no game about.

"Patience, my brother," replied he; "we shall soon reach the spot where I eat my dinner, and you will then see how I am provided."

After walking on a long time they came to a place where several fine mats were spread, and there they sat down to refresh themselves. At this place there was a hole in the sky and O-na-wut-a-qut-o, at his companion's request, looked through it down upon the earth. He saw below the great lakes and the villages of the Indians. In one place he saw a war-party stealing on the camp of their enemies. In another he saw feasting and dancing. On a green plain some young men were playing at ball, and along the banks of a stream were women employed in gathering the a-puk-wa for mats.

"Do you see," asked the brother, "that group of children playing beside a lodge? Observe that beautiful and active lad," said he, at the same time darting something from his hand. The child immediately fell on the ground, and was carried by his companions into the lodge.

O-na-wut-a-qut-o and his companion watched and saw the people below gathering about the lodge. They listened to the she-she-gwau of the meeta, to the song he sang asking that the child's life might be spared. To this request O-na-wut-a-qut-o's companion made answer—

"Send me up the sacrifice of a white dog."

A feast was immediately ordered by the parents of the child. The white dog was killed, his carcass was roasted, all the wise men and medicine-men of the village assembling to witness the ceremony.

"There are many below," said O-na-wut-a-qut-o's companion, "whom you call great in medical skill. They are so, because their ears are open; and they are able to succeed, because when I call they hear my voice. When I have struck one with sickness they direct the people to look to me, and when they make me the offering I ask, I remove my hand from off the sick person and he becomes well."

While he was saying this, the feast below had been served. Then the master of the feast said—

"We send this to thee, Great Manito," and immediately the roasted animal came up. Thus O-na-wut-a-qut-o and his companion got their dinner, and after they had eaten they returned to the lodge by a different path.

In this manner they lived for some time, but at last the youth got weary of the life. He thought of his friends, and wished to go back to them. He could not forget his native village and his father's lodge, and he asked his wife's permission to return. After some persuasion she consented.

"Since you are better pleased," she said, "with the cares and ills and poverty of the world, than with the peaceful delights of the sky and its boundless prairies, go. I give you my permission, and since I have brought you hither I will conduct you back. Remember, however, that you are still my husband. I hold a chain in my hand by which I can, whenever I will, draw you back to me. My power over you will be in no way diminished. Beware, therefore, how you venture to take a wife among the people below. Should you ever do so, you will feel what a grievous thing it is to arouse my anger."

As she uttered these words her eyes sparkled, and she drew herself up with a majestic air. In the same moment

O-na-wut-a-qut-o awoke. He found himself on the ground near his father's lodge, on the very spot where he had thrown himself down to sleep. Instead of the brighter beings of a higher world, he found around him his parents and their friends. His mother told him that he had been absent a year. For some time O-na-wut-a-qut-o remained gloomy and silent, but by degrees he recovered his spirits, and he began to doubt the reality of all he had seen and heard above. At last he even ventured to marry a beautiful girl of his own tribe. But within four days she died. Still he was forgetful of his first wife's command, and he married again. Then one night he left his lodge, to which he never returned. His wife, it is believed, recalled him to the sky, where he still dwells, walking the vast plains.

GREAT HEAD AND THE TEN BROTHERS

In a remote Indian village at the edge of the forest, an orphaned family of ten boys lived in a small lodge with their uncle. The five elder brothers went out to hunt every day, but the younger ones, not yet ready for so rigorous a life, remained at home with their uncle, never daring to venture too far from their home.

One day, the group of elder brothers, who had been away deer-hunting, failed to return at the usual hour. As the evening wore on, there was still no sign of them, and by nightfall their uncle had become extremely worried for their safety. It was agreed among the remaining family that the eldest boy should go out on the following morning in search of his brothers. He readily accepted the challenge and he set off after sunrise, confident that he would locate them before long. But the boy did not return, and his disappearance caused even greater consternation among the household.

'We must find out what is happening to them,' said the next in line. 'Though I am young and ill-prepared for adventure, I cannot bear to picture any of my family lying wounded in some fearful, hostile place.'

And so, having obtained his uncle's permission, he too set off enthusiastically, though he was not so self-assured as his brother before him. Just like the others, however, the youth failed to reappear, and an identical fate awaited the two more after him who took it upon themselves to go out in search of the lost hunters. At length, only one small brother remained with his uncle at the lodge, and fearing he might lose the last of his young nephews, the old man became very protective of him, turning a deaf ear to his persistent pleas to be allowed take his turn in the search.

The youngest brother was now obliged to accompany his uncle everywhere. He was even forced to walk with the old man the short distance to the wood-pile, and he longed for the day when adventure would come knocking on his door. He had almost resigned himself to the fact that this would never happen when, one morning, as the pair stooped to gather firewood, the young boy imagined he heard a deep groan coming from the earth beneath his feet. He called upon his uncle to listen and the sound, unmistakably a human groan, soon repeated itself. Both were deeply shocked by the discovery and began clawing frantically at the earth with their bare hands. Shortly afterwards, a human face revealed itself and before long, they had uncovered the entire body of a man, caked in mould and scarcely able to breathe.

Carefully, they lifted the unfortunate creature from the soil and carried him into their lodge where they rubbed his skin down with bear oil until he slowly began to revive. It was several hours before the man could bring himself to speak, but then, at last, he began mouthing a few words, informing his hosts that he had been out hunting when his mind had suddenly become entirely blank. He could remember nothing more, he told them, neither his name, nor the village he had come from. The old man and his nephew begged the stranger to stay with them, hoping that soon his memory would be restored and that then, perhaps, he could help them in their own search.

The days passed by, but after only a very short time, the young boy and his uncle began to observe that the person they had rescued was no ordinary mortal like themselves. He did not eat any of the food they served him, but his strength increased daily none the less. He had no need of sleep, and often when it rained he behaved very strangely, tossing restlessly in his chair and calling aloud in a curious language.

One night, a particularly violent storm raged outside. As the rain pelted down and the winds howled fiercely, the boy and his uncle were awoken by the loud cries of their guest:

'Do you hear that noise?' he yelled. 'That is my brother, Great Head, riding on the wind. Can you not hear him wailing?'

'Yes, we can,' said the old man. 'Would you like us to invite him here? Would he come if you sent for him?'

'I would certainly like to see him,' replied the strange guest, 'but he will not come unless I bring him here by magic. You should prepare for him a welcoming meal, ten large blocks of maple-wood, for that is the food he lives on.' And saying this, the stranger departed in search of his brother, taking with him his bow and a selection of arrows, carved from the roots of a hickory-tree.

At about midday, he drew near to Great Head's dwelling and quickly transformed himself into a mole, so that his brother would not notice his approach. Silently, he crept through the grass until he spotted Great Head up ahead, perched on a cliff-face, glowering fiercely at an owl.

'I see you!' shouted Great Head, 'now you shall die.' And he lunged forward, ready to devour the helpless creature.

Just at that moment, the mole stood up, and taking aim with his bow, shot an arrow in Great Head's direction. The arrow became larger and larger as it sped through the air towards the monstrous creature, but then, when it had almost reached its target, it turned back on itself and returned to the mole, regaining its normal size. Great Head was soon in pursuit, puffing and snorting like a hurricane as he trampled through the trees. Once more, the mole shot an arrow and again it returned to him, luring Great Head further and further onwards towards the lodge where the young boy and his uncle nervously awaited their arrival.

As soon as the door to their house burst open, its terrified occupants began attacking Great Head with wooden mallets. But the more vigorously they struck him, the more Great Head broke into peals of laughter, for he was not only impervious to pain, but the sight of his brother standing before him had put him in the best of moods. The two embraced warmly and Great Head sat down to his meal of maple-blocks which he devoured with great relish.

When he had done, he thanked his hosts for their hospitality and enquired of them how he might return their kindness. They began telling him the story of their missing relatives, but had only uttered a few words before Great Head interrupted them:

'You need tell me no more,' he said to them, 'I know precisely what has become of them. They have fallen into the hands of a woodland witch. Now if this boy will accompany me, I will point out her dwelling and show him the bones of his brothers.'

Although reluctant to release him, the uncle perceived how anxious his nephew was to learn the fate of his brothers. Finally, he gave his consent, and the young boy started off with Great Head, smiling broadly at the thought of the adventure which lay ahead.

They did not once pause for rest and after a time they came upon a ramshackle hut, in front of which were strewn dry bones of every size and description. In the doorway sat a crooked old witch, rocking back and forth, singing to herself. When she looked up and saw her visitors, she flew into a rage and began chanting her spell to change the living into dry bones. But her magic had no effect on Great Head, and because his companion stood in his shadow, he too was protected from the charm. The youth sprang forward and began to attack the frail, old witch, beating her with his fists until she fell lifeless to the ground. As soon as she lay dead, a loud shriek pierced the silence, and her flesh was transformed into black-feathered birds that rose squawking into the air.

The young boy now set about the task of selecting the bones of his brothers. It was slow and difficult work, but, at last, he had gathered together nine white mounds. Great Head came forward to examine each of them and when he was satisfied that no bone was missing he spoke to his young companion:

'I am going back to my rock,' he told him. 'But do not despair or think I have abandoned you, for soon you will see me again.'

The boy stood alone, guarding the heaps of bones, trying to decide whether he should make his way back home before daylight faded. Looking upwards, he noticed that a huge storm was gathering and began walking towards the hut for shelter. The hail beat on his back even as he walked the short distance and soon sharp needles of rain pricked his skin all over. The thunder now clashed and lightning struck the ground wherever he attempted to step. The young boy grew fearful and flung himself to the earth, but suddenly he heard a familiar voice calling to him, and lifting his eyes, he saw Great Head riding at the centre of the storm.

'Arise you bones,' Great Head yelled, 'I bid you come to life.' The hurricane passed overhead in an instant, as rapidly as it had first appeared. The young boy felt certain that he must have been dreaming, but then, he observed that the mounds had disappeared. In a moment he was surrounded by his brothers and huge tears of relief and joy flooded down his cheeks.

WHITE FEATHER AND THE SIX GIANTS

There was once an old man living in the depths of the great forest with his young grandson whom he had taken charge of when the boy was still an infant. The child had never encountered any other human being apart from his grandfather. He had no parents, brothers or sisters, no friends or relatives, and although he frequently questioned the old man on the subject of his family, he could not get even the smallest scrap of information from him.

His guardian insisted upon this silence for the boy's own protection, for he felt certain that he would attempt to avenge the death of his brothers and sisters before long. They had perished at the hands of six great giants after the villagers had challenged the giants to a race they believed they would win, casually offering their children as the forfeit. All were slain by the victorious giants except for the old man's grandson who, by some miracle, managed to escape through the trees to the safety of the isolated lodge.

Here the boy, who was named Chacopee, grew up relatively content. He learned to fish and he learned to hunt, beginning with smaller animals such as rabbits, until he became so highly accomplished with his bow and arrow that he could bring down deer and larger game almost with his eyes closed. Of course, as he developed into a more expert hunter, he longed to roam even further and his curiosity to know what lay beyond the tiny lodge increased with every passing day.

One day he wandered to the edge of the prairie where he happened upon several mounds of ashes, encircled by lodge-poles left standing in the earth. Returning home, he described to his grandfather what he had seen and asked him to explain the presence of these things. But the old man grew agitated and responded that the boy had surely lost his senses, for nothing of the kind existed except in his imagination.

Another day, however, Chacopee had followed a different path through the forest when suddenly he heard a voice calling to him: 'You do not wear the white feather yet, but the hour is not far off when you will prove yourself worthy of it. Go home now and sleep. Soon you will dream of a pipe, a smoking-sack, and a large white feather. When you awake you will find these items by your side.'

Chacopee turned in the direction of the voice and came face to face with a man, an encounter in itself quite shocking for a boy who had only ever seen his grandfather, but made even worse by the man's very peculiar body which was carved of wood from the breast downwards. 'Put the white feather on your head,' the stranger continued, 'and you will become a great hunter, a great warrior and a great leader. If you need proof of my words, smoke the pipe and soon you will see the smoke turn into pigeons.'

After this, the stranger informed Chacopee of his real identity and told him the story of how his family had perished at the hands of the giants, urging him to avenge the wrongs of his kindred.

'Take this enchanted vine,' he told him, 'you will need it when your enemy challenges you to a race. No giant can see it for it is invisible. You must throw it over your opponent's head while he runs. It will entangle him and bring him crashing to the ground.'

Chacopee listened keenly to all of this advice and then returned homeward, extremely bewildered by the meeting. Everything happened just as the Man of Wood had predicted, however. As soon as he lay down the boy fell into a deep sleep and when he awoke he was surrounded by the promised gifts. The old grandfather was greatly surprised to see a flock of pigeons emerge from his own lodge, followed by his grandson wearing on his head a white feather, but then he remembered the old tribal prophecy, and knowing that the day would soon come when he would be forced to relinquish control of Chacopee, he sat down and began to weep inconsolably.

Next morning the young boy set off in search of his enemies. The giants, he had learned, lived in a very tall lodge at the centre of the woods, but this lodge was surrounded by little spirits who carried news to the giants of Chacopee's arrival. The monstrous creatures hastened out of doors and spotted the young boy approaching in the distance.

'Here comes the little man we are supposed to call White Feather,' they mocked among themselves. 'Haven't we been warned that he is destined to achieve great things. Let us welcome him as a great hero and encourage him to attempt some foolhardy trial of strength.'

But Chacopee paid no heed to the giants' fine speeches, and without awaiting an invitation, marched fearlessly into their lodge where he challenged every one of them to a race. It was eventually agreed that the youngest among the giants would be the first to run against him and without wasting any more time, they set off across the fields in search of an appropriate starting-point.

They had soon mapped out a course which extended from an old, rugged tree as far as the edge of the horizon and back again. A war-club of iron was placed at the foot of the tree, to be used by the winner on his defeated opponent. As soon as they had taken their places, a gong was sounded and each of the runners shot off with as much speed as he could muster. Chacopee knew that his little legs would not carry him to victory over such a great distance and so he waited for the giant to overtake him and cast his vine out in front of him, tugging on it sharply as it wrapped itself around the giant's ankles. The hideous creature fell to the ground and when he attempted to rise again, Chacopee lifted the war-club high in the air, bringing it down on the giant's great skull over and over again until he was certain that the giant lay dead.

The next morning, Chacopee ran against a second giant and killed him in exactly the same manner. For five mornings he managed to conquer his foes in this way, but then, on the sixth morning, as he set off confidently to meet the last of the giants, he was met by his old counsellor, the Man of Wood, who informed him that his last opponent was far more cunning than any of the others.

'He is out to deceive you, White Feather,' he told the boy. 'Before you even reach his lodge you will encounter a very beautiful young woman. Do not pay her any attention, for she is there for your destruction. As soon as you catch her eye, you must transform yourself into an elk. Lower your head and feed on the grass and do not look at the maiden again.'

White Feather thanked his kind adviser and walked on towards the lodge, mindful of the advice he had received. Before long, as had been foretold, he met the most beautiful woman. Quickly he transformed himself into an elk and began rooting in the earth, his eyes lowered as he had been instructed. But the woman only moved closer to him and began weeping softly.

'I have travelled a very long way to meet you,' she sobbed. 'Your great achievements have made you famous throughout the land, and I wanted, more than anything, to offer myself as your bride.'

Filled with compassion and remorse, White Feather raised his eyes towards the woman and wished aloud that he might resume his natural shape. At once, he became a man again and sat down under a tree with the beautiful maiden, wrapping her in his arms to comfort her. Soon her tears and sighs had abated and he lay his head in her lap and fell into a peaceful slumber.

After she had listened awhile to his deep breathing and had satisfied herself that White Feather was not likely to wake up, the beautiful woman transformed herself into the sixth giant and, taking up an axe, struck the young man on his back, changing him into a dog. The white plume immediately fell from his hair unto the earth, but as soon as he noticed it, the giant stooped and picked it up, putting it in his own hair. Now stripped of his powers, Chacopee gave a pitiful whimper, and followed wretchedly in the path of the giant towards the neighbouring village.

There were living in this particular village two sisters, the daughters of a chief, who had been bitter rivals for many years. Having heard the prophecy concerning the wearer of the white feather, each had made up her mind to have him for her husband and each was constantly on the look-out from her lodge door, hoping that White Feather would soon appear. When the day finally arrived and the sisters spotted a stranger wearing a white plume heading towards their home, they were filled with excitement. The eldest sister, who was the more ambitious of the two, dressed herself up in all her finery and ran ahead to meet the giant, inviting him into her lodge. The youngest, who did not possess any flamboyant clothes, remained dressed in her simple shawl and moccasins and invited the poor dog into her home where she prepared for him a good supper and a neat bed. The giant, pleased with the attention lavished upon him by the eldest sister, soon agreed to marry her and together they mocked the younger sister for having landed herself a dishevelled old dog as a life-long companion.

It was not long, however, before the villagers began to demand a demonstration of the skill and courage they had come to associate with the famous name of White Feather. The giant, who readily supposed that whoever wore the white plume would possess all of its virtues, boasted of the fact that he could bring back enough food in one day to supply the entire village and set off with the dog across the plains towards the forest.

Immediately, he began shouting and waving his great hands in the air, calling to the animals to come and be killed. But they fled in terror at the sight of him and he failed to catch a single one of them. The dog, on the other hand, stepped into a nearby river and drew out a stone which instantly changed into a fine, fat beaver. The giant stood staring in amazement, but as soon as he had recovered himself, he waded into the water and successfully performed the same feat. He was delighted with himself and having tied the animal to his belt, he called for the dog to accompany him back home.

When he had been seated a short time, savouring in advance the impact of his great achievement on the villagers, he called to his wife to come and examine his hunting girdle. Obediently, she knelt on the floor, but when she lifted his shirt to reveal his belt, she discovered only a massive stone secured to it. The giant stood up furiously and ordered his wife to keep her silence until he had gone out again and returned with the food he had promised.

Next morning, he took the dog along with him as before and watched its every movement closely. This time, the dog plucked a charred branch from a burned-out tree and threw it to the ground where it instantly transformed itself into a bear. The giant did exactly as the dog had done, and managed to produce a bear in precisely the same fashion. He carried the creature homewards to his wife, but again, as soon as he had called for her to inspect it, the bear disappeared and all the woman found was a black stick tied to her husband's belt.

And so it continued on. Everything the giant attempted failed miserably, while everything the dog undertook was a great success. Every day the youngest sister had more and more reason to be proud of the poor dog she had adopted, while every day the eldest sister received yet another reminder that the man she had married did not possess any of the virtues associated with the white feather. But in spite of this, the eldest sister insisted on keeping up appearances and departed the following morning for her father's lodge to inform him what a skilful hunter her new husband was.

As soon as she had set off, the dog began making signs to the younger sister that he wished to be sweated in the traditional manner of the Indians. Accordingly, his mistress built a little lodge just large enough for him to creep into and placed within it a number of heated stones on which she poured water until a thick vapour rose up into the air. When she imagined the dog had been completely sweated, she stooped down to unblock the entrance and was astonished to find, in place of the dog, a handsome young warrior lying on the earth. But she could not get a word out of him and realizing that he was quite dumb, she decided to lead him to the village where she hoped one of the medicine-people might be able to help restore his voice.

As soon as the chief heard his youngest daughter's story, he assembled all the old and wise heads of the tribe for a general meeting. He was now convinced, he told them, that there was some kind of magic at work and was keener than ever to discover the truth about the giant and the young man. And so he called for a pipe to be brought forward and began passing it among the circle. One after another, the elders puffed on the pipe, handing it around until eventually it was the young man's turn. But the handsome warrior signalled politely that it should be given to the giant first. The giant took the pipe and began smoking, swelling his chest and shaking the white feather on his head. But nothing came of this exhibition except a great cloud of smoke. Then the handsome young warrior took hold of the pipe and made a sign to them to put the white feather upon his head. As he drew the smoke deep into his lungs, his voice suddenly returned, and as he breathed out, the smoke became a flock of white and blue pigeons.

From that moment, the villagers turned on the giant and after the young man had recounted his strange adventures, indignation rose to a fever pitch. The chief then ordered that the giant should be transformed into a dog and stoned to death by the people. The villagers were more than delighted to carry out this instruction and danced in a circle around the dead body, greatly relieved that the six giants would trouble them no longer.

The handsome young warrior now gave them all the proof they needed of his right to wear the white feather. Calling for a buffalo robe to be brought to him, he cut it into thin strips and scattered them on the prairie in every direction. Next day he summoned the braves of the tribe to accompany him on a hunt. When they arrived at the edge of the prairie they found it covered with a great herd of buffalo. The people hunted as many of these buffalo as they pleased and afterwards a great feast was held to celebrate White Feather's triumph over the giant.

THE GIFT OF CORN

Long ago, there lived a poor Indian who dwelt with his wife and children in a tiny lodge in the heart of the forest. The family relied on hunting for their food, and although the father was never lacking in courage and skill, there were often times when he returned home without provisions, so that his wife and children had only the leaves on the trees to satisfy their hunger. The eldest son of the family, a boy of fourteen, had inherited the same kind and gentle disposition as his father, and as he watched the old man struggle to take care of them all, he longed only for the time when he would be able to help out in some way.

At last, the young boy reached the age of the great fast, when he was obliged to shut himself away without food, praying night and day to the Great Spirit in preparation for the coming of his spirit-guide and guardian through life. This solemn and sacred event demanded that he empty his mind and heart of every evil thought and he now began to meditate earnestly on the generosity of the Great Spirit who never ceased to provide mankind with everything good and wholesome. As he roamed the fields and mountains during the first few days of his retreat, he was deeply moved by the beauty of his surroundings, the glorious flowers, the succulent berries, and he felt the strong desire to make his own contribution to this remarkable world.

The young boy was well aware that both he and his family were deeply indebted to the Great Spirit, but at the same time, he began asking himself why it was that the divine ruler had not made it easier for them to find enough food to survive on.

'Perhaps if I pray very hard,' the boy thought to himself, 'the Great Spirit will reveal to me in a dream the means by which I can ease the hardship my family now suffers.' And with that he lay down and kept to his bed for a full day and a night.

It was now the fifth day of his fast and the boy lay feeble with hunger, drifting in and out of sleep and hoping that some sort of vision would soon come to him. Suddenly the room in which he lay became filled with a dazzling light, out of which emerged a beautiful young man who moved gracefully towards him. The stranger's slender form was draped in a luxurious, satin robe of green and yellow, his complexion was the purest marble-white and on his head he wore an exotic plume of jade-green feathers. The boy was startled by the apparition, but the stranger's eyes conveyed the gentlest, warmest expression and his voice was as sweet as music as he spoke.

'The Great Spirit has been listening to your prayers,' he said softly. 'He understands how deeply you care for your family and he knows that you have always been a loyal and obedient child. For these reasons he has sent me to guide you in your pursuit and to ensure that your desire is fulfilled.'

'Arise young warrior,' added the beautiful stranger, 'and prepare yourself to wrestle with me, for such is the wish of the Great Spirit.'

Even though his limbs were weak from fasting, the young boy stood up courageously and did as the stranger commanded him. The struggle which followed was long and punishing and at length the boy began to grow faint. But just at this precise moment, the stranger called a halt to the conflict, promising to return on the following day when the boy had replenished his strength.

At exactly the same hour next morning, the celestial visitor reappeared and the two took up the fighting once more. As they battled on, the young boy felt his strength improve and his courage increase. He threw himself wholeheartedly into the struggle, wrestling fiercely with his visitor, until the latter was forced to cry out in pain.

'You have certainly proven your worth today,' the stranger declared, 'now it is my turn to rest before we begin our final trial. Tomorrow will be the seventh day of your fast,' he continued, 'and your father will bring you food to strengthen you. In the evening, you will wrestle with me and easily overcome me, for you have succeeded in winning the favour of the Great Spirit.

'As soon as I have fallen, you must strip me of my garments and bury me in the earth. Once a month, come and cover me with fresh soil and make certain that no weeds or grass are allowed to grow upon my grave. If you do all this, I shall return to life and I promise that you will see me again, splendidly clothed in a garment of green.'

The stranger had no sooner spoken these words than he vanished into thin air, leaving his opponent to fathom the meaning of all that he had been told.

Shortly after dawn on the following day, the young boy's father filled a small basket with nourishing food and set off in search of his son. He was greatly relieved to see the boy again, but noticed that he had grown thin and frail.

'My son, you must eat something,' he urged him. 'You have fasted long enough and I feel certain that the Great Spirit does not require you to sacrifice your own life.'

'Father,' the boy replied, 'please be patient with me until sundown, and at that hour I will happily partake of the meal you have brought me.'

For the young boy was determined to prove his hero's strength without assistance, resolving to rely on his inner strength alone during the trial ahead.

Once again, at the usual hour, the stranger appeared and the contest was renewed as before. Though he had not eaten any of his father's food, or allowed even a drop of water to pass his lips, the boy felt invigorated and irrepressible. Fired by the need to achieve some great purpose, he lunged at his handsome opponent, pushing him violently against a rock in the ground. The stranger did not rise up again to challenge him and, as he bent over to examine him where he lay, the boy could find no trace of life in the handsome youth. A deep sadness and regret suddenly invaded his soul as he began digging the earth to bury the body and he swore to himself that he would tend the grave as lovingly as if it were that of his own mother.

Throughout the spring which followed, the boy never once allowed a day to slip past without visiting the burial place of his friend. He stooped and carefully weeded out the grass and carried fresh soil up the mountain to replace the old, just as he had vowed he would. By summertime, tiny green shoots began to appear in the earth, but because they so reminded the young boy of the feather plume his visitor always wore, he was loathe to remove them and so they continued to rise in height as the months progressed.

The days and weeks passed by and during all of this time, the boy never once revealed to a single soul the purpose of his regular excursions up into the mountains. Then one day, he gingerly approached his father requesting that he follow him on his mysterious ramble. Though he was surprised and a little apprehensive, the old man agreed to accompany his son and soon they had reached the spot where the handsome stranger lay buried.

The sight which now greeted them was truly the most astonishing and gratifying they had ever witnessed. Overnight, the green shoots on the grave had broadened out into beautiful, graceful plants with velvet-soft foliage, each one bearing a generous golden cluster crowned by a majestic plume.

Leaping for joy, the young boy began shouting aloud: 'It is my friend, the friend of my vision who promised he would return to me.'

'It is Mondamin,' [From the words moedo, meaning 'spirit' and min, meaning 'grain' or 'berry'.] replied his father, filled with admiration for his son. 'It is the spirit grain the old ones have sometimes spoken of, the Indian corn which the Merciful Master has sent to nourish us because he is greatly pleased with you.'

And the two began to gather the golden ears of corn, tearing away the green husks from the stalks as once the young boy had torn away the garments of his extraordinary wrestling companion.

From that day forward, the people no longer depended entirely on hunting and were blessed with beautiful fields of healthy grain which they harvested every year just as soon as the long hot summer had begun to fade into autumn.

MICHABO DEFEATS THE KING OF FISHES

One morning, Michabo went out upon the lake in his canoe to fish. Casting his line into the middle of the water, he began to shout: 'Meshenahmahgwai, King of Fishes, grab hold of my bait, you cannot escape me forever.'

For a full hour he continued to call out these words until, at last, the King of Fishes, who had been attempting to rest at the bottom of the lake, could bear the dreadful commotion no longer.

'Michabo is beginning to irritate me,' he complained. 'Here, trout, take hold of the bait and keep this fellow silent.'

The trout obeyed the request and sunk its jaws into the hook as Michabo commenced drawing in his catch. The line, which was very heavy, caused his canoe to stand almost perpendicular in the water, but he persevered bravely until the fish appeared above the surface. As soon as he saw the trout, however, he began to roar angrily: 'Esa, Esa! Shame! Shame! Why did you take hold of my hook, you ugly creature?'

The trout let go at once and swam back down to the bottom of the lake. Michabo then cast his line into the water once more saying: 'King of Fishes, I am still waiting and I will remain here for as long as it takes.'

This time the King of Fishes caught hold of a giant sunfish and commanded him to do exactly as the trout had done before him. The sunfish obeyed and Michabo again drew up his line, his canoe turning in swift circles with the weight of the monstrous creature. Michabo felt certain he had succeeded and began crying out in excitement:

'Wha-wee-he! Wha-wee-he!' But he was quickly made to realize that he had been deceived once more and his face turned a bright shade of crimson as he screamed into the water:

'Esa! Esa! You hideous fish. You have contaminated my hook by placing it in your big mouth. Let go of it, you filthy brute.' The sunfish dropped the hook and disappeared below the surface of the lake.

'Meshenahmahgwai! I have reached the end of my patience,' Michabo bellowed with increasing fury. 'Do as I have bid you and take hold of my hook.'

By now, the King of Fishes was himself seething with anger and he grabbed hold of the bait, allowing himself to be tugged upwards through the water. He had no sooner reached the surface, however, when he opened his mouth wide, and in one gulp, swallowed Michabo, his fishing rod and his little wooden canoe.

Michabo stumbled about in the belly of the fish wondering, for an instant, who had turned the lights out in the sky. But then, he felt a sudden motion and a tremendous rumbling noise and it dawned on him that the King of Fishes had helped himself to an early supper. Michabo glanced around him and seeing his war-club lying in his canoe, lifted it above his shoulders and brought it down mercilessly wherever he could find a solid wall. He was hurled to and fro as the King of Fishes responded to these blows and complained to those around him:

'I am sick in my stomach for having swallowed that troublemaker, Michabo. He has not provided a satisfying meal.' And as he spoke, Michabo continued with his attack, delivering a number of very severe blows to the fish's heart.

The King of Fishes began to heave violently and, fearing that he would be thrown up into the lake to drown, Michabo quickly rammed his canoe lengthways into the fish's throat. The pain induced by the obstruction, combined with the repeated beating he suffered internally, caused the King's heart to stop beating, and soon his great body, battered and lifeless, was tossed up by the waves upon the shore.

Michabo sat down in the darkness, faced now with an even greater problem, for he had not paused to consider how he would manage to free himself from the bowels of the King of Fishes once his victim lay dead. Had he been ejected, he might have stood some small chance of survival in spite of the fact that he could not swim, but now, there seemed little or no hope.

He chastized himself for his own folly and had begun to come to terms with his sorry fate when, all of a sudden, his ears were filled with the sound of tapping noises above his head. Certain that the King of Fishes lay dead, he was puzzled by the rhythm, but its source was soon revealed to him, as light began to filter in through an opening in the fleshy roof and the heads of gulls peered into the darkness below.

'What a good thing that you have come, my friends,' cried Michabo. 'Quickly, make the opening larger so that I can get out.' The birds, utterly astonished to discover Michabo in the belly of a fish, chattered excitedly as they obeyed the god's command. In no time at all Michabo found himself at liberty and smiled broadly to find his feet touching firm soil once more.

'I have been foolish,' he told the gulls, 'and you have shown great kindness in releasing me from my confinement. From this day forth, you shall not be looked upon as scavengers, but shall be known as Kayosk, Noble Scratchers, and receive my special blessing.'

Then, walking towards the shores of the lake, Michabo breathed life into the King of Fishes, restoring him to his former glory. The King took up his usual place at the bottom of the water and in this silent world, undisturbed by the cries of a keen fisherman, he carried on with his rest.

THE SUN ENSNARED

At the very beginning of time, when chaos and darkness reigned and hordes of bloodthirsty animals roamed the earth devouring mankind, there remained only two survivors of the human race. A young brother and sister, who managed to flee from the jaws of the ferocious beasts, took refuge in a secluded part of the forest where they built for themselves a little wooden lodge. Here, they carved out a meagre existence, relying on nature's kindness for their survival. The young girl, who was strong and hardworking, bravely accepted the responsibility of keeping the household together, for her younger brother had never grown beyond the size of an infant and demanded her constant care. Every morning she would go out in search of firewood, taking her brother with her and seating him on a comfortable bed of leaves while she chopped and stacked the logs they needed to keep a warm fire burning. Then, before heading homeward, she would gather the ripest berries from the surrounding hedgerows and both would sit down together to enjoy their first meal of the day.

They had passed many pleasant years in this way before the young girl began to grow anxious for her brother's future, fearing that she might not always be able to care for him. She had never considered it wise in the past to leave him alone while she went about her chores, but now she felt she must take that risk for his own good.

'Little brother,' she said to him, 'I will leave you behind today while I go out to gather wood, but you need not be afraid and I promise to return shortly.'

And saying this, she handed him a bow and several small arrows.

'Hide yourself behind that bush,' she added, 'and soon you will see a snowbird coming to pick worms from the newly cut logs. When the bird appears, try your skill and see if you can shoot it.'

Delighted at the opportunity to prove himself, the young boy sat down excitedly, ready to draw his bow as soon as the bird alighted on the logs. But the first arrow he shot went astray and before he was able to launch a second, the creature had risen again into the air. The little brother felt defeated and discouraged and bowed his head in shame, fully expecting that his sister would mock his failure. As soon as she returned, however, she began to reassure him, offering him encouragement and insisting that he try again on the following day.

Next morning, the little brother crouched down once more behind the bush and waited for the snowbird to appear. He was now more determined than ever to prove his skill and, on this occasion, his arrow shot swiftly through the air, piercing the bird's breast. Seeing his sister approach in the distance, he ran forward to meet her, his face beaming with pride and joy.

'I have killed a fine, large bird,' he announced triumphantly. 'Please will you skin it for me and stretch the skin out to dry in the sunshine. When I have killed more birds, there will be enough skins to make me a fine, long coat.'

'I would be very happy to do this for you,' his sister smiled. 'But what shall I do with the body when I have skinned it?'

The young boy searched for an answer, and as he stood thinking his stomach groaned with hunger. It seemed wasteful to burn such a plump bird and he now began to wonder what it would be like to taste something other than wild berries and greens: 'We have never before eaten flesh,' he said, 'but let us cut the body in two and cook one half of it in a pot over the fire. Then, if the food is good, we can savour the remaining half later.'

His sister agreed that this was a wise decision and prepared for them their very first dish of game which they both ate with great relish that same evening.

The little brother had passed his very first test of manhood and with each passing day he grew more confident of his ability to survive in the wilderness. Soon he had killed ten birds whose skins were sewn into the coat he had been promised. Fiercely proud of his hunting skills, he wore this new garment both day and night and felt himself ready to meet any challenge life might throw at him.

'Are we really all alone in the world, sister?' he asked one day as he paraded up and down the lodge in his bird-skin coat, 'since I cannot believe that this great broad earth with its fine blue sky was created simply for the pair of us.'

'There may be other people living,' answered his sister, 'but they can only be terrible beings, very unlike us. It would be most unwise to go in search of these people, little brother, and you must never be tempted to stray too far from home.'

But his sister's words only added to the young boy's curiosity, and he grew more impatient than ever to slip away quietly and explore the surrounding forests and countryside for himself.

Before the sun had risen on the following morning, he grabbed his bow and arrows and set off enthusiastically in the direction of the open hills. By midday, he had walked a very great distance, but still he hadn't discovered any other human beings. At length, he decided to rest for a while and lay down on the grass in the warmth of the sun's golden rays. He had happened upon a very beautiful spot, and was soon lulled gently to sleep by the tinkling sound of the waters dancing over the pebbles of a nearby stream. He slept for many hours in the heat of the brilliant sunshine and would have remained in this position a good while longer had he not been disturbed by the sensation that something close to him had begun to shrink and shrivel. At first, he thought he had been dreaming, but as he opened his eyes wider and gazed upon his bird-skin coat, he soon realized that it had tightened itself upon his body, so much so that he was scarcely able to breathe.

The young boy stood up in horror and began to examine his seared and singed coat more closely. The garment he had been so proud of was now totally ruined and he flew into a great passion, vowing to take vengeance on the sun for what it had done.

'Do not imagine that you can escape me because you are so high up in the sky,' he shouted angrily. 'What you have done will not go unpunished. I will pay you back before long.' And after he had sworn this oath, he trudged back home wearily to tell his sister of the dreadful misfortune that had befallen his new coat.

The young girl was now more worried than ever for her little brother. Ever since his return, he had fallen into a deep depression, refusing all food and laying down on his side, as still as a corpse, for a full ten days, at the end of which he turned over and lay on his other side for a further ten days. When he eventually arose, he was pale and drawn, but his voice was firm and resolute as he informed his sister that she must make a snare for him with which he intended to catch the sun.

'Find me some material suitable for making a noose,' he told her, but when his sister returned with a piece of dried deer sinew, he shook his head and said it would not do. Racking her brains, she searched again through their belongings, and came forward with a bird skin, left over from the coat she had made.

'This won't do either,' her brother declared agitatedly, 'the sun has had enough of my bird skins already. Go and find me something else.'

Finally, his sister thought of her own beautiful long hair, and pulling several glossy strands from her head, she began to weave a thick black cord which she handed to her brother.

'This is exactly what I need,' he said delightedly and began to draw it back and forth through his fingers until it grew rigid and strong. Then, having coiled it round his shoulders, he kissed his sister goodbye and set off to catch the sun, just as the last light began to fade in the sky.

Under cover of darkness, the little brother set his trap, fixing the snare on a spot where he knew the sun would first strike the land as it rose above the earth. He waited patiently, offering up many prayers. These were answered as soon as the sun attempted to rise from its sleepy bed, for it became fastened to the ground by the cord and could not ascend any higher. No light twinkled on the horizon and the land remained in deep shadow, deprived of the sun's warm rays.

Fear and panic erupted among the animals who ruled the earth as they awoke to discover a world totally submerged in darkness. They ran about blindly, calling to each other, desperate to find some explanation for what had happened. The most powerful among them immediately formed a council and it was agreed that someone would have to go forward to the edge of the horizon to investigate why the sun had not risen. This was a very dangerous undertaking, since whoever ventured so close to the sun risked severe burning and possible death. Only the dormouse, at that time the largest animal in the world, taller than any mountain, stood up bravely, offering to risk her life so that the others might be saved.

Hurriedly, she made her way to the place where the sun lay captive and quickly spotted the cord pinning it to the ground. Even now, though the dormouse was not yet close enough to begin gnawing the cord, her back began to smoke and the intense heat was almost overwhelming. Still she persevered, chewing the cord with her two front teeth while at the same time her huge bulk was turned into an enormous heap of ashes. When, at last, the sun was freed, it shot up into the sky as dazzling as it had ever been. But the dormouse, now shrunken to become one of the tiniest creatures in the world, fled in terror from its light and from that day forward she became known as Kug-e-been-gwa-kwa, or Blind Woman.

As soon as he discovered that the sun had escaped his snare, the little brother returned home once more to his sister. But he was now no longer anxious to take revenge, since his adventure had brought him greater wisdom and the knowledge that he had not been born to interfere with the ways of nature. For the rest of his life, he devoted himself to hunting, and within a very short time had shot enough snowbirds to make himself a new coat, even finer than the one which had led him to challenge the sun.

THE SPIRITS AND THE LOVERS

At the distance of a woman's walk of a day from the mouth of the river, called by the pale-faces the Whitestone, in the country of the Sioux, in the middle of a large plain, stands a lofty hill or mound. Its wonderful roundness, together with the circumstance of its standing apart from all other hills, like a fir-tree in the midst of a wide prairie, or a man whose friends and kindred have all descended to the dust, has made it known to all the tribes of the West. Whether it was created by the Great Spirit or filled up by the sons of men, whether it was done in the morning of the world, ask not me, for I cannot tell you. Know it is called by all the tribes of the land the Hill of Little People, or the Mountain of Little Spirits. No gifts can induce an Indian to visit it; for why should he incur the anger of the Little People who dwell in it, and, sacrificed upon the fire of their wrath, behold his wife and children no more? In all the marches and counter-marches of the Indians, in all their goings and returnings, in all their wanderings by day or by night to and from lands which lie beyond it, their paths are so ordered that none approaches near enough to disturb the tiny inhabitants of the hill. The memory of the red-man of the forest has preserved but one instance when their privacy was violated, since it was known through the tribes that they wished for no intercourse with mortals. Before that time many Indians were missing each year. No one knew what became of them, but they were gone, and left no trace nor story behind. Valiant warriors filled their quivers with arrows, put new strings to their bows, new shod their moccasins, and sallied out to acquire glory in combat; but there was no wailing in the camp of our foes: their arrows were not felt, their shouts were not heard. Yet they fell not by the hands of our foes, but perished we know not how.

Many seasons ago there lived within the limits of the great council-fire of the Mahas a chief who was renowned for his valour and victories in the field, his wisdom in the council, his dexterity and success in the chase. His name was Mahtoree, or the White Crane. He was celebrated throughout the vast regions of the West, from the Mississippi to the Hills of the Serpent, from the Missouri to the Plains of Bitter Frost, for all those qualities which render an Indian warrior famous and feared.

In one of the war expeditions of the Pawnee Mahas against the Burntwood Tetons, it was the good fortune of the former to overcome and to make many prisoners—men, women, and children. One of the captives, Sakeajah, or the Bird-Girl, a beautiful creature in the morning of life, after being adopted into one of the Mahas families, became the wife of the chief warrior of the nation. Great was the love which the White Crane had for his wife, and it grew yet stronger when she had brought him four sons and a daughter, Tatokah, or the Antelope. She was beautiful. Her skin was fair, her eyes were large and bright as those of the bison-ox, and her hair black, and braided with beads, brushed, as she walked, the dew from the flowers upon the prairies. Her temper was gentle and her voice sweet.

It may not be doubted that the beautiful Tatokah had many lovers; but the heart of the maiden was touched by none of the noble youths who sought her. She bade them all depart as they came; she rejected them all. With the perverseness which is often seen among women, she had placed her affections upon a youth who had distinguished himself by no valiant deeds in war, nor by industry or dexterity in the chase. His name had never reached the surrounding nations. His own nation knew him not, unless as a weak and imbecile man. He was poor in everything which constitutes the riches of Indian life. Who had heard the twanging of Karkapaha's bow in the retreat of the bear, or who had beheld the war-paint on his cheek or brow? Where were the scalps or the prisoners that betokened his valour or daring?

No song of valiant exploits had been heard from his lips, for he had none to boast of—if he had done aught becoming a man, he had done it when none was by. The beautiful Tatokah, who knew and lamented the deficiencies of her lover, strove long to conquer her passion without success. At length, since her father would not agree to her union with her lover, the two agreed to fly together. The night fixed came, and they left the village of the Mahas and the lodge of Mahtoree for the wilderness.

Their flight was not unmarked, and when the father was made acquainted with the disgrace which had befallen him, he called his young men around him, and bade them pursue the fugitives, promising his daughter to whomsoever should slay the Karkapaha. Immediately pursuit was made, and soon a hundred eager youths were on the track of the hapless pair. With that unerring skill and sagacity in discovering footprints which mark their race, their steps were tracked, and themselves soon discovered flying. What was the surprise of the pursuers when they found that the path taken by the hapless pair would carry them to the mountain of little spirits, and that they were sufficiently in advance to reach it before they could be overtaken. None of them durst venture within the supposed limits, and they halted till the White Crane should be informed of his daughter and her lover having placed themselves under the protection of the spirits.

In the meantime the lovers pursued their journey towards the fearful residence of the little people. Despair lent them courage to perform an act to which the stoutest Indian resolution had hitherto been unequal. They determined to tell their tale to the spirits and ask their protection. They were within a few feet of the hill when, on a sudden, its brow, on which no object had till now been visible, became covered with little people, the tallest of whom was not higher than the knee of the maiden, while many of them—but these were children—were of lower stature than the squirrel. Their voice was sharp and quick, like the barking of the prairie dog. A little wing came out at each shoulder; each had a single eye, which eye was to the right in the men, and to the left in the women, and their feet stood out at each side. They were armed like Indians, with tomahawks, spears, bows, and arrows. He who appeared to be the head chief—for he wore an air of command, and had the eagle feather—came up to the fugitives and said—

"Why have you invaded the village of our race whose wrath has been so fatal to your people? How dare you venture within the limits of our residence? Know you not that your lives are forfeited?"

Tatokah, for her lover had less than the heart of a doe and was speechless, related their story. She told them how they had loved, how wroth her father had been, how they had stolen away and been pursued, and concluded her tale of sorrow with a flood of tears. The little man who wore the eagle feather appeared moved by what she said, and calling around him a large number of men, who were doubtless the chiefs and counsellors of the nation, a long consultation took place. The result was a determination to favour and protect the lovers.

At this moment Shongotongo, or the Big Horse, one of the braves whom Mahtoree had despatched in quest of his daughter, appeared in view in pursuit of the fugitives. It was not till Mahtoree had taxed his courage that Big Horse had ventured on the perilous quest. He approached with the strength of heart and singleness of purpose which accompany an Indian warrior who deems the eyes of his nation upon him. When first the brave was discovered thus wantonly, and with no other purpose but the shedding of blood, intruding on the dominions of the spirits, no words can tell the rage which appeared to possess their bosoms. Secure in the knowledge of their power to repel the attacks of every living thing, the intrepid Maha was permitted to advance within a few steps of Karkapaha. He had just raised his spear to strike the unmanly lover, when, all at once, he found himself riveted to the ground. His feet refused to move, his hands hung powerless at his side, his tongue refused to utter a word. The bow and arrow fell from his hand, and his spear lay powerless. A little child, not so high as the fourth leaf of the thistle, came and spat on him, and a company of the spirits danced around him singing a taunting song. When they had thus finished their task of preparatory torture, a thousand little spirits drew their bows, and a thousand arrows pierced his heart. In a moment innumerable mattocks were employed in preparing him a grave, and he was hidden from the eyes of the living ere Tatokah could have thrice counted over the fingers of her hand.

When this was done, the chief of the little spirits called Karkapaha before him, and said—

"Maha, you have the heart of a doe. You would fly from a roused wren. We have not spared you because you deserve to be spared, but because the maiden loves you. It is for this purpose that we will give you the heart of a man, that you may return to the village of the Mahas, and find favour in the eyes of Mahtoree and the braves of the nation. We will take away your cowardly spirit, and will give you the spirit of the warrior whom we slew, whose heart was firm as a rock. Sleep, man of little soul, and wake to be better worthy the love of the beautiful Antelope."

Then a deep sleep came over the Maha lover. How long he slept he knew not, but when he woke he felt at once that a change had taken place in his feelings and temper. The first thought that came to his mind was of a bow and arrow, the second was of the beautiful maiden who lay sleeping at his side. The little spirits had disappeared—not a solitary being of the many thousands who, but a few minutes before, had filled the air with their discordant cries was now to be seen or heard. At the feet of Karkapaha lay a tremendous bow, larger than any warrior ever yet used, a sheaf of arrows of proportionate size, and a spear of a weight which no Maha could wield. Karkapaha drew the bow as an Indian boy bends a willow twig, and the spear seemed in his hand but a reed or a feather. The shrill war-whoop burst unconsciously from his lips, and his nostrils seemed dilated with the fire and impatience of a newly-awakened courage. The heart of the fond Indian girl dissolved in tears when she saw these proofs of strength and these evidences of spirit which, she knew, if they were coupled with valour—and how could she doubt the completeness of the gift to effect the purposes of the giver?—would thaw the iced feelings of her father and tune his heart to the song of forgiveness. Yet it was not without many fears, tears, and misgivings on the part of the maiden that they began their journey to the Mahas village. The lover, now a stranger to fear, used his endeavours to quiet the beautiful Tatokah, and in some measure succeeded. Upon finding that his daughter and her lover had gone to the Hill of the Spirits, and that Shongotongo did not return from his perilous adventure, the chief of the Mahas had recalled his braves from the pursuit, and was listening to the history of the pair, as far as the returned warriors were acquainted with it, when his daughter and her lover made their appearance. With a bold and fearless step the once faint-hearted Karkapaha walked up to the offended father, and, folding his arms upon his breast, stood erect as a pine, and motionless as that tree when the winds of the earth are chained. It was the first time that Karkapaha had ever looked on angry men without trembling, and a demeanour so unusual in him excited universal surprise.

"Karkapaha is a thief," said the White Crane.

"It is the father of Tatokah that says it," answered the lover, "else would Karkapaha say it was the song of a bird that has flown over."

"My warriors say it."

"Your warriors are singing-birds; they are wrens. Karkapaha says they do not speak the truth. Karkapaha has a brave heart and the strength of a bear. Let the braves try him. He has thrown away the woman's heart, and become a man."

"Karkapaha is changed," said the chief thoughtfully, "but how and when?"

"The Little Spirits of the mountain have given him a new soul. Bid your braves draw this bow. Bid them poise this spear. Their eyes say they can do neither. Then is Karkapaha the strong man of his tribe?" As he said this he flourished the ponderous spear over his head as a man would poise a reed, and drew the bow as a child would bend a twig.

"Karkapaha is the husband of Tatokah," said Mahtoree, springing to his feet, and he gave the maiden to her lover.

The traditionary lore of the Mahas is full of the exploits, both in war and in the chase, of Karkapaha, who was made a man by the Spirits of the Mountain.

SAYADIO AND THE MAGIC CUP

Many months had passed since the young brave, Sayadio, lost his beautiful young sister to a fatal illness. She had been only twelve years old when she died, and her abrupt departure to the Land of Souls had left a deep sadness in the hearts of all who had known her. Sayadio occupied himself as best he could after her death and attempted to carry on a normal life, but often he could not prevent himself falling into the blackest of moods from which it took several long weeks to rouse himself.

Worried that his grief would never be silenced, he decided the time had come to call upon his manitto for help. He found a place of solitude and meditated hard, and soon he heard a voice calling to him:

'Your mourning will only cease', it told him, 'when you have followed the path your sister has taken to the Land of Souls.' Sayadio welcomed the advice of his manitto and in great haste he began making preparations for his journey, resolving to be reunited with his sister before long and to bring her back with him on his return.

But the path ahead was never-ending and the months crept by without offering any sign of improvement. Sayadio began to despair and was just about ready to abandon his quest when, quite unexpectedly, he encountered a stooped old man moving slowly towards him along the same track. The stranger's great white beard trailed the ground and in his right hand he carried a heavy, silver object which, on closer inspection, proved to be a curious type of drinking vessel.

'Can I help you on your way,' Sayadio offered, 'perhaps I can carry something for you.'

'I need go no further,' replied the old man, 'for I have set out to meet you so that I might give you this gourd. If ever you find your sister, use the gourd to catch her spirit and hold it captive until you have returned to your earthly home.'

Delighted to receive such a valuable gift, Sayadio travelled onwards, his mood brighter than it had been for many weeks. It was not long before he approached the outskirts of the Land of Souls and, filled with excitement, he began to call his sister's name over and over again. He received no answer, but he did not feel dejected, for up ahead, in the distance, he suddenly noticed a group of spirits playing in the meadow. Respectfully he advanced towards them, expecting that they would greet him kindly, but to his utter dismay, the spirits fled in horror as soon as they set eyes on him.

At that particular time of year, according to ancient custom, the dead were due to gather together for a great dance ceremony presided over by the Holder of the Heavens, Tarenyawago. Soon the spirit-drum began to beat loudly and the sound of an Indian flute filled the air. The effect of these instruments was almost instantaneous, for the spirits immediately abandoned their hiding places and thronged into a circle anxious to commence their bewildering ritual. Sayadio peered from behind the trees and quickly spotted his sister among the spirits. Without warning, he sprang forward, uncorked his gourd, and attempted to sweep her into the vessel. But she eluded his grasp without any trouble and dissolved into thin air before he knew quite what had happened.

Defeated and despondent, Sayadio made a desperate appeal to the Holder of the Heavens:

'I have come a very long way', he informed the great and

powerful spirit, 'because my sister was taken from us before her time. Please will you help me to capture her soul, so that she may be returned to her earthly home and to those who love her.'

Observing the deep perplexity and sadness of the young man, Tarenyawago took pity on him and kindly offered his assistance.

'Take this magic rattle', he told Sayadio, 'and shake it as soon as you catch sight of the spirits gathering again to complete their dance. Be patient, yet swift, and you will succeed in your ambition.'

Shortly before sunset, just as the Holder of the Heavens had promised, the spirits began floating on the air like a thick mist, descending one by one on exactly the same spot as before. Once more, Sayadio saw his sister among the group, stepping lightly, round and round, to the sound of the eerie melody. She appeared to be wholly entranced by the music, and he took this opportunity to step forward cautiously with his magic rattle. As soon as she passed before him again, he shook it delicately in her ear and this time, to his great relief, he found that she came to an abrupt halt, frozen in motion like a graceful statue. Quick as a flash, he swooped her off the ground and into his gourd, securely fastening the lid and ignoring the pitiful cries of the captured soul struggling to regain its liberty.

Retracing his steps homeward, Sayadio soon reached his native village where he summoned his friends and relatives to come and examine the strange gourd housing his precious charge. He called for the body of his sister to be brought forth from its burial-place, for he intended, without further delay, to enact the ceremony that would reunite her spirit with her body. Everything was almost ready for the sacred rite of resurrection when, out of nowhere, the most witless Indian in the village rushed forward and removed the lid of the gourd, no longer able to control his immoderate curiosity.

Without any hesitation, the imprisoned spirit rose up into the air, and failing to look back, glided high up into the sky, disappearing over the horizon. Sayadio gazed helplessly in the direction of its frantic flight, calling upon the departed spirit to return to him, but it made no response to his plea. Overwhelmed with despair, he retreated to his lodge, but soon he heard the familiar voice of his manitto whispering in his ear:

'The spirit of your sister was not destined for this mortal world,' the voice explained. 'She is happy in her new home, so be at peace and cease your mourning.'

Sayadio listened and his grief suddenly abandoned him. And from that day forth, he never again attempted to recall his sister from the dead. This is a legend from the Wyandot tribe of the Iroquois.

THE LAND OF SOULS

The **wedding ceremony** of a handsome, young Algonquin chief was fast approaching. He had chosen for his bride a very beautiful woman from a neighbouring tribe. The two had fallen deeply in love and looked forward to a long and happy life together, but sadly this was not to be, for on the eve of their wedding the young woman succumbed to a raging fever and within hours she had passed away, leaving her intended husband grief-stricken and distraught.

The handsome chief, who had once been famous for his courage and heroism throughout the land, now spent all of his time in mourning, making a daily pilgrimage to the burial place of his beloved where he threw himself on the soft mound and sobbed helplessly. Hunting and warfare no longer held any charm for him and he cast aside his bow and arrow, resolving never to use his weapon again. The situation appeared hopeless and even the chief's closest friends began to believe that he would never mend his broken heart or recover his brave reputation.

One day, however, the chief overheard a conversation among the elders of his tribe which, for the first time in many months, prompted him to join the circle and listen attentively. The old men were discussing their loved ones who had died, and they also spoke of a path leading to the spirit-world which, if a man was lucky enough to find it, enabled the living to visit the dead. The grieving young lover eagerly welcomed this unexpected news and, taking up his weapon and a few meagre belongings, set off immediately to discover the path that would lead him to the Land of Souls.

He had no firm idea which direction he should take, but instinct informed him that he must keep travelling southward until he observed some change in the landscape. His journey over the snow-covered fields and hills was both difficult and wearisome, but after fourteen days, he became convinced of a difference in the appearance of the surrounding countryside. Certainly, the thick snow had begun to melt. The sky, too, was of a more radiant blue and the trees had begun to reveal tiny leaf-buds. Moving onwards, as if by enchantment, delicate and colourful flowers emerged from the soil, birds began to chirp sweet melodies and the air grew warm and fragrant. The young chief's heart began to beat with excitement at these changes, for he knew that he must be nearing the Land of Souls.

A rugged path wound its way through the trees of the spreading forest before him and he felt sure that he must follow this path. Passing through a dark grove, he came upon a little lodge set high up on a hill. In the doorway stood an old man, his hair as white as snow and his eyes as bright as sapphires. He wore a robe of swan-skin and in his right hand he carried a long staff with which he beckoned the young chief forward.

'I have been expecting you,' said the old man. 'Come inside the lodge and I will answer all the questions I know you wish to ask me.'

There was no need for the chief to inform the stranger of his quest, since the old man already knew every detail of his misfortune.

'Only a few days ago the beautiful woman you seek rested here within my lodge,' he said to the chief. 'Now she has gone to the Land of Souls and you can follow her there if you do as I say and listen carefully to my counsel.'

'You cannot take your body along with you, nor will your bow and arrow be of any use,' the old man told him. 'Leave them here and they will be returned to you when we meet again. I must warn you that the journey ahead is a perilous one. You now stand at the border of the Land of Souls and you must cross that vast lake beyond to reach the Island of the Blessed where it will be possible for you to visit your loved one again.'

The young chief, who was in no way frightened by the old man's words of caution, grew impatient to be on his way once more. He found, as he travelled onwards, that the forests, rivers and mountains had taken on an almost ethereal quality. Animals bounded along gleefully by his side and as he moved swiftly through thickets and dense woodlands, he realized that he was now a weightless spirit floating effortlessly and fearlessly through the air in the Land of Souls.

It was not long before he reached the broad lake the old man had described to him. Gazing across its waters, he caught sight of a very beautiful island shimmering in the midday sunshine. A canoe of white, shining stone lay tied upon the shore, and the young chief lost no time jumping aboard it and grasping the paddles. He was just about to pull away in the direction of the island when he was struck by a powerful sense that he was no longer alone on the water. Turning to confront his mysterious companion, he was utterly amazed and delighted to see his young bride seated in an identical canoe alongside him, ready to accompany him on his crossing to the Island of the Blessed.

At first, the surface of the silver lake remained as smooth as glass, disturbed only by tiny ripples of frolicking trout anxious to join in the excursion. But then, as the couple approached the half-way mark, the waves of the lake began to swell dramatically in strength and size. The water now changed to a steely-grey colour and as the young chief peered over the side of his canoe, he was shocked to discover several human skulls floating on the spray. He remembered the old man's words, that it would be a hazardous journey, and thought now of those who had attempted it before him, battling on bravely, yet eventually drowning in the furious tempest.

Though he was filled with terror and fear for the safety of both himself and his bride, the young chief did not alter his course but continued to row boldly towards the shore, never once losing sight of his loved one. The Master of Life kept a watchful eye on them from above and, knowing that they were innocent children whose deeds in life had been free of evil, he decreed that they should reach the island unharmed. Suddenly the winds began to ease, the water grew calm and the young couple at last felt their canoes grating on the golden sand.

Leaping on to the island, they embraced each other rapturously, shedding many tears of relief and joy. Then, as they stood hand in hand, they surveyed the perfect world they now occupied where everything seemed designed to bring them the utmost pleasure. The air itself was like an exquisite, mouth-watering food sent to nourish and strengthen them. Walking through the beautiful countryside, they could find no trace of suffering or sadness, no cold or discomfort, no war or destruction, only the sights and sounds of a perfect paradise of nature.

For three days and three nights, the young lovers remained free to enjoy this blissful land, each of them hoping that their happiness would last forever. But on the third evening, the young chief was awoken by a gentle voice calling to him on the breeze:

'Your time has not yet come,' whispered the Master of Life. 'You must return to your own people and fulfil your mortal destiny. Rule them wisely and well, for they need your guidance at this time, and when you have completed your duty to them, you may return here and join forever the bride you must now abandon.'

The young chief rose obediently and, making his way to the old man's lodge on the far side of the lake, re-entered the body he had left behind. Although he was heavy-hearted, he was not resentful of his departure, but felt honoured that the Master of Life had intervened to set him on the correct path.

Returning to his people, the young chief became a just and kindly ruler, winning the admiration and loyalty of all who knew him. Often, at the end of a long hunt, he would call for a great fire to be built and ordering his people to sit around it, he would tell them of the Land of Souls and describe to them the path he knew he would follow once more as soon as he had served his time as father to his people.

THE STRANGE GUESTS

Many years ago there lived, near the borders of Lake Superior, a noted hunter, who had a wife and one child. His lodge stood in a remote part of the forest, several days' journey from that of any other person. He spent his days in hunting, and his evenings in relating to his wife the incidents that had befallen him in the chase. As game was very abundant, he seldom failed to bring home in the evening an ample store of meat to last them until the succeeding evening; and while they were seated by the fire in his lodge partaking the fruits of his day's labour, he entertained his wife with conversation, or by occasionally relating those tales, or enforcing those precepts, which every good Indian esteems necessary for the instruction of his wife and children. Thus, far removed from all sources of disquiet, surrounded by all they deemed necessary to their comfort, and happy in one another's society, their lives passed away in cheerful solitude and sweet contentment. The breast of the hunter had never felt the compunctions of remorse, for he was a just man in all his dealings. He had never violated the laws of his tribe by encroaching upon the hunting-grounds of his neighbours, by taking that which did not belong to him, or by any act calculated to displease the village chiefs or offend the Great Spirit. His chief ambition was to support his family with a sufficiency of food and skins by his own unaided exertions, and to share their happiness around his cheerful fire at night. The white man had not yet taught them that blankets and clothes were necessary to their comfort, or that guns could be used in the killing of game.

The life of the Chippewa hunter peacefully glided away.

One evening during the winter season, it chanced that he remained out later than usual, and his wife sat lonely in the lodge, and began to be agitated with fears lest some accident had befallen him. Darkness had already fallen. She listened attentively to hear the sound of coming footsteps; but nothing could be heard but the wind mournfully whistling around the sides of the lodge. Time passed away while she remained in this state of suspense, every moment augmenting her fears and adding to her disappointment.

Suddenly she heard the sound of approaching footsteps upon the frozen surface of the snow. Not doubting that it was her husband, she quickly unfastened the loop which held, by an inner fastening, the skin door of the lodge, and throwing it open she saw two strange women standing before it.

Courtesy left the hunter's wife no time for deliberation. She invited the strangers to enter and warm themselves, thinking, from the distance to the nearest neighbours, they must have walked a considerable way. When they were entered she invited them to remain. They seemed to be total strangers to that part of the country, and the more closely she observed them the more curious the hunter's wife became respecting her guests.

No efforts could induce them to come near the fire. They took their seats in a remote part of the lodge, and drew their garments about them in such a manner as to almost completely hide their faces. They seemed shy and reserved, and when a glimpse could be had of their faces they appeared pale, even of a deathly hue. Their eyes were bright but sunken: their cheekbones were prominent, and their persons slender and emaciated.

Seeing that her guests avoided conversation as well as observation, the woman forbore to question them, and sat in silence until her husband entered. He had been led further than usual in the pursuit of game, but had returned with the carcass of a large and fat deer. The moment he entered the lodge, the mysterious women exclaimed—

"Behold! what a fine and fat animal!" and they immediately ran and pulled off pieces of the whitest fat, which they ate with avidity.

Such conduct appeared very strange to the hunter, but supposing the strangers had been a long time without food, he made no remark; and his wife, taking example from her husband, likewise restrained herself.

On the following evening the same scene was repeated. The hunter brought home the best portions of the game he had killed, and while he was laying it down before his wife, according to custom, the two strange women came quickly up, tore off large pieces of fat, and ate them with greediness. Such behaviour might well have aroused the hunter's displeasure; but the deference due to strange guests induced him to pass it over in silence.

Observing the parts to which the strangers were most partial, the hunter resolved the next day to anticipate their wants by cutting off and tying up a portion of the fat for each. This he did: and having placed the two portions of fat upon the top of his burden, as soon as he entered the lodge he gave to each stranger the part that was hers. Still the guests appeared to be dissatisfied, and took more from the carcass lying before the wife.

Except for this remarkable behaviour, the conduct of the guests was unexceptionable, although marked by some peculiarities. They were quiet, modest, and discreet. They maintained a cautious silence during the day, neither uttering a word nor moving from the lodge. At night they would get up, and, taking those implements which were then used in breaking and preparing wood, repair to the forest. Here they would busy themselves in seeking dry branches and pieces of trees blown down by the wind. When a sufficient quantity had been gathered to last until the succeeding night they carried it home upon their shoulders. Then carefully putting everything in its place within the lodge, they resumed their seats and their studied silence. They were always careful to return from their labours before the dawn of day, and were never known to stay out beyond that hour. In this manner they repaid, in some measure, the kindness of the hunter, and relieved his wife from one of her most laborious duties.

Thus nearly the whole year passed away, every day leading to some new development of character which served to endear the parties to each other. The visitors began to assume a more hale and healthy aspect; their faces daily lost something of that deathly hue which had at first marked them, and they visibly improved in strength, and threw off some of that cold reserve and forbidding austerity which had kept the hunter so long in ignorance of their true character.

One evening the hunter returned very late after having spent the day in toilsome exertion, and having laid the produce of his hunt at his wife's feet, the silent women seized it and began to tear off the fat in such an unceremonious manner that the wife could no longer control her feelings of disgust, and said to herself—

"This is really too bad. How can I bear it any longer!"

She did not, however, put her thought into words, but an immediate change was observed in the two visitors. They became unusually reserved, and showed evident signs of being uneasy in their situation. The good hunter immediately perceived this change, and, fearful that they had taken offence, as soon as they had retired demanded of his wife whether any harsh expression had escaped her lips during the day. She replied that she had uttered nothing to give the least offence. The hunter tried to compose himself to sleep, but he felt restive and uneasy, for he could hear the sighs and lamentations of the two strangers. Every moment added to his conviction that his guests had taken some deep offence; and, as he could not banish this idea from his mind, he arose, and, going to the strangers, thus addressed them—

"Tell me, ye women, what is it that causes you pain of mind, and makes you utter these unceasing sighs? Has my wife given you any cause of offence during the day while I was absent in the chase? My fears persuade me that, in some unguarded moment, she has forgotten what is due to the rights of hospitality, and used expressions ill-befitting the mysterious character you sustain. Tell me, ye strangers from a strange country, ye women who appear not to be of this world, what it is that causes you pain of mind, and makes you utter these unceasing sighs."

They replied that no unkind expression had ever been used towards them during their residence in the lodge, that they had received all the affectionate attention they could reasonably expect.

"It is not for ourselves," they continued, "it is not for ourselves that we weep. We are weeping for the fate of mankind; we are weeping for the fate of mortals whom Death awaits at every stage of their existence. Proud mortals, whom disease attacks in youth and in age. Vain men, whom hunger pinches, cold benumbs, and poverty emaciates. Weak beings, who are born in tears, who are nurtured in tears, and whose whole course is marked upon the thirsty sands of life in a broad line of tears. It is for these we weep.

"You have spoken truly, brother; we are not of this world. We are spirits from the land of the dead, sent upon the earth to try the sincerity of the living. It is not for the dead but for the living that we mourn. It was by no means necessary that your wife should express her thoughts to us. We knew them as soon as they were formed. We saw that for once displeasure had arisen in her heart. It is enough. Our mission is ended. We came but to try you, and we knew before we came that you were a kind husband, an affectionate father, and a good friend. Still, you have the weaknesses of a mortal, and your wife is wanting in our eyes; but it is not alone for you we weep, it is for the fate of mankind.

"Often, very often, has the widower exclaimed, 'O Death, how cruel, how relentless thou art to take away my beloved friend in the spring of her youth, in the pride of her strength, and in the bloom of her beauty! If thou wilt permit her once more to return to my abode, my gratitude shall never cease; I will raise up my voice continually to thank the Master of Life for so excellent a boon. I will devote my time to study how I can best promote her happiness while she is permitted to remain; and our lives shall roll away like a pleasant stream through a flowing valley!' Thus also has the father prayed for his son, the mother for her daughter, the wife for her husband, the sister for her brother, the lover for his mistress, the friend for his bosom companion, until the sounds of mourning and the cries of the living have pierced the very recesses of the dead.

"The Great Spirit has at length consented to make a trial of the sincerity of these prayers by sending us upon the earth. He has done this to see how we should be received,—coming as strangers, no one knowing from where. Three moons were allotted to us to make the trial, and if, during that time, no impatience had been evinced, no angry passions excited at the place where we took up our abode, all those in the land of spirits, whom their relatives had desired to return, would have been restored. More than two moons have already passed, and as soon as the leaves began to bud our mission would have been successfully terminated. It is now too late. Our trial is finished, and we are called to the pleasant fields whence we came.

"Brother, it is proper that one man should die to make room for another. Otherwise, the world would be filled to overflowing. It is just that the goods gathered by one should be left to be divided among others; for in the land of spirits there is no want, there is neither sorrow nor hunger, pain nor death. Pleasant fields, filled with game spread before the eye, with birds of beautiful form. Every stream has good fish in it, and every hill is crowned with groves of fruit-trees, sweet and pleasant to the taste. It is not here, brother, but there that men begin truly to live. It is not for those who rejoice in those pleasant groves but for you that are left behind that we weep.

"Brother, take our thanks for your hospitable treatment. Regret not our departure. Fear not evil. Thy luck shall still be good in the chase, and there shall ever be a bright sky over thy lodge. Mourn not for us, for no corn will spring up from tears."

The spirits ceased, but the hunter had no power over his voice to reply. As they had proceeded in their address he saw a light gradually beaming from their faces, and a blue vapour filled the lodge with an unnatural light. As soon as they ceased, darkness gradually closed around. The hunter listened, but the sobs of the spirits had ceased. He heard the door of his tent open and shut, but he never saw more of his mysterious visitors.

The success promised him was his. He became a celebrated hunter, and never wanted for anything necessary to his ease. He became the father of many boys, all of whom grew up to manhood, and health, peace, and long life were the rewards of his hospitality.

THE UNDYING HEAD

In a remote part of the north lived a man and his only sister who had never seen human being. Seldom, if ever, had the man any cause to go from home, for if he wanted food he had only to go a little distance from the lodge, and there place his arrows with their barbs in the ground. He would then return to the lodge and tell his sister where the arrows had been placed, when she would go in search of them, and never fail to find each struck through the heart of a deer. These she dragged to the lodge and dressed for food. Thus she lived until she attained womanhood. One day her brother, who was named Iamo, said to her—

"Sister, the time is near when you will be ill. Listen to my advice, for if you do not it will probably be the cause of my death. Take the implements with which we kindle our fires, go some distance from our lodge and build a separate fire. When you are in want of food I will tell you where to find it. You must cook for yourself and I for myself. When you are ill do not attempt to come near the lodge or bring to it any of the utensils you use. Be sure to always have fastened to your belt whatever you will need in your sickness, for you do not know when the time of your indisposition will come. As for myself, I must do the best I can." His sister promised to obey him in all he said.

Shortly after her brother had cause to go from home. His sister was alone in the lodge combing her hair, and she had just untied and laid aside the belt to which the implements were fastened when suddenly she felt unwell. She ran out of the lodge, but in her haste forgot the belt. Afraid to return she stood some time thinking, and finally she determined to return to the lodge and get it, for she said to herself—

"My brother is not at home, and I will stay but a moment to catch hold of it."

She went back, and, running in, suddenly seized the belt, and was coming out, when her brother met her. He knew what had happened.

"Did I not tell you," said he, "to take care? Now you have killed me."

His sister would have gone away, but he spoke to her again.

"What can you do now? What I feared has happened. Go in, and stay where you have always lived. You have killed me."

He then laid aside his hunting dress and accoutrements, and soon after both his feet began to inflame and turn black, so that he could not move. He directed his sister where to place his arrows, so that she might always have food. The inflammation continued to increase, and had now reached his first rib.

"Sister," said he, "my end is near. You must do as I tell you.

You see my medicine-sack and my war-club tied to it. It contains all my medicines, my war-plumes, and my paints of all colours. As soon as the inflammation reaches my chest, you will take my war-club, and with the sharp point of it cut off my head. When it is free from my body, take it, place its neck in the sack, which you must open at one end. Then hang it up in its former place. Do not forget my bow and arrows. One of the last you will take to procure food. Tie the others to my sack, and then hang it up so that I can look towards the door. Now and then I will speak to you, but not often."

His sister again promised to obey.

In a little time his chest became affected.

"Now," cried he, "take the club and strike off my head."

His sister was afraid, but he told her to muster up courage.

"Strike," said he, with a smile upon his face.

Calling up all her courage, his sister struck and cut off the head.

"Now," said the head, "place me where I told you."

Fearful, she obeyed it in all its commands.

Retaining its animation, it looked round the lodge as usual, and it would command its sister to go to such places where it thought she could best procure the flesh of the different animals she needed. One day the head said—

"The time is not distant when I shall be freed from this situation, but I shall have to undergo many sore evils. So the Superior Manito decrees, and I must bear all patiently."

In a certain part of the country was a village inhabited by a numerous and warlike band of Indians. In this village was a family of ten young men, brothers. In the spring of the year the youngest of these blackened his face and fasted. His dreams were propitious, and having ended his fast, he sent secretly for his brothers at night, so that the people in the village should not be aware of their meeting. He told them how favourable his dreams had been, and that he had called them together to ask them if they would accompany him in a war excursion. They all answered they would. The third son, noted for his oddities, swinging his war-club when his brother had ceased speaking, jumped up: "Yes," said he, "I will go, and this will be the way I will treat those we go to fight with." With those words he struck the post in the centre of the lodge, and gave a yell. The other brothers spoke to him, saying—

"Gently, gently, Mudjikewis, when you are in other people's lodges." So he sat down. Then, in turn, they took the drum, sang their songs, and closed the meeting with a feast. The youngest told them not to whisper their intention to their wives, but to prepare secretly for their journey. They all promised obedience, and Mudjikewis was the first to do so.

The time for departure drew near. The youngest gave the word for them to assemble on a certain night, when they would commence their journey. Mudjikewis was loud in his demands for his moccasins, and his wife several times demanded the reason of his impatience.

"Besides," said she, "you have a good pair on."

"Quick, quick," replied Mudjikewis; "since you must know, we are going on a war excursion."

Thus he revealed the secret.

That night they met and started. The snow was on the ground, and they travelled all night lest others should follow them. When it was daylight, the leader took snow, made a ball of it, and tossing it up in the air, said—

"It was in this way I saw snow fall in my dream, so that we could not be tracked."

Immediately snow began to fall in large flakes, so that the leader commanded the brothers to keep close together for fear of losing one another. Close as they walked together it was with difficulty they could see one another. The snow continued falling all that day and the next night, so that it was impossible for any one to follow their track.

They walked for several days, and Mudjikewis was always in the rear. One day, running suddenly forward, he gave the Saw-saw-quan (war-cry), and struck a tree with his war-club, breaking the tree in pieces as if it had been struck by lightning.

"Brothers," said he, "this is the way I will serve those we are going to fight."

The leader answered—

"Slowly, slowly, Mudjikewis. The one I lead you to is not to be thought of so lightly."

Again Mudjikewis fell back and thought to himself—

"What, what! Who can this be he is leading us to?"

He felt fearful, and was silent. Day after day they travelled on till they came to an extensive plain, on the borders of which human bones were bleaching in the sun. The leader said—

"These are the bones of those who have gone before us. None has ever yet returned to tell the sad tale of their fate."

Again Mudjikewis became restless, and, running forward, gave the accustomed yell. Advancing to a large rock which stood above the ground he struck it, and it fell to pieces.

"See, brothers," said he, "thus will I treat those we are going to fight."

"Be quiet," said the leader. "He to whom I am leading you is not to be compared to that rock."

Mudjikewis fell back quite thoughtful, saying to himself—

"I wonder who this can be that he is going to attack;" and he was afraid.

They continued to see the remains of former warriors who had been to the place to which they were now going, and had retreated thus far back again. At last they came to a piece of rising ground, from which they plainly saw on a distant mountain an enormous bear. The distance between them was very great, but the size of the animal caused it to be seen very clearly.

"There," said the leader; "it is to him I am leading you. Here our troubles will only commence, for he is a mishemokwa" (a she-bear, or a male-bear as ferocious as a she-bear) "and a manito. It is he who has what we prize so dearly, to obtain which the warriors whose bones we saw sacrificed their lives. You must not be fearful. Be manly; we shall find him asleep."

The warriors advanced boldly till they came near to the bear, when they stopped to look at it more closely. It was asleep, and there was a belt around its neck.

"This," said the leader, touching the belt, "is what we must get. It contains what we want."

The eldest brother then tried to slip the belt over the bear's head, the animal appearing to be fast asleep, and not at all disturbed by his efforts. He could not, however, remove the belt, nor was any of the brothers more successful till the one next to the youngest tried in his turn. He slipped the belt nearly over the beast's head, but could not get it quite off. Then the youngest laid his hands on it, and with a pull succeeded. Placing the belt on the eldest brother's back, he said—

"Now we must run," and they started off at their best pace. When one became tired with the weight of the belt another carried it. Thus they ran till they had passed the bones of all the warriors, and when they were some distance beyond, looking back, they saw the monster slowly rising. For some time it stood still, not missing the belt. Then they heard a tremendous howl, like distant thunder, slowly filling the sky. At last they heard the bear cry—

"Who can it be that has dared to steal my belt? Earth is not so large but I can find them," and it descended the hill in pursuit. With every jump of the bear the earth shook as if it were convulsed. Very soon it approached the party. They, however, kept the belt, exchanging it from one to another, and encouraging each other. The bear, however, gained on them fast.

"Brothers," said the leader, "have none of you, when fasting, ever dreamed of some friendly spirit who would aid you as a guardian?"

A dead silence followed.

"Well," continued he, "once when I was fasting I dreamed of being in danger of instant death, when I saw a small lodge, with smoke curling up from its top. An old man lived in it, and I dreamed that he helped me, and may my dream be verified soon."

Having said this, he ran forward and gave a yell and howl. They came upon a piece of rising ground, and, behold! a lodge with smoke curling from its top appeared before them. This gave them all new strength, and they ran forward and entered the lodge. In it they found an old man, to whom the leader said—

"Nemesho (my grandfather), help us. We ask your protection, for the great bear would kill us."

"Sit down and eat, my grandchildren," said the old man. "Who is a great manito? There is none but me; but let me look;" and he opened the door of the lodge, and saw at a little distance the enraged bear coming on with slow but great leaps. The old man closed the door.

"Yes," said he; "he is indeed a great manito. My grandchildren, you will be the cause of my losing my life. You asked my protection, and I granted it; so now, come what may, I will protect you. When the bear arrives at the door you must run out at the other end of the lodge."

Putting his hand to the side of the lodge where he sat, he took down a bag, and, opening it, took out of it two small black dogs, which he placed before him.

"These are the ones I use when I fight," said he, and he commenced patting with both hands the sides of one of the dogs, which at once commenced to swell out until it filled the lodge, and it had great strong teeth. When the dog had attained its full size it growled, and, springing out at the door, met the bear, which, in another leap, would have reached the lodge. A terrible combat ensued. The sky rang with the howls of the monsters. In a little while the second dog took the field. At the commencement of the battle the brothers, acting on the advice of the old man, escaped through the opposite side of the lodge. They had not proceeded far in their flight before they heard the death-cry of one of the dogs, and soon after that of the other.

"Well," said the leader, "the old man will soon share their fate, so run, run! the bear will soon be after us."

The brothers started with fresh vigour, for the old man had refreshed them with food; but the bear very soon came in sight again, and was evidently fast gaining upon them. Again the leader asked the warriors if they knew of any way in which to save themselves. All were silent. Running forward with a yell and a howl, the leader said—

"I dreamed once that, being in great trouble, an old man, who was a manito, helped me. We shall soon see his lodge."

Taking courage, the brothers still went on, and, after going a short distance, they saw a lodge. Entering it, they found an old man, whose protection they claimed, saying that a manito was pursuing them.

"Eat," said the old man, putting meat before them. "Who is a manito? There is no manito but me. There is none whom I fear."

Then he felt the earth tremble as the bear approached, and, opening the door of the lodge, he saw it coming. The old man shut the door slowly, and said—

"Yes, my grandchildren, you have brought trouble upon me."

Taking his medicine sack, he took out some small war-clubs of black stone, and told the young men to run through the other side of the lodge. As he handled the clubs they became an enormous size, and the old man stepped out as the bear reached the door. He struck the beast with one of his clubs, which broke in pieces, and the bear stumbled. The old man struck it again with the other club, and that also broke, but the bear fell insensible. Each blow the old man struck sounded like a clap of thunder, and the howls of the bear ran along the skies.

The brothers had gone some distance before they looked back. They then saw that the bear was recovering from the blows. First it moved its paws, and then they saw it rise to its feet. The old man shared the fate of the first, for the warriors heard his cries as he was torn in pieces. Again the monster was in pursuit, and fast overtaking them. Not yet discouraged, the young men kept on their way, but the bear was so close to them that the leader once more applied to his brothers, but they could do nothing.

"Well," said he, "my dreams will soon be exhausted. After this I have but one more."

He advanced, invoking his guardian spirit to aid him.

"Once," said he, "I dreamed that, being sorely pressed, I came to a large lake, on the shore of which was a canoe, partly out of water, and having ten paddles all in readiness. Do not fear," he cried, "we shall soon get to it."

It happened as he had said. Coming to the lake, the warriors found the canoe with the ten paddles, and immediately took their places in it. Putting off, they paddled to the centre of the lake, when they saw the bear on the shore. Lifting itself on its hind-legs, it looked all around. Then it waded into the water until, losing its footing, it turned back, and commenced making the circuit of the lake. Meanwhile the warriors remained stationary in the centre watching the animal's movements. It travelled round till it came to the place whence it started. Then it commenced drinking up the water, and the young men saw a strong current fast setting in towards the bear's mouth. The leader encouraged them to paddle hard for the opposite shore. This they had nearly reached, when the current became too strong for them, and they were drawn back by it, and the stream carried them onwards to the bear.

Then the leader again spoke, telling his comrades to meet their fate bravely.

"Now is the time, Mudjikewis," said he, "to show your prowess. Take courage, and sit in the bow of the canoe, and, when it approaches the bear's mouth, try what effect your club will have on the beast's head."

Mudjikewis obeyed, and, taking his place, stood ready to give the blow, while the leader, who steered, directed the canoe to the open mouth of the monster.

Rapidly advancing, the canoe was just about to enter the bear's mouth, when Mudjikewis struck the beast a tremendous blow on the head, and gave the saw-saw-quan. The bear's limbs doubled under it, and it fell stunned by the blow, but before Mudjikewis could strike again the monster sent from its mouth all the water it had swallowed with such force that the canoe was immediately carried by the stream to the other side of the lake. Leaving the canoe, the brothers fled, and on they went till they were completely exhausted. Again they felt the earth shake, and, looking back, saw the monster hard after them. The young men's spirits drooped, and they felt faint-hearted. With words and actions the leader exerted himself to cheer them, and once more he asked them if they could do nothing, or think of nothing, that might save them. All were silent as before.

"Then," said he, "this is the last time I can apply to my guardian spirit. If we do not now succeed, our fate is decided."

He ran forward, invoking his spirit with great earnestness, and gave the yell.

"We shall soon arrive," said he to his brothers, "at the place where my last guardian spirit dwells. In him I place great confidence. Do not be afraid, or your limbs will be fear-bound. We shall soon reach his lodge. Run, run!"

What had in the meantime passed in the lodge of Iamo? He had remained in the same condition, his head in the sack, directing his sister where to place the arrows to procure food, and speaking at long intervals.

One day the girl saw the eyes of the head brighten as if with pleasure. At last it spoke.

"O sister!" it said, "in what a pitiful situation you have been the cause of placing me! Soon, very soon, a band of young men will arrive and apply to me for aid; but alas! how can I give what I would with so much pleasure have afforded them? Nevertheless, take two arrows, and place them where you have been in the habit of placing the others, and have meat cooked and prepared before they arrive. When you hear them coming, and calling on my name, go out and say, 'Alas! it is long ago since an accident befell him. I was the cause of it.' If they still come near, ask them in, and set meat before them. Follow my directions strictly. A bear will come. Go out and meet him, taking my medicine sack, bow and arrows, and my head. You must then untie the sack, and spread out before you my paints of all colours, my war eagle-feathers, my tufts of dried hair, and whatsoever else the sack contains. As the bear approaches take these articles, one by one, and say to him, 'This is my dead brother's paint,' and so on with all the articles, throwing each of them as far from you as you can. The virtue contained in the things will cause him to totter. Then, to complete his destruction, you must take my head and cast it as far off as you can, crying aloud, 'See, this is my dead brother's head!' He will then fall senseless. While this is taking place the young men will have eaten, and you must call them to your aid. You will, with their assistance, cut the carcass of the bear into pieces—into small pieces—and scatter them to the winds, for unless you do this he will again come to life."

The sister promised that all should be done as he commanded, and she had only time to prepare the meal when the voice of the leader of the band of warriors was heard calling on Iamo for aid. The girl went out and did as she had been directed. She invited the brothers in and placed meat before them, and while they were eating the bear was heard approaching. Untying the medicine sack and taking the head the girl made all ready for its approach. When it came up she did as her brother directed, and before she had cast down all the paints the bear began to totter, but, still advancing, came close to her. Then she took the head and cast it from her as far as she could, and as it rolled upon the ground the bear, tottering, fell with a tremendous noise. The girl cried for help, and the young men rushed out.

Mudjikewis, stepping up, gave a yell, and struck the bear a blow on the head. This he repeated till he had dashed out its brains. Then the others, as quickly as possible, cut the monster up into very small pieces and scattered them in all directions. As they were engaged in this they were surprised to find that wherever the flesh was thrown small black bears appeared, such as are seen at the present day, which, starting up, ran away. Thus from this monster the present race of bears derives its origin.

Having overcome their pursuer the brothers returned to the lodge, and the girl gathered together the articles she had used, and placed the head in the sack again. The head remained silent, probably from its being fatigued with its exertion in overcoming the bear.

Having spent so much time, and having traversed so vast a country in their flight, the young men gave up the idea of ever returning to their own country, and game being plentiful about the lodge, they determined to remain where they were. One day they moved off some distance from the lodge for the purpose of hunting, and left the belt with the girl. They were very successful, and amused themselves with talking and jesting. One of them said—

"We have all this sport to ourselves. Let us go and ask our sister if she will not let us bring the head to this place, for it is still alive."

So they went and asked for the head. The girl told them to take it, and they carried it to their hunting-grounds and tried to amuse it, but only at times did they see its eyes beam with pleasure. One day, while they were busy in their encampments, they were unexpectedly attacked by unknown enemies. The fight was long and fierce. Many of the foes were slain, but there were thirty of them to each warrior. The young men fought desperately till they were all killed, and then the attacking party retreated to a high place to muster their men and count the missing and the slain. One of the men had strayed away, and happened to come to where the head was hung up. Seeing that it was alive he eyed it for some time with fear and surprise. Then he took it down, and having opened the sack he was much pleased to see the beautiful feathers, one of which he placed on his head.

It waved gracefully over him as he walked to his companions' camp, and when he came there he threw down the head and sack and told his friends how he had found them, and how the sack was full of paints and feathers. The men all took the head and made sport of it. Many of the young men took the paint and painted themselves with it; and one of the band, taking the head by the hair, said—

"Look, you ugly thing, and see your paints on the faces of warriors."

The feathers were so beautiful that many of the young men placed them on their heads, and they again subjected the head to all kinds of indignity. They were, however, soon punished for their insulting conduct, for all who had worn the feathers became sick and died. Then the chief commanded the men to throw all the paints and feathers away.

"As for the head," he said, "we will keep that and take it home with us; we will there see what we can do with it. We will try to make it shut its eyes."

Meanwhile for several days the sister had been waiting for the brothers to bring back the head; till at last, getting impatient, she went in search of them. She found them lying within short distances of one another, dead, and covered with wounds. Other bodies lay scattered around. She searched for the head and sack, but they were nowhere to be found, so she raised her voice and wept, and blackened her face. Then she walked in different directions till she came to the place whence the head had been taken, and there she found the bow and arrows, which had been left behind. She searched further, hoping to find her brother's head, and, when she came to a piece of rising ground she found some of his paints and feathers. These she carefully put by, hanging them to the branch of a tree.

At dusk she came to the first lodge of a large village. Here she used a charm employed by Indians when they wish to meet with a kind reception, and on applying to the old man and the woman who occupied the lodge she was made welcome by them. She told them her errand, and the old man, promising to help her, told her that the head was hung up before the council fire, and that the chiefs and young men of the village kept watch over it continually. The girl said she only desired to see the head, and would be satisfied if she could only get to the door of the lodge in which it was hung, for she knew she could not take it by force.

"Come with me," said the old man, "I will take you there."

So they went and took their seats in the lodge near to the door.

The council lodge was filled with warriors amusing themselves with games, and constantly keeping up the fire to smoke the head to dry it. As the girl entered the lodge the men saw the features of the head move, and, not knowing what to make of it, one spoke and said—

"Ha! ha! it is beginning to feel the effects of the smoke."

The sister looked up from the seat by the door; her eyes met those of her brother, and tears began to roll down the cheeks of the head.

"Well," said the chief, "I thought we would make you do something at last. Look! look at it shedding tears," said he to those around him, and they all laughed and made jokes upon it. The chief, looking around, observed the strange girl, and after some time said to the old man who brought her in—

"Who have you got there? I have never seen that woman before in our village."

"Yes," replied the old man, "you have seen her. She is a relation of mine, and seldom goes out. She stays in my lodge, and she asked me to bring her here."

In the centre of the lodge sat one of those young men who are always forward, and fond of boasting and displaying themselves before others.

"Why," said he, "I have seen her often, and it is to his lodge I go almost every night to court her."

All the others laughed and continued their games. The young man did not know he was telling a lie to the girl's advantage, who by means of it escaped.

She returned to the old man's lodge, and immediately set out for her own country. Coming to the spot where the bodies of her adopted brothers lay, she placed them together with their feet towards the east. Then taking an axe she had she cast it up into the air, crying out—

"Brothers, get up from under it or it will fall on you!"

This she repeated three times, and the third time all the brothers rose and stood on their feet. Mudjikewis commenced rubbing his eyes and stretching himself.

"Why," said he, "I have overslept myself."

"No, indeed," said one of the others. "Do you not know we were all killed, and that it is our sister who has brought us to life?"

The brothers then took the bodies of their enemies and burned them. Soon after the girl went to a far country, they knew not where, to procure wives for them, and she returned with the women, whom she gave to the young men, beginning with the eldest. Mudjikewis stepped to and fro, uneasy lest he should not get the one he liked, but he was not disappointed, for she fell to his lot; and the two were well matched, for she was a female magician.

The young men and their wives all moved into a very large lodge, and their sister told them that one of the women must go in turns every night to try and recover the head of her brother, untying the knots by which it was hung up in the council lodge. The women all said they would go with pleasure. The eldest made the first attempt. With a rushing noise she disappeared through the air.

Towards daylight she returned. She had failed, having only succeeded in untying one of the knots. All the women save the youngest went in turn, and each one succeeded in untying only one knot each time. At length the youngest went. As soon as she arrived at the lodge she went to work. The smoke from the fire in the lodge had not ascended for ten nights. It now filled the place and drove all the men out. The girl was alone, and she carried off the head.

The brothers and Iamo's sister heard the young woman coming high through the air, and they heard her say—

"Prepare the body of our brother."

As soon as they heard that they went to where Iamo's body lay, and, having got it ready, as soon as the young woman arrived with the head they placed it to the body, and Iamo was restored in all his former manliness and beauty. All rejoiced in the happy termination of their troubles, and when they had spent some time joyfully together, Iamo said—

"Now I will divide the treasure," and taking the bear's belt he commenced dividing what it contained amongst the brothers, beginning with the eldest. The youngest brother, however, got the most splendid part of the spoil, for the bottom of the belt held what was richest and rarest.

Then Iamo told them that, since they had all died and been restored to life again, they were no longer mortals but spirits, and he assigned to each of them a station in the invisible world. Only Mudjikewis' place was, however, named. He was to direct the west wind. The brothers were commanded, as they had it in their power, to do good to the inhabitants of the earth, and to give all things with a liberal hand.

The spirits then, amid songs and shouts, took their flight to their respective places, while Iamo and his sister, Iamoqua, descended into the depths below.

THE MAN WHO SHOT A GHOST

In the olden time, a man was travelling alone, and in a forest he killed several rabbits. After sunset he was in the midst of the forest. He had to spend the night there, so he made a fire.

He thought this: "Should I meet any danger by and by, I will shoot. I am a man who ought not to regard anything."

He cooked a rabbit, so he was no longer hungry. Just then he heard many voices. They were talking about their own affairs. But the man could see no one.

So he thought: "It seems now that at last I have encountered ghosts."

Then he went and lay under a fallen tree, which was a great distance from the fire. They came around him and whistled, "Hyu! hyu! hyu!"

"He has gone yonder," said one of the ghosts. Then they came and stood around the man, just as people do when they hunt rabbits. The man lay flat beneath the fallen tree, and one ghost came and climbed on the trunk of that tree. Suddenly the ghost gave the cry that a man does when he hits an enemy, "A-he!" Then the ghost kicked the man in the back.

Before the ghost could get away, very suddenly the man shot at him and wounded him in the legs. So the ghost cried as men do in pain, "Au! au! au!" At last he went off, crying as women do, "Yun! yun! yun! yun!"

The other ghosts said to him, "Where did he shoot?"

The wounded ghost said, "He shot me through the head and I have come apart." Then the other ghosts were wailing on the hillside.

The man decided he would go to the place where the ghosts were wailing. So when day came, he went there. He found some graves. Into one of them a wolf had dug, so that the bones could be seen; and there was a wound in the skull.

THE WOMAN OF STONE

In one of the niches or recesses formed by a precipice in the cavern of Kickapoo Creek, which is a tributary of the Wisconsin, there is a gigantic mass of stone presenting the appearance of a human figure. It is so sheltered by the overhanging rocks and by the sides of the recess in which it stands as to assume a dark and gloomy character. Of the figure the following legend is related:—

Once upon a time there lived a woman who was called Shenanska, or the White Buffalo Robe. She was an inhabitant of the prairie, a dweller in the cabins which stand upon the verge of the hills. She was the pride of her people, not only for her beauty, which was very great, but for her goodness. The breath of the summer wind was not milder than the temper of Shenanska, the face of the sun was not fairer than her countenance.

At length the tribe was surprised in its encampment on the banks of the Kickapoo by a numerous band of the fierce Mengwe. Many of them fell fighting bravely, the greater part of the women and children were made prisoners, and the others fled to the wilds for safety. It was the fortune of Shenanska to escape from death or captivity. When the alarm of the war-whoop reached her ear as she was sleeping in her lodge with her husband, she had rushed forth with him and gone with the braves to meet their assailants. When she saw half of the men of her nation lying dead around, then she fled. She had been wounded in the battle, but she still succeeded in effecting her escape to the hills. Weakened by loss of blood, she had not strength enough left to hunt for a supply of food, and she was near perishing with hunger.

While she lay beneath the shade of a tree there came to her a being not of this world.

"Shenanska," said he, in a gentle voice, "thou art wounded and hungry, shall I heal thee and feed thee? Wilt thou return to the lands of thy tribe and live to be old, a widow and alone, or go now to the land of departed spirits and join the shade of thy husband? The choice is thine. If thou wilt live, crippled, and bowed down by wounds and disease, thou mayest. If it would please thee better to rejoin thy friends in the country beyond the Great River, say so."

Shenanska replied that she wished to die. The spirit took her, and placed her in one of the recesses of the cavern, overshadowed by hanging rocks. He then spoke some words in a low voice, and, breathing on her, she became stone. Determined that a woman so good and beautiful should not be forgotten by the world, he made her into a statue, to which he gave the power of killing suddenly any one who irreverently approached it. For a long time the statue relentlessly exercised this power. Many an unconscious Indian, venturing too near to it, fell dead without any perceptible wound. At length, tired of the havoc the statue made, the guardian spirit took away the power he had given to it. At this day the statue may be approached with safety, but the Indians hold it in fear, not intruding rashly upon it, and when in its presence treating it with great respect.

THE INDIAN WHO WRESTLED WITH A GHOST

A young Teton man went alone on the warpath. At length he reached a wood. One day, as he was going along, he heard a voice. He said, "I shall have company." As he was approaching a forest, he heard some one halloo. Behold, it was an owl.

By and by he drew near another wood, and as night was coming on he lay down to rest. At the edge of the trees he lay down in the open air. At midnight he was aroused by the voice of a woman. She was wailing, "My son! my son!" Still he remained where he was, and put more wood on the fire. He lay with his back to the fire. He tore a hole in his blanket large enough to peep through.

Soon he heard twigs break under the feet of one approaching, so he looked through his blanket without rising. Behold, a woman of the olden days was coming. She wore a skin dress with long fringe. A buffalo robe was fastened around her at the waist. Her necklace was of very large beads, and her leggings were covered with beads or porcupine work. Her robe was drawn over her head and she was snuffing as she came.

The man lay with his legs stretched out, and she stood by him. She took him by one foot, which she raised very slowly. When she let it go, it fell with a thud as though he were dead. She raised it a second time; then a third time. Still the man did not move. Then the woman pulled a very rusty knife from the front of her belt, seized his foot suddenly and was about to lift it and cut it, when up sprang the man. He said, "What are you doing?" Then he shot at her suddenly. She ran into the forest screaming, "Yun! yun! yun! yun! yun!" She plunged into the forest and was seen no more.

Again the man covered his head with his blanket but he did not sleep. When day came, he raised his eyes. Behold, there was a burial scaffold, with the blankets all ragged and dangling. He thought, "Was this the ghost that came to me?"

Again he came to a wood where he had to remain for the night. He started a fire. As he sat there, suddenly he heard someone singing. He made the woods ring. The man shouted to the singer, but no answer was paid. The man had a small quantity of wasna, which was grease mixed with pounded buffalo meat, and wild cherry; he also had plenty of tobacco.

So when the singer came and asked him for food, the man said, "I have nothing." The ghost said, "Not so; I know you have some wasna."

Then the man gave some of it to the ghost and filled his pipe. After the meal, when the stranger took the pipe and held it by the stem, the traveler saw that it was nothing but bones. There was no flesh. Then the stranger's robe dropped back from his shoulders. Behold, all his ribs were visible. There was no flesh on them. The ghost did not open his lips when he smoked. The smoke came pouring out through his ribs.

When he had finished smoking, the ghost said, "Ho! we must wrestle together. If you can throw me, you shall kill the enemy without hindrance and steal some horses."

The young man agreed. But first he threw an armful of brush on the fire. He put plenty of brush near the fire.

Then the ghost rushed at the man. He seized him with his bony hands, which was very painful; but this mattered not. The man tried to push off the ghost, whose legs were very powerful. When the ghost was pulled near the fire, he became weak; but when he pulled the young man toward the darkness, he became strong. As the fire got low, the strength of the ghost increased. Just as the man began to get weary, the day broke. Then the struggle began again. As they drew near the fire again, the man made a last effort; with his foot he pushed more brush into the fire. The fire blazed up again suddenly. Then the ghost fell, just as if he was coming to pieces.

So the man won in wrestling. Also he killed his enemy and stole some horses. It came out just as the ghost said. That is why people believe what ghosts say.

THE GHOST'S RESENTMENT

Long, long ago, a Dakota died and his parents made a death lodge for him on the bluff. In the lodge they made a grave scaffold, on which they laid the body of their son.

Now in that same village of Dakotas lived a young married man. His father lived with him, and there were two old men who used to visit the father and smoke with him, and talk with him about many things.

One night the father of the young man said, "My friends, let us go to the death scaffold and cut off summer robes for ourselves from the tent skins."

The young man said, "No! Do not do so. It was a pity the young man died, and as his parents had nothing else to give up for him they made the death lodge and left it there."

"What use can he get from the tent?" asked the father. "We have no robes, so we wish to use part of the tent skins for ourselves."

"Well, then," said the young man. "Go as you have said and we shall see what will happen."

The old men arose without saying a word and went to the lodge on the bluff. As soon as they were gone, the young man said, "Oh, wife, get my piece of white clay. I must scare one of those old men nearly to death."

But the woman was unwilling, saying, "Let them alone. They have no robes. Let them cut off robes for themselves."

But as the husband would not stop talking about it, the wife got the piece of white clay for him. He whitened his whole body and his face and hands. Then he went to the lodge in a course parallel to that taken by the old men. He went very quickly and reached there before they did.

He climbed the scaffold and lay on it, thrusting his head out through the tent skins just above the doorway.

At last the old men approached, ascending the hill, and talking together in a low tone. The young man lay still, listening to them. When they reached the lodge, they sat down.

The leader said, "Fill your pipe, friends. We must smoke this last time with our friend up there."

"Yes, your friend has spoken well. That should be done," answered one of them.

So he filled the pipe. He drew a whiff, and when the fire glowed, he turned the pipe stem toward the seam of the skins above the doorway. He looked up towards the sky, saying, "Ho, friend, here is the pipe. We must smoke with you this last time. And then we must separate. Here is the pipe."

As he said this, he gazed above the doorway and saw a head looking out from the tent.

"Oh! My friends!" he cried. "Look at this place behind you."

When the two looked, they said, "Really! Friends, it is he!" And all fled.

Then the young man leaped down and pursued them. Two of them fell to the ground in terror, but he did not disturb them, going on in pursuit of his father. When the old man was overtaken, he fell to the ground. He was terrified. The young man sat astride of him. He said, "You have been very disobedient! Fill the pipe for me!"

The old man said, "Oh! My grandchild! Oh! My grandchild!" hoping that the ghost would pity him. Then he filled the pipe as he lay stretched there and gave it to his son.

The young man smoked. When he stopped smoking, the old man said, "Oh! My grandchild! Oh! My grandchild! Pity me, and let me go. We thought we must smoke with you this last time, so we went to the place where you were. Oh! My grandchild, pity me."

"If that be so, arise and extend your hands to me in entreaty," said the young man.

The old man arose and did so, saying continually, "Oh! My grandchild! Oh! My grandchild!"

It was as much as the young man could do to keep from laughing. At length he said, "Well! Begone! Beware lest you come again and go around my resting place very often! Do not visit it again!" Then he let the old man go.

On returning to the burial lodge, he found the two old men still lying where they had fallen. When he approached them, they slipped off, with their heads covered, as they were terrified, and he let them go undisturbed. When they had gone, the young man hurried home. He reached there first and after washing himself, reclined at full length.

He said to his wife, "When they return, be sure not to laugh. Make an effort to control yourself. I came very near making them die of fright."

When the old men returned, the young people seemed to be asleep. The old men did not lie down; all sat in silence, smoking together until daylight. When the young man arose in the morning, the old men appeared very sorrowful.

Then he said, "Give me one of the robes that you and your

friends cut off and brought back. I, too, have no robe at all."

His father said, "Why! We went there, but we did not get anything at all. We were attacked. We came very near being killed."

To this the son replied, "Why! I was unwilling for this to happen, so I said, 'Do not go,' but you paid no attention to me, and went. But now you think differently and you weep."

When it was night, the young man said, "Go again and make another attempt. Bring back a piece for me, as I have no robe at all."

The old men were unwilling to go again, and they lost their patience, as he teased them so often.

LOVE & MARRIAGE

Though **love and marriage** have obviously had a part to play in other stories already related in this book, the following tales exemplify the typical themes and treatment of these subjects. This does not mean, of course, that all stories about such things were happy ones, as seen in 'Moowis, the Snow-husband'. Whilst these stories were a way to explore and explain human relationships with each other; as we have already seen with animal marriages, relationships were not exclusively between humans, serving to also explore mankind's relationship with nature on a very spiritual level.

MOOWIS, THE SNOW-HUSBAND

In **a northern village** of the Algonquin tribe there lived a young maiden whose exquisite beauty had won her great fame throughout the region. Every day a whole host of admirers made their way to her father's lodge hoping for an opportunity to feast their eyes on the beautiful young woman. The path to his door was now so well worn, the old man had often considered sending his daughter away but, at the same time, he was fiercely proud of his child and was certain that one day a deserving young warrior would appear and carry her off as his bride.

The young maiden was not so easily satisfied, however, and as the months passed by, she became more and more conscious of her charms, treating her suitors as mere playthings no matter how sincere their intentions towards her. One noble brave, in particular, greatly desired to take the young maiden for his wife. He was of a very kind and sensitive nature, and it was many weeks before he managed to pluck up the courage to visit her at her father's lodge. Kneeling before the beautiful girl, he poured forth from the depths of his soul every agonizing detail of his passion, revealing that he could no longer sleep for love of her, nor partake of any activity without heaviness in his heart. But the young maiden laughed aloud to hear all of this and, failing to consider the appalling cruelty of her response, called to a group of friends nearby and carried on loudly mocking her rejected lover.

By sundown, the entire village had been informed of the morning's events and the noble brave was forced to retire to the solitude of his lodge, overwhelmed by feelings of shame and humiliation. A deep melancholy invaded his spirit and for days on end he remained seated in a fixed position, staring blankly at the walls and refusing to eat, drink or speak. Even when his family and friends began making preparations for the annual migration to their summer camp, he refused to join them, but took to his couch instead, where he lay completely still even as his possessions were packed up for transport around him.

At last, when his family had moved off into the distance and all was silent, the young brave began praying earnestly to his manitto (a potent spirit), calling for his assistance in a plot to avenge himself on the maiden who had shunned and disgraced him. Before long, his prayer was answered, for his despondency began to ease and he felt impelled to move from lodge to lodge gathering up old scraps of cloth and personal ornaments left behind by his tribe. He took whatever he could find of these items outdoors and began sewing them into a coat and leggings which he trimmed elaborately with beads and feathers. Then he cast around him for any left-over animal bones and, after he had assembled these in the form of a human skeleton, began coating them with snow, pressing and smoothing it with his fingers until he had moulded the shape of a tall and handsome man. Again, he called upon his manitto for aid and, breathing upon the image, brought it to life. Next, he placed a bow and arrows in its hands and stood back to admire his creation of snow and rags.

'I will call you Moowis,' said the young man, delighted by the figure. 'Come handsome stranger, follow me, and I will explain to you why you have been sent here and how you are destined to help me.'

The two walked forward together in the direction of the tribe's summer camp. Their arrival generated tremendous excitement, not only because people were pleased to see the young brave returned to health, but also because they all desired to know the identity of his elegant companion. The chief of the tribe immediately invited the stranger to feast with his family that evening, while all the maidens of the camp lined up to catch even the slightest glimpse of him.

None was so infatuated by the striking visitor as the beautiful young maiden who had so haughtily refused the noble brave. Confidently, she strode forward and requested the company of her discarded lover and his companion at her lodge early that same afternoon. The two appeared at the appointed time and it seemed as if a transformation had occurred in the maiden, for she could not do enough to please the handsome stranger, even urging him to take up her father's place in the most comfortable chair by the fire. Not wishing to run the risk of melting during the visit, Moowis refused her kind offer, but this in itself was interpreted as the most humble and magnanimous of gestures. The noble brave smiled to see these things, for he knew that his plan was unfolding nicely and that, before long, the tribe would be celebrating a wedding feast.

On the following day, Moowis announced his intention to marry the beautiful young maiden and within a week the chief had proclaimed the couple man and wife. They remained very happy together for a short time, but then, one morning, Moowis turned to his wife and, gathering up his bow and arrows, declared that he must depart on a long and arduous journey.

'May I not come with you?' his wife pleaded.

But Moowis had been instructed by the young brave not to allow her to accompany him as punishment for her cruel actions towards him.

'The way is too difficult and dangerous,' Moowis told his bride. 'It is far better for you that you remain behind.'

'But there are no dangers I would not fully share with you,' she responded, stirring a wave of pity within her husband's breast. Disturbed and confused, Moowis went to his master's lodge and related to him his wife's request.

'It is good to see that she is so devoted to you,' the noble brave answered him, 'but she has never listened to the voice of prudence and still she will not listen. It is her own folly that drives her to accompany you and now she must submit to her fate.'

A rough and rugged road lay ahead for the newly wedded pair. The beautiful young wife was unaccustomed to hardship of any kind and it was not long before she had fallen behind, her feet torn and bleeding from the severe uphill struggle. Moowis continued his rapid pace, passing through thick, shady trees until he reached the broad, open plains. He had been long out of sight when the first rays of sun began to disperse the dull, grey clouds overhead, gradually warming the air and causing the snow to melt under his feet. Soon he observed a number of tiny glass beads appear on his white body, gently rolling to the ground through his fingers which had begun wasting away to reveal ivory-coloured bones. Moowis was helpless to prevent himself melting in the heat and, as he slowly dissolved, his splendid garments began to disintegrate also, dropping piece by piece on to the green grass below.

At length, the young bride arose and resumed her gruelling pursuit, crossing over rocks and marshland, until eventually she encountered fragments of clothing scattered on the earth. Quickly recognizing the tattered garments to be those of her husband, she was thrown into a frenzy of concern, but then, believing that some trick had been played on her, she began crying out:

'Moowis! Moowis! Nin ge won e win ig; ne won e wig!' (You have led me astray; I cannot find my way.) But the young wife received no reply. Now frantic with fear, she began running about wildly, through the forests, among the thickets, over the rocks, in every possible direction, hoping to catch sight of her handsome husband walking in the distance.

The years passed and still she roamed the countryside, calling aloud to the air, her face lined with exhaustion, her body stooped and twisted in sorrow. On and on she wandered until the day finally arrived for her to be released from her punishment. Falling wearily to the ground, she uttered her husband's name one last time before passing away. In an instant, her spirit rose from her body, ascending high above the spot in the deep recesses of the wood where she had eventually come to rest. But even to this day, it is said that her unhappy voice is often heard on the breeze, calling through the trees in search of her snow-husband:

'Moowis! Moowis! Nin ge won e win ig; ne won e wig!'

OSSEO, SON OF EVENING STAR

There once lived a tribal chief who had ten daughters, all of whom turned out to be extremely beautiful young women. None was more captivating, however, than the very youngest daughter, the chief's favourite, who was named Oweenee. Unlike her sisters, Oweenee was both spirited and independent, and nothing delighted her more than to do what was least expected of her. She loved, for instance, to roam the open countryside while the rain pelted down upon her, or to run barefoot through the camp in winter, paying little or no heed to the raw, biting cold.

Her elder sisters had all found husbands for themselves and now they were keen that Oweenee should follow their example and choose for herself a man who might succeed in taming her wild and unpredictable nature. Oweenee had rejected many suitors in the past and seemed deaf to all proposals, until the day she set eyes on Osseo, a feeble old man, scarcely able to walk, whose offer of marriage had been refused by every other single woman of her tribe. Oweenee cared only for the fact that Osseo was a kind, devout man who remained obedient in all things to the Great Spirit. It did not trouble her that his walking stick appeared to be his only material possession, or that he was decrepit and his body almost bent in two. Graciously, she decided to accept him as her husband, resolving to care for him as best she could until the day when death would force them to separate.

The announcement that the couple would soon marry was greeted by a chorus of laughter. The nine remaining sisters, each of whom considered their own husbands fine and handsome young men, made a special mockery of Osseo's walking stick and referred derisively to the old man as 'the great timber-chief'.

'He may not carry an elaborately carved staff of precious wood,' Oweenee challenged them, 'but if his simple stick supports him as he walks, then it is of more value to me than all the forests of the north.'

And she never failed to show her husband the greatest respect, which he always returned, teaching her that real love was above all circumstance of physical beauty.

The time was drawing near for the great annual feast in honour of Evening Star. A large party would soon gather at a chosen lodge for celebrations that were set to continue into the small hours. It was an occasion demanding the stamina of youth, but Oweenee would not be put off by the jibes and sneers of the other guests who maintained that her husband would not even survive the short journey to the festivities. Hand in hand, the two set off together, pausing as often as necessary for Osseo to catch his breath.

Presently, they passed a large hollow log where Osseo began muttering to himself, his eyes raised towards the sky. One of the elder sisters overheard the words, 'pity me, my father' and, turning to her husband, she declared furiously:

'Look at him, the silly old fool, praying to the air. It would be a blessing if he should fall down now and break his puny neck. Then, at least, my sister would have the chance to marry a younger, more deserving man.'

She had scarcely finished her tirade before Osseo gave a loud, piercing cry and as he fell trembling to the earth, he was transformed into a beautiful youth with dark, shining hair and a flawless complexion. He stood up regally, proud and ready to greet his beautiful young wife, but to his horror he discovered that their fate had been reversed and that Oweenee stood old and shrivelled before him, clinging to the simple wooden staff he no longer needed.

It was now Osseo's turn to bestow on his wife the love and devotion she had so generously shown him. Carefully, he guided her along the path towards the feast, gazing fondly into her eyes, not noticing the thousands of creases that surrounded them.

When at length they arrived at the lodge, the celebrations were well under way and they took up their places at the end of the table, filling the last two remaining seats. Although the meat was of the finest quality and the fruit of a most delicious fragrance, Osseo would not be persuaded to sample anything that was placed in front of him. He had fallen into a sombre mood, his heart torn apart with sorrow, and as he looked towards his aged wife, he could not prevent his eyes brimming with tears.

Suddenly, in the distance, the sound of a strange, ethereal voice was heard on the air, becoming louder and plainer until its words were clearly distinguishable.

'My son,' the voice spoke gently, 'I have come to call you away from this life filled with pain and sorrow. I see that you have suffered cruelty and abuse, but you will be a victim no more, for the Power of Evil, which condemned you to this wretched earthly domain has now been overcome.

'Ascend, my son, ascend into the skies, know that it is your father, Evening Star, who beckons you. Bring those you love with you and partake of the feast I have prepared for you in the stars.

'Doubt not and delay not. Eat the food that has been put before you, for it is enchanted and will bring you the gift of immortality. No longer will your kettles be moulded from the earth, no longer will your bowls be made of wood. They shall be made of silver and shine like fire. Your wife and those around you shall take on the radiance of stars and become transformed into magnificent birds of the air. They shall dance and never work, they shall sing and never cry. Come, it is time for you to return to happiness and to your celestial reward.'

The lodge began to shake violently as it rose up into the air. Peering through the windows, Osseo observed that they were already high above the tree-tops, moving swiftly in the direction of the clouds. His parents and brothers, his friends and relatives, even Oweenee's sisters who had treated him so unkindly, now soared through the windows into the night air, their wings extended in ecstatic flight, their bodies covered in the most glorious plumage. Oweenee rose and stood by her husband's side, no longer a fragile old woman, but more beautiful than ever before, dressed in a robe of green silk, with silver feathers plaited into her long, silken tresses.

Evening Star waited patiently to greet his son and beamed brightly to see the couple approach. Everything that would make it easier for them to settle into their new home was speedily provided. Then, when he was certain that their every wish had been attended to, the father called for his son to visit him and began conversing with him earnestly.

'My son,' said the old man, 'hang that cage of birds which you have brought with you at the door for protection and I will tell you why you have been sent for.'

Osseo obeyed his father's command and took a seat next to him in the lodge.

'The Power of Evil which transformed you and your beautiful wife into frail and withered creatures lives in the lodge to the left of mine. He is known as the Small Star, a wicked spirit, who has always felt envious of our family because of our greater power. I have removed the curse he placed on you, but I cannot guarantee that he will not try to harm you again. A single ray of his light serves as his bow and arrow, and all of you must be careful not to let the light of his beams fall on you while you are here with me, for those beams contain the source of his enchantment.'

Osseo and Oweenee remained faithful to Evening Star's wishes and lived a happy and peaceful life, enriched by the birth of their son who was the very likeness of his father. The boy, always hungry for knowledge and adventure, quickly mastered every celestial skill his grandfather taught him, but he wished, more than anything, to learn the art of using a bow and arrow, for he had heard that it was the favourite pursuit of all men on the earth below. Osseo agreed that his son was now old enough to begin hunting and presented him with the weapon he had himself used as a youth. Then, he began releasing into the air some of the birds from the cage hanging by the lodge, instructing his son to practise his shooting on them.

He little imagined that the child would be successful, but the young boy became quite expert after only a few attempts, and in no time at all one of the birds plummeted to the ground. But when he went to retrieve his catch, to his amazement the boy discovered that it had changed to a beautiful woman, his young aunt, who lay with an arrow he did not recognize as his own protruding from her breast.

As soon as her blood fell upon the surface of the pure and spotless Evening Star, the charm which had allowed Osseo and his family to remain there in safety was immediately dissolved. The boy suddenly found himself sinking through the lower clouds until he landed upon a large, rocky island. Looking upwards, he saw all his aunts and uncles following him in the shape of birds, and in mid-air he caught sight of a silver lodge descending gracefully to the earth in which his mother and father were seated.

The lodge came to rest on the steepest cliff of the island and as soon as each of them touched the soil they resumed their natural shape. They could never now return to the skies, but Evening Star still watched over them and, wishing to help them preserve their immortality, he reduced them all to the size of fairies.

From that day forward they lived quite happily among the rocks, never failing on a summer's evening to join hands and dance upon the summit of the cliff as a mark of respect to Evening Star. Their shimmering silver lodge can always be seen on a starry night when the moon is full and its beams touch the horizon. Fishermen who climb the high cliffs at night say they have heard very clearly the merry voices of Osseo, Oweenee and the other little dancers, and because of this they have christened the island Mish-in-e-nok-inokong, land of Little Spirits.

THE FIRE PLUME

Wassamo was living with his parents on the shores of a large bay on the east coast of Lake Michigan. It was at a period when nature spontaneously furnished everything that was wanted, when the Indians used skins for clothing, and flints for arrow heads. It was long before the time that the flag of the white man had first been seen in these lakes, or the sound of an iron axe had been heard. The skill of our people supplied them with weapons to kill game, with instruments to procure bark for their canoes, and they knew to dress and cook their victuals.

One day, when the season had commenced for fish to be plentiful near the shore of the lake, Wassamo's mother said to him—

"My son, I wish you would go to yonder point, and see if you cannot procure me some fish. You may ask your cousin to accompany you."

He did so. They set out, and, in the course of the afternoon, arrived at the fishing-ground. His cousin attended to the nets, for he was grown up to manhood, but Wassamo had not yet reached that age. They put their nets in the water, and encamped near them, using only a few pieces of birch-bark for a lodge to shelter them at night. They lit a fire, and, while they were conversing together, the moon arose. Not a breath of wind disturbed the smooth and bright surface of the lake. Not a cloud was seen. Wassamo looked out on the water towards their nets, and saw that almost all the floats had disappeared.

"Cousin," he said, "let us visit our nets. Perhaps we are fortunate."

They did so, and were rejoiced, as they drew them up, to see the meshes white here and there with fish. They landed in good spirits, and put away their canoe in safety from the winds.

"Wassamo," said his cousin, "you cook that we may eat."

Wassamo set about it immediately, and soon got his kettle on the flames, while his cousin was lying at his ease on the opposite side of the fire.

"Cousin," said Wassamo, "tell me stories, or sing me some love-songs."

The other obeyed, and sang his plaintive songs. He would frequently break off, and tell parts of stories, and would then sing again, as suited his feelings or fancy. While thus employed, he unconsciously fell asleep. Wassamo had scarcely noticed it in his care to watch the kettle, and, when the fish were done, he took the kettle off. He spoke to his cousin, but received no answer. He took the wooden ladle to skim off the oil, for the fish were very fat. He had a flambeau of twisted bark in one hand to give light; but, when he came to take out the fish, he did not know how to manage to hold the light, so he took off his garters, and tied them tight round his head, and then placed the lighted flambeau above his forehead, so that it was firmly held by the bandage, and threw its light brilliantly about him. Having both hands thus at liberty, he began to take out the fish. Suddenly he heard a laugh.

"Cousin," said he, "some one is near us. Awake, and let us look out."

His cousin, however, continued asleep. Again Wassamo heard the laughter, and, looking, he beheld two beautiful girls.

"Awake, awake," said he to his cousin. "Here are two young women;" but he received no answer, for his cousin was locked in his deepest slumbers.

Wassamo started up and advanced to the strange women. He was about to speak to them, when he fell senseless to the earth.

A short while after his cousin awoke. He looked around and called Wassamo, but could not find him.

"Netawis, Netawis (Cousin, cousin)!" he cried; but there was no answer. He searched the woods and all the shores around, but could not find him. He did not know what to do.

"Although," he reasoned, "his parents are my relations, and they know he and I were great friends, they will not believe me if I go home and say that he is lost. They will say that I killed him, and will require blood for blood."

However, he resolved to return home, and, arriving there, he told them what had occurred. Some said, "He has killed him treacherously," others said, "It is impossible. They were like brothers."

Search was made on every side, and when at length it became certain that Wassamo was not to be found, his parents demanded the life of Netawis.

Meanwhile, what had happened to Wassamo? When he recovered his senses, he found himself stretched on a bed in a spacious lodge.

"Stranger," said some one, "awake, and take something to eat."

Looking around him he saw many people, and an old spirit man, addressing him, said:

"My daughters saw you at the fishing-ground, and brought you here. I am the guardian spirit of Nagow Wudjoo (the sand mountains). We will make your visit here agreeable, and if you will remain I will give you one of my daughters in marriage."

The young man consented to the match, and remained for

some time with the spirit of the sand-hills in his lodge at the bottom of the lake, for there was it situated. At last, however, approached the season of sleep, when the spirit and his relations lay down for their long rest.

"Son-in-law," said the old spirit, "you can now, in a few days, start with your wife to visit your relations. You can be absent one year, but after that you must return."

Wassamo promised to obey, and set out with his wife. When he was near his village, he left her in a thicket and advanced alone. As he did so, who should he meet but his cousin.

"Netawis, Netawis," cried his cousin, "you have come just in time to save me!"

Then he ran off to the lodge of Wassamo's parents.

"I have seen him," said he, "whom you accuse me of having killed. He will be here in a few minutes."

All the village was soon in a bustle, and Wassamo and his wife excited universal attention, and the people strove who should entertain them best. So the time passed happily till the season came that Wassamo and his wife should return to the spirits. Netawis accompanied them to the shores of the lake, and would have gone with them to their strange abode, but Wassamo sent him back. With him Wassamo took offerings from the Indians to his father-in-law.

The old spirit was delighted to see the two return, and he was also much pleased with the presents Wassamo brought. He told his son-in-law that he and his wife should go once more to visit his people.

"It is merely," said he, "to assure them of my friendship, and to bid them farewell for ever."

Some time afterwards Wassamo and his wife made this visit.

Having delivered his message, he said—

"I must now bid you all farewell for ever."

His parents and friends raised their voices in loud lamentation, and they accompanied him and his wife to the sand-banks to see them take their departure.

The day was mild, the sky clear, not a cloud appeared, nor was there a breath of wind to disturb the bright surface of the water. The most perfect silence reigned throughout the company. They gazed intently upon Wassamo and his wife as they waded out into the water, waving their hands. They saw them go into deeper and deeper water. They saw the wave close over their heads. All at once they raised a loud and piercing wail. They looked again. A red flame, as if the sun had glanced on a billow, marked the spot for an instant; but the Feather-of-Flames and his wife had disappeared for ever.

THE SOUTHERN BRIDE

North went travelling, and after a long time, and after visiting many tribes, he fell in love with the daughter of South.

South and his wife said, "No. Ever since you came the weather has been cold. If you stay we will all freeze."

North said he would go back to his own country. So South let his daughter marry him. Then North went back to his own country with South's daughter. All the people there lived in ice houses.

The next day, after sunrise, the houses began to leak. The ice began to melt. It grew warmer and warmer. Then North's people came to him. They said, "It is the daughter of the South.

If she lives here all the lodges will melt. You must send her back to her father."

North said, "No."

But every day it grew hotter. The lodges began to melt away. The people said North must send his wife home. Therefore North had to send her back to South.

AGGO-DAH-GAUDA

Aggo-dah-gauda had one leg hooped up to his thigh so that he was obliged to get along by hopping. He had a beautiful daughter, and his chief care was to secure her from being carried off by the king of the buffaloes. He was peculiar in his habits, and lived in a loghouse, and he advised his daughter to keep indoors, and never go out for fear she should be stolen away.

One sunshiny morning Aggo-dah-gauda prepared to go out fishing, but before he left the lodge he reminded his daughter of her strange lover.

"My daughter," said he, "I am going out to fish, and as the day will be a pleasant one, you must recollect that we have an enemy near who is constantly going about, and so you must not leave the lodge."

When he reached his fishing-place, he heard a voice singing:

> *"Man with the leg tied up,*
> *Man with the leg tied up,*
> *Broken hip—hip—*
> *Hipped.*
> *Man with the leg tied up,*

> *Man with the leg tied up,*
> *Broken leg—leg—*
> *Legged."*

He looked round but saw no one, so he suspected the words were sung by his enemies the buffaloes, and hastened home.

The girl's father had not been long absent from the lodge when she began to think to herself—

"It is hard to be for ever kept indoors. The spring is coming on, and the days are so sunny and warm, that it would be very pleasant to sit out of doors. My father says it is dangerous. I know what I will do: I will get on the top of the house, and there I can comb and dress my hair."

She accordingly got up on the roof of the small house, and busied herself in untying and combing her beautiful hair, which was not only fine and shining, but so long that it reached down to the ground, hanging over the eaves of the house as she combed it. She was so intent upon this that she forgot all ideas of danger. All of a sudden the king of the buffaloes came dashing by with his herd of followers, and, taking her between his horns, away he cantered over the plains, and then, plunging into a river that bounded his land, he carried her safely to his lodge on the other side. Here he paid her every attention in order to gain her affections, but all to no purpose, for she sat pensive and disconsolate in the lodge among the other females, and scarcely ever spoke. The buffalo king did all he could to please her, and told the others in the lodge to give her everything she wanted, and to study her in every way. They set before her the choicest food, and gave her the seat of honour in the lodge. The king himself went out hunting to obtain the most delicate bits of meat both of animals and wild-fowl, and, not content with these proofs of his love, he fasted himself and would often take his pib-be-gwun (Indian flute) and sit near the lodge singing:

> "My sweetheart,
> My sweetheart,
> Ah me!
> When I think of you,
> When I think of you,
> Ah me!
> How I love you,
> How I love you,
> Ah me!
> Do not hate me,
> Do not hate me,
> Ah me!"

In the meantime Aggo-dah-gauda came home, and finding his daughter had been stolen he determined to get her back. For this purpose he immediately set out. He could easily trace the king till he came to the banks of the river, and then he saw he had plunged in and swum over. When Aggo-dah-gauda came to the river, however, he found it covered with a thin coating of ice, so that he could not swim across nor walk over. He therefore determined to wait on the bank a day or two till the ice might melt or become strong enough to bear him. Very soon the ice was strong enough, and Aggo-dah-gauda crossed over. On the other side, as he went along, he found branches torn off and cast down, and these had been strewn thus by his daughter to aid him in following her. The way in which she managed it was this. Her hair was all untied when she was captured, and as she was carried along it caught in the branches as she passed, so she took the pieces out of her hair and threw them down on the path.

When Aggo-dah-gauda came to the king's lodge it was evening. Carefully approaching it, he peeped through the sides and saw his daughter sitting there disconsolately. She saw him, and knowing that it was her father come for her, she said to the king, giving him a tender glance—

"I will go and get you a drink of water."

The king was delighted at what he thought was a mark of her affection, and the girl left the lodge with a dipper in her hand. The king waited a long time for her, and as she did not return he went out with his followers, but nothing could be seen or heard of the girl. The buffaloes sallied out into the plains, and had not gone far by the light of the moon, when they were attacked by a party of hunters. Many of them fell, but the buffalo-king, being stronger and swifter than the others, escaped, and, flying to the west, was never seen more.

THE GIRL WHO MARRIED THE PINE-TREE

Upon the side of a certain mountain grew some pines, under the shade of which the Puckwudjinies, or sprites, were accustomed to sport at times. Now it happened that in the neighbourhood of these trees was a lodge in which dwelt a beautiful girl and her father and mother. One day a man came to the lodge of the father, and seeing the girl he loved her, and said—

"Give me Leelinau for my wife," and the old man consented.

Now it happened that the girl did not like her lover, so she escaped from the lodge and went and hid herself, and as the sun was setting she came to the pine-trees, and leaning against one of them she lamented her hard fate. On a sudden she heard a voice, which seemed to come from the tree, saying—

"Be my wife, maiden, beautiful Leelinau, beautiful Leelinau."

The girl was astonished, not knowing whence the voice could have come. She listened again, and the words were repeated, evidently by the tree against which she leaned. Then the maid consented to be the wife of the pine-tree.

Meanwhile her parents had missed her, and had sent out parties to see if she could be found, but she was nowhere.

Time passed on, but Leelinau never returned to her home. Hunters who have been crossing the mountain, and have come to the trees at sunset, say that they have seen a beautiful girl there in company with a handsome youth, who vanished as they approached.

THE SUN AND THE MOON

There were once ten brothers who hunted together, and at night they occupied the same lodge. One day, after they had been hunting, coming home they found sitting inside the lodge near the door a beautiful woman.

She appeared to be a stranger, and was so lovely that all the hunters loved her, and as she could only be the wife of one, they agreed that he should have her who was most successful in the next day's hunt.

Accordingly, the next day, they each took different ways, and hunted till the sun went down, when they met at the lodge. Nine of the hunters had found nothing, but the youngest brought home a deer, so the woman was given to him for his wife.

The hunter had not been married more than a year when he was seized with sickness and died. Then the next brother took the girl for his wife. Shortly after he died also, and the woman married the next brother.

In a short time all the brothers died save the eldest, and he married the girl. She did not, however, love him, for he was of a churlish disposition, and one day it came into the woman's head that she would leave him and see what fortune she would meet with in the world.

So she went, taking only a dog with her, and travelled all day. She went on and on, but towards evening she heard some one coming after her who, she imagined, must be her husband. In great fear she knew not which way to turn, when she perceived a hole in the ground before her.

There she thought she might hide herself, and entering it with her dog she suddenly found herself going lower and lower, until she passed through the earth and came up on the other side. Near to her there was a lake, and a man fishing in it.

"My grandfather," cried the woman, "I am pursued by a spirit."

"Leave me," cried Manabozho, for it was he, "leave me. Let me be quiet."

The woman still begged him to protect her, and Manabozho at length said:

"Go that way, and you shall be safe."

Hardly had she disappeared when the husband, who had discovered the hole by which his wife had descended, came on the scene.

"Tell me," said he to Manabozho, "where has the woman gone?"

"Leave me," cried Manabozho, "don't trouble me."

"Tell me," said the man, "where is the woman?" Manabozho was silent, and the husband, at last getting angry, abused him with all his might.

"The woman went that way," said Manabozho at last. "Run after her, but you shall never catch her, and you shall be called Gizhigooke (day sun), and the woman shall be called Tibikgizis (night sun)."

So the man went on running after his wife to the west, but he has never caught her, and he pursues her to this day.

THE FAITHFUL LOVERS

There once lived a chief's daughter who had many relations. All the young men in the village wanted to have her for wife, and were all eager to fill her skin bucket when she went to the brook for water.

There was a young man in the village who was industrious and a good hunter; but he was poor and of a mean family. He loved the maiden and when she went for water, he threw his robe over her head while he whispered in her ear:

"Be my wife. I have little but I am young and strong. I will treat you well, for I love you."

For a long time the maiden did not answer, but one day she whispered back.

"Yes, you may ask my father's leave to marry me. But first you must do something noble. I belong to a great family and have many relations. You must go on a war party and bring back the scalp of an enemy."

The young man answered modestly, "I will try to do as you bid me. I am only a hunter, not a warrior. Whether I shall be brave or not I do not know. But I will try to take a scalp for your sake."

So he made a war party of seven, himself and six other young men. They wandered through the enemy's country, hoping to get a chance to strike a blow. But none came, for they found no one of the enemy.

"Our medicine is unfavorable," said their leader at last. "We shall have to return home."

Before they started they sat down to smoke and rest beside a beautiful lake at the foot of a green knoll that rose from its shore. The knoll was covered with green grass and somehow as they looked at it they had a feeling that there was something about it that was mysterious or uncanny.

But there was a young man in the party named the jester, for he was venturesome and full of fun. Gazing at the knoll he said: "Let's run and jump on its top."

"No," said the young lover, "it looks mysterious. Sit still and finish your smoke."

"Oh, come on, who's afraid," said the jester, laughing. "Come on you – come on!" and springing to his feet he ran up the side of the knoll.

Four of the young men followed. Having reached the top of the knoll all five began to jump and stamp about in sport, calling, "Come on, come on," to the others. Suddenly they stopped – the knoll had begun to move toward the water. It was a gigantic turtle. The five men cried out in alarm and tried to run – too late! Their feet by some power were held fast to the monster's back.

"Help us – drag us away," they cried; but the others could do nothing. In a few moments the waves had closed over them.

The other two men, the lover and his friend, went on, but with heavy hearts, for they had forebodings of evil. After some days, they came to a river. Worn with fatigue the lover threw himself down on the bank.

"I will sleep awhile," he said, "for I am wearied and worn out."

"And I will go down to the water and see if I can chance upon a dead fish. At this time of the year the high water may have left one stranded on the sea-shore," said his friend.

And as he had said, he found a fish which he cleaned, and then called to the lover.

"Come and eat the fish with me. I have cleaned it and made a fire and it is now cooking."

"No, you eat it; let me rest," said the lover.

"Oh, come on."

"No, let me rest."

"But you are my friend. I will not eat unless you share it with me."

"Very well," said the lover, "I will eat the fish with you, but you must first make me a promise. If I eat the fish, you must promise, pledge yourself, to fetch me all the water that I can drink."

"I promise," said the other, and the two ate the fish out of their war-kettle. For there had been but one kettle for the party.

When they had eaten, the kettle was rinsed out and the lover's friend brought it back full of water. This the lover drank at a draught.

"Bring me more," he said.

Again his friend filled the kettle at the river and again the lover drank it dry.

"More!" he cried.

"Oh, I am tired. Cannot you go to the river and drink your fill from the stream?" asked his friend.

"Remember your promise."

"Yes, but I am weary. Go now and drink."

"Ek-hey, I feared it would be so. Now trouble is coming upon us," said the lover sadly. He walked to the river, sprang in, and lying down in the water with his head toward land, drank greedily. By and by he called to his friend.

"Come hither, you who have been my sworn friend. See what comes of your broken promise."

The friend came and was amazed to see that the lover was now a fish from his feet to his middle.

Sick at heart he ran off a little way and threw himself upon the ground in grief. By and by he returned. The lover was now a fish to his neck.

"Cannot I cut off the part and restore you by a sweat bath?" the friend asked.

"No, it is too late. But tell the chief's daughter that I loved her to the last and that I die for her sake. Take this belt and give it to her. She gave it to me as a pledge of her love for me," and he being then turned to a great fish, swam to the middle of the river and there remained, only his great fin remaining above the water.

The friend went home and told his story. There was great mourning over the death of the five young men, and for the lost lover. In the river the great fish remained, its fin just above the surface, and was called by the Indians 'Fish that Bars,' because it bar'd navigation. Canoes had to be portaged at great labor around the obstruction.

The chief's daughter mourned for her lover as for a husband, nor would she be comforted. "He was lost for love of me, and I shall remain as his widow," she wailed.

In her mother's tepee she sat, with her head covered with her robe, silent, working, working. "What is my daughter doing," her mother asked. But the maiden did not reply.

The days lengthened into moons until a year had passed. And then the maiden arose. In her hands were beautiful articles of clothing, enough for three men. There were three pairs of moccasins, three pairs of leggings, three belts, three shirts, three head dresses with beautiful feathers, and sweet smelling tobacco.

"Make a new canoe of bark," she said, which was made for her.

Into the canoe she stepped and floated slowly down the river toward the great fish.

"Come back my daughter," her mother cried in agony. "Come back. The great fish will eat you."

She answered nothing. Her canoe came to the place where the great fin arose and stopped, its prow grating on the monster's back. The maiden stepped out boldly. One by one she laid her presents on the fish's back, scattering the feathers and tobacco over his broad spine.

"Oh, fish," she cried, "Oh, fish, you who were my lover, I shall not forget you. Because you were lost for love of me, I shall never marry. All my life I shall remain a widow. Take these presents. And now leave the river, and let the waters run free, so my people may once more descend in their canoes."

She stepped into her canoe and waited. Slowly the great fish sank, his broad fin disappeared, and the waters of the St. Croix (Stillwater) were free.

SUKONIA'S WIVES AND THE ICHPUL SISTERS

Old Jahtaneno had a great many daughters, and all but two of these were married.

At that time Sukonia was a great chief in this country about us. He had a large sweat-house, and many people to serve him.

One day Jahtaneno called his daughters and said: "My girls, I want you to go to Sukonia's house. I have heard that he is very rich; go and see him. He has no wife yet; he may marry you. Rise early in the morning, bathe, comb your hair, go and see the chief Sukonia."

The two sisters made no answer, said nothing, obeyed their father. They rose early next morning, bathed, combed their hair, painted their faces red (young people painted red always). Their mother gave each girl a nice basket; she hung beads on their necks, and put food in their baskets.

"If any man meets you on the road," said Jahtaneno, at parting, "do not look at him. A man richly dressed and wearing many beads will come toward you, will speak to you; do not look at that man; he is no one but Metsi."

The two girls began to sing when they started, and their song was:

> "Au ni á, au ni á, mo a wé, he ló,
> Au ni á, au ni á, mo a wé, he ló."

They went northeast, the way which the old man had told them to go. He warned them further, saying, "There is a house this side of Sukonia's, and not very far from it; two women live in that house, two old maids. Be sure not to stop at that house. Do

LOVE & MARRIAGE

not go near these women; pass their place quickly, do not stop before it, do not talk to the women. They are bad, evil women. If you go into their house, you will never come out of it; if you go, you will be killed there."

Jahtaneno's daughters started, walked away quickly, singing as they went:

> "Au ni á, au ni á, mo a wé, he ló,
> Au ni á, au ni á, mo a wé, he ló."

Metsi heard the song; he listened and said to himself, "That is a good song, that is nice singing; I like to hear that song. I think those two girls are going to the chief I think they are going to visit Sukonia Mujaupa. Now, otter-skins be here before me, and beads in plenty, and beautiful shells."

He wished for all other things that he liked. Metsi dressed himself richly and waited.

Jahtaneno's daughters walked and walked on without stopping, met no one on the way till they came to where Metsi was waiting. The younger sister was walking ahead; she saw Metsi at one side of the trail, but would not look at him a second time. The elder sister looked a second and a third time.

"I think that is Sukonia Mujaupa," said she.

"Your father would not say so," answered the younger sister; "that is Metsi."

But the elder sister liked the stranger's appearance; she looked at him many times.

"I think this is Sukonia," said she.

"Come on with me," said the younger sister.

"Have you lost your eyes? That is Metsi."

The younger girl was ahead now some distance; the elder stopped to look at the stranger more closely.

"Which way are you going?" asked Metsi.

"Our father sent us to Sukonia the chief."

"Oh, I am chief," said Metsi; "you are to come with me. I will start for home very soon."

"My sister is ahead, she is waiting. I must hurry and tell her first. I will come back to you then."

She caught up with her sister and said: "I will go with this man; this is Sukonia, the chief. He said he was chief."

"You must have lost your mind," answered the younger sister; "that is Metsi. He is no chief, he is not Sukonia."

The elder sister went with the younger, but she wanted to go back to Metsi, she wished to go with him; she liked his dress, his words pleased her, she believed him. Both went on, though the elder went against her will.

"You will see two black bearskins hanging over the sweat-house door," said the father, when his daughters were starting. "Stop there; that is Sukonia's house, that is the house to which you are going."

Toward sunset they came near the place where the Ichpuls lived.

"Let us stop here," said the elder sister, "and get something to eat. I am hungry."

"Our father told us to pass this house; he told us not to stop near it, not to go to it, not to look at it," said the younger sister; and she went on without looking, she went straight ahead.

The elder sister followed her, but followed unwillingly. At last both came near Sukonia's, and saw the two bearskins hanging out over the sweat-house.

Chikpitpa, Sukonia's little brother, was on the roof, and Tsore Jowa, his sister, was at work making a house for herself a little way off at one side. Chikpitpa ran into the house, calling loudly:

"Two girls are coming! Two girls are coming with baskets!"

The old man, Sukonia's father, brought bearskins for the young women to sit on, and waited. The sisters came in and took the places shown them. Chikpitpa was in a corner when the sisters sat down. He ran to one and then to the other, looked at them, sat on their laps. He was very glad that the sisters had come; he liked to be with them and talk to them.

Old Sukonia went out and called to Tsore Jowa, "Come! my daughter; bring food to our guests, to the young women who have come to us."

She brought deer's marrow; she brought other kinds of food, too. The sisters had put down their baskets outside, near the door. On the way they had said to the baskets, "Let the food in you be nice;" and when leaving them at the door, they said, "Be large and be full."

The two small baskets stood outside now, very large and full of every good food. Sukonia came home with his men about sunset. Chikpitpa sprang up to the roof of the house, and called to his brother, "Two guests have come to our house. Two women are sitting inside. They are sitting in your place."

The men came in, and Sukonia sat down with the sisters. They pleased him; he liked their looks.

"Have you brought food to our guests?" asked Sukonia.

"I brought some," said Tsore Jowa.

"Oh, give more. Bring plenty of everything!"

The two baskets which Jahtaneno's daughters had brought were carried into the house. The sisters invited all present to try their food. All the men ate food from the baskets and praised it, Sukonia, the chief, was pleased more and more with the sisters that evening, and married them.

After all the people had eaten next morning, Sukonia went to hunt. He took many men with him.

That day Sukonia's sisters showed his wives every place in the house and outside it – showed them where venison, roots, and acorns were kept; showed them where the water was. The spring was in the house in one corner, carefully covered.

After some days Sukonia said to his wives: "I want you to tell me what your father said when you were leaving him. When does he want you to go back? When does he wish you to visit him?"

"He did not tell us when to go to him. He did not tell us to go back at all, he only told us to come here; but we want to see him. We want to tell him how we live here."

"Well," said Sukonia, "go to-morrow; go to see your father. What does he eat? What does he like?"

"He eats salmon; he likes nice beads, furs, and shells."

"I will send him some of my meat, I will send him venison. I will send him beads and furs."

"May I go with my sisters-in-law?" asked Chikpitpa.

"No. I want you here," said Sukonia. "I want you here, my little brother."

The two women rose early next morning, and Tsore Jowa helped them to make ready. Sukonia gave them fat venison, and every kind of bright beads and rich presents for their father.

They started; went as far as the Ichpul house, where the two frog sisters lived. The two old maids were in the road and spoke to Sukonia's wives. They were very kind and pleasant.

"Put down your baskets and sit a while with us to talk," said they.

The Jahtaneno sisters were frightened. They did not wish to stop. They feared the Ichpul women, did not like to make them angry by refusing. They were afraid to sit down, afraid to refuse.

"Oh, how your hair looks! let me see your head," said one Ichpul woman to the elder sister.

"Oh, how your hair looks!" said the other to the younger sister; "let me look at your head."

"Put your head on my lap," said each Ichpul sister to each of Sukonia's wives.

Each was afraid, but still put her head on the old maid's lap. The Ichpul sisters killed Sukonia's wives, flayed their bodies, and put their skins on themselves.

About sunset next day the two frog women went to Sukonia's house; went in and sat where Jahtaneno's daughters had always sat; took the place of Sukonia's wives; looked just like them because they had their skins on.

About dusk Sukonia came home from the hunt. Chikpitpa, who ran ahead, rushed into the sweat-house to see if his sisters-in-law had come back from their father's. He saw the two women, looked at them; they seemed like his sisters-in-law, but when he came near he cried out at once:

"Phu! they smell like frogs! The Ichpul sisters are here: these are the frog old maids!"

He cried and ran out to meet his brother.

"Brother," said he, "the Ichpul women are in our house. They killed my sisters-in-law to-day. I know they did." And he kept crying, "They killed my sisters-in-law, they killed my poor sisters-in-law!" and he cried without stopping, cried bitterly.

The two old maids wearing the skins of Sukonia's wives were making acorn porridge. When it was almost ready, Sukonia looked at the two women. They seemed like his wives, and he was in doubt, till all at once he thought: "I will ask them to bring water from the spring. If they know where the water is, they are my wives; if not, they are false."

"Bring me water, my wife," said he to one of the women.

She stood up, took a water basket, turned toward the door, and said to Chikpitpa, "Come out with me for water, my little brother-in-law."

"Wait," said Sukonia. "You need not go now."

She came back to the fire and sat down with her sister. Sukonia knew now that those were strange women.

"Whip me," said Chikpitpa to his brother, "I will cry, roll around and kick. I will kick those nasty frogs! I will kill them."

When the acorn porridge was boiling hard, Sukonia struck Chikpitpa with a switch and scolded him: "Why are you crying? I can do nothing, you cry so."

The boy rolled on the floor, cried more than ever, kicked, rolled around, kicked as hard as he could, rolled toward the fire and kicked, kicked one woman into the boiling porridge, kicked the other one into the burning fire, and in this way he killed the false sisters.

Chikpitpa was glad; he laughed. Sukonia threw the two women out doors, and mourned all that night for his wives. Next morning early he rose and said, "Stay home to-day, all of you."

"Where are you going?" asked Chikpitpa.

"Stay here, my little brother," said Sukonia. "I am going somewhere."

Sukonia followed the trail of his wives, reached the place

where the Ichpul sisters had stopped them, and found their dead bodies. He took out his bowstring of deer sinew, struck the two women, called them, raised them to life.

"How were you killed?" asked Sukonia; "how did it happen? Did you go to the Ichpul house?"

"We did not go to that house; those two women were out on the road and they stopped us. They asked us to sit down and talk with them. We were afraid to sit, afraid to refuse. We sat down, and they killed us."

Sukonia took his wives home. When they were in sight of the house, Chikpitpa was on the roof watching.

"Oh, those are your sisters-in-law," said he to Tsore Jowa; and he ran out to meet them.

"Go, now, to your father," said Sukonia, next morning. "Carry presents and venison to him, and be here at sunset."

The two sisters rose early, took two baskets, and started. At noon they were at their father's house. Old Jahtaneno was glad when he looked at his daughters and saw the nice presents.

"Our husband told us to go home to-day, and we cannot stay long with you."

They took back many presents from their father, and were home at sunset. They met no trouble on the way. The Ichpul sisters were dead, and Metsi did not meet them a second time.

THE TWO SISTERS, HAKA LASI AND TSORE JOWA

At some distance east of **Jigul Matu**, lived old Juka. He had a great many sons and two daughters – a big house full of children.

Juka's two daughters were Tsore Jowa, the elder, and Haka Lasi, the younger. After a time Haka Lasi fell in love with her brother Hitchinna. One day she fell asleep and dreamed that he had married her.

Metsi lived, too, in Juka's house. He was no relative; he just lived as a guest there.

One day all the men were out hunting. It was then that Haka Lasi saw Hitchinna in a dream. She began to sing about him, and she sang: "I dream of Hitchinna; I dream that he is my husband. I dream of Hitchinna; I dream that he is my husband."

All the men came back from the hunt at night. At daylight next morning they went to swim, and Tsore Jowa made ready food for them. Haka Lasi took a very nice staff in her hand, and went on top of the sweat-house. She looked in and sang:

"Where is my husband? Send him up here to me. I will take him away. We must go on a journey. Where is my husband? Send him up here to me."

All knew that she had no husband.

"You have no husband," said they.

Hitchina was lying in one corner wrapped up in the skin of a wildcat.

"You have no husband in this house; all here are your brothers," said Juka.

"I have a husband, and I want him to come here to me," answered Haka Lasi.

"Well," said the eldest son, "I will go up to her. Let us hear what she will say." He went up.

"You are not my husband," said Haka Lasi. "Do not come near me."

She drove that one down, and called again: "Where is my husband? Send him up to me."

"Go you," said Juka to the second son.

"I don't want you," said Haka Lasi to the second son.

She refused one after another, and drove them away until none was left but Hitchinna. Juka went then to Hitchinna and said, "My son, get up and go to her; it looks as though you were the one she wants."

"He is the one," said Haka Lasi; "he is my husband. I want him to go away with me."

Hitchinna said not a word, but rose, washed, dressed himself nicely, and went to the woman.

"The sun is high now," said Haka Lasi; "we must go quickly."

She was glad when taking away the one she wanted. They travelled along, and she sang of Hitchinna as they travelled, sang of him all the time. They went a long distance, and at night she fixed a bed and they lay down on it.

Young Hitchinna could not sleep, he was frightened. When Haka Lasi was asleep, he rose very quickly, took a piece of soft rotten wood, put it on her arm where she had held his head, covered it, and then ran away quickly, hurried back toward Juka's sweat-house with all his might. About daylight he was at the sweat-house.

Now Chuhna, Juka's sister, lived with him. She was the greatest person in the world to spin threads and twist ropes. She had a willow basket as big as a house, and a rope which reached, up to the sky and was fastened there.

"My nephew," said she to Hitchinna, "I will save you and save all from your terrible sister. She will be here very soon; she may come any moment. She will kill all in this house; she will kill every one if she finds us here. Let all go into my basket. I will take you up to the sky. She cannot find us there; she cannot follow us to that place."

"I will lie lowest," said Metsi. "I am a good man, I will go in first, I will go in before others; I will be at the bottom of the basket."

Metsi went in first; every one in the sweat-house followed him. Then Chuhna ran up, rose on her rope, and pulled the basket after her.

The sweat-house was empty; no one stayed behind. Chuhna kept rising and rising, going higher and higher.

When Haka Lasi woke up and saw that she had a block of rotten wood on her arm instead of Hitchinna, she said, "You won't get away from me, I will catch you wherever you are."

She rushed back to the sweat-house. It was empty; no one there. She ran around in every direction looking for tracks, to find which way they had gone. She found nothing on the ground; then she looked into the sky, and far up, very high, close to the sun. she saw the basket rising, going up steadily.

Haka Lasi was raging; she was so awfully angry that she set fire to the house. It burned quickly, was soon a heap of coals.

The basket was almost at the sky when Metsi said to himself, "I wonder how far up we are; I want to see." And he made a little hole in the bottom of the basket to peep through and look down.

That instant the basket burst open; all came out, poured down, a great stream of people, and all fell straight into the fire of the sweat-house.

Now, Tsore Jowa was outside on top of the basket. She caught at the sun, held to it, and saved herself.

Hitchinna went down with the rest, fell into the burning coals, and was burned like his brothers.

Haka Lasi was glad that they had not escaped her; she took a stick, fixed a net on it, and watched.

All were in the fire now and were burning. After a while one body burst, and the heart flew out of it. Haka Lasi caught this heart in her net. Soon a second and a third body burst, and two more hearts flew out. She caught those as well as the first one. She caught all the hearts except two – Juka's own heart and his eldest son's heart.

Juka's heart flew high, went away far in the sky, and came down on the island of a river near Klamath Lake. It turned into Juka himself there. He sank in the ground to his chin; only his head was sticking out.

The heart of the eldest son flew off to the foot of Wahkalu and turned to be himself again. He fell so deep into the earth that only his face was sticking out on the surface.

Now Haka Lasi put all the hearts which she had caught on a string, hung them around her neck, and went to a lake east of Jigulmatu. She wanted to live at the bottom of the lake, but could not find a place deep enough. So she went northwest of Klamath Lake to Crater Lake, where she could live in deep water.

Two Tsanunewa brothers lived near the lake with their old grandmother. One morning early these brothers were out catching ducks, and just at daybreak they heard some one call.

"Who is that?" asked the elder brother. "I don't know," answered the younger.

Soon they saw Haka Lasi spring up on the water and call. She had a large string of hearts around her neck. Then she sank again in the water. Again she came up at some distance and called a second time.

Now Tsore Jowa came down from the sun and went to the old sweat-house, where she found nothing but a heap of bones and ashes. Putting pitch on her head and on her arms, and strips of deerskin around her neck with pitch on them, she cried and went around mourning. After a time she began to look for her sister. She went everywhere; went to Klamath Lake.

For some time the two Tsanunewa brothers had heard a voice singing:

*"Li-wa-éh, li-wa-há,
Li-wa-éh, li-wa-há."*

This was old Juka. He was lying in the ground where he had fallen, and was crying.

Tsore Jowa searched, inquired, asked every one about Haka Lasi, and told what she had done – that she had killed her own brothers and father.

Tsore Jowa came at last to the house of the two Tsanunewa brothers one day about sunset, and spoke to their grandmother. "My sister, Haka Lasi, has killed all my brothers and my father," said she; and she told the whole story.

The old woman cried when she heard what Tsore Jowa told her. The two brothers were away hunting; they came home about dark with a large string of ducks. "This woman," said the grandmother, "is looking for her sister, who has killed all her people."

The two brothers cried when the story was told to them. When they had finished crying, they said to the old woman. "Cook ducks and let this woman have plenty to eat."

When all had eaten, the two brothers said to Tsore Jowa: "Tell us what kind of a person your sister is. Which way did she go?"

"I don't know which way she went," said Tsore Jowa.

"Three days ago," said the elder brother, "just as daylight was coming, we saw a woman jump up in the lake where we were fishing. She seemed to have large beads around her neck. That woman may be your sister."

"Catch that woman for me. I will give you otter-skins and beads. I will give bearskins. If you wish, I will stay with you here, if you catch her."

"We want no beads nor otter-skins nor bearskins," said the brothers.

"What do you want?"

"We want red deer-bones and green deer-bones; small, sharp ones to stab fish with."

"You shall have all you want of both kinds," said Tsore Jowa.

Next morning she set out with a sack, went away to high mountains, gathered deer-bones, red and green leg-bones, and put them in her sack. At sunset she went back to the house, with the sack full.

The two brothers were glad, now. The elder took red, and the younger green bones. (The fat on the leg-bones of deer turns some red and others green.)

"You must catch her bad sister for Tsore Jowa," said the old woman to her grandsons.

All that night the brothers sat sharpening the bones and then fastening them to the spear-shafts. They did not stop for a moment. "Let us go now; it is near daylight," said the elder brother.

They started. When they reached the lake, they went out on the water. Every morning at daybreak Haka Lasi sprang up to the surface and called from the lake. The elder brother took a stem of tule grass, opened it, placed it on the water, made himself small, and sat down in the middle of it. The younger brother fixed himself in another stem of tule in the same way. The two tule stems floated away on the water, till they came near the place where the brothers had seen Haka Lasi spring up the first time.

"Let me shoot before you," said the elder brother.

"Oh, you cannot shoot; you will miss her," said the younger. "Let me shoot first. You will miss; you will not hit her heart."

"I will hit," said the elder.

They watched and watched. Each had his bow drawn ready to shoot. Daylight came now. Haka Lasi rose quickly, came to the top of the water, and held out her arms before calling.

The younger brother sent the first arrow, struck her in the neck; the elder shot, struck her right under the arm. Haka Lasi dropped back and sank in the water.

The brothers watched and watched. After a time they saw two arrows floating, and were afraid they had lost her. She had pulled them out of her body, and they rose to the surface. After a while the body rose. Haka Lasi was dead.

The brothers saw that she had a great many hearts on a string around her neck. They drew her to the shore then, and carried her home. They left the body hidden outside the house, and went in.

"We did not see her," said the elder Tsanunewa, to his grandmother.

All sat down to eat fish, and when they were through eating, the elder said to Tsore Jowa, "Come out and see what we caught this morning."

She ran out with them, and saw her dead sister with a string of hearts on her neck. Tsore Jowa, took off her buckskin skirt, wrapped up the body, and put it in the house. She counted the hearts.

"My eldest brother's heart is not here, and my father's is not here," said she.

"Every morning we hear some one crying, far away toward the north; that may be one of them," said the two Tsanunewas.

Tsore Jowa started out to find this one, if she could, who was calling. She left the body and hearts at the old grandmother's house, and hurried off toward the north. She heard the cry soon and knew it. "That is my father," said she.

Tsore Jowa came near the place from which the cry rose; saw no one. Still she heard the cry. At last she saw a face; it was the face of Juka, her father.

Tsore Jowa took a sharp stick and dug. She dug down to Juka's waist; tried to pull him up, but could not stir him. She dug again, dug a good while; pulled and pulled, until at last she drew him out.

Juka was very poor, all bones, no flesh at all on him. Tsore Jowa put down a deerskin, wrapped her father in it, and carried him to the old woman's house; then she put him with Haka Lasi's body, and carried them home to the old burned sweat-house east of Jigulmatu.

She was crying yet, since one brother was missing. She put down the basket in which she had carried them, hid it away, covered it carefully.

At the foot of Wahkalu lived a certain Jamuka, an old man who had a wife and two daughters.

"Bring in some wood," said the old man one day to his daughters,

The two girls took their baskets and went to bring wood. Soon they heard some one singing:

> "I-nó i-nó, I-no mi-ná
> I-nó i-nó, I-no mi-ná."

"Listen," said the younger sister; "some one is singing."

They listened, heard the singing; it seemed right at the foot of Wahkalu. They went toward the place from which the sound came.

"That is a nice song," said the younger sister. "I should like to see the one who sings so."

They went near, saw no one yet. "Let us take the wood home," said the elder sister, "then come back here; our father may be angry if we stay away longer."

They took the wood home, put it down, and said nothing. Both went back to the place where the singing was and listened. At last the younger sister came to the right place, and said, "I think this is he who is singing."

There was a head sticking out of the ground, and the face was covered with water. The man had cried so much that he looked dirty and ugly.

The sisters took sharp sticks, and dug all around the head. dug deeply. They could not pull out the person; they had only dug to his waist when night came and they must go.

"Why did you stay out so late?" asked their father.

"We heard some one singing, and wanted to know who it was, but were not able. We will go back in the morning and search again."

"That is well," said Jamuka. He had heard how Juka's sons had been killed. "Perhaps one of those people is alive yet," said he; "you must look for him."

They went early next morning to dig, and drew the man out. They took off their buckskin skirts then and wrapped him up carefully. He was nothing but bones, no flesh at all on his body. The younger sister ran home to get wildcat skins to wrap around him.

"We have found a man, but he is all bones," said she to her father.

"Take good care of the stranger, feed and nurse him well," said Jamuka; "he may be Juka himself, and he is a good man."

They wrapped the man in wildcat skins. A great stream of water was running from his eyes, and deer came down the hill to drink of that water.

The girls lay on each side of the man, and gave him food; stayed all night with him. Next morning they went home for more food.

"Feed him, give him plenty," said Jamuka; "he may get health and strength yet."

The sisters went back and stayed a second night. The man began to look better, but he cried all the time, and many deer came to drink the water that flowed from his eyes. The girls went home the second morning. "The man looks better," said they to their father.

"I have heard," said old Jamuka, "that Juka's sons were killed. This must be one of them."

They went back right away, and stayed another day and night with the stranger. The man looked as though he might get his health again. He began to talk. "Has your father a bow and arrows?" asked he of the sisters.

"He has; he has many."

"Bring me a bow and arrows; many deer come near me to drink, I may shoot one."

They took the man's words to their father. Jamuka gave them a bow and some arrows, and they went back to the sick man.

"You may go home to-night," said he. "I wish to be alone."

The girls left him. At sundown a great buck came and drank of the tears, he killed him; later another came, he killed that one; at midnight a third came, he killed the third; now he had three. At daylight a fourth buck was killed; he had four now. "That is enough," thought he.

When the girls came and saw four great bucks lying dead near the stranger, they were frightened; they ran home and told their father. Old Jamuka was glad when they told him. He sharpened his knife, hurried out to the woods and looked at the stranger. "That is Juka's son," said he; "take good care of him, daughters."

Jamuka dressed the deer, carried them home, and cut up the venison for drying. Next evening Juka's son sent the girls home a second time, and killed five great deer that night. Next morning the girls came to see him, and ran home in wonder.

Their father was very glad. He dressed the five deer as he had the four, and cut up the venison.

Tsore Jowa was hunting everywhere all this time to find her brother. She had left the hearts, her sister's body, and her father hidden away carefully; had done nothing yet to save them.

The night after Juka's son killed the five deer the two girls took him home to their father. He was well now and beautiful, in good health and strong. He cried no more after that. A salt spring was formed in the place where he had fallen and shed so many tears. The spring is in that place till this day, and deer go in herds to drink from it. People watch near the spring and kill them, as Juka's son did.

Tsore Jowa went to every house inquiring about her brother. At last she came to Jamuka's house, and there she found him. She was glad now and satisfied. She left her brother with his two wives and hurried home.

Tsore Jowa made in one night a great sweat-house, prepared a big basket, and filled it with water. When the second night came, she dropped hot stones into the water; put all the hearts into the basket. Opening her sister's body, she took out her heart and put it in with the others. At this time the water in the basket was boiling. She covered the basket and placed it on top of the sweat-house. Then she went in, lay down and slept.

The water was seething all night. At daybreak the basket turned over, and there was a crowding and hurrying of people around the sweat-house. They began to talk briskly.

"We are cold, we are cold!" said they. "Let us in!"

Soon broad daylight came. Tsore Jowa opened the door, and all crowded into the sweat-house. Tsore Jowa said not a word yet. All the brothers came; behind them Haka Lasi. She looked well, she was good. Her heart was clean; there was nothing bad now in it.

"Where is our eldest brother?" asked all.

"He is well; I have found him. He has two wives," said Tsore Jowa.

Juka was in good health and strong. She had washed him and given him good food.

All were happy, and they went hunting.

"I think your husband would like to go home," said Jamuka one day to his daughters.

Juka's son and his two wives set out to visit his father; Juka saw his son coming; took a big blanket quickly, caught him, placed him in it, and put him right away.

Now the wives of Juka's son came in and sat down in the house. Two other brothers took them for wives. They stayed a long time, never saw their first husband again. Old Juka kept him secreted, made him a Weanmauna, a hidden one.

After a time the two women wished to go home to visit Jamuka. They took beads and blankets, nice things of all kinds, and went to their father at the foot of Wahkalu.

"We have never seen our husband," said they, "since we went to his father's. We have new husbands now."

"I think that is well enough," said Jamuka.

His father has put him away. His brothers are as good for you as he was."

The sisters agreed with their father, and went back and lived at Juka's house after that.

THE SIOUX WHO MARRIED THE CROW CHIEF'S DAUGHTER

A **war party of seven young men**, seeing a lone tepee standing on the edge of a heavy belt of timber, stopped and waited for darkness, in order to send one of their scouts ahead to ascertain whether the camp which they had seen was the camp of friend or enemy.

When darkness had settled down on them, and they felt secure in not being detected, they chose one of their scouts to go on alone and find out what would be the best direction for them to advance upon the camp, should it prove to be an enemy.

Among the scouts was one who was noted for his bravery, and many were the brave acts he had performed. His name was Big Eagle. This man they selected to go to the lone camp and obtain the information for which they were waiting.

Big Eagle was told to look carefully over the ground and select the best direction from which they should make the attack. The other six would await his return. He started on his mission, being careful not to make any noise. He stealthily approached the camp. As he drew near to the tent he was surprised to note the absence of any dogs, as these animals are always kept by the Sioux to notify the owners by their barking of the approach of anyone. He crawled up to the tepee door, and peeping through a small aperture, he saw three persons sitting inside.

An elderly man and woman were sitting at the right of the fireplace, and a young woman at the seat of honor, opposite the door.

Big Eagle had been married and his wife had died five winters previous to the time of this episode. He had never thought of marrying again, but when he looked upon this young woman he thought he was looking upon the face of his dead wife. He removed his cartridge belts and knife, and placing them, along with his rifle, at the side of the tent, he at once boldly stepped inside the tepee, and going over to the man, extended his hand and shook first the man's hand, then the old woman's, and lastly the young woman's. Then he seated himself by the side of the girl, and thus they sat, no one speaking.

Finally, Big Eagle made signs to the man, explaining as well as possible by signs, that his wife had died long ago, and when he saw the girl she so strongly resembled his dead wife that he wished to marry her, and he would go back to the enemy's camp and live with them, if they would consent to the marriage of their daughter.

The old man seemed to understand, and Big Eagle again made signs to him that a party were lying in wait just a short distance from his camp. Noiselessly they brought in the horses, and taking down the tent, they at once moved off in the direction from whence they had come. The war party waited all night, and when the first rays of dawn disclosed to them the absence of the tepee, they at once concluded that Big Eagle had been discovered and killed, so they hurriedly started on their trail for home.

In the meantime, the hunting party, for this it was that Big Eagle had joined, made very good time in putting a good distance between themselves and the war party. All day they traveled, and when evening came they ascended a high hill, looking down into the valley on the other side. There stretched for two miles, along the banks of a small stream, an immense camp. The old man made signs for Big Eagle to remain with the two women where he was, until he could go to the camp and prepare them to receive an enemy into their village.

The old man rode through the camp and drew up at the largest tepee in the village. Soon Big Eagle could see men gathering around the tepee. The crowd grew larger and larger, until the whole village had assembled at the large tepee. Finally they dispersed, and catching their horses, mounted and advanced to the hill on which Big Eagle and the two women were waiting. They formed a circle around them and slowly they returned to the village, singing and riding in a circle around them.

LOVE & MARRIAGE

When they arrived at the village they advanced to the large tepee, and motioned Big Eagle to the seat of honor in the tepee. In the village was a man who understood and spoke the Sioux language. He was sent for, and through him the oath of allegiance to the Crow tribe was taken by Big Eagle. This done he was presented with the girl to wife, and also with many spotted ponies.

Big Eagle lived with his wife among her people for two years, and during this time he joined in four different battles between his own people (the Sioux) and the Crow people, to whom his wife belonged.

In no battle with his own people would he carry any weapons, only a long willow coup-stick, with which he struck the fallen Sioux.

At the expiration of two years he concluded to pay a visit to his own tribe, and his father-in-law, being a chief of high standing, at once had it heralded through the village that his son-in-law would visit his own people, and for them to show their good will and respect for him by bringing ponies for his son-in-law to take back to his people.

Hearing this, the herds were all driven in and all day long horses were brought to the tent of Big Eagle, and when he was ready to start on his homeward trip, twenty young men were elected to accompany him to within a safe distance of his village. The twenty young men drove the gift horses, amounting to two hundred and twenty head, to within one day's journey of the village of Big Eagle, and fearing for their safety from his people, Big Eagle sent them back to their own village.

On his arrival at his home village, they received him as one returned from the dead, as they were sure he had been killed the night he had been sent to reconnoiter the lone camp. There was great feasting and dancing in honor of his return, and the horses were distributed among the needy ones of the village.

Remaining at his home village for a year, he one day made up his mind to return to his wife's people. A great many fancy robes, dresses, war bonnets, moccasins, and a great drove of horses were given him, and his wife, and he bade farewell to his people for good, saying, "I will never return to you again, as I have decided to live the remainder of my days with my wife's people."

On his arrival at the village of the Crows, he found his father-in-law at the point of death. A few days later the old man died, and Big Eagle was appointed to fill the vacancy of chief made by the death of his father-in-law.

Subsequently he took part in battles against his own people, and in the third battle was killed on the field. Tenderly the Crow warriors bore him back to their camp, and great was the mourning in the Crow village for the brave man who always went into battle unarmed, save only the willow wand which he carried.

Thus ended the career of one of the bravest of Sioux warriors who ever took the scalp of an enemy, and who for the love of his dead wife, gave up home, parents, and friends, to be killed on the field of battle by his own tribe.

DEETA KWAY, OR THE FOAM WOMAN

There once lived a woman called **Monedo Kway** on the sand mountains called 'the Sleeping Bear,' of Lake Michigan, who had a daughter as beautiful as she was modest and discreet. Everybody spoke of the beauty of this daughter. She was so handsome that her mother feared she would be carried off, and to prevent it she put her in a box on the lake, which was tied by a long string to a stake on the shore. Every morning the mother pulled the box ashore, and combed her daughter's long, shining hair, gave her food, and then put her out again on the lake.

One day a handsome young man chanced to come to the spot at the moment she was receiving her morning's attentions from her mother. He was struck with her beauty, and immediately went home and told his feelings to his uncle, who was a great chief and a powerful magician. "My nephew," replied the old man, "go to the mother's lodge, and sit down in a modest manner, without saying a word. You need not ask her the question. But whatever you think she will understand, and what she thinks in answer you will also understand." The young man did so. He sat down, with his head dropped in a thoughtful manner, without uttering a word. He then thought, "I wish she would give me her daughter." Very soon he understood the mother's thoughts in reply. "Give you my daughter?" thought she; "you! No, indeed, my daughter shall never marry you." The young man went away and reported the result to his uncle. "Woman without good sense;" said he, "who is she keeping her daughter for? Does she think she will marry the Mudjikewis? Proud heart! we will try her magic skill, and see whether she can withstand our power." The pride and haughtiness of the mother was talked of by the spirits living on that part of the lake. They met together and determined to exert their power in humbling her. For this purpose they resolved to raise a great storm on the lake. The water began to toss and roar, and the tempest became so severe, that the string broke, and the box floated off through the straits down Lake Huron, and struck against the sandy shores at its outlet. The place where it struck was near the lodge of a superannuated old spirit called Ishkwon Daimeka, or the keeper of the gate of the lakes. He opened the box and let out the beautiful daughter, took her into his lodge, and married her.

When the mother found that her daughter had been blown off by the storm, she raised very loud cries and lamented exceedingly. This she continued to do for a long time, and would not be comforted. At length, after two or three years, the spirits had pity on her, and determined to raise another storm and bring her back. It was even a greater storm than the first; and when it began to wash away the ground and encroach on the lodge of Ishkwon Daimeka, she leaped into the box, and the waves carried her back to the very spot of her mother's lodge on the shore. Monedo Equa was overjoyed; but when she opened the box, she found that her daughter's beauty had almost all departed. However, she loved her still because she was her daughter, and now thought of the young man who had made her the offer of marriage. She sent a formal message to him, but he had altered his mind, for he knew that she had been the wife of another: "I marry your daughter?" said he; "your daughter! No, indeed! I shall never marry her."

The storm that brought her back was so strong and powerful, that it tore away a large part of the shore of the lake, and swept off Ishkwon Daimeka's lodge, the fragments of which, lodging in the straits, formed those beautiful islands which are scattered in the St. Clair and Detroit rivers. The old man himself was drowned, and his bones are buried under them. They heard him singing his songs of lamentation as he was driven off on a portion of his lodge; as if he had been called to testify his bravery and sing his war song at the stake.

No storms can blench my heart.

A LAZY MAN

In Geneseo there was a young man, an orphan, who went around among the people, staying wherever kindhearted persons would keep him, sleeping on the ground by a brush fire, and eating whatever was given to him. When he was twenty years old, he was as much of a boy as ever.

A chief, who was rich and proud, lived in Geneseo. He had a daughter and two or three sons. One day the orphan stopped near the chief's house where people were burning brush.

One of the chief's sons came out and said to him, "Don't you feel poor and lonely sitting around so?"

"No," said the young man, "I feel as rich as you do."

"Don't you sometimes think you would like to have a wife?"

"Yes, I sometimes think I would like a wife if I could get one."

"What would you think of my sister for a wife? Many men have tried to marry her, but she refuses everyone."

"Oh," said the orphan, looking up, "I would as soon have her as any woman; she is handsome and rich."

"I will ask her to marry you," said the brother, thinking to have fun with his sister.

He went to the house and said to her, "There is a young man out there by the fire, who would like to marry you. Will you be his wife?"

"I will. I would rather marry him than anyone else."

"Shall I tell him so?"

"You may."

He told the young man, who said, "I shall be glad to have her for my wife."

The brother, in fun, repeated this to his sister, who said, "I will go and ask him myself."

She went to the orphan, and asked, "What did my brother say to you?"

He told her, and she said, "I will go with you. Come tomorrow at this time and I'll marry you."

The next morning the girl got leggings and moccasins for the young man. (He had never worn moccasins in Summer.) In the evening he came to where she was. He washed, put on the leggings and embroidered moccasins and tied up his hair. She told him then that he could go home with her, but he must not talk with any of the men, that one of her brothers was always fooling.

The girl became the orphan's wife and he lived in the chief's house. In the Fall when the chief's sons were ready to go deer hunting, the young woman wanted to go. She had a husband and she thought he might be a good hunter.

The man had never hunted but he said, "I will go and try."

When the party had gone some distance, they camped and began to hunt. The young man found a place where there were wild grape vines. He made a swing, then sat in it and swung all day, didn't try to hunt. At night he went home without game. Each morning he went to the swing and each evening he went home without game.

The brothers killed many deer. One day one brother said to the other, "Our brother-in-law gets no game, maybe he doesn't hunt." They agreed to watch him.

The next morning they followed the young man, found him swinging and saw that the ground was smooth around the swing. Then they said, "We will not live with him and feed him. We will leave him, go a day's journey away and camp."

They left the man and woman with only one leg of deer meat.

The young man never ate much; the woman ate most of the meat. When it was gone, she began to be afraid of starving.

One day, while the man was swinging, a horned owl lighted on a tree nearby. He shot the owl and put it under the swing where he could look at it as he swung. His wife was getting very hungry.

That night when he came home without game, she said, "If I have nothing to eat to-morrow, I will be too weak to get up. You ought to kill something."

"Well, maybe to-morrow I will kill something."

The next morning the man went, as usual, to the swing. While swinging he heard a woman crying. He was frightened and stopped swinging. Soon he saw a female panther coming with three cubs. She was crying. As she approached, he heard a terrible roar in the North, the direction from which the panther had come. Then the man saw Whirlwind coming, tearing down all the trees in his path. He stopped on a tree near the swing.

"You know now what harm you have done," said Whirlwind to Panther.

"Why are you angry with the panther?" asked the young man. "What has she done to you?"

"She has torn up my best feather cap."

"Why do you think so much of your cap? It must have been a nice one."

"It was nice."

"What kind of feathers was it made of?"

"It was the skin and feathers of a horned owl."

"What would you think if I gave you another cap?"

"How can you get one?"

The young man picked up the horned owl that he had killed and threw it at Whirlwind. Whirlwind caught it, said, "Thank you, this is better than the one Panther destroyed," and away he flew.

Panther thanked the man, and said, "I am glad that you had the owl, you have saved my life. Now I will help you. Go to that knoll yonder, behind it you will find two bucks fighting. Shoot them both. The one you shoot first will not run; they will fight till they die."

The young man found the bucks and watched them till they killed each other. Then, taking a large piece of meat, He went home to his wife, who was almost starved.

"I have brought you meat," said he, "I had good luck to-day."

The woman sprang up, threw the meat on the fire and hardly waited for it to cook till she began to eat.

They dragged the bucks home, skinned them, and had plenty of meat. The young woman dried the meat and tanned the skins.

Panther told the man to always hunt near the swing and he would kill a great deal of game.

When they had a large quantity of meat, the man said to his wife, "Your brothers are good hunters. No doubt they have plenty of meat, but I will find them and see."

He started. On the way he killed a deer, and he carried the carcass along. He found the camp and looking in saw the brothers; they were poor and weak.

He went in, and asked, "How are you?"

"We are almost starved," said one of them. "We can find nothing to kill."

"Your sister and I have a plenty. Come and live with us. I have meat here. Eat and then come to my camp."

He gave them the deer and they ate the meat nearly raw, they were so hungry.

When they started for the young man's camp he went ahead, got home quickly and told his wife he had found her brothers nearer starvation than she had been. During the night the brothers came. They were satisfied and remained with their sister and brother-in-law.

After a while they all went back to the village loaded with skins and venison. Now the young man was rich; and he and his wife lived ever after in Geneseo Valley.

THE INVISIBLE ONE

There was once a large Indian village situated on the border of a lake – Nameskeek' oodun Kuspemku. At the end of the place was a lodge, in which dwelt a being who was always invisible. He had a sister who attended to his wants, and it was known that any girl who could see him might marry him. Therefore there were indeed few who did not make the trial, but it was long ere one succeeded.

And it passed in this wise. Towards evening, when the Invisible One was supposed to be returning home, his sister would walk with any girls who came down to the shore of the lake. She indeed could see her brother, since to her he was always visible, and beholding him she would say to her companions, "Do you see my brother?" And then they would mostly answer, "Yes," though some said, "Nay," – alt telovejich, aa alttelooejik. And then the sister would say, "Cogoowa' wiskobooksich?" "Of what is his shoulder-strap made?" But as some tell the tale, she would inquire other things, such as, "What is his moose-runner''s haul?" or, "With what does he draw his sled?" And they would reply, "A strip of rawhide," or "A green withe," or something of the kind. And then she, knowing they had not told the truth, would reply quietly, "Very well, let us return to the wigwam!"

And when they entered the place she would bid them not to take a certain seat, for it was his. And after they had helped to cook the supper they would wait with great curiosity to see him eat. Truly he gave proof that he was a real person, for as he took off his moccasins they became visible, and his sister hung them up; but beyond this they beheld nothing not even when they remained all night, as many did.

There dwelt in the village an old man, a widower, with three daughters. The youngest of these was very small, weak, and often ill, which did not prevent her sisters, especially the eldest, treating her with great cruelty. The second daughter was kinder, and sometimes took the part of the poor abused little girl, but the other would burn her hands and face with hot coals; yes, her whole body was scarred with the marks made by torture, so that people called her Oochigeaskw (the rough-faced girl). And when her father, coming home, asked what it meant that the child was so disfigured, her sister would promptly say that it was the fault of the girl herself, for that, having been forbidden to go near the fire, she had disobeyed and fallen in.

Now it came to pass that it entered the heads of the two elder sisters of this poor girl that they would go and try their fortune at seeing the Invisible One. So they clad themselves in their finest and strove to look their fairest; and finding his sister at home went with her to take the wonted walk down to the water. Then when He came, being, asked if they saw him, they said, "Certainly," and also replied to the question of the shoulder-strap or sled cord, "A piece of rawhide." In saying which, they lied, like the rest, for they had seen nothing and got nothing for their pains.

When their father returned home the next evening he brought with him many of the pretty little shells from which weiopeskool, or wampum, was made, and they were soon engaged napawejik (in stringing them).

That day poor little Oochigeaskw', the burnt-faced girl, who had always run barefoot, got a pair of her father's old moccasins, and put them into water that they might become flexible to wear. And begging her sisters for a few wampum shells, the eldest did but call her "a lying little pest," but the other gave her a few. And having no clothes beyond a few paltry rags, the poor creature went forth and got herself from the woods a few sheets of birch bark, of which she made a dress, putting some figures on the bark. And this dress she shaped like those worn of old. So she made a petticoat and a loose gown, a cap, leggins, and handkerchief, and, having put on her father's great old moccasins – which came nearly up to her knees – she went forth to try her luck. For even this little thing would see the Invisible One in the great wigwam at the end of the village.

Truly her luck had a most inauspicious beginning, for there was one long storm of ridicule and hisses, yells and hoots, from her own door to that which she went to seek. Her sisters tried to shame her, and bade her stay at home, but she would not obey; and all the idlers, seeing this strange little creature in her odd array, cried, "Shame!" But she went on, for she was greatly resolved; it may be that some spirit had inspired her.

Now this poor small wretch in her mad attire, with her hair singed off and her little face as full of burns and sears as there are holes in a sieve, was, for all this, most kindly received by the sister of the Invisible One; for this noble girl knew more than the mere outside of things as the world knows them. And as the brown of the evening sky became black, she took her down to the lake. And erelong the girls knew that He had come. Then the sister said, "Do you see him?" And the other replied with awe, "Truly I do – and He is wonderful." "And what is his sled-string?" "It is," she replied, "the Rainbow." And great fear was on her. "But, my sister," said the other, "what is his bow-string?" "His bowstring is Ketaksoowowcht" (the Spirits' Road, the Milky Way).

"Thou hast seen him," said the sister. And, taking the girl home, she bathed her, and as she washed all the scars disappeared from face and body. Her hair grew again; it was very long, and like a blackbird's wing. Her eyes were like stars. In all the world was no such beauty. Then from her treasures she gave her a wedding garment, and adorned her. Under the comb, as she combed her, her hair grew. It was a great marvel to behold.

Then, having done this, she bade her take the wife's seat in the wigwam – that by which her brother sat, the seat next the door. And when He entered, terrible and beautiful, he smiled and said, "Wajoolkoos!" "So we are found out!" "Alajulaa." "Yes," was her reply. So she became his wife.

SNOWBIRD AND THE WATER-TIGER

Snowbird was the much-loved wife of **Brown Bear**, the brave hunter whose home was on the shore of the Great Lake. He kept the wigwam well supplied with food; and Snowbird's moccasins were the finest in the tribe, save only those of the Chief's daughters. Even those owed much of their beauty to the lovely feathers that Snowbird had given them. If you had asked her where she got them she would have answered proudly, "My husband brought them from the chase."

Besides Brown Bear and his wife, there lived in the wigwam their own, dear, little papoose whom they called "Pigeon," because he was always saying, "Goo, goo;" but they hoped that he would win a nobler name some day, when he should fight the enemy, or kill some beast that was a terror to the tribe, and so take its name for his own.

These three would have been a very happy family; nor would the little orphan boy whom they had adopted long before Pigeon was born, have made them any trouble; he was a great help to them. But there was still another inmate, Brown Bear's mother, a wicked, old squaw, whom none of the other sons' wives would have in their wigwams. Brown Bear was her youngest son, and had always been her favorite. She was kind to him when she was not to any one else; and he loved her and took good care of her, just as much after he brought Snowbird home to be his wife, as he had done before. But the old woman was jealous; and when Brown Bear brought in dainty bits, such as the moose's lip and the bear's kidney, and gave them to his wife, she hated her and grumbled and mumbled to herself in the corner by the fire.

Day after day she sat thinking how she could get rid of the "intruder," as she called her daughter-in-law. She forgot how she had married the only son of a brave Chief and had gone to be the mistress of his wigwam; and he had been as kind and good to her as her son was to Snowbird.

One day when the work was all done, the old woman asked her daughter-in-law to go out to see a swing she had found near the Great Lake. It was a twisted grapevine, that hung over a high rock; but it was stout and strong, for it had been there many years and was securely fastened about the roots of two large trees. The old woman got in first and grasping the vine tightly, swung herself further and further until she was clear out over the water. "It is delightful," said she; "just try it."

So Snowbird got into the swing. While she was enjoying the cool breeze that rose from the lake, the old woman crept behind the trees, and, as soon as the swing was in full motion, and Snowbird was far out over the water, she cut the vine and let her drop down, down, down, not stopping to see what became of her.

She went home and putting on her daughter-in-law's clothes sat in Snowbird's place by the fire, hiding her face as much as possible, so that no one should see her wrinkles.

When Brown Bear came home he gave her the dainties, supposing she was his wife; and she ate them greedily, paying no attention to the baby, who was crying as if its heart would break.

"Why does little Pigeon cry so?" asked the father.

I don't know," said the old woman, "I suppose he's hungry."

Thereat, she picked up the baby, shook it soundly and made believe to nurse it. It cried louder than ever. She boxed its ears and stuffed something into its mouth to keep it quiet.

Brown Bear thought his wife very cross, so he took his pipe and left the wigwam.

The orphan boy had watched all these doings and had grown suspicious. Going to the fire he pretended to brush away the ashes; and, when he thought the old woman was not looking at him, he stirred the logs and made a bright flame leap up so that he could plainly see her face. He was sure there was something wrong.

"Where is Snowbird?" asked he.

"Sh–!" said the old woman; "she is by the lake, swinging." The boy said no more, but went out of the wigwam and down to the lake. There he saw the broken swing, and guessing what had happened, he went in search of Brown Bear and told him what he had discovered.

Brown Bear did not like to think any wrong of his mother, and therefore asked her no questions. Sadly he paced up and down outside the door of his wigwam. Then taking some black paint he smeared his face and body with it as a sign of mourning. When this was done he turned his long spear upside down, and pressing it into the earth, prayed for lightning, thunder and rain, so that his wife's body might rise from the lake.

Every day he went thither, but saw no sign of his dear Snowbird, though the thunder rolled heavily and the lightning had split a great oak near the wigwam from the top to the base. He watched in the rain, in the sunlight, and when the great, white moon shone over the lake, but he saw nothing.

Meanwhile the orphan boy looked after little Pigeon, letting him suck the dantiest, juiciest bits of meat, and bringing him milk to drink. On bright afternoons he would take the baby to the lake shore and amuse him by throwing pebbles into the water. Little Pigeon would laugh and crow and stretch out his tiny hands, then taking a pebble would try to throw it into the water himself, and, though it always dropped at his feet, he was just as well pleased.

One day as they were playing in this manner they saw a white gull rise from the center of the lake and fly towards the part of the shore where they were. When it reached them it circled above their heads, flying down close to them until little Pigeon could almost touch its great, white wings. Then, all of a sudden, it changed to a woman—Snowbird, little Pigeon's mother!

The baby crowed with delight and caught at two belts, one of leather and one of white metal, that his mother wore about her waist. She could not speak; but she took the baby in her arms, fondled it and nursed it. Then she made signs to the boy by which he understood that he was to bring the child there every day.

When Brown Bear came home that night the boy told him all that had happened.

The next afternoon when the baby cried for food the boy took him to the lake shore, Brown Bear following and hiding behind the bushes. The boy stood where he had before, close to the water's edge, and, choosing a smooth, round pebble, raised his arm slowly and with careful aim threw it far out into the lake.

Soon the gull, with a long, shining belt around its body, was seen rising from the water. It came ashore, hovered above them a moment, and, as on the previous day, changed into a woman and took the child in her arms.

While she was nursing it her husband appeared. The black paint was still on his body, but he held his spear in his hand.

"Why have you not come home?" he cried, and sprang forward to embrace her.

She could not speak, but pointed to the shining belt she wore.

Brown Bear raised his spear carefully and struck a great blow at the links. They were shivered to fragments and dropped on the sands, where any one seeing them would have supposed they were pieces of a large shell.

Then Snowbird's speech returned and she told how when she fell into the lake, a water-tiger seized her and twisting his tail around her waist, drew her to the bottom.

There she found a grand lodge whose walls were blue like the bluejay's back when the sun shines upon it, green like the first leaves of the maize and golden like the bright sands on the island of the Caribs; and the floor was of sand, white as the snows of winter. This was the wigwam of the Chief of the water-tigers, whose mother was the Horned Serpent and lived with him.

The Serpent lay on a great, white shell which had knobs of copper that shone like distant campfires. But these were nothing to the red stone that sparkled on her forehead. It was covered with a thin skin like a man's eyelid, which was drawn down when she went to sleep. Her horns were very wonderful, for they were possessed of magic. When they touched a great rock the stone fell apart and there was a pathway made through it wherever the Serpent wanted to go.

There were forests in the Water-Tiger's country, trees with leaves like the willow, only longer, finer and broader, bushes and clumps of soft, dark grass.

When night came and the sun no longer shone down into the lodge and the color went out of the walls, there were fireflies—green, blue, crimson, and orange—that lighted on the bushes outside the Water-Tiger's wigwam; and the most beautiful s of them passed inside and fluttered about the throne of the

Serpent, standing guard over her while the purple snails, the day sentinels, slept.

Snowbird trembled when she saw these things and fell down in a faint before the great Horned Serpent. But the Water-Tiger soothed her, for he loved her and wanted her to become his wife. This she consented to do at last on condition that she should be allowed to go back sometimes to the lake shore to see her child.

The Water-Tiger consulted his mother, who agreed to lend him a sea-gull's wing which should cover his wife all over and enable her to fly to the shore. He was told, however, to fasten his tail securely about her waist, lest she should desert him when she found herself near her old home. He did so, taking care to put a leather belt around her, for fear the links of white metal might hurt her delicate skin.

So she lived with the Water-Tiger, kept his lodge in order and made moccasins for the little water-tigers out of beaver skin and dried fish scales, and was as happy as she could have been anywhere away from her own Brown Bear and Little Pigeon.

When the old woman, Brown Bear's mother, saw them at the door of the wigwam, she leaped up and flew out of the lodge and was never seen again.

A GLOSSARY OF MYTH & FOLKLORE

Aaru Heavenly paradise where the blessed go after death.

Ab Heart or mind.

Abiku (Yoruba) Person predestined to die. Also known as ogbanje.

Absál Nurse to Saláman, who died after their brief love affair.

Achilles The son of Peleus and the sea-nymph Thetis, who distinguished himself in the Trojan War. He was made almost immortal by his mother, who dipped him in the River Styx, and he was invincible except for a portion of his heel which remained out of the water.

Acropolis Citadel in a Greek city.

Adad-Ea Ferryman to Ut-Napishtim, who carried Gilgamesh to visit his ancestor.

Adapa Son of Ea and a wise sage.

Adar God of the sun, who is worshipped primarily in Nippur.

Aditi Sky goddess and mother of the gods.

Adityas Vishnu, children of Aditi, including Indra, Mitra, Rudra, Tvashtar, Varuna and Vishnu.

Aeneas The son of Anchises and the goddess Aphrodite, reared by a nymph. He led the Dardanian troops in the Trojan War According to legend, he became the founder of Rome.

Aengus Óg Son of Dagda and Boann (a woman said to have given the Boyne river its name), Aengus is the Irish god of love whose stronghold is reputed to have been at New Grange. The famous tale 'Dream of Aengus' tells of how he fell in love with a maiden he had dreamt of. He eventually discovered that she was to be found at the Lake of the Dragon's Mouth in Co. Tipperary, but that she lived every alternate year in the form of a swan. Aengus thus plunged into the lake transforming himself also into the shape of a swan. Then the two flew back together to his palace on the Boyne where they lived out their days as guardians of would-be lovers.

Aesir Northern gods who made their home in Asgard; there are twelve in number.

Afrásiyáb Son of Poshang, king of Túrán, who led an army against the ruling shah Nauder. Afrásiyáb became ruler of Persia on defeating Nauder.

Afterlife Life after death or paradise, reached only by the process of preserving the body from decay through embalming and preparing it for reincarnation.

Agamemnon A famous King of Mycenae. He married Helen of Sparta's sister Clytemnestra. When Paris abducted Helen, beginning the Trojan War, Menelaus called on Agamemnon to raise the Greek troops. He had to sacrifice his daughter Iphigenia in order to get a fair wind to travel to Troy.

Agastya A rishi (sage). Leads hermits to Rama.

Agemo (Yoruba) A chameleon who aided Olorun in outwitting Olokun, who was angry at him for letting Obatala create life on her lands without her permission. Agemo outwitted Olokun by changing colour, letting her think that he and Olorun were better cloth dyers than she was. She admitted defeat and there was peace between the gods once again.

Aghasur A dragon sent by Kans to destroy Krishna.

Aghríras Son of Poshang and brother of Afrásiyáb, who was killed by his brother.

Agni The god of fire.

Agora Greek marketplace.

Ahura-Mazda Supreme god of the Persians, god of the sky. Similar to the Hindu god Varuna.

Ajax Ajax the Greater was the bravest, after Achilles, of all warriors at Troy, fighting Hector in single combat and distinguishing himself in the Battle of the Ships. He was not chosen as the bravest warrior and eventually went mad.

Ajax of Locris Another warrior at Troy. When Troy was captured, he committed the ultimate sacrilege by seizing Cassandra from her sanctuary with the Palladium.

Aje (Igbo) Goddess of the earth and the underworld.

Aje (Yoruba) Goddess of the River Niger, daughter of Yemoja.

Akhet Season of the year when the River Nile traditionally flooded.

Akkadian Person of the first Mesopotamian empire, centred in Akkad.

Akwán Diw An evil spirit who appeared as a wild ass in the court of Kai-khosráu. Rustem fought and defeated the demon, presenting its head to Kai-khosráu.

Alba Irish and Scottish Gaelic word for Scotland.

Alberich King of the dwarfs.

Alcinous King of the Phaeacians.

Alf-heim Home of the elves, ruled by Frey.

All Hallowmass All Saints' Day.

Allfather Another name for Odin; Yggdrasill was created by Allfather.

Alsvider Steed of the moon (Mani) chariot.

Alsvin Steed of the sun (Sol) chariot.

Amado Outer panelling of a dwelling, usually made of wood.

Ama-no-uzume Goddess of the dawn, meditation and the arts, who showed courage when faced with a giant who scared the other deities, including Ninigi. Also known as Uzume.

Amaterasu Goddess of the sun and daughter of Izanagi after Izanami's death; she became ruler of the High Plains of Heaven on her father's withdrawal from the world. Sister of Tsuki-yomi and Susanoo.

Ambalika Daughter of the king of Benares.
Ambika Daughter of the king of Benares.
Ambrosia Food of the gods.
Amemet Eater of the dead, monster who devoured the souls of the unworthy.
Amen Original creator deity.
Amen-Ra A being created from the fusion of Ra and Osiris. He champions the poor and those in trouble. Similar to the Greek god Zeus.
Ananda Disciple of Buddha.
Anansi One of the most popular African animal myths, Anansi the spider is a clever and shrewd character who outwits his fellow animals to get his own way. He is an entertaining but morally dubious character. Many African countries tell Anansi stories.
Ananta Thousand-headed snake that sprang from Balarama's mouth, Vishnu's attendant, serpent of infinite time.
Andhrímnir Cook at Valhalla.
Andvaranaut Ring of Andvari, the King of the dwarfs.
Angada Son of Vali, one of the monkey host.
Anger-Chamber Room designated for an angry queen.
Angurboda Loki's first wife, and the mother of Hel, Fenris and Jormungander.
Aniruddha Son of Pradyumna.
Anjana Mother of Hanuman.
Anunnaki Great spirits or gods of Earth.
Ansar God of the sky and father of Ea and Anu. Brother-husband to Kishar. Also known as Anshar or Asshur.
Anshumat A mighty chariot fighter.
Anu God of the sky and lord of heaven, son of Ansar and Kishar.

Anubis Guider of souls and ruler of the underworld before Osiris; he was one of the divinities who brought Osiris back to life. He is portrayed as a canid, African wolf or jackal.

Apep Serpent and emblem of chaos.

Apollo One of the twelve Olympian gods, son of Zeus and Leto. He is attributed with being the god of plague, music, song and prophecy.

Apsaras Dancing girls of Indra's court and heavenly nymphs.

Apsu Primeval domain of fresh water, originally part of Tiawath with whom he mated to have Mummu. The term is also used for the abyss from which creation came.

Aquila The divine eagle.

Arachne A Lydian woman with great skill in weaving. She was challenged in a competition by the jealous Athene who destroyed her work and when she killed herself, turned her into a spider destined to weave for eternity.

Aralu Goddess of the underworld, also known as Eres-ki-Gal. Married to Nergal.

Ares God of War, 'gold-changer of corpses', and the son of Zeus and Hera.

Argonauts Heroes who sailed with Jason on the ship Argo to fetch the golden fleece from Colchis.

Ariki A high chief, a leader, a master, a lord.

Arjuna The third of the Pandavas.

Aroha Affection, love.

Artemis The virgin goddess of the chase, attributed with being the moon goddess and the primitive mother-goddess. She was daughter of Zeus and Leto.

Arundhati The Northern Crown.

Asamanja Son of Sagara.

Asclepius God of healing who often took the form of a snake. He is the son of Apollo by Coronis.

Asgard Home of the gods, at one root of Yggdrasill.

Ashvatthaman Son of Drona.

Ashvins Twin horsemen, sons of the sun, benevolent gods and related to the divine.

Ashwapati Uncle of Bharata and Satrughna.

Asipû Wizard.

Asopus The god of the River Asopus.

Assagai Spear, usually made from hardwood tipped with iron and used in battle.

Astrolabe Instrument for making astronomical measurements.

Asuras Titans, demons, and enemies of the gods with magical powers.

Atef crown White crown made up of the Hedjet, the white crown of Upper Egypt, and red feathers.

Atem The first creator-deity, he is also thought to be the finisher of the world. Also known as Tem.

Athene Virgin warrior-goddess, born from the forehead of Zeus when he swallowed his wife Metis. Plays a key role in the travels of Odysseus, and Perseus.

Atlatl Spear-thrower.

Atua A supernatural being, a god.

Atua-toko A small carved stick, the symbol of the god whom it represents. It was stuck in the ground whilst holding incantations to its presiding god.

Augeas King of Elis, one of the Argonauts.

Augsburg Tyr's city.

Avalon Legendary island where Excalibur was created and where Arthur went to recover from his wounds. It is said he will return from Avalon one day to reclaim his kingdom.

Ba Dead person or soul. Also known as ka.

Bairn Little child, also called bairnie.

Balarama Brother of Krishna.

Balder Son of Frigga; his murder causes Ragnarok. Also spelled as Baldur.

Bali Brother of Sugriva and one of the five great monkeys in the *Ramayana*.

Balor The evil, one-eyed King of the Fomorians and also grandfather of Lugh of the Long Arm. It was prophesied that Balor would one day be slain by his own grandson so he locked his daughter away on a remote island where he intended that she would never fall pregnant. But Cian, father of Lugh, managed to reach the island disguised as a woman, and Balor's daughter eventually bore him a child. During the second battle of Mag Tured (or Moytura), Balor was killed by Lugh who slung a stone into his giant eye.

Ban King of Benwick, father of Lancelot and brother of King Bors.

Bannock Flat loaf of bread, typically of oat or barley, usually cooked on a griddle.

Banshee Mythical spirit, usually female, who bears tales of imminent death. They often deliver the news by wailing or keening outside homes. Spelled *bean sí* in Gaelic.

Bard Traditionally a storyteller, poet or music composer whose work often focused on legends.

Barû Seer.

Basswood Any of several North American linden trees with a soft light-coloured wood.

Bastet Goddess of love, fertility and sex and a solar deity. She is often portrayed with the head of a cat.

Bateta (Yoruba) The first human, created alongside Hanna by the Toad and reshaped into human form by the Moon.

Bau Goddess of humankind and the sick, and known as the 'divine physician'. Daughter of Anu.

Bawn Fortified enclosure surrounding a castle.

Beaver Largest rodent in the United States of America, held in high esteem by Native American people. Although a land mammal, it spends a great deal of time in water and has a dense waterproof fur coat to protect it from harsh weather conditions.

Behula Daughter of Saha.

Bel Name for the god En-lil, the word is also used as a title meaning 'lord'.

Belus Deity who helped form the heavens and earth and created animals and celestial beings. Similar to Zeus in Greek mythology.

Benten Goddess of the sea and one of the Seven Divinities of Luck. Also referred to as the goddess of love, beauty and eloquence and as being the personification of wisdom.

Bere Barley.

Berossus Priest of Bel who wrote a history of Babylon.

Berserker Norse warrior who fights with a frenzied rage.

Bestla Giant mother of Aesir's mortal element.

Bhadra A mighty elephant.

Bhagavati Shiva's wife, also known as Parvati.

Bhagiratha Son of Dilipa.

Bharadhwaja Father of Drona and a hermit.

Bharata One of Dasharatha's four sons.

Bhaumasur A demon, slain by Krishna.

Bhima The second of the Pandavas.

Bhimasha King of Rajagriha and disciple of Buddha.

Bier Frame on which a coffin or dead body is placed before being carried to the grave.

Bifrost Rainbow bridge presided over by Heimdall.

Big-Belly One of Ravana's monsters.

Bilskirnir Thor's palace.

Bodach The term means 'old man'. The Highlanders believed that the Bodach crept down chimneys in order to steal naughty children. In other territories, he was a spirit who warned of death.

Bodkin Large, blunt needle used for threading strips of cloth or tape through cloth; short pointed dagger or blade.

Boer Person of Dutch origin who settled in southern Africa in the late seventeenth century. The term means 'farmer'. Boer people are often called Afrikaners.

Bogle Ghost or phantom; goblin-like creature.

Boliaun Ragwort, a weed with ragged leaves.

Book of the Dead Book for the dead, thought to be written by Thoth, texts from which were written on papyrus and buried with the dead, or carved on the walls of tombs, pyramids or sarcophagi.

Bors King of Gaul and brother of King Ban.

Bothy Small cottage or hut.

Brahma Creator of the world, mythical origin of colour (caste).

Brahmadatta King of Benares.

Brahman Member of the highest Hindu caste, traditionally a priest.

Bran In Scottish legend, Bran is the great hunting hound of Fionn Mac Chumail. In Irish mythology, he is a great hero.

Branstock Giant oak tree in the Volsung's hall; Odin placed a sword in it and challenged the guests of a wedding to withdraw it.

Brave Young warrior of Native American descent, sometimes also referred to as a 'buck'.

Bree Thin broth or soup.

Breidablik Balder's palace.

Brigit Scottish saint or spirit associated with the coming of spring.
Brisingamen Freyia's necklace.
Britomartis A Cretan goddess, also known as Dictynna.
Brocéliande Legendary enchanted forest and the supposed burial place of Merlin.
Brokki Dwarf who makes a deal with Loki, and who makes Miolnir, Draupnir and Gulinbursti.
Brollachan A shapeless spirit of unknown origin. One of the most frightening in Scottish mythology, it spoke only two words, 'Myself' and 'Thyself', taking the shape of whatever it sat upon.
Brownie A household spirit or creature which took the form of a small man (usually hideously ugly) who undertakes household chores, and mill or farm work, in exchange for a bowl of milk.
Brugh Borough or town.
Brunhilde A Valkyrie found by Sigurd.
Buddha Founder of buddhism, Gautama, avatar of Vishnu in Hinduism.
Buddhism Buddhism arrived in China in the first century BCE via the silk trading route from India and Central Asia. Its founder was Guatama Siddhartha (the Buddha), a religious teacher in northern India. Buddhist doctrine declared that by destroying the causes of all suffering, mankind could attain perfect enlightenment. The religion encouraged a new respect for all living things and brought with it the idea of reincarnation; i.e. that the soul returns to the earth after death in another form, dictated by the individual's behaviour in his previous life. By the fourth century, Buddhism was the dominant religion in China, retaining its powerful influence over the nation until the mid-ninth century.
Buffalo A type of wild ox, once widely scattered over the Great Plains of North America. Also known as a 'bison', the buffalo

was an important food source for Native American tribes and its hide was also used in the construction of tepees and to make clothing. The buffalo was also sometimes revered as a totem animal, i.e. venerated as a direct ancestor of the tribesmen, and its skull used in ceremonial fashion.

Bull of Apis Sacred bull, thought to be the son of Hathor.

Bulu Sacrificial rite.

Bundles, sacred These bundles contained various venerated objects of the tribe, believed to have supernatural powers. Custody or ownership of the bundle was never lightly entered upon, but involved the learning of endless songs and ritual dances.

Bushel Unit of measurement, usually used for agricultural products or food.

Bushi Warrior.

Byre Barn for keeping cattle.

Byrny Coat of mail.

Cacique King or prince.

Cailleach Bheur A witch with a blue face who represents winter. When she is reborn each autumn, snow falls. She is mother of the god of youth (Angus mac Og).

Calabash Gourd from the calabash tree, commonly used as a bottle.

Calchas The seer of Mycenae who accompanied the Greek fleet to Troy. It was his prophecy which stated that Troy would never be taken without the aid of Achilles.

Calpulli Village house, or group or clan of families.

Calumet Ceremonial pipe used by Native Americans.

Calypso A nymph who lived on the island of Ogygia.

Camaxtli Tlascalan god of war and the chase, similar to Huitzilopochtli.

Camelot King Arthur's castle and centre of his realm.

Caoineag A banshee.

Caravanserai Traveller's inn, traditionally found in Asia or North Africa.

Carle Term for a man, often old; peasant.

Cat A black cat has great mythological significance, is often the bearer of bad luck, a symbol of black magic, and the familiar of a witch. Cats were also the totem for many tribes.

Cath Sith A fairy cat who was believed to be a witch transformed.

Cazi Magical person or influence.

Ceasg A Scottish mermaid with the body of a maiden and the tail of a salmon.

Ceilidh Party.

Cerberus The three-headed dog who guarded the entrance to the Underworld.

Chalchiuhtlicue Goddess of water and the sick or newborn, and wife of Tlaloc. She is often symbolized as a small frog.

Changeling A fairy substitute-child left by fairies in place of a human child they have stolen.

Channa Guatama's charioteer.

Chaos A state from which the universe was created – caused by fire and ice meeting.

Charon The ferryman of the dead who carries souls across the River Styx to Hades.

Charybdis *See* Scylla and Charybdis.

Chicomecohuatl Chief goddess of maize and one of a group of deities called Centeotl, who care for all aspects of agriculture.

Chicomoztoc Legendary mountain and place of origin of the Aztecs. The name means 'seven caves'.

Chinawezi Primordial serpent.

Chinvat Bridge Bridge of the Gatherer, which the souls of the righteous cross to reach Mount Alborz or the world of the dead. Unworthy beings who try to cross Chinvat Bridge fall or are dragged into a place of eternal punishment.

Chitambaram Sacred city of Shiva's dance.

Chrysaor Son of Poseidon and Medusa, born from the severed neck of Medusa when Perseus beheaded her.

Chryseis Daughter of Chryses who was taken by Agamemnon in the battle of Troy.

Chullasubhadda Wife of Buddha-elect (Sumedha).

Chunda A good smith who entertains Buddha.

Churl Mean or unkind person.

Circe An enchantress and the daughter of Helius. She lived on the island of Aeaea with the power to change men to beasts.

Citlalpol The Mexican name for Venus, or the Great Star, and one of the only stars they worshipped. Also known as Tlauizcalpantecutli, or Lord of the Dawn.

Cleobis and Biton Two men of Argos who dragged the wagon carrying their mother, priestess of Hera, from Argos to the sanctuary.

Clio Muse of history and prophecy.

Clytemnestra Daughter of Tyndareus, sister of Helen, who married Agamemnon but deserted him when he sacrificed Iphigenia, their daughter, at the beginning of the Trojan War.

Coatepetl Mythical mountain, known as the 'serpent mountain'.

Coatl Serpent.

Coatlicue Earth mother and celestial goddess, she gave birth to Huitzilopochtli and his sister, Coyolxauhqui, and the moon and stars.

Codex Ancient book, often a list with pages folded into a zigzag pattern.

Confucius (Kong Fuzi) Regarded as China's greatest sage and ethical teacher, Confucius (551–479 BCE) was not especially revered during his lifetime and had a small following of some three thousand people. After the Burning of the Books in 213 BCE, interest in his philosophies became widespread. Confucius believed that mankind was essentially good, but argued for a highly structured society, presided over by a strong central government which would set the highest moral standards. The individual's sense of duty and obligation, he argued, would play a vital role in maintaining a well-run state.

Coracle Small, round boat, similar to a canoe. Also known as curragh or currach.

Coyolxauhqui Goddess of the moon and sister to Huitzilopochtli, she was decapitated by her brother after trying to kill their mother.

Creel Large basket made of wicker, usually used for fish.

Crodhmara Fairy cattle.

Cronan Musical humming, thought to resemble a cat purring or the drone of bagpipes.

Crow Usually associated with battle and death, but many mythological figures take this form.

Cu Sith A great fairy dog, usually green and oversized.

Cubit Ancient measurement, equal to the approximate length of a forearm.

Cuculain Irish warrior and hero. Also known as Cuchulainn.

Cutty Girl.

Cyclopes One-eyed giants who were imprisoned in Tartarus by Uranus and Cronus, but released by Zeus, for whom they made thunderbolts. Also a tribe of pastoralists who live without laws, and on, whenever possible, human flesh.

A GLOSSARY OF MYTH & FOLKLORE

Daedalus Descendant of the Athenian King Erechtheus and son of Eupalamus. He killed his nephew and apprentice. Famed for constructing the labyrinth to house the Minotaur, in which he was later imprisoned. He constructed wings for himself and his son to make their escape.

Dagda One of the principal gods of the Tuatha De Danann, the father and chief, the Celtic equivalent of Zeus. He was the god reputed to have led the People of Dana in their successful conquest of the Fir Bolg.

Dagon God of fish and fertility; he is sometimes described as a sea-monster or chthonic god.

Daikoku God of wealth and one of the gods of luck.

Daimyō Powerful lord or magnate.

Daksha The chief Prajapati.

Dana Also known as Danu, a goddess worshipped from antiquity by the Celts and considered to be the ancestor of the Tuatha De Danann.

Danae Daughter of Acrisius, King of Argos. Acrisius trapped her in a cave when he was warned that his grandson would be the cause of his ultimate death. Zeus came to her and Perseus was born.

Danaids The fifty daughters of Danaus of Argos, by ten mothers.

Daoine Sidhe The people of the Hollow Hills, or Otherworld.

Dardanus Son of Zeus and Electra, daughter of Atlas.

Dasharatha A Manu amongst men, King of Koshala, father of Santa.

Deianeira Daughter of Oeneus, who married Heracles after he won her in a battle with the River Achelous.

Deirdre A beautiful woman doomed to cause the deaths of three Irish heroes and bring war to the whole country. After a soothsayer prophesied her fate, Deidre's father hid her away from the world to prevent it. However, fate finds its way and the events come to pass before Deidre eventually commits suicide to remain with her love.

Demeter Goddess of agriculture and nutrition, whose name means earth mother. She is the mother of Persephone.

Demophoon Son of King Celeus of Eleusis, who was nursed by Demeter and then dropped in the fire when she tried to make him immortal.

Dervish Member of a religious order, often Sufi, known for their wild dancing and whirling.

Desire The god of love.

Deva A god other than the supreme God.

Devadatta Buddha's cousin, plots evil against Buddha.

Dhrishtadyumna Twin brother of Draupadi, slays Drona.

Dibarra God of plague. Also a demonic character or evil spirit.

Dik-dik Dwarf antelope native to eastern and southern Africa.

Dilipa Son of Anshumat, father of Bhagiratha.

Dionysus The god of wine, vegetation and the life force, and of ecstasy. He was considered to be outside the Greek pantheon, and generally thought to have begun life as a mortal.

Dioscuri Castor and Polydeuces, the twin sons of Zeus and Leda, who are important deities.

Distaff Tool used when spinning which holds the wool or flax and keeps the fibres from tangling.

Divan Privy council.

Divots Turfs.

Dog The dog is a symbol of humanity, and usually has a role helping the hero of the myth or legend. Fionn's Bran and Grey Dog are two examples of wild beasts transformed to become invaluable servants.

Dōshin Government official.

Dossal Ornamental altar cloth.

Doughty Persistent and brave person.

Dragon Important animal in Japanese culture, symbolizing power, wealth, luck and success.

Draiglin' Hogney Ogre.

Draupadi Daughter of Drupada.

Draupnir Odin's famous ring, fashioned by Brokki.

Drona A Brahma, son of the great sage Bharadwaja.

Druid An ancient order of Celtic priests held in high esteem who flourished in the pre-Christian era. The word 'druid' is derived from an ancient Celtic one meaning 'very knowledgeable'. These individuals were believed to have mystical powers and in ancient Irish literature possess the ability to conjure up magical charms, to create tempests, to curse and debilitate their enemies and to perform as soothsayers to the royal courts.

Drupada King of the Panchalas.

Dryads Nymphs of the trees.

Dun A stronghold or royal abode surrounded by an earthen wall.

Durga Goddess, wife of Shiva.

Durk Knife. Also spelled as dirk.

Duryodhana One of Drona's pupils.

Dvalin Dwarf visited by Loki; also the name for the stag on Yggdrasill.

Dwarfie Stone Prehistoric tomb or boulder.

Dwarfs Fairies and black elves are called dwarfs.

Dwarkanath The Lord of Dwaraka; Krishna.

Dyumatsena King of the Shalwas and father of Satyavan.

Ea God of water, light and wisdom, and one of the creator deities. He brought arts and civilization to humankind. Also known as Oannes and Nudimmud.

Eabani Hero originally created by Aruru to defeat Gilgamesh, the two became friends and destroyed Khumbaba together. He personifies the natural world.

Each Uisge The mythical water-horse which haunts lochs and appears in various forms.

Ebisu One of the gods of luck. He is also the god of labour and fishermen.

Echo A nymph who was punished by Hera for her endless stories told to distract Hera from Zeus's infidelity.

Ector King Arthur's foster father, who raised Arthur to protect him.

Edda Collection of prose and poetic myths and stories from the Norsemen.

Eight Immortals Three of these are reputed to be historical: Han Chung-li, born in Shaanxi, who rose to become a Marshal of the Empire in 21 BCE. Chang Kuo-Lao, who lived in the seventh to eighth century CE, and Lü Tung-pin, who was born in 755 CE.

Einheriear Odin's guests at Valhalla.

Eisa Loki's daughter.

Ekake (Ibani) Person of great intelligence, which means 'tortoise'. Also known as Mbai (Igbo).

Ekalavya Son of the king of the Nishadas.

Electra Daughter of Agamemnon and Clytemnestra.

Eleusis A town in which the cult of Demeter is centred.

Elf Sigmund is buried by an elf; there are light and dark elves (the latter called dwarfs).

Elokos (Central African) Imps of dwarf-demons who eat human flesh.

Elpenor The youngest of Odysseus's crew who fell from the roof of Circe's house on Aeaea and visited with Odysseus at Hades.

Elysium The home of the blessed dead.

Emain Macha The capital of ancient Ulster.

Emma Dai-o King of hell and judge of the dead.

En-lil God of the lower world, storms and mist, who held sway over the ghostly animistic spirits, which at his bidding might pose as the friends or enemies of men. Also known as Bel.

Eos Goddess of the dawn and sister of the sun and moon.

Erichthonius A child born of the semen spilled when Hephaestus tried to rape Athene on the Acropolis.

Eridu The home of Ea and one of the two major cities of Babylonian civilization.

Erin Term for Ireland, originally spelled Éirinn.

Erirogho Magical mixture made from the ashes of the dead.

Eros God of Love, the son of Aphrodite.

Erpa Hereditary chief.

Erysichthon A Thessalian who cut down a grove sacred to Demeter, who punished him with eternal hunger.

Eshu (Yoruba) God of mischief. He also tests people's characters and controls law enforcement.

Eteocles Son of Oedipus.

Eumaeus Swineherd of Odysseus's family at Ithaca.

Euphemus A son of Poseidon who could walk on water. He sailed with the Argonauts.

Europa Daughter of King Agenor of Tyre, who was taken by Zeus to Crete.

Eurydice A Thracian nymph married to Orpheus.

Excalibur The magical sword given to Arthur by the Lady of the Lake. In some versions of the myths, Excalibur is also the sword that the young Arthur pulls from the stone to become king.

Fabulist Person who composes or tells fables.

Fafnir Shape-changer who kills his father and becomes a dragon to guard the family jewels. Slain by Sigurd.

Fairy The word is derived from 'Fays' which means Fates. They are immortal, with the gift of prophecy and of music, and their role changes according to the origin of the myth. They were often considered to be little people, with enormous propensity for mischief, but they are central to many myths and legends, with important powers.

Faro (Mali, Guinea) God of the sky.

Fates In Greek mythology, daughters of Zeus and Themis, who spin the thread of a mortal's life and cut it when his time is due. Called Norns in Viking mythology.

Fenris A wild wolf, who is the son of Loki. He roams the earth after Ragnarok.

Ferhad Sculptor who fell in love with Shireen, the wife of Khosru, and undertook a seemingly impossible task to clear a passage through the mountain of Beysitoun and join the rivers in return for winning Shireen's hand.

Fialar Red cock of Valhalla.

Fianna/Fenians The word 'fianna' was used in early times to describe young warrior-hunters. These youths evolved under the leadership of Finn Mac Cumaill as a highly skilled band of military men who took up service with various kings throughout Ireland.

Filheim Land of mist, at the end of one of Yggdrasill's roots.

Fingal Another name for Fionn Mac Chumail, used after MacPherson's Ossian in the eighteenth century.

Fionn Mac Chumail Irish and Scottish warrior, with great powers of fairness and wisdom. He is known not for physical strength but for knowledge, sense of justice, generosity and canny instinct. He had two hounds, which were later discovered to be his nephews transformed. He became head of the Fianna, or Féinn, fighting the enemies of Ireland and Scotland. He was the father of Oisin (also called Ossian, or other derivatives), and father or grandfather of Osgar.

Fir Bolg One of the ancient, pre-Gaelic peoples of Ireland who were reputed to have worshipped the god Bulga, meaning god of lighting. They are thought to have colonized Ireland around 1970 BCE, after the death of Nemed and to have reigned for a short period of thirty-seven years before their defeat by the Tuatha De Danann.

Fir Chlis Nimble men or merry dancers, who are the souls of fallen angels.

Flitch Side of salted and cured bacon.

Folkvang Freyia's palace.

Fomorians A race of monstrous beings, popularly conceived as sea-pirates with some supernatural characteristics who opposed the earliest settlers in Ireland, including the Nemedians and the Tuatha De Danann.

Frey Comes to Asgard with Freyia as a hostage following the war between the Aesir and the Vanir.

Freyia Comes to Asgard with Frey as a hostage following the war between the Aesir and the Vanir. Goddess of beauty and love.

Frigga Odin's wife and mother of gods; she is goddess of the earth.

Fuath Evil spirits which lived in or near the water.

Fulla Frigga's maidservant.

Furies Creatures born from the blood of Cronus, guarding the greatest sinners of the Underworld. Their power lay in their ability to drive mortals mad. Snakes writhed in their hair and around their waists.

Furoshiki Cloths used to wrap things.

Gae Bolg Cuchulainn alone learned the use of this weapon from the woman-warrior, Scathach and with it he slew his own son Connla and his closest friend, Ferdia. Gae Bolg translates as 'harpoon-like javelin' and the deadly weapon was reported to have been created by Bulga, the god of lighting.

Gaea Goddess of Earth, born from Chaos, and the mother of Uranus and Pontus. Also spelled as Gaia.

Gage Object of value presented to a challenger to symbolize good faith.

Galahad Knight of the Round Table, who took up the search for the Holy Grail. Son of Lancelot, Galahad is considered the purest and most perfect knight.

Galatea Daughter of Nereus and Doris, a sea-nymph loved by Polyphemus, the Cyclops.

Gandhari Mother of Duryodhana.

Gandharvas Demi-gods and musicians.

Gandjharva Musical ministrants of the upper air.

Ganesha Elephant-headed god of scribes and son of Shiva.

Ganges Sacred river personified by the goddess Ganga, wife of Shiva and daughter of the mount Himalaya.

Gareth of Orkney King Arthur's nephew and knight of the Round Table.

Garm Hel's hound.

Garuda King of the birds and mount Vishnu, the divine bird, attendant of Narayana.

Gautama Son of Suddhodana and also known as Siddhartha.

Gawain Nephew of King Arthur and knight of the Round Table, he is best known for his adventure with the Green Knight, who challenges one of Arthur's knights to cut off his head, but only if he agrees to be beheaded in turn in a year and a day, if the Green Knight survives. Gawain beheads the Green Knight, who simply replaces his head. At the appointed time, they meet, and the Green Knight swings his axe but merely nicks Gawain's skin instead of beheading him.

Geisha Performance artist or entertainer, usually female.

Geri Odin's wolf.

Ghommid (Yoruba) Term for mythological creatures such as goblins or ogres.

Giallar Bridge in Filheim.

Giallarhorn Heimdall's trumpet – the final call signifies Ragnarok.

Giants In Greek mythology, a race of beings born from Gaea, grown from the blood that dropped from the castrated Uranus. Usually represent evil in Viking mythology.

Gilgamesh King of Erech known as a half-human, half-god hero similar to the Greek Heracles, and often listed with the gods. He is the personification of the sun and is protected by the god Shamash, who in some texts is described as his father. He is also portrayed as an evil tyrant at times.

Gillie Someone who works for a Scottish chief, usually as an attendant or servant; guide for fishing or hunting parties.

Gladheim Where the twelve deities of Asgard hold their thrones. Also called Gladsheim.

Gled Bird of prey.

Golden Fleece Fleece of the ram sent by Poseidon to substitute for Phrixus when his father was going to sacrifice him. The Argonauts went in search of the fleece.

Goodman Man of the house.

Goodwife Woman of the house.

Gopis Lovers of the young Krishna and milkmaids.

Gorgon One of the three sisters, including Medusa, whose frightening looks could turn mortals to stone.

Graces Daughters of Aphrodite by Zeus.

Gramercy Expression of surprise or strong feeling.

Great Head The Iroquois believed in the existence of a curious being known as Great Head, a creature with an enormous head poised on slender legs.

Great Spirit The name given to the Creator of all life, as well as the term used to describe the omnipotent force of the Creator existing in every living thing.

Great-Flank One of Ravana's monsters.

Green Knight A knight dressed all in green and with green hair and skin who challenged one of Arthur's knights to strike him a blow with an axe and that, if he survived, he would return to behead the knight in a year and a day. He turned out to be Lord Bertilak and was under an enchantment cast by Morgan le Fay to test Arthur's knights.

Gruagach Mythical creature, often a giant or ogre similar to a wild man of the woods. The term can also refer to other mythical creatures such as brownies or fairies. As a brownie, he is usually dressed in red or green as opposed to the traditional brown. He has great power to enchant the hapless, or to help mortals who are worthy (usually heroes). He often appears to challenge a boy-hero, during his period of education.

Gudea High priest of Lagash, known to be a patron of the arts and a writer himself.

Guebre Religion founded by Zoroaster, the Persian prophet.

Gugumatz Creator god who, with Huracan, formed the sky, earth and everything on it.

Guha King of Nishadha.

A GLOSSARY OF MYTH & FOLKLORE

Guidewife Woman.

Guinevere Wife of King Arthur; she is often portrayed as a virtuous lady and wife, but is perhaps best known for having a love affair with Lancelot, one of Arthur's friends and knights of the Round Table. Her name is also spelled Guenever.

Gulistan *Rose Garden*, written by the poet Sa'di

Gungnir Odin's spear, made of Yggdrasill wood, and the tip fashioned by Dvalin.

Gylfi A wandering king to whom the Eddas are narrated.

Haab Mayan solar calendar that consisted of eighteen twenty-day months.

Hades One of the three sons of Cronus; brother of Poseidon and Zeus. Hades is King of the Underworld, which is also known as the House of Hades.

Haere-mai Maori phrase meaning 'come here, welcome.'

Haere-mai-ra, me o tatou mate Maori phrase meaning 'come here, that I may sorrow with you.'

Haere-ra Maori phrase meaning 'goodbye, go, farewell.'

Haji Muslim pilgrim who has been to Mecca.

Hakama Traditional Japanese clothing, worn on the bottom half of the body.

Hanuman General of the monkey people.

Harakiri Suicide, usually by cutting or stabbing the abdomen. Also known as seppuku.

Hari-Hara Shiva and Vishnu as one god.

Harmonia Daughter of Ares and Aphrodite, wife of Cadmus.

Hatamoto High-ranking samurai.

Hathor Great cosmic mother and patroness of lovers. She is portrayed as a cow.

Hati The wolf who pursues the sun and moon.

Hatshepsut Second female pharaoh.

Hauberk Armour to protect the neck and shoulders, sometimes a full-length coat of mail.

Hector Eldest son of King Priam who defended Troy from the Greeks. He was killed by Achilles.

Hecuba The second wife of Priam, King of Troy. She was turned into a dog after Troy was lost.

Heimdall White god who guards the Bifrost bridge.

Hel Goddess of death and Loki's daughter. Also known as Hela.

Helen Daughter of Leda and Tyndareus, King of Sparta, and the most beautiful woman in the world. She was responsible for starting the Trojan War.

Heliopolis City in modern-day Cairo, known as the City of the Sun and the central place of worship of Ra. Also known as Anu.

Helius The sun, son of Hyperion and Theia.

Henwife Witch.

Hephaestus or **Hephaistos** The Smith of Heaven.

Hera A Mycenaean palace goddess, married to Zeus.

Heracles An important Greek hero, the son of Zeus and Alcmena. His name means 'Glory of Hera'. He performed twelve labours for King Eurystheus, and later became a god.

Hermes The conductor of souls of the dead to Hades, and god of trickery and of trade. He acts as messenger to the gods.

Hermod Son of Frigga and Odin who travelled to see Hel in order to reclaim Balder for Asgard.

Hero and Leander Hero was a priestess of Aphrodite, loved by Leander, a young man of Abydos. He drowned trying to see her.

Hestia Goddess of the hearth, daughter of Cronus and Rhea.

Hieroglyphs Type of writing that combines symbols and pictures, usually cut into tombs or rocks, or written on papyrus.

Himalaya Great mountain and range, father of Parvati.

Hiordis Wife of Sigmund and mother of Sigurd.

Hoderi A fisher and son of Okuninushi.

Hodur Balder's blind twin; known as the personification of darkness.

Hoenir Also called Vili; produced the first humans with Odin and Loki, and was one of the triad responsible for the creation of the world.

Hōichi the Earless A biwa hōshi, a blind storyteller who played the biwa or lute. Also a priest.

Holger Danske Legendary Viking warrior who is thought to never die. He sleeps until he is needed by his people and then he will rise to protect them.

Homayi Phoenix.

Hoodie Mythical creature which often appears as a crow.

Hoori A hunter and son of Okuninushi.

Horus God of the sky and kinship, son of Isis and Osiris. He captained the boat that carried Ra across the sky. He is depicted with the head of a falcon.

Hotei One of the gods of luck. He also personifies humour and contentment.

Houlet Owl.

Houri Beautiful virgin from paradise.

Hrim-faxi Steed of the night.

Hubris Presumptuous behaviour which causes the wrath of the gods to be brought on to mortals.

Hueytozoztli Festival dedicated to Tlaloc and, at times, Chicomecohuatl or other deities. Also the fourth month of the Aztec calendar.

Hugin Odin's raven.

Huitzilopochtli God of war and the sun, also connected with the summer and crops; one of the principal Aztec deities. He was born a full-grown adult to save his mother, Coatlicue, from the jealousy of his sister, Coyolxauhqui, who tried to kill Coatlicue. The Mars of the Aztec gods. In some origin stories he is one of four offspring of Ometeotl and Omecihuatl.

Hurley A traditional Irish game played with sticks and balls, quite similar to hockey.

Hurons A tribe of Iroquois stock, originally one people with the Iroquois.

Huveane (Pedi, Venda) Creator of humankind, who made a baby from clay into which he breathed life. He is known as the High God or Great God. He is also known as a trickster god.

Hymir Giant who fishes with Thor and is drowned by him.

Iambe Daughter of Pan and Echo, servant to King Celeus of Eleusis and Metaeira.

Icarus Son of Daedalus, who plunged to his death after escaping from the labyrinth.

Ichneumon Mongoose.

Idunn Guardian of the youth-giving apples.

Ifa (Yoruba) God of wisdom and divination. Also the term for a Yoruban religion.

Ife (Yoruba) The place Obatala first arrived on Earth and took for his home.

Igigi Great spirits or gods of Heaven and the sky.

Igraine Wife of the duke of Tintagel, enemy of Uther Pendragon, who marries Uther when her first husband dies. She is King Arthur's mother.

Ile (Yoruba) Goddess of the earth.

Imhetep High priest and wise sage. He is sometimes thought to be the son of Ptah.

Imam Person who leads prayers in a mosque.

Imana (Banyarwanda) Creator or sky god.

In The male principle who, joined with Yo, the female side, brought about creation and the first gods. In and Yo correspond to the Chinese Yang and Yin.

Inari God of rice, fertility, agriculture and, later, the fox god. Inari has both good and evil attributes but is often presented as an evil trickster.

Indra The King of Heaven.

Indrajit Son of Ravana.

Indrasen Daughter of Nala and Damayanti.

Indrasena Son of Nala and Damayanti.

Inundation Annual flooding of the River Nile.

Iphigenia The eldest daughter of Agamemnon and Clytemnestra who was sacrificed to appease Artemis and obtain a fair wind for Troy.

Iris Messenger of the gods who took the form of a rainbow.

Iseult Princess of Ireland and niece of the Morholt. She falls in love with Tristan after consuming a love potion but is forced to marry King Mark of Cornwall.

Ishtar Goddess of love, beauty, justice and war, especially in Ninevah, and earth mother who symbolizes fertility. Married to Tammuz, she is similar to the Greek goddess Aphrodite. Ishtar is sometimes known as Innana or Irnina.

Isis Goddess of the Nile and the moon, sister-wife of Osiris. She and her son, Horus, are sometimes thought of in a similar way to Mary and Jesus. She was one of the most worshipped female

Egyptian deities and was instrumental in returning Osiris to life after he was killed by his brother, Set.

Istakbál Deputation of warriors.

Izanagi Deity and brother-husband to Izanami, who together created the Japanese islands from the Floating Bridge of Heaven. Their offspring populated Japan.

Izanami Deity and sister-wife of Izanagi, creator of Japan. Their children include Amaterasu, Tsuki-yomi and Susanoo.

Jade It was believed that jade emerged from the mountains as a liquid which then solidified after ten thousand years to become a precious hard stone, green in colour. If the correct herbs were added to it, it could return to its liquid state and when swallowed increase the individual's chances of immortality.

Jambavan A noble monkey.

Jason Son of Aeson, King of Iolcus and leader of the voyage of the Argonauts.

Jatayu King of all the eagle-tribes.

Jesseraunt Flexible coat of armour or mail.

Jimmo Legendary first emperor of Japan. He is thought to be descended from Hoori, while other tales claim him to be descended from Amaterasu through her grandson, Ninigi.

Jizo God of little children and the god who calms the troubled sea.

Jord Daughter of Nott; wife of Odin.

Jormungander The world serpent; son of Loki. Legends tell that when his tail is removed from his mouth, Ragnarok has arrived.

Jorō Geisha who also worked as a prostitute.

Jotunheim Home of the giants.

Ju Ju tree Deciduous tree that produces edible fruit.

Jurasindhu A rakshasa, father-in-law of Kans.

Jyeshtha Goddess of bad luck.

Ka Life power or soul. Also known as ba.

Kai-káús Son of Kai-kobád. He led an army to invade Mázinderán, home of the demon-sorcerers, after being persuaded by a demon. Known for his ambitious schemes, he later tried to reach Heaven by trapping eagles to fly him there on his throne.

Kaikeyi Mother of Bharata, one of Dasharatha's three wives.

Kai-khosrau Son of Saiawúsh, who killed Afrásiyáb in revenge for the death of his father.

Kai-kobád Descendant of Feridún, he was selected by Zál to lead an army against Afrásiyáb. Their powerful army, led by Zál and Rustem, drove back Afrásiyáb's army, who then agreed to peace.

Kailyard Kitchen garden or small plot, usually used for growing vegetables.

Kali The Black, wife of Shiva.

Kalindi Daughter of the sun, wife of Krishna.

Kaliya A poisonous hydra that lived in the jamna.

Kalki Incarnation of Vishnu yet to come.

Kalnagini Serpent who kills Lakshmindara.

Kal-Purush The Time-man, Bengali name for Orion.

Kaluda A disciple of Buddha.

Kalunga-ngombe (Mbundu) Death, also depicted as the king of the netherworld.

Kama God of desire.

Kamadeva Desire, the god of love.

Kami Spirits, deities or forces of nature.

Kamund Lasso.

Kans King of Mathura, son of Ugrasena and Pavandrekha.

Kanva Father of Shakuntala.

Kappa River goblin with the body of a tortoise and the head of an ape. Kappa love to challenge human beings to single combat.

Karakia Invocation, ceremony, prayer.

Karna Pupil of Drona.

Kaross Blanket or rug, also worn as a traditional garment. It is often made from the skins of animals which have been sewn together.

Kasbu A period of twenty-four hours.

Kashyapa One of Dasharatha's counsellors.

Kauravas or Kurus Sons of Dhritarashtra, pupils of Drona.

Kaushalya Mother of Rama, one of Dasharatha's three wives.

Kay Son of Ector and adopted brother to King Arthur, he becomes one of Arthur's knights of the Round Table.

Keb God of the earth and father of Osiris and Isis, married to Nut. Keb is identified with Kronos, the Greek god of time.

Kehua Spirit, ghost.

Kelpie Another word for each uisge, the water-horse.

Ken Know.

Keres Black-winged demons or daughters of the night.

Keshini Wife of Sagara.

Khalif Leader.

Khara Younger brother of Ravana.

Khepera God who represents the rising sun. He is portrayed as a scarab. Also known as Nebertcher.

Kher-heb Priest and magician who officiated over rituals and ceremonies.

Khnemu God of the source of the Nile and one of the original Egyptian deities. He is thought to be the creator of children and of other gods. He is portrayed as a ram.

Khosru King and husband to Shireen, daughter of Maurice, the Greek Emperor. He was murdered by his own son, who wanted his kingdom and his wife.

A GLOSSARY OF MYTH & FOLKLORE

Khumbaba Monster and guardian of the goddess Irnina, a form of the goddess Ishtar. Khumbaba is likened to the Greek gorgon.

Kia-ora Welcome, good luck. A greeting.

Kiboko Hippopotamus.

Kikinu Soul.

Kimbanda (Mbundu) Doctor.

Kimono Traditional Japanese clothing, similar to a robe.

King Arthur Legendary king of Britain who plucked the magical sword from the stone, marking him as the heir of Uther Pendragon and 'true king' of Britain. He and his knights of the Round Table defended Britain from the Saxons and had many adventures, including searching for the Holy Grail. Finally wounded in battle, he left Britain for the mythical Avalon, vowing to one day return to reclaim his kingdom.

Kingu Tiawath's husband, a god and warrior who she promised would rule Heaven once he helped her defeat the 'gods of light'. He was killed by Merodach who used his blood to make clay, from which he formed the first humans. In some tales, Kingu is Tiawath's son as well as her consort.

Kinnaras Human birds with musical instruments under their wings.

Kinyamkela (Zaramo) Ghost of a child.

Kirk Church, usually a term for Church of Scotland churches.

Kirtle One-piece garment, similar to a tunic, which was worn by men or women.

Kis Solar deity, usually depicted as an eagle.

Kishar Earth mother and sister-wife to Anshar.

Kist Trunk or large chest.

Kitamba (Mbundu) Chief who made his whole village go into mourning when his head-wife, Queen Muhongo, died. He also pledged that no one should speak or eat until she was returned to him.

Knowe Knoll or hillock.

Kojiki One of two myth-histories of Japan, along with the *Nihon Shoki*.

Ko-no-Hana Goddess of Mount Fuji, princess and wife of Ninigi.

Kore 'Maiden', another name for Persephone.

Kraal Traditional rural African village, usually consisting of huts surrounded by a fence or wall. Also an animal enclosure.

Krishna The Dark one, worshipped as an incarnation of Vishnu.

Kui-see Edible root.

Kumara Son of Shiva and Paravati, slays demon Taraka.

Kumbha-karna Ravana's brother.

Kunti Mother of the Pandavas.

Kura Red. The sacred colour of the Maori.

Kusha or Kusi One of Sita's two sons.

Kvasir Clever warrior and colleague of Odin. He was responsible for finally outwitting Loki.

Kwannon Goddess of mercy.

Labyrinth A prison built at Knossos for the Minotaur by Daedalus.

Lady of the Lake Enchantress who presents Arthur with Excalibur.

Laertes King of Ithaca and father of Odysseus.

Laestrygonians Savage giants encountered by Odysseus on his travels.

Laili In love with Majnun but unable to marry him, she was given to the prince, Ibn Salam, to marry. When he died, she escaped and found Majnun, but they could not be legally married. The couple died of grief and were buried together. Also known as Laila.

Laird Person who owns a significant estate in Scotland.

Lakshmana Brother of Rama and his companion in exile.

Lakshmi Consort of Vishnu and a goddess of beauty and good fortune.

Lakshmindara Son of Chand resurrected by Manasa Devi.

Lancelot Knight of the Round Table. Lancelot was raised by the Lady of the Lake. While he went on many quests, he is perhaps best known for his affair with Guinevere, King Arthur's wife.

Land of Light One of the names for the realm of the fairies. If a piece of metal welded by human hands is put in the doorway to their land, the door cannot close. The door to this realm is only open at night, and usually at a full moon.

Lang syne The days of old.

Lao Tzu (Laozi) The ancient Taoist philosopher thought to have been born in 571 BCE a contemporary of Confucius with whom, it is said, he discussed the tenets of Tao. Lao Tzu was an advocate of simple rural existence and looked to the Yellow Emperor and Shun as models of efficient government. His philosophies were recorded in the Tao Te Ching. Legends surrounding his birth suggest that he emerged from the left-hand side of his mother's body, with white hair and a long white beard, after a confinement lasting eighty years.

Laocoon A Trojan wiseman who predicted that the wooden horse contained Greek soldiers.

Laomedon The King of Troy who hired Apollo and Poseidon to build the impregnable walls of Troy.

Lava Son of Sita.

Leda Daughter of the King of Aetolia, who married Tyndareus. Helen and Clytemnestra were her daughters.

Legba (Dahomey) Youngest offspring of Mawu-Lisa. He was given the gift of all languages. It was through him that humans could converse with the gods.

Leman Lover.

Leprechaun Mythical creature from Irish folk tales who often appears as a mischievous and sometimes drunken old man.

Lethe One of the four rivers of the Underworld, also called the River of Forgetfulness.

Lif The female survivor of Ragnarok.

Lifthrasir The male survivor of Ragnarok.

Lil Demon.

Liongo (Swahili) Warrior and hero.

Lofty mountain Home of Ahura-Mazda.

Logi Utgard-loki's cook.

Loki God of fire and mischief-maker of Asgard; he eventually brings about Ragnarok. Also spelled as Loptur.

Lotus-Eaters A race of people who live a dazed, drugged existence, the result of eating the lotus flower.

Ma'at State of order meaning truth, order or justice. Personified by the goddess Ma'at, who was Thoth's consort.

Macha There are thought to be several different Machas who appear in quite a number of ancient Irish stories. For the purposes of this book, however, the Macha referred to is the wife of Crunnchu. The story unfolds that after her husband had boasted of her great athletic ability to the King, she was subsequently forced to run against his horses in spite of the fact that she was heavily pregnant. Macha died giving birth to her twin babies and with her dying breath she cursed Ulster for nine generations, proclaiming that it would suffer the weakness of a woman in childbirth in times of great stress. This curse had its most disastrous effect when Medb of Connacht invaded Ulster with her great army.

Machi-bugyō Senior official or magistrate, usually samurai.

Macuilxochitl God of art, dance and games, and the patron of luck in gaming. His name means 'source of flowers' or 'prince of flowers'. Also known as Xochipilli, meaning 'five-flower'.

Madake Weapon used for whipping, made of bamboo.

Maduma Taro tuber.

Mag Muirthemne Cuchulainn's inheritance. A plain extending from River Boyne to the mountain range of Cualgne, close to Emain Macha in Ulster.

Magni Thor's son.

Mahaparshwa One of Ravana's generals.

Maharaksha Son of Khara, slain at Lanka.

Mahasubhadda Wife of Buddha-select (Sumedha).

Majnun Son of a chief, who fell in love with Laili and followed her tribe through the desert, becoming mad with love until they were briefly reunited before dying.

Makaras Mythical fish-reptiles of the sea.

Makoma (Senna) Folk hero who defeated five mighty giants.

Mana Power, authority, prestige, influence, sanctity, luck.

Manasa Devi Goddess of snakes, daughter of Shiva by a mortal woman.

Manasha Goddess of snakes.

Mandavya Daughter of Kushadhwaja.

Man-Devourer One of Ravana's monsters.

Mandodari Wife of Ravana.

Mandrake Poisonous plant from the nightshade family which has hallucinogenic and hypnotic qualities if ingested. Its roots resemble the human form and it has supposedly magical qualities.

Mani The moon.

Manitto Broad term used to describe the supernatural or a potent spirit among the Algonquins, the Iroquois and the Sioux.

Man-Slayer One of Ravana's counsellors.

Manthara Kaikeyi's evil nurse, who plots Rama's ruin.

Mantle Cloak or shawl.

Manu Lawgiver.

Manu Mythical mountain on which the sun sets.

Mara The evil one, tempts Gautama.

Markandeya One of Dasharatha's counsellors.

Mashu Mountain of the Sunset, which lies between Earth and the underworld. Guarded by scorpion-men.

Matali Sakra's charioteer.

Mawu-Lisa (Dahomey) Twin offspring of Nana Baluka. Mawu (female) and Lisa (male) are often joined to form one being. Their own offspring populated the world.

Mbai (Igbo) Person of great intelligence, also known as Ekake (Ibani), which means 'tortoise'.

Medea Witch and priestess of Hecate, daughter of Aeetes and sister of Circe. She helped Jason in his quest for the Golden Fleece.

Medusa One of the three Gorgons whose head had the power to turn onlookers to stone.

Melpomene One of the muses, and mother of the Sirens.

Menaka One of the most beautiful dancers in Heaven.

Menat Amulet, usually worn for protection.

Mendicant Beggar.

Menelaus King of Sparta, brother of Agamemnon. Married Helen and called war against Troy when she eloped with Paris.

Menthu Lord of Thebes and god of war. He is portrayed as a hawk or falcon.

Mere-pounamu A native weapon made of a rare green stone.

Merlin Wizard and advisor to King Arthur. He is thought to be the son of a human female and an incubus (male demon). He brought about Arthur's birth and ascension to king, then acted as his mentor.

Merodach God who battled Tiawath and defeated her by cutting out her heart and dividing her corpse into two pieces. He used these pieces to divide the upper and lower waters once controlled by Tiawath, making a dwelling for the gods of light. He also created humankind. Also known as Marduk.

Merrow Mythical mermaid-like creature, often depicted with an enchanted cap called a cohuleen driuth which allows it to travel between land and the depths of the sea. Also known as murúch.

Metaneira Wife of Celeus, King of Eleusis, who hired Demeter in disguise as her nurse.

Metztli Goddess of the moon, her name means 'lady of the night'. Also known as Yohualtictl.

Michabo Also known as Manobozho, or the Great Hare, the principal deity of the Algonquins, maker and preserver of the earth, sun and moon.

Mictlan God of the dead and ruler of the underworld. He was married to Mictecaciuatl and is often represented as a bat. He is also the Aztec lord of Hades. Also known as Mictlantecutli. Mictlan is also the name for the underworld.

Midgard Dwelling place of humans (Earth).

Midsummer A time when fairies dance and claim human victims.

Mihrab Father of Rúdábeh and descendant of Zohák, the serpent-king.

Milesians A group of iron-age invaders led by the sons of Mil, who arrived in Ireland from Spain around 500 BCE and overcame the Tuatha De Danann.

Mimir God of the ocean. His head guards a well; reincarnated after Ragnarok.

Minos King of Crete, son of Zeus and Europa. He was considered to have been the ruler of a sea empire.

Minotaur A creature born of the union between Pasiphae and a Cretan Bull.

Minúchihr King who lives to be one hundred and twenty years old. Father of Nauder.

Miolnir *See* Mjolnir.

Mithra God of the sun and light in Iran, protector of truth and guardian of pastures and cattle. Alo known as Mitra in Hindu mythology and Mithras in Roman mythology.

Mixcoatl God of the chase or the hunt. Sometimes depicted as the god of air and thunder, he introduced fire to humankind. His name means 'cloud serpent'.

Mjolnir Hammer belonging to the Norse god of thunder, which is used as a fearsome weapon which always returns to Thor's hand, and as an instrument of consecration.

Mnoatia Forest spirits.

Moccasins One-piece shoes made of soft leather, especially deerskin.

Modi Thor's son.

Moly A magical plant given to Odysseus by Hermes as protection against Circe's powers.

Montezuma Great emperor who consolidated the Aztec Empire.

Mordred Bastard son of King Arthur and Morgawse, Queen of Orkney, who, unknown to Arthur, was his half-sister. Mordred becomes one of King Arthur's knights of the Round Table before betraying and fatally wounding Arthur, causing him to leave Britain for Avalon.

Morgan le Fay Enchantress and half-sister to King Arthur, Morgan was an apprentice of Merlin's. She is generally depicted as benevolent, yet did pit herself against Arthur and his knights on occasion. She escorts Arthur on his final journey to Avalon. Also known as Morgain le Fay.

Morholt The knight sent to Cornwall to force King Mark to pay tribute to Ireland. He is killed by Tristan.

Morongoe the brave (Lesotho) Man who was turned into a snake by evil spirits because Tau was jealous that he had married the beautiful Mokete, the chief's daughter. Morongoe was returned to human form after his son, Tsietse, returned him to their family.

Mosima (Bapedi) The underworld or abyss.

Mount Fuji Highest mountain in Japan, on the island of Honshū.

Mount Kunlun This mountain features in many Chinese legends as the home of the great emperors on Earth. It is written in the *Shanghaijing (The Classic of Mountains and Seas)* that this towering structure measured no less than 3300 miles in circumference and 4000 miles in height. It acted both as a central pillar to support the heavens, and as a gateway between Heaven and Earth.

Moving Finger Expression for taking responsibility for one's life and actions, which cannot be undone.

Moytura Translated as the 'Plain of Weeping', Mag Tured, or Moytura, was where the Tuatha De Danann fought two of their most significant battles.

Mua An old-time Polynesian god.

Muezzin Person who performs the Muslim call to prayer.

Mugalana A disciple of Buddha.

Muilearteach The Cailleach Bheur of the water, who appears as a witch or a sea-serpent. On land she grew larger and stronger by fire.

Mul-lil God of Nippur, who took the form of a gazelle.

Muloyi Sorcerer, also called mulaki, murozi, ndozi or ndoki.

Mummu Son of Tiawath and Apsu. He formed a trinity with them to battle the gods. Also known as Moumis. In some tales, Mummu is also Merodach, who eventually destroyed Tiawath.

Munin Odin's raven.

Murile (Chaga) Man who dug up a taro tuber that resembled his baby brother, which turned into a living boy. His mother killed the baby when she saw Murile was starving himself to feed it.

Murtough Mac Erca King who ruled Ireland when many of its people – including his wife and family – were converting to Christianity. He remained a pagan.

Muses Goddesses of poetry and song, daughters of Zeus and Mnemosyne.

Musha Expression, often of surprise.

Muskrat North American beaver-like, amphibious rodent.

Muspell Home of fire, and the fire-giants.

Mwidzilo Taboo which, if broken, can cause death.

Nabu God of writing and wisdom. Also known as Nebo. Thought to be the son of Merodach.

Nahua Ancient Mexicans.

Nakula Pandava twin skilled in horsemanship.

Nala One of the monkey host, son of Vishvakarma.

Nana Baluka (Dahomey) Mother of all creation. She gave birth to an androgynous being with two faces. The female face was Mawu, who controlled the night and lands to the west. The male face was Lisa and he controlled the day and the east.

Nanahuatl Also known as Nanauatzin. Presided over skin diseases and known as Leprous, which in Nahua meant 'divine'.

Nandi Shiva's bull.

Nanna Balder's wife.

Nannar God of the moon and patron of the city of Ur.

Naram-Sin Son or ancestor of Sargon and king of the Four Zones or Quarters of Babylon.

A GLOSSARY OF MYTH & FOLKLORE

Narcissus Son of the River Cephisus. He fell in love with himself and died as a result.

Narve Son of Loki.

Nataraja Manifestation of Shiva, Lord of the Dance.

Natron Preservative used in embalming, mined from the Natron Valley in Egypt.

Nauder Son of Minúchihr, who became king on his death and was tyrannical and hated until Sám begged him to follow in the footsteps of his ancestors.

Nausicaa Daughter of Alcinous, King of Phaeacia, who fell in love with Odysseus.

Nebuchadnezzar Famous king of Babylon. Also known as Nebuchadrezzar.

Necromancy Communicating with the dead.

Nectar Drink of the gods.

Neith Goddess of hunting, fate and war. Neith is sometimes known as the creator of the universe.

Nemesis Goddess of retribution and daughter of night.

Neoptolemus Son of Achilles and Deidameia, he came to Troy at the end of the war to wear his father's armour. He sacrificed Polyxena at the tomb of Achilles.

Nephthys Goddess of the air, night and the dead. Sister of Isis and sister-wife to Seth, she is also the mother of Anubis.

Nereids Sea-nymphs who are the daughters of Nereus and Doris. Thetis, mother of Achilles, was a Nereid.

Nergal God of death and patron god of Cuthah, which was often known as a burial place. He is also known as the god of fire. Married to Aralu, the goddess of the underworld.

Nestor Wise King of Pylus, who led the ships to Troy with Agamemnon and Menelaus.

Neta Daughter of Shiva, friend of Manasa.

Ngai (Gikuyu) Creator god.

Ngaka (Lesotho) Witch doctor.

Niflheim The underworld In Norse mythology, ruled over by Hel.

Night Daughter of Norvi.

Nikumbha One of Ravana's generals.

Nila One of the monkey host, son of Agni.

Nin-Girsu God of fertility and war, patron god of Girsu. Also known as Shul-gur.

Ninigi Grandson of Amaterasu, Ninigi came to Earth bringing rice and order to found the Imperial family. He is known as the August Grandchild.

Niord God of the sea; marries Skadi.

Nippur The home of En-lil and one of the two major cities of Babylonian civilization.

Nirig God of war and storms, and son of Bel. Also known as Enu-Restu.

Nirvana Transcendent state and the final goal of Buddhism.

Nis Mythological creature, similar to a brownie or goblin, usually harmless or even friendly, but can be easily offended. They are often associated with Christmas or the winter solstice.

Noatun Niord's home.

Noisy-Throat One of Ravana's counsellors.

Noondah (Zanzibar) Cannibalistic cat which attacked and killed animals and humans.

Norns The fates and protectors of Yggdrasill. Many believe them to be the same as the Valkyries.

Norvi Father of the night.

Nott Goddess of night.

Nsasak bird Small bird who became chief of all small birds after winning a competition to go without food for seven days. The

Nsasak bird beat the Odudu bird by sneaking out of his home to feed.

Nü Wa The Goddess Nü Wa, who in some versions of the Creation myths is the sole creator of mankind, and in other tales is associated with the God Fu Xi, also a great benefactor of the human race. Some accounts represent Fu Xi as the brother of Nü Wa, but others describe the pair as lovers who lie together to create the very first human beings. Fu Xi is also considered to be the first of the Chinese emperors of mythical times who reigned from 2953 to 2838 BCE.

Nuada The first king of the Tuatha De Danann in Ireland, who lost an arm in the first battle of Moytura against the Fomorians. He became known as 'Nuada of the Silver Hand' when Diancecht, the great physician of the Tuatha De Danann, replaced his hand with a silver one after the battle.

Nunda (Swahili, East Africa) Slayer that took the form of a cat and grew so big that it consumed everyone in the town except the sultan's wife, who locked herself away. Her son, Mohammed, killed Nunda and cut open its leg, setting free everyone Nunda had eaten.

Nut Goddess of the sky, stars and astronomy. Sister-wife of Keb and mother of Osiris, Isis, Set and Nephthys. She often appears in the form of a cow.

Nyame (Ashanti) God of the sky, who sees and knows everything.

Nymphs Minor female deities associated with particular parts of the land and sea.

Obassi Osaw (Ekoi) Creator god with his twin, Obassi Nsi. Originally, Obassi Osaw ruled the skies while Obassi Nsi ruled the Earth.

Obatala (Yoruba) Creator of humankind. He climbed down a golden chain from the sky to the earth, then a watery abyss, and formed land and humankind. When Olorun heard of his success, he created the sun for Obatala and his creations.

Oberon Fairy king.

Odin Allfather and king of all gods, he is known for travelling the nine worlds in disguise and recognized only by his single eye; dies at Ragnarok.

Oduduwa (Yoruba) Divine king of Ile-Ife, the holy city of Yoruba.

Odur Freyia's husband.

Odysseus Greek hero, son of Laertes and Anticleia, who was renowned for his cunning, the master behind the victory at Troy, and known for his long voyage home.

Oedipus Son of Leius, King of Thebes and Jocasta. Became King of Thebes and married his mother.

Ogdoad Group of eight deities who were formed into four male-female couples who joined to create the gods and the world.

Ogham One of the earliest known forms of Irish writing, originally used to inscribe upright pillar stones.

Oiran Courtesan.

Oisin Also called Ossian (particularly by James Macpherson who wrote a set of Gaelic Romances about this character, supposedly garnered from oral tradition). Ossian was the son of Fionn and Sadbh, and had various brothers, according to different legends. He was a man of great wisdom, became immortal for many centuries, but in the end he became mad.

Ojibwe Another name for the Chippewa, a tribe of Algonquin stock.

Okuninushi Deity and descendant of Susanoo, who married Suseri-hime, Susanoo's daughter, without his consent. Susanoo tried to kill him many times but did not succeed and eventually forgave Okuninushi. He is sometimes thought to be the son or grandson of Susanoo.

Olokun (Yoruba) Most powerful goddess who ruled the seas and marshes. When Obatala created Earth in her domain, other gods began to divide it up between them. Angered at their presumption, she caused a great flood to destroy the land.

Olorun (Yoruba) Supreme god and ruler of the sky. He sees and controls everything, but others, such as Obatala, carry out the work for him. Also known as Olodumare.

Olympia Zeus's home in Elis.

Olympus The highest mountain in Greece and the ancient home of the gods.

Omecihuatl Female half of the first being, combined with Ometeotl. Together they are the lords of duality or lords of the two sexes. Also known as Ometecutli and Omeciuatl or Tonacatecutli and Tonacaciuatl. Their offspring were Xipe Totec, Huitzilopochtli, Quetzalcoatl and Tezcatlipoca.

Ometeotl Male half of the first being, combined with Omecihuatl.

Ometochtli Collective name for the pulque-gods or drink-gods. These were often associated with rabbits as they were thought to be senseless creatures.

Onygate Anyway.

Opening of the Mouth Ceremony in which mummies or statues were prayed over and anointed with incense before their mouths were opened, allowing them to eat and drink in the afterlife.

Oracle The response of a god or priest to a request for advice – also a prophecy; the place where such advice was sought; the person or thing from whom such advice was sought.

Oranyan (Yoruba) Youngest grandson of King Oduduwa, who later became king himself.

Orestes Son of Agamemnon and Clytemnestra who escaped following Agamemnon's murder to King Strophius. He later returned to Argos to murder his mother and avenge the death of his father.

Orpheus Thracian singer and poet, son of Oeagrus and a Muse. Married Eurydice and when she died tried to retrieve her from the Underworld.

Orunmila (Yoruba) Eldest son of Olorun, he helped Obatala create land and humanity, which he then rescued after Olokun flooded the lands. He has the power to see the future.

Osiris God of fertility, the afterlife and death. Thought to be the first of the pharaohs. He was murdered by his brother, Set, after which he was conjured back to life by Isis, Anubis and others before becoming lord of the afterworld. Married to Isis, who was also his sister.

Otherworld The world of deities and spirits, also known as the Land of Promise, or the Land of Eternal Youth, a place of everlasting life where all earthly dreams come to be fulfilled.

Owuo (Krachi, West Africa) Giant who personifies death. He causes a person to die every time he blinks his eye.

Palamedes Hero of Nauplia, believed to have created part of the ancient Greek alphabet. He tricked Odysseus into joining the fleet setting out for Troy by placing the infant Telemachus in the path of his plough.

Palermo Stone Stone carved with hieroglyphs, which came from the Royal Annals of ancient Egypt and contains a list of the kings of Egypt from the first to the early fifth dynasties.

Palfrey Docile and light horse, often used by women.

Palladium Wooden image of Athene, created by her as a monument to her friend Pallas who she accidentally killed. While in Troy it protected the city from invaders.

Pallas Athene's best friend, whom she killed.

Pan God of Arcadia, half-goat and half-man. Son of Hermes. He is connected with fertility, masturbation and sexual drive. He is also associated with music, particularly his pipes, and with laughter.

Pan Gu Some ancient writers suggest that this God is the offspring of the opposing forces of nature, the yin and the yang. The yin (female) is associated with the cold and darkness of the earth, while the yang (male) is associated with the sun and the warmth of the heavens. 'Pan' means 'shell of an egg' and 'Gu' means 'to secure' or 'to achieve'. Pan Gu came into existence so that he might create order from chaos.

Pandareus Cretan King killed by the gods for stealing the shrine of Zeus.

Pandavas Alternative name for sons of Pandu, pupils of Drona.

Pandora The first woman, created by the gods, to punish man for Prometheus's theft of fire. Her dowry was a box full of powerful evil.

Papyrus Paper-like material made from the pith of the papyrus plant, first manufactured in Egypt. Used as a type of paper as well as for making mats, rope and sandals.

Paramahamsa The supreme swan.

Parashurama Human incarnation of Vishnu, 'Rama with an axe'.

Paris Handsome son of Priam and Hecuba of Troy, who was left for dead on Mount Ida but raised by shepherds. Was reclaimed by his family, then brought them shame and caused the Trojan War by eloping with Helen.

Parsa Holy man. Also known as a zahid.

Parvati Consort of Shiva and daughter of Himalaya.

Passion Wife of desire.

Pavanarekha Wife of Ugrasena, mother of Kans.

Peerie Folk Fairy or little folk.

Pegasus The winged horse born from the severed neck of Medusa.

Peggin Wooden vessel with a handle, often shaped like a tub and used for drinking.

Peleus Father of Achilles. He married Antigone, caused her death, and then became King of Phthia. Saved from death himself by Jason and the Argonauts. Married Thetis, a sea nymph.

Penelope The long-suffering but equally clever wife of Odysseus who managed to keep at bay suitors who longed for Ithaca while Odysseus was at the Trojan War and on his ten-year voyage home.

Pentangle Pentagram or five-pointed star.

Pentecost Christian festival held on the seventh Sunday after Easter. It celebrates the holy spirit descending on the disciples after Jesus's ascension.

Percivale Knight of the Round Table and original seeker of the Holy Grail.

Persephone Daughter of Zeus and Demeter who was raped by Hades and forced to live in the Underworld as his queen for three months of every year.

Perseus Son of Danae, who was made pregnant by Zeus. He fought the Gorgons and brought home the head of Medusa. He eventually founded the city of Mycenae and married Andromeda.

Pesh Kef Spooned blade used in the Opening the Mouth ceremony.

Phaeacia The Kingdom of Alcinous on which Odysseus landed after a shipwreck which claimed the last of his men as he left Calypso's island.

Pharaoh King or ruler of Egypt.

Philoctetes Malian hero, son of Poeas, received Heracles's bow and arrows as a gift when he lit the great hero's pyre on Mount Oeta. He was involved in the last part of the Trojan War, killing Paris.

Philtre Magic potion, usually a love potion.

Pibroch Bagpipe music.

Pintura Native manuscript or painting.

Pipiltin Noble class of the Aztecs.

Pismire Ant.

Piu-piu Short mat made from flax leaves and neatly decorated.

Po Gloom, darkness, the lower world.

Polyphemus A Cyclops, but a son of Poseidon. He fell in love with Galatea, but she spurned him. He was blinded by Odysseus.

Polyxena Daughter of Priam and Hecuba of Troy. She was sacrificed on the grave of Achilles by Neoptolemus.

Pooka Mythical creature with the ability to shapeshift. Often appears as a horse, but also as a bull, dog or in human form, and has the ability to talk. Also known as púca.

Popol Vuh Sacred 'book of counsel' of the Quiché or K'iche' Maya people.

Poseidon God of the sea, and of sweet waters. Also the god of earthquakes. His is brother to Zeus and Hades, who divided the earth between them.

Pradyumna Son of Krishna and Rukmini.

Prahasta (Long-Hand) One of Ravana's generals.

Prajapati Creator of the universe, father of the gods, demons and all creatures, later known as Brahma.

Priam King of Troy, married to Hecuba, who bore him Hector, Paris, Helenus, Cassandra, Polyxena, Deiphobus and Troilus. He was murdered by Neoptolemus.

Pritha Mother of Karna and of the Pandavas.

Prithivi Consort of Dyaus and goddess of the earth.

Proetus King of Argos, son of Abas.

Prometheus A Titan, son of Iapetus and Themus. He was champion of mortal men, which he created from clay. He stole fire from the gods and was universally hated by them.

Prose Edda Collection of Norse myths and poems, thought to have been compiled in the 1200s by Icelandic historian Snorri Sturluson.

Proteus The old man of the sea who watched Poseidon's seals.

Psyche A beautiful nymph who was the secret wife of Eros, against the wishes of his mother Aphrodite, who sent Psyche to perform many tasks in hope of causing her death. She eventually married Eros and was allowed to become partly immortal.

Ptah Creator god and deity of Memphis who was married to Sekhmet. Ptah built the boats to carry the souls of the dead to the afterlife.

Puddock Frog.

Pulque Alcoholic drink made from fermented agave.

Purusha The cosmic man, he was sacrificed and his dismembered body became all the parts of the cosmos, including the four classes of society.

Purvey To provide or supply.

Pushkara Nala's brother.

Pushpaka Rama's chariot.

Putana A rakshasi.

Pygmalion A sculptor who was so lonely he carved a statue of a beautiful woman, and eventually fell in love with it. Aphrodite brought the image to life.

Quauhtli Eagle.

Quern Hand mill used for grinding corn.

Quetzalcoatl Deity and god of wind. He is represented as a feathered or plumed serpent and is usually a wise and benevolent god. Offspring of Ometeotl and Omecihuatl, he is also known as Kukulkan.

Ra God of the sun, ruling male deity of Egypt whose name means 'sole creator'.

Radha The principal mistress of Krishna.

Ragnarok The end of the world.

Rahula Son of Siddhartha and Yashodhara.

Raiden God of thunder. He traditionally has a fierce and demonic appearance.

Rakshasas Demons and devils.

Ram of Mendes Sacred symbol of fatherhood and fertility.

Rama or **Ramachandra** A prince and hero of the *Ramayana*, worshipped as an incarnation of Vishnu.

Ra-Molo (Lesotho) Father of fire, a chief who ruled by fear. When trying to kill his brother, Tau the lion, he was turned into a monster with the head of a sheep and the body of a snake.

Rangatira Chief, warrior, gentleman.

Regin A blacksmith who educated Sigurd.

Reinga The spirit land, the home of the dead.

Reservations Tracts of land allocated to the Native American people by the United States Government with the purpose of bringing the many separate tribes under state control.

Rewati Daughter of Raja, marries Balarama.

Rhadha Wife of Adiratha, a gopi of Brindaban and lover of Krishna.

Rhea Mother of the Olympian gods. Cronus ate each of her children, but she concealed Zeus and gave Cronus a swaddled rock in his place.

Rill Small stream.

Rimu (Chaga) Monster known to feed off human flesh, which sometimes takes the form of a werewolf.

Rishis Sacrificial priests associated with the devas in Swarga.
Rituparna King of Ayodhya.
Rohini The wife of Vasudeva, mother of Balarama and Subhadra, and carer of the young Krishna. Another Rohini is a goddess and consort of Chandra.
Rōnin Samurai whose master had died or fallen out of favour.
Rubáiyát Collection of poems written by Omar Khayyám.
Rúdábeh Wife of Zál and mother of Rustem.
Rudra Lord of Beasts and disease, later evolved into Shiva.
Rukma Rukmini's eldest brother.
Rustem Son of Zál and Rúdábeh, he was a brave and mighty warrior who undertook seven labours to travel to Mázinderán to rescue Kai-káús. Once there, he defeated the White Demon and rescued Kai-káús. He rode the fabled stallion Rakhsh and is also known as Rustam.
Ryō Traditional gold currency.
Sabdh Mother of Ossian, or Oisin.
Sabitu Goddess of the sea.
Sagara King of Ayodhya.
Sahadeva Pandava twin skilled in swordsmanship.
Sahib diwan Lord high treasurer or chief royal executive.
Saiawúsh Son of Kai-káús, who was put through trial by fire when Sudaveh, Kai-káús's wife, told him that Saiawúsh had taken advantage of her. His innocence was proven when the fire did not harm him. He was eventually killed by Afrásiyáb.
Saithe Blessed.
Sajara (Mali) God of rainbows. He takes the form of a multi-coloured serpent.
Sake Japanese rice wine.
Sakuni Cousin of Duryodhana.

Salam Greeting or salutation.

Saláman Son of the Shah of Yunan, who fell in love with Absál, his nurse. She died after they had a brief love affair and he returned to his father.

Salmali tree Cotton tree.

Salmon A symbol of great wisdom, around which many Scottish legends revolve.

Sám Mighty warrior who fought and won many battles. Father of Zál and grandfather to Rustem.

Sambu Son of Krishna.

Sampati Elder brother of Jatayu.

Samurai Noblemen who were part of the military in medieval Japan.

Sanehat Member of the royal bodyguard.

Sango (Yoruba) God of war and thunder.

Sangu (Mozambique) Goddess who protects pregnant women, depicted as a hippopotamus.

Santa Daughter of Dasharatha.

Sarapis Composite deity of Apis and Osiris, sometimes known as Serapis. Thought to be created to unify Greek and Egyptian citizens under the Greek pharaoh Ptolemy.

Sarasvati The tongue of Rama.

Sarcophagus Stone coffin.

Sargon of Akkad Raised by Akki, a husbandman, after being hidden at birth. Sargon became King of Assyria and a great hero. He founded the first library in Babylon. Similar to King Arthur or Perseus.

Sarsar Harsh, whistling wind.

Sasabonsam (Ashanti) Forest ogre.

Sassun Scottish word for England.

Sati Daughter of Daksha and Prasuti, first wife of Shiva.

Satrughna One of Dasharatha's four sons.

Satyavan Truth speaker, husband of Savitri.

Satyavati A fisher-maid, wife of Bhishma's father, Shamtanu.

Satyrs Elemental spirits which took great pleasure in chasing nymphs. They had horns, a hairy body and cloven hooves.

Saumanasa A mighty elephant.

Scamander River running across the Trojan plain, and father of Teucer.

Scarab Dung beetle, often used as a symbol of the immortal human soul and regeneration.

Scylla and Charybdis Scylla was a monster who lived on a rock of the same name in the Straits of Messina, devouring sailors. Charybdis was a whirlpool in the Straits which was supposedly inhabited by the hateful daughter of Poseidon.

Seal Often believed that seals were fallen angels. Many families are descended from seals, some of which had webbed hands or feet. Some seals were the children of sea-kings who had become enchanted (selkies).

Seelie-Court The court of the Fairies, who travelled around their realm. They were usually fair to humans, doling out punishment that was morally sound, but they were quick to avenge insults to fairies.

Segu (Swahili, East Africa) Guide who informs humans where honey can be found.

Sekhmet Solar deity who led the pharaohs in war. She is goddess of healing and was sent by Ra to destroy humanity when people turned against the sun god. She is portrayed with the head of a lion.

Selene Moon-goddess, daughter of Hyperion and Theia. She was seduced by Pan, but loved Endymion.

Selkie Mythical creature which is seal-like when in water but can shed its skin to take on human form when on land.

Seneschal Steward of a royal or noble household.

Sensei Teacher.

Seriyut A disciple of Buddha.

Sessrymnir Freyia's home.

Set God of chaos and evil, brother of Osiris, who killed him by tricking him into getting into a chest, which he then threw in the Nile, before cutting Osiris's body into fourteen separate pieces. Also known as Seth.

Sgeulachd Stories.

Sháhnámeh *The Book of Kings* written by Ferdowsi, one of the world's longest epic poems, which describes the mythology and history of the Persian Empire.

Shaikh Respected religious man.

Shaivas or Shaivites Worshippers of Shiva.

Shakti Power or wife of a god and Shiva's consort as his feminine aspect.

Shaman Also known as the 'Medicine Men' of Native American tribes, it is the shaman's role to cultivate communication with the spirit world. They are endowed with knowledge of all healing herbs, and learn to diagnose and cure disease. They are believed to foretell the future, find lost property and have power over animals, plants and stones.

Shamash God of the sun and protector of Gilgamesh, the great Babylonian hero. Known as the son of Sin, the moon god, he is also portrayed as a judge of good and evil.

Shamtanu Father of Bhishma.

Shankara A great magician, friend of Chand Sadagar.

Shashti The Sixth, goddess who protects children and women in childbirth.

Sheen Beautiful and enchanted woman who casts a spell on Murtough, King of Ireland, causing him to fall in love with her and cast out his family. He dies at her hands, half burned and half drowned, but she then dies of grief as she returns his love. Sheen is known by many names, including Storm, Sigh and Rough Wind.

Shesh A serpent that takes human birth through Devaki.

Shi-en Fairy dwelling.

Shinto Indigenous religion of Japan, from the pre-sixth century to the present day.

Shireen Married to Khosru. Her beauty meant that she was desired by many, including Khosru's own son by his previous marriage. She killed herself rather than give in to her stepson.

Shitala The Cool One and goddess of smallpox.

Shiva One of the two great gods of post-Vedic Hinduism with Vishnu.

Shogun Military ruler or overlord.

Shoji Sliding door, usually a lattice screen of paper.

Shu God of the air and half of the first divine couple created by Atem. Brother and husband to Tefnut, father to Keb and Nut.

Shubistán Household.

Shudra One of the four fundamental colours (caste).

Shuttle Part of a machine used for spinning cloth, used for passing weft threads between warp threads.

Siddhas Musical ministrants of the upper air.

Sif Thor's wife; known for her beautiful hair.

Sigi Son of Odin.

Sigmund Warrior able to pull the sword from Branstock in the Volsung's hall.

Signy Volsung's daughter.

Sigurd Son of Sigmund, and bearer of his sword. Slays Fafnir the dragon.

Sigyn Loki's faithful wife.

Símúrgh Griffin, an animal with the body of a lion and the head and wings of an eagle. Known to hold great wisdom. Also called a symurgh.

Sin God of the moon, worshipped primarily in Ur.

Sindri Dwarf who worked with Brokki to fashion gifts for the gods; commissioned by Loki.

Sirens Sea nymphs who are half-bird, half-woman, whose song lures hapless sailors to their death.

Sisyphus King of Ephyra and a trickster who outwitted Autolycus. He was one of the greatest sinners in Hades.

Sita Daughter of the earth, adopted by Janaka, wife of Rama.

Skadi Goddess of winter and the wife of Niord for a short time.

Skanda Six-headed son of Shiva and a warrior god.

Skraeling Person native to Canada and Greenland. The name was given to them by Viking settlers and can be translated as 'barbarian'.

Skrymir Giant who battled against Thor.

Sleipnir Odin's steed.

Sluagh The host of the dead, seen fighting in the sky and heard by mortals.

Smote Struck with a heavy blow.

Sohráb Son of Rustem and Tahmineh, Sohráb was slain in battle by his own father, who killed him by mistake.

Sol The sun-maiden.

Soma A god and a drug, the elixir of life.

Somerled Lord of the Isles, and legendary ancestor of the Clan MacDonald.

Soothsayer Someone with the ability to predict or see the future, by the use of magic, special knowledge or intuition. Known as seanagal in Scottish myths.

Squaw A Native American woman or wife (now offensive).

Squint-Eye One of Ramana's monsters.

Squire Shield- or armour-bearer of a knight.

Srutakirti Daughter of Kushadhwaja.

Stirabout Porridge made by stirring oatmeal into boiling milk or water.

Stone Giants A malignant race of stone beings whom the Iroquois believed invaded their territory, threatening the Confederation of the Five Nations. These fierce and hostile creatures lived off human flesh and were intent on exterminating the human race.

Stoorworm A great water monster which frequented lochs. When it thrust its great body from the sea, it could engulf islands and whole ships. Its appearance prophesied devastation.

Stot Bullock.

Styx River in Arcadia and one of the four rivers in the Underworld. Charon ferried dead souls across it into Hades, and Achilles was dipped into it to make him immortal.

Subrahmanian Son of Shiva, a mountain deity.

Sugriva The chief of the five great monkeys in the *Ramayana*.

Sukanya The wife of Chyavana.

Suman Son of Asamanja.

Sumantra A noble Brahman.

Sumati Wife of Sagara.

Sumedha A righteous Brahman who dwelt in the city of Amara.

Sumitra One of Dasharatha's three wives, mother of Lakshmana and Satrughna.

Suniti Mother of Dhruva.

Suparshwa One of Ravana's counsellors.

Supranakha A rakshasi, sister of Ravana.

Surabhi The wish-bestowing cow.

Surcoat Loose robe, traditionally worn over armour.

Surtr Fire-giant who eventually destroys the world at Ragnarok.

Surya God of the sun.

Susanoo God of the storm. He is depicted as a contradictory character with both good and bad characteristics. He was banished from Heaven after trying to kill his sister, Amaterasu.

Sushena A monkey chief.

Svasud Father of summer.

Swarga An Olympian paradise, where all wishes and desires are gratified.

Sweating A ritual customarily associated with spiritual purification and prayer practised by most tribes throughout North America prior to sacred ceremonies or vision quests. Steam was produced within a 'sweat lodge', a low, dome-shaped hut, by sprinkling water on heated stones.

Syrinx An Arcadian nymph who was the object of Pan's love.

Tablet of Destinies Cuneiform clay tablet on which the fates were written. Tiawath had given this to Kingu, but it was taken by Merodach when he defeated them. The storm god Zu later stole it for himself.

Taiaha A weapon made of wood.

Tailtiu One of the most famous royal residences of ancient Ireland. Possibly also a goddess linked to this site.

Tall One of Ravana's counsellors.

Tammuz Solar deity of Eridu who, with Gishzida, guards the gates of Heaven. Protector of Anu.

Tamsil Example or guidance.

Tangi Funeral, dirge. Assembly to cry over the dead.

Taniwha Sea monster, water spirit.

Tantalus Son of Zeus who told the secrets of the gods to mortals and stole their nectar and ambrosia. He was condemned to eternal torture in Hades, where he was tempted by food and water but allowed to partake of neither.

Taoism Taoism (or Daoism) came into being at roughly the same time as Confucianism, although its tenets were radically different and were largely founded on the philosophies of Lao Tzu (Laozi). While Confucius argued for a system of state discipline, Taoism strongly favoured self-discipline and looked upon nature as the architect of essential laws. A newer form of Taoism evolved after the Burning of the Books, placing great emphasis on spirit worship and pacification of the gods.

Tapu Sacred, supernatural possession of power. Involves spiritual rules and restrictions.

Tara Also known as Temair, the Hill of Tara was the popular seat of the ancient High-Kings of Ireland from the earliest times to the sixth century. Located in Co. Meath, it was also the place where great noblemen and chieftains congregated during wartime, or for significant events.

Tara Sugriva's wife.

Tartarus Dark region, below Hades.

Tau (Lesotho) Brother to Ra-Molo, depicted as a lion.

Taua War party.

Tefnut Goddess of water and rain. Married to Shu, who was also her brother. She, like Sekhmet, is portrayed with the head of a lion. Also known as Tefenet.

Telegonus Son of Odysseus and Circe. He was allegedly responsible for his father's death.

Telemachus Son of Odysseus and Penelope who was aided by Athene in helping his mother to keep away the suitors in Odysseus's absence.

Temu The evening form of Ra, the Sun god.

Tengu Goblin or gnome, often depicted as bird-like. A powerful fighter with weapons.

Tenochtitlán Capital city of the Aztecs, founded around 1350 CE and the site of the 'Great Temple'. Now Mexico City.

Teo-Amoxtli Divine book.

Teocalli Great temple built in Tenochtitlán, now Mexico City.

Teotleco Festival of the Coming of the Gods; also the twelfth month of the Aztec calendar.

Tepee A conical-shaped dwelling constructed of buffalo hide stretched over lodge-poles. Mostly used by Native American tribes living on the plains.

Tepeyollotl God of caves, desert places and earthquakes, whose name means 'heart of the mountain'. He is depicted as a jaguar, often leaping at the sun. Also known as Tepeolotlec.

Tepitoton Household gods.

Tereus King of Daulis who married Procne, daughter of Pandion King of Athens. He fell in love with Philomela, raped her and cut out her tongue.

Tezcatlipoca Supreme deity and Lord of the Smoking Mirror. He was also patron of royalty and warriors. Invented human sacrifice to the gods. Offspring of Ometeotl and Omecihuatl, he is known as the Jupiter of the Aztec gods.

Thalia Muse of pastoral poetry and comedy.

Theia Goddess of many names, and mother of the sun.

Theseus Son of King Aegeus of Athens. A cycle of legends has been woven around his travels and life.

Thetis Chief of the Nereids loved by both Zeus and Poseidon. They married her to a mortal, Peleus, and their child was Achilles. She tried to make him immortal by dipping him in the River Styx.

Thialfi Thor's servant, taken when his peasant father unwittingly harms Thor's goat.

Thiassi Giant and father of Skadi, he tricked Loki into bringing Idunn to him. Thrymheim is his kingdom.

Thomas the Rhymer Also called 'True Thomas', he was Thomas of Ercledoune, who lived in the thirteenth century. He met with the Queen of Elfland, and visited her country, was given clothes and a tongue that could tell no lie. He was also given the gift of prophecy, and many of his predictions were proven true.

Thor God of thunder and of war (with Tyr). Known for his huge size, and red hair and beard. Carries the hammer Miolnir. Slays Jormungander at Ragnarok.

Thoth God of the moon. Invented the arts and sciences and regulated the seasons. He is portrayed with the head of an ibis or a baboon.

Three-Heads One of Ravana's monsters.

Thrud Thor's daughter.

Thrudheim Thor's realm. Also called Thrudvang.

Thunder-Tooth Leader of the rakshasas at the siege of Lanka.

Tiawath Primeval dark ocean or abyss, Tiawath is also a monster and evil deity of the deep. She took the form of a dragon or sea serpent and battled the gods of light for supremacy over all living beings. She was eventually defeated by Merodach, who used her body to create Heaven and Earth.

Tiglath-Pileser I King of Assyria, who made it a leading power for centuries.

Tiki First man created, a figure carved of wood, or other representation of man.

Tirawa The name given to the Great Creator (*see* Great Spirit) by the Pawnee tribe who believed that four direct paths led from his house in the sky to the four semi-cardinal points: north-east, north-west, south-east and south-west.

Tiresias A Theban who was given the gift of prophecy by Zeus. He was blinded for seeing Athene bathing. He continued to use his prophetic talents after his death, advising Odysseus.

Tirfing Sword made by dwarves which was cursed to kill every time it was drawn, be the cause of three great atrocities, and kill Suaforlami (Odin's grandson), for whom it was made.

Tisamenus Son of Orestes, who inherited the Kingdom of Argos and Sparta.

Titania Queen of the fairies.

Tlaloc God of rain and fertility, so important to the people, because he ensured a good harvest, that the Aztec heaven or paradise was named Tlalocan in his honour.

Tlazolteotl Goddess of ordure, filth and vice. Also known as the earth-goddess or Tlaelquani, meaning 'filth-eater'. She acted as a confessor of sins or wrongdoings.

Tohu-mate Omen of death.

Tohunga A priest; a possessor of supernatural powers.

Toltec Civilization that preceded the Aztecs.

Tomahawk Hatchet with a stone or iron head used in war or hunting.

Tonalamatl Record of the Aztec calendar, which was recorded in books made from bark paper.

Tonalpohualli Aztec calendar composed of twenty thirteen-day weeks called trecenas.

Totec Solar deity known as Our Great Chief.

Totemism System of belief in which people share a relationship with a spirit animal or natural being with whom they interact. Examples include Ea, who is represented by a fish.

Toxilmolpilia The binding up of the years.

Tristan Nephew of King Mark of Cornwall, who travels to Ireland to bring Iseult back to marry his uncle. On the way, he and Iseult consume a love potion and fall madly in love before their story ends tragically.

Triton A sea-god, and son of Poseidon and Amphitrite. He led the Argonauts to the sea from Lake Tritonis.

Trojan War War waged by the Greeks against Troy, in order to reclaim Menelaus's wife Helen, who had eloped with the Trojan prince Paris. Many important heroes took part, and form the basis of many legends and myths.

Troll Unfriendly mythological creature of varying size and strength. Usually dwells in mountainous areas, among rocks or caves.

Truage Tribute or pledge of peace or truth, usually made on payment of a tax.

Tsuki-yomi God of the moon, brother of Amaterasu and Susanoo.

Tuat The other world or land of the dead.

Tupuna Ancestor.

Tvashtar Craftsman of the gods.

Tyndareus King of Sparta, perhaps the son of Perseus's daughter Grogphone. Expelled from Sparta but restored by Heracles. Married Leda and fathered Helen and Clytemnestra, among others.

Tyr Son of Frigga and the god of war (with Thor). Eventually kills Garm at Ragnarok.

Tzompantli Pyramid of Skulls.

Uayeb The five unlucky days of the Mayan calendar, which were believed to be when demons from the underworld could reach Earth. People would often avoid leaving their houses on uayeb days.

Ubaaner Magician, whose name meant 'splitter of stones', who created a wax crocodile that came to life to swallow up the man who was trying to seduce his wife.

Uile Bheist Mythical creature, usually some form of wild beast.

Uisneach A hill formation between Mullingar and Athlone said to mark the centre of Ireland.

uKqili (Zulu) Creator god.

Uller God of winter, whom Skadi eventually marries.

Ulster Cycle Compilation of folk tales and legends telling of the Ulaids, people from the northeast of Ireland, now named Ulster. Also known as the *Uliad Cycle*, it is one of four Irish cycles of mythology.

Unseelie Court An unholy court comprising a kind of fairies, antagonistic to humans. They took the form of a kind of Sluagh, and shot humans and animals with elf-shots.

Urd One of the Norns.

Urien King of Gore, husband of Morgan le Fey and father to Yvain.

Urmila Second daughter of Janaka.

Usha Wife of Aniruddha, daughter of Vanasur.

Ushas Goddess of the dawn.

Utgard-loki King of the giants. Tricked Thor.

Uther Pendragon King of England in sub-Roman Britain; father of King Arthur.

Utixo (Hottentot) Creator god.

Ut-Napishtim Ancestor of Gilgamesh, whom Gilgamesh sought out to discover how to prevent death. Similar to Noah in that he was sent a vision warning him of a great deluge. He built an ark in seven days, filling it with his family, possessions and all kinds of animals.

Uz Deity symbolized by a goat.

Vach Goddess of speech.

Vajrahanu One of Ravana's generals.

Vala Another name for Norns.

Valfreya Another name for Freyia.

Valhalla Odin's hall for the celebrated dead warriors chosen by the Valkyries.

Vali The cruel brother of Sugriva, dethroned by Rama.

Valkyries Odin's attendants, led by Freyia. Chose dead warriors to live at Valhalla. Also spelled as Valkyrs.

Vamadeva One of Dasharatha's priests.

Vanaheim Home of the Vanir.

Vanir Race of gods in conflict with the Aesir; they are gods of the sea and wind.

Varuna Ancient god of the sky and cosmos, later, god of the waters.

Vasishtha One of Dasharatha's priests.

Vassal Person under the protection of a feudal lord.

Vasudev Descendant of Yadu, husband of Rohini and Devaki, father of Krishna.

Vasudeva A name of Narayana or Vishnu.

Vavasor Vassal or tenant of a baron or lord who himself has vassals.

Vedic Mantras, hymns.

Vernandi One of the Norns.

Vichitravirya Bhishma's half-brother.

Vidar Slays Fenris.

Vidura Friend of the Pandavas.

Vigrid The plain where the final battle is held.

Vijaya Karna's bow.

Vikramaditya A king identified with Chandragupta II.

Vintail Moveable front of a helmet.

Virabhadra A demon that sprang from Shiva's lock of hair.

Viradha A fierce rakshasa, seizes Sita, slain by Rama.

Virupaksha The elephant who bears the whole world.

Vishnu The Preserver, Vedic sun god and one of the two great gods of post-Vedic Hinduism.

Vision Quest A sacred ceremony undergone by Native Americans to establish communication with the spirit set to direct them in life. The quest lasted up to four days and nights and was preceded by a period of solitary fasting and prayer.

Vivasvat The sun.

Vizier High-ranking official or adviser. Also known as vizir or vazir.

Volsung Family of great warriors about whom a great saga was spun.

Vrishadarbha King of Benares.

Vrishasena Son of Karna, slain by Arjuna.

Vyasa Chief of the royal chaplains.

Wairua Spirit, soul.

Wanjiru (Kikuyu) Maiden who was sacrificed by her village to appease the gods and make it rain after years of drought.

Weighing of the Heart Procedure carried out after death to assess whether the deceased was free from sin. If the deceased's heart weighed less than the feather of Ma'at, they would join Osiris in the Fields of Peace.

Whare Hut made of fern stems tied together with flax and vines, and roofed in with raupo (reeds).

White Demon Protector of Mázinderán. He prevented Kai-káús and his army from invading.

Withy Thin twig or branch which is very flexible and strong.

Wolverine Large mammal of the musteline family with dark, very thick, water-resistant fur, inhabiting the forests of North America and Eurasia.

Wroth Angry.

Wyrd One of the Norns.

Xanthus & Balius Horses of Achilles, immortal offspring of Zephyrus the west wind. A gift to Achilles's father Peleus.

Xipe Totec High priest and son of Ometeotl and Omecihuatl. Also known as the god of the seasons.

Xiupohualli Solar year, composed of eighteen twenty-day months. Also spelt Xiuhpōhualli.

Yadu A prince of the Lunar dynasty.

Yakshas Same as rakshasas.

Yakunin Government official.

Yama God of Death, king of the dead and son of the sun.

Yamato Take Legendary warrior and prince. Also known as Yamato Takeru.

Yashiki Residence or estate, usually of a daimyō.

Yasoda Wife of Nand.

Yemaya (Yoruba) Wife of Obatala.

Yemoja (Yoruba) Goddess of water and protector of women.

Yggdrasill The World Ash, holding up the Nine Worlds. Does not fall at Ragnarok.

Ymir Giant created from fire and ice; his body created the world.

Yo The female principle who, joined with In, the male side, brought about creation and the first gods. In and Yo correspond to the Chinese Yang and Yin.

Yomi The underworld.

Yudhishthira The eldest of the Pandavas, a great soldier.

Yuki-Onna The Snow-Bride or Lady of the Snow, who represents death.

Yvain Son of Morgan le Fay and knight of the Round Table, who goes on chivalric quests with a lion he rescued from a dragon.

Zahid Holy man.

Zál Son of Sám, who was born with pure white hair. Sám abandoned Zál, who was raised by the Símúrgh, or griffins. Zal became a great warrior, second only to his son, Rustem. Also known as Ním-rúz and Dustán.

Zephyr Gentle breeze.

Zeus King of gods, god of sky, weather, thunder, lightning, home, hearth and hospitality. He plays an important role as the voice of justice, arbitrator between man and gods, and among them. Married to Hera, but lover of dozens of others.

Zohák Serpent-king and figure of evil. Father of Mihrab.

Zu God of the storm, who took the form of a huge bird. Similar to the Persian símúrgh.

Zukin Head covering.

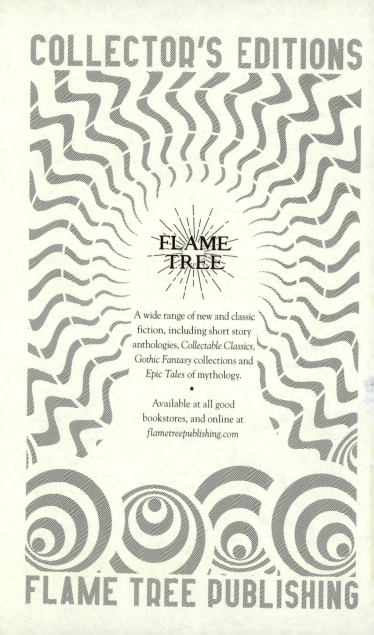